Praise for Peter Hanington

'Topical, authoritative and gripping'   Charles Cumming

'Thoughtful, atmospheric and grippingly plotted'   *Guardian*

'Another page-turner from a writer who can take you into gripping worlds, real and virtual'   Mishal Husain

'Shot-through with great authenticity and insider knowledge – wholly compelling and shrewdly wise'   William Boyd

'A panoramic thriller that shuttles with aplomb between four continents . . . chockful of vivid characters'
John Dugdale, *Sunday Times*

'An intriguing, timely and unsettling new thriller'   Sam Bourne

'A tremendously good debut with characters who leap to life . . . I have not read anything that has taken me anywhere near as close to Afghanistan as a place – amazingly gripping'
Melvyn Bragg

'The multi-layered plot moves excitingly and entertainingly but also raises serious current issues . . . Hanington has true talent'
The Times

Also by Peter Hanington

A Dying Breed
A Single Source

A CURSED PLACE

First published in Great Britain in 2021 by Two Roads
An Imprint of John Murray (Publishers)
An Hachette UK company

This paperback edition published in 2023 by Baskerville
An imprint of John Murray (Publishers)
An Hachette UK company

1

A CIP catalogue record for this title is available from the British Library

Paperback ISBN 9781529305241
eBook ISBN 9781529305234

Printed and bound in Great Britain by Clays Ltd, Elcograf S.p.A.

John Murray policy is to use papers that are natural, renewable and
recyclable products and made from wood grown in sustainable forests.
The logging and manufacturing processes are expected to conform
to the environmental regulations of the country of origin.

Baskerville, an imprint of John Murray
Carmelite House
50 Victoria Embankment
London EC4Y 0DZ

www.johnmurraypress.co.uk

PETER HANINGTON

A CURSED PLACE

BASKERVILLE
An imprint of JOHN MURRAY

For Euan, Zoe, Mark and Nick

It is their prayer that good seed sown may bring forth a good harvest, that all things hostile to peace or purity may be banished from this house, and that the people, inclining their ear to whatsoever things are beautiful and honest and of good report, may tread the path of wisdom and uprightness.

Latin inscription in the reception of BBC Broadcasting House

PART ONE

Evil comes at leisure like the disease;
good comes in a hurry like the doctor.

G.K. Chesterton

1 In the Shadow of the Dam

The town was sleeping. No sign of dawn except for the occasional squawk of a hopeful cockerel from a far-off farm. Jags slowed and brought the Chevy to a stop in the gravel lay-by next to a pockmarked green metal sign announcing your imminent arrival in Brochu. He switched off the engine and stared down at the town. The moon was bright and just a sliver short of full. Brochu looked all right in this light, he thought. Like any other Chilean shithole town, anyhow. Maybe even a little prettier than most – *picturesque* – seeing as how you had the foothills of the Andes mountains there in the background and the river running through. He lit a cigarette and cracked the window open, letting the smoke out and a blast of cold early morning air in. He took a long drag on his Marlboro. This must've been what Brochu looked like back in the old days. Rolling hills, a river running through the valley, sleepy little town with a handful of stores, surrounded by farms. He glanced at his watch – in an hour from now you'd see things differently. You'd see the deep scars cut into the mountain, you'd notice that the river wasn't running right. Most of all, you'd figure

3

out that that dark shadow in the middle distance wasn't another hill, but rather the steep side of a one hundred and eighty metre-high dam, containing one thousand, seven hundred tons of toxic shit. If the dam broke – earthquake, structural failure, whatever – then the people of Brochu had ten minutes to run like hell before all that shit landed smack on their heads. That's why, on his regular visits, Jags took a room at a guesthouse outside of town. The drive back was a pain, especially when he had to start early, like today, but it was worth it – for peace of mind. Nothing was more important than peace of mind. He took a couple more drags then flicked the half-smoked cigarette out of the window. He pulled a notepad and pencil from inside his bomber jacket and wrote.

> *Through a car window*
> *A moonlit mining town, hills*
> *No one awake but me*

He counted the syllables off on his thick fingers.

'Bullshit.' He looked again at his scribbled poem, flipped the pencil and erased the last line. Tried again.

> *Through a car window*
> *A moonlit mining town, hills*
> *One man awake, me*

He read it through again, out loud. 'Nah.' Jags shut the notebook and stuffed it back inside his jacket. Stupid to try and write something decent when he was on a job, working to a deadline and with his mind whirring. One thing at a time. He clicked the glove compartment open and pulled out a white plastic carrier bag. A handful of blurry-looking photographs tumbled out of an envelope and fell to the floor; Jags picked them up and put them back in the glove. Inside the plastic bag were half a dozen mobile phones, a variety of makes, shapes and sizes. He tipped them out onto the passenger seat and shuffled through them. Each phone had a sticker on the reverse with dates and three-letter codes written on them, all in upper case: LAX, LHR, PEK, JRS, SCL . . . He found the phone he was looking for and switched it on; its blue screen reflected off the windscreen and lit the car. Jags turned the brightness down, selected his contacts and scrolled down until he found the name he was looking for. He scratched at his stubbled cheek, constructing as short a sentence as possible in one language before translating it into another, then he typed. *Hora de trabajar.* He checked the time once more and pressed send. The message left his phone with a satisfying swishing sound and made its digital way a mile and a half down the road into Brochu.

Pablo Mistral ate no breakfast. Better to throw up a mug of sour coffee than a plateful of egg and bread and onions, and he almost always threw up. The nature of the work he did for the American, combined with a weak stomach, made it all but inevitable. He filled a saucepan with water from the plastic jerrycan, lit the gas hob and walked back down the short hall to his bedroom to get dressed while the water boiled. He edged round the double bed in the direction of the metal roll-along clothes rail that held his and his wife's clothes. Francesca had been full of praise when Pablo first bought the rail and brought it home, but in recent months its limitations had become obvious. The only place to put it was alongside the bed, hard against the wall, and the wall was damp. Francesca had sewn a cover for it out of recycled fertiliser sacks, scrubbed clean, but the damp somehow worked its way through this as well. He pulled a musty-smelling sweatshirt and shirt from their hangers, together with his best pair of jeans. The clothes he wore when working for the American were different from the clothes he wore at the mine, smarter, although Mr Jags had never shown any sign of noticing or caring what Pablo wore.

He sat down heavily on the end of the bed and pulled his jeans on over his grey long johns. Francesca turned in her sleep and he heard her soft snore. He thought about waking his wife and saying a brief goodbye; also this would allow her to see how early he was up, how hard he had to work. He decided to let her be; he didn't want to have a pointless conversation or have to explain himself – better just to go.

He finished dressing then reached for his wife's hand mirror. His moustache was growing in slowly; a thick black hairy cater-pillar covered his top lip, while the attempted handlebars – although a little wispy – were coming along. Pablo had overheard his daughter commenting that the moustache just drew attention to his bulbous nose, rather than distracting from it, which she guessed was the intention. He wet his thumb and finger with his tongue and curled the wisps of handlebar hair upwards. She could go to hell; he was growing the moustache for himself, not to please her. He'd given up trying to please Soledad long ago. Pablo left the room, pulling the door shut behind him.

Louder snores drifted from behind the next door down the hall. His two teenage boys and their big sister, plus his favourite – ten-year-old Claudio – all still sharing the one room, still in bunk beds. This knowledge pricked at his pride. Three or four more jobs like this morning's and perhaps they could think about moving to a bigger place. Still in Brochu – everyone who worked at the mine lived in the town – but maybe they could move to the other side. The houses were better there and they'd be a mile or two further from the dam instead of right in the shadow of the devilish thing. He would keep the next envelope of money Mr Jags gave him in his pocket, or give it to Francesca instead of taking it to the bar and spending it all in one go on himself and his fair-weather friends. Or even worse, his mistress. She could spend in a weekend what Francesca would make last a month. Pablo nodded his head vigorously. He was in complete agreement with this new plan of his. From now on he would save his money and focus on his family: his three boys, the girl and Francesca. He would forget about the other plan – the one that involved airline tickets and passports and the other woman. It wasn't really a plan anyway. It was a foolish dream.

He made the coffee, pouring the oily film on the top of the boiled water down the plughole before adding the cleaner-looking water to a chipped mug with two spoons of coffee granules and three spoons of white sugar. His boots, black beanie hat and puffer jacket were by the front door, but even with all these on and a mug of hot coffee inside him, it felt bitterly cold out on the street. He stuck his hands in his pockets and trudged through the dark, past one breeze block and tin-roofed house after another, each almost identical to his own.

Ten minutes of walking and he was on the outskirts of Brochu. Up on the hill, just about visible, thanks to the brightness of the moon, Pablo saw the familiar outline of a Chevrolet and, standing next to it, a hunched form. A man. His master and fellow murderer.

2 Revolution 2.0

If you loved cities then Hong Kong was heaven, if you didn't it was a hellish place. Most of the time, Patrick belonged to the former group. But not today. He needed a cup of tea and another dose of painkillers. His blue eyes were bloodshot and his feet throbbed. His feet and his head; a hangover from last night's session in the bar at the Headland Hotel. He'd started drinking during happy hour but continued long after with his reporter, John Brandon, egging him on. Several pints of beer, then dragon cocktails, then something else that he couldn't even remember. Sambuca? He remembered it had an aniseed taste to it. Whatever it was, it had been a bad idea. Patrick winced at the memory before consoling himself with the thought that at least he hadn't let this thumping hangover get in the way of his work. He'd spent the day with a thousand-strong crowd of pro-democracy demonstrators, who had gathered in a park on the edge of the city before marching here, to the Central business district. As they'd walked, their numbers had grown until eventually they had enough people to successfully block an eight-lane highway. In between swallowing paracetamol and getting rained on, Patrick had interviewed dozens of the protestors. One more interview and he'd be done. Just then an earnest-looking young man, a boy really, wearing a dark T-shirt and thick black-rimmed spectacles, shouted in Patrick's direction.

'Man from the BBC? Mr Reid? I have some time now if you are ready?' The boy's hair was plastered to his head by the rain. The humidity had steamed his glasses and he was squinting to see if Patrick had heard him and was coming.

'Yes, thanks. Just call me Patrick, Eric. I'll be right with you.'

In the course of just a few days, Eric Fung had emerged as the de facto leader of a student-led protest group calling itself *Scholastic*. Patrick gathered up his stuff and walked over to where Eric and his young comrades were gathered. 'I can stay here and speak to you, is that correct?'

Patrick nodded. The mizzling rain had eased a little and here was as good as anywhere.

'Sure, I'll just need to be a bit careful with the levels.' Eric was standing at the very front of the demonstration, yards from a thick line of Hong Kong police. He was wearing what looked a lot like school trousers and his T-shirt had green fluorescent graffiti-style writing on it, calling for *Freedom Now!* The cops wore full riot gear and had their shields raised, although Patrick had the feeling that this was largely for show, at least for now. The atmosphere this side of the police line was more festive than threatening, but Patrick had learnt from experience how quickly that could change. Eric and his gang were standing behind a long waterproof canvas banner that read *Occupy Central with Love and Peace* in English and Cantonese. Patrick slipped his headphones on and asked Eric for his name and title and, while listening to the answer, adjusted the levels on his digital tape recorder. When that wasn't quite enough, he asked the hardy perennial question about breakfast. Eric frowned. 'It was an awfully long time ago, but I had a boiled egg for my breakfast.'

The levels looked fine.

'Great, so here we go. Eric Fung, what makes you think that Hong Kong's pro-democracy protest can succeed when so many other similar movements have failed?' Listening to his own voice though the headphones, Patrick was aware that he sounded tired. More than tired in fact – cynical. Eric, by contrast, was upbeat.

'I believe that we have learnt useful lessons from North Africa and the Middle East. We are resolute.' As he spoke his fellow revolutionaries nodded and passed around the hand sanitiser. Patrick had noticed that the Hongkongers' revolutionary fervour came coupled with a deep-seated fear of germs. Earlier, he'd watched as wave after wave of protestors – marching hand in hand – arrived at the gridlocked stretch of motorway and promptly reached into their backpacks for baby wipes and hand gel. The ever-entrepreneurial locals had noticed this too, and there were makeshift stalls selling hand sanitiser, a variety of snacks and, of course, plastic umbrellas of every conceivable colour; the brighter they were the better they sold. The umbrella had become the symbol of this new revolution and it was a powerful one. But it would take more than plastic umbrellas to defeat the Hong Kong authorities and, at their back, the Chinese state. Patrick pressed his young interviewee on this point.

'The protestors I met in Tahrir Square were resolute too. The young Egyptians that we called *Generation Revolution* now refer to themselves as *Generation Jail*. Why will things be any different here?'

Eric nodded. 'Hong Kong has a long history of protest. We are good at this. We know how to organise and we understand that success will take time. This is a process, not a moment. We understand that.'

Patrick could see why these kids had picked Eric to represent them. He was impressive.

'I heard the same thing in Cairo and Istanbul, in Bahrain. I heard people saying similar things in Ukraine just the other week.'

Eric pushed the thick bottle-top glasses back up the bridge of his nose and smiled.

'Perhaps you are an unlucky charm, Mr Reid? I hope you're not here to bring us bad luck . . .' He smiled at his colleagues. Patrick got the impression that Eric didn't often crack jokes. 'Maybe I should be asking you the questions. Why do you think all those other protests failed?' Patrick shrugged. 'If we can learn these lessons then we might have a better chance of success.'

Patrick shook his head.

'I'm better at asking questions than answering them I'm sorry to say.' He asked a few more and Eric did a good job of answering them. They *had* learnt lessons from other protest movements, a few at least, although Patrick still sensed a certain naivety, especially in the rather amateurish the way they were communicating with each other and organising themselves – text message and Facebook and so on. It reminded him of things he'd seen in Turkey and some of the mistakes the protestors had made there. Deadly mistakes as it had turned out. But he had the quotes he needed and he'd rained on these idealistic Hongkongers' parade long enough. He thanked Eric, slipped his headphones down around his neck and switched off the digital recorder. Once it was off, Eric relaxed and his manner became less formal.

'I meant what I said about being interested in what you have seen elsewhere. In Egypt and Turkey. Perhaps it would be possible to talk again?'

'Sure.' It would be useful to have a contact right at the front line of the protests; Patrick had tried to make similar connections in all the countries where he'd been working. He took a BBC business card from inside his wallet and handed it to Eric. Swapping business cards was a popular hobby in Hong Kong, even the students had them, but it seemed Eric Fung was the exception. He pocketed Patrick's card but offered nothing in return. Patrick got a pen out instead. 'Do you want to scribble your number down?'

Eric shook his head. 'I'm in between phones at the moment, but I'll contact you. I assume you're staying at the Headland Hotel with all the other media people?' Patrick acknowledged, slightly reluctantly, that yes, he was.

Hovering nearby and clearly hoping to talk to Eric next was a square-jawed American, a newspaper reporter by the look of him, in camo pants and a black flak jacket with *PRESS* printed on it in white capital letters. Patrick had seen this guy approach several of the same protestors that he'd been speaking to right after he'd finished talking to them. He'd found this more than a little irritating; going after all the same interviews was either lazy or, at the very least, poor form. If William Carver, his former boss and a journalist of the old school, had been here, he'd have flayed the bloke alive. Patrick checked himself; maybe he was just in a bad mood? Perhaps the guy was new, he had that look about him – *all the gear, no idea* – that would have been Carver's verdict. Patrick pushed through the crowd, away from the heart of the demo and found a quieter spot next to a thick white water-filled crash barrier. As he moved, Patrick could feel the American's eyes following him. He knelt down next to the barrier and studied the digital display on the front of his recording machine, flicking through the audio files and listening back to snatches of some. He had at least ten interviews and plenty of wild track: chanting, the pounding sound of rain on umbrellas, police announcements on a tinny-sounding tannoy, traffic noise. It was more than enough to make a decent radio package. He just needed to dig John Brandon out of bed or prise him away from the bar long enough to write and record his script and he'd be done. Then a hot bath and an early night. Sleep was what he really needed. He packed his kit up, tucked it away carefully at the bottom of his shoulder bag and stood. His own, slightly battered, navy blue flak jacket felt heavy – the thing seemed to absorb water like a sponge – the white cotton shirt he had on underneath was sodden and cold. He walked back down the hard shoulder, past streams of predominantly young people, lots of them still wearing school uniforms and carrying umbrellas, striding towards the heart of the demonstration. Eventually the crowds began to thin. Patrick removed his flak jacket and put that in his bag too, then set off in the direction of the harbour and his hotel.

Hong Kong was unlike any other city he had been to. Every buildable bit of land was built on, every pavement filled with quickstepping pedestrians, every road filled with traffic – long lines of battered Toyotas and flashy Mercedes jostling for space alongside the double-decker buses, red and white taxis and the Hong Kong police weaving between the chaos on flatulent-sounding motorcycles. A labyrinth of flyovers, underpasses, tunnels and towering skyscrapers. It was the evening rush hour now and the streets were a chaos of commuters, food and tea stalls. Patrick smiled, recalling something Carver had told him on a previous visit, the only other time that he'd been to the city, but one of William's many visits: *Fragrant Harbour my arse.* As different as Hong Kong was from the rest of China – as different as it believed itself to be – as far as Carver was concerned, it still smelt the same. *Duck shit, fried food and petrol.*

As well as this bouquet, which William had identified, there was also the simple smell of *people*. Too many people living too close together. Patrick didn't have a great memory for statistics but he remembered this one . . . more than seventeen thousand people were squeezed into every square mile of Hong Kong. For a while he just followed the crowd, his face inches from the person in front, more people pushing at his back. A dizzying mix of sweat, bad breath, aftershave and cheap perfume. There was a commotion on the pavement up ahead and a loose knot of Englishmen came crashing through the crowd, stolen beer glasses still in hand.

They were mad drunk and drenched with rain, blue shirts stuck to their flabby bellies. Patrick moved to one side and let them pass, staring down at his feet.

Above the sound of the rain and the traffic he heard the deep basso call of a foghorn from the harbour. He made his way in that direction, up Connaught Road, past the Hing Yip Centre and on. Then he stopped, unsure at first exactly why or rather what had brought him to such a sudden halt. He looked around. In a city where almost everything was strange, something here was familiar. He glanced up and saw that he was standing underneath the sign for Mrs Wang's – Carver's favourite Hong Kong café. Last time he was here, William had brought Patrick to Mrs Wang's for a corned beef bun and milk tea – the best on the island in Carver's opinion. William had been greeted like the prodigal son.

Patrick received no such welcome this time, but waiting in line he recognised the owner, an elegant, white-haired woman who was standing at the counter taking orders. William had introduced them. When his turn came, he ordered his food in clunky Cantonese then switched to English.

'I have been here before.'

Mrs Wang didn't look up from her note making. 'We are a popular restaurant.'

'Yes, but not just me. I was here with William Carver.' Now she looked.

'You're here with Car-ver-ah?' She pronounced every letter in the name, adding syllables. 'I guessed he would come. Any time there is trouble here in Hong Kong – he comes. Where is he?' She gazed past Patrick at the rows of plastic tables, scanning the faces. While she looked for William, Patrick studied her. You could still see the young, very beautiful woman in the older woman's face. If you took the time to look. Patrick wondered how long Carver had been coming here. How long he'd known her. 'I cannot see him.'

14

'No, I'm sorry, it's just me this time.'

'Just you? Why is he not here?'

Patrick paused, looking for a proper explanation. He paused too long.

'Car-ver-ah is dead?'

'What? No, he isn't dead. He's just taking some time off. He's having a rest.'

The woman tried this idea out for size.

'Car-ver-ah is having a rest?' She seemed unconvinced. 'Why would he want a rest?' She shook her head. Much more likely that he was dead. A sweaty-faced cook, wearing a hairnet, appeared at the service hatch behind the woman and palmed a hotel reception bell, yelling something that sounded vaguely like Patrick's order. She went and collected Patrick's corned beef roll and tea, plated up and steaming hot. She put the food down on a red plastic tray and pushed it across the metal counter.

'That looks amazing, thank you.' There was an awkward pause. 'So, I'll tell William I was here. I'll tell him I saw you and that you said hi.' Mrs Wang shrugged. If this lanky, blond English boy believed that he could commune with the dead then so be it. She nodded politely and turned her attention to the next customer in line.

3 The Golden Rules

STOCKWELL ROAD, LONDON

William Carver pressed a fresh crease into his trousers with the iron then spent some time hopping around his living room in a stiff-legged fashion, trying to put them on without undoing his good work. The radio was on and the Right Reverend somebody was talking about her local parish flower show. Bit of an obvious choice for any *Thought For The Day*-er, Carver thought – ripe with religious metaphor. Overripe. Having said that, she was doing a good enough job. Usually he tuned out during *Thought For the Day* – either mentally or literally.

'All flowers begin as simple seeds and, once grown, all flowers bend towards the sun . . .' It was an ear-catching phrase and William wondered who had coined it. The Right Reverend lost him a little after that. The garden was God's garden of course, we were the seeds, the rain was just the rain, Jesus got to be chief gardener, as per usual. He wandered back into the bedroom to finish getting dressed. Since starting his work at the College of Journalism, Carver had made some adjustments to his wardrobe. To be more accurate, he'd thought about the clothes he wore for the first time in a long time. It seemed to him that teaching required a level of smartness several notches higher than that of a jobbing journalist. He'd spent the best part of one month's pay in John Lewis on a new raincoat, a brown corduroy jacket, blue shirts and two new chalk-stripe suits, plus a pair of brogues and a leather briefcase. The overall effect made him look, in his friend McCluskey's words, '. . . *a proper blueberry. John Lewis really saw yous coming, didn't they? I bet they've been waiting thirty years to sell tha' cord jacket. They certainly haven't manufactured any with leather elbow patches this century.*'

William was supposed to see McCluskey, a long-serving employee of the BBC Monitoring service at Caversham, later that day but that would not affect his choice of clothes. Carver was happy with the new wardrobe, which to his mind made him look rather like his old geography teacher – a kind man in a school full of sadists and, moreover, a good teacher. Brushing his teeth, he glanced up at his reflection in the bathroom mirror, then winced. The jabbing pain in his right hip would sometimes agree to be walked off, but it seemed as though it was settling in for the duration today. He popped a couple more ibuprofen into his mouth and washed them down with a swallow of water from the tooth mug. This number of pills risked unsettling his stomach. He'd be farting his way up the Northern line, but he and the rest of the morning commute were just going to have to grin and bear it.

Taking his raincoat from a coat hanger on the back of the front door, Carver noticed his grab bag – a brown leather and canvas shoulder bag that contained three changes of clothes, two passports, four hundred pounds in a variety of currencies and a washbag. Most importantly, it contained his old recording equipment – a MiniDisc recorder and a Marantz the size and weight of a brick, but almost impossible to break, wrapped up inside a yellow plastic bag. He shoved the somewhat dusty-looking bag back into the corner between the door jamb and wall with the side of his foot. He should really put the thing away in a cupboard. Maybe later. Carver picked up his new briefcase, inside the tools of his current trade: a laptop and a few acetate slides. Not as exciting, maybe, but no less important. More important some might say. Nurturing tomorrow's talent.

The College of Journalism occupied the top floor of a 1970s-built tower block overlooking the Elephant and Castle roundabout. The rest of the building was home to other *more arty* types: painters, potters, ceramicists, sculptors. He'd been a bit intimidated by this lot when he first started, but now Carver rather enjoyed hanging around in the basement café, watching the students and other teachers and trying to guess which subjects they were studying or teaching.

Half an hour before the lesson was due to begin he caught the lift up to the top floor and settled in. The overhead projector that he'd requested was sitting there on his desk and Carver gave a satisfied grunt of approval. He'd found the machine and a box of unused transparencies and red and blue markers at the back of the college storeroom and decided to give it a whirl. He knew that most of his students wouldn't recognise a landline telephone if they saw one and so were unlikely to be familiar with the *3M 2000* projector, but that could be a good thing. Shake them out of their stupor long enough to learn a thing or two.

The buttery light in the room reminded William of the classrooms he'd known as a child – back in the Triassic. He took another look at his slides and typed notes and when the clock on the wall reached ten a.m. he opened the door to a line of anxious-looking young faces.

'Good morning.'

Carver stood just inside the classroom, a red metal fire bucket held out in front of him. The students filed in. 'You remember the drill, stick your phones in the bucket.'

The first student in line was Derek, an odd-looking kid, his round face decorated with multiple piercings including studs around his cheeks, chin, nose, ears and tongue. The boy reminded Carver of a Christmas decoration his mother used to make: a whole orange punctured with cloves arranged in symmetrical patterns. It hung from the Christmas tree throughout the holiday and then in his mother's clothes cupboard. Derek looked like a human version of this homemade decoration, while smelling significantly less aromatic. Carver stared at Derek, whose hand was hovering above the bucket.

'There's loads of sand and cigarettes and shit in there sir.' Carver glanced inside and, taking a clean-ish handkerchief from his breast pocket, lined the bottom of the bucket.

'There you go.' The young man remained unconvinced. 'Get a move on, Derek, you know the score, either put your phone in the fire bucket or bugger off.'

William had tried getting his students to switch their phones off, to put them away in their bags or inside the old-fashioned hinged desks that they sat at, but none of this had worked. If they were within an arm's length of their mobiles, then they were incapable of focussing on anything else.

Once the bucket was filled and the class was seated, Carver went to sort out the window blinds. He lifted and lowered them with several jerky pulls of the toggled cord before eventually the blinds fell to the sill with a metallic crash.

'Right, listen up.' Carver looked at the rows of expectant faces. 'The first couple of weeks we've done some journalistic history, a few of the big scoops and stories that've changed things here in this country and elsewhere.' Sitting in the middle of the front row, Naz had her hand up. Naz often had her hand up.

'Yes?'

'Watergate.'

'That's right.'

'Watergate, Vietnam and then quite a few of your own stories.'

'That's right. Is there a point to this intervention Miss Shah, or are you just showing me what a good memory you've got?'

'No sir.'

'Good. So today, we're getting down to brass tacks. The basics. The things you lot will need to remember if you ever want to produce anything of value during your careers.' Heads nodded. Carver turned to the overhead projector and shuffled it around on the desk, aiming the square head directly at the whiteboard. When Naz inevitably piped up again, asking what on earth this thing was, Carver was ready.

'It's like one of those Power Point presentations. Just not as flash.' His students eyed the machine warily. William flicked the switch on the side of the projector on and it whirred into life. The smell of burnt dust filled the small classroom and a square of bright yellow light appeared on the whiteboard behind him. Carver slapped the first transparency down and glanced behind him.

SELUR NEDLOG EHT

'Are you teaching us in Welsh today sir?' Naz again.

'Very funny, good one. Technical hitch . . .' He flipped the transparency over.

THE GOLDEN RULES

He read the three words and waited while the students did the same, then he turned to face them.

'If you remember nothing else after these next six months are up, then I want you to remember this. Two rules . . .' He removed the first slide and slid the second into place.

1. Make it interesting
2. Don't make it up

'If you can manage these two things then there's a chance you'll make a living. Who knows? You might even make a difference.'

Clove-boy had his hand up.

'If you gave us our phones back sir, we could take a picture of that.'

'I don't want you to take a bloody picture of it, I want you to remember it.'

He looked around the class; several of his pupils had already lost interest, one or two were repeating the rules back to themselves, their mouths moving. Down at the front, Naz had opened what looked like an old spiral-bound reporter's notebook, the sort Carver himself preferred, although it was getting harder to find them. She was writing the rules down in careful capitals.

The ping of a mobile phone broke the silence and Carver gave the fire bucket an accusing stare before realising that the sound had come from inside his trouser pocket. He took the phone out and glanced at the screen before switching it off. The news it was alerting Carver to had something to do with naked pictures of an actress William had never heard of.

'It's another one of those bloody news alerts.' Carver found the increasing frequency with which these urgent alerts popped up on his phone annoying and their choice of story, for the most part, baffling. 'Does anyone know how to switch those things off?' Naz's arm went up.

'I do.'

'Fine. You can show me after the lesson.'

21

4 A Cursed Place

As Pablo walked up the side of the tarmac road in the direction of the old white Chevy, a shiver climbed his spine. A combination of the cold wind that cut right through four layers of clothes and straightforward fear. His boss had parked where he always parked, on the rise in the road just next to the Brochu sign, a sign that the local kids liked to take pot shots at with their rabbit-hunting rifles. Jags was standing next to the car, pushing against it and causing it to rock gently to and fro. He was broad in the shoulder and appeared slightly hunched in the back, although not in a way that suggested weakness or age, but rather a readiness. Tree trunks for legs and a barrel-like torso in grey T-shirt and black bomber jacket. His arms looked a little short in comparison with the rest of his frame, but they were the strongest thing about him. Pablo had seen this. A kid that the two men had taken for a drive one time had slipped from Pablo's grip and run straight into Jags' lifted arm. It was as though the boy had tried running through a steel joist. He hit the ground like a sack of rocks, his nose bleeding.

'Dias.'

'Dias.'

'You look cold, smoke a cigarette.' Jags offered the pack of Marlboro and Pablo fumbled one from the soft crumpled packet. His fingers were shaking as he placed the cigarette between moustache and lower lip. He waited patiently while Jags went through half the contents of an American motel-branded matchbook. The flame wouldn't take in the damp morning air and Jags cussed repeatedly. When he eventually coaxed a flame, cupping it in his large hand and raising it up, Pablo studied his employer's face. In the US, people assumed Jags was part Italian. South of the border he passed for Argentinian. In fact, he had no connection with either place. The long nose, slightly off-centred, was the first thing you noticed, followed by the eyes. These had no discernible colour, just two black slots in a weathered brown face. His dark curly hair was cut short, not military short but almost. Other than that, the face was solid and, at first glance, handsome.

While Pablo smoked, Jags took in the view. The sun was beginning to rise now – a ribbon of amethyst-coloured light appearing at the horizon. He felt his stomach rumble and turned to Pablo.

'We should get some food. Eat something decent 'fore we do anything else.'

Pablo looked dubious.

'Where?'

There was only one place in Brochu where outsiders like Jags ate – a barbeque restaurant done up to look like an old American diner, serving overpriced food for overpaid Yankees. Pablo had never eaten there, no one from the town ever did.

'I passed a little roadside place. Ten miles back. We can head there and then take the freeway north afterwards.' A route like this would take them in the opposite direction to town, away from where they usually worked.

'The freeway north to where?'

'I'll lay it all out for you later. After we eat.' Jags stamped the cold out of his feet and climbed back into the Chevy.

Once on the road, Pablo tried a little small talk, speaking in the slowed down Spanish that he usually used when they were together. Jags had told him in the past that he liked the practice. Pablo commented on the cold weather and the empty roads. His boss nodded along, understanding everything, but his half of the stilted conversation all came in English.

'You do not want to speak your Spanish today?'

'Not today.'

Pablo remembered something that Jags had said soon after they'd started working together. Something about men finding it harder to lie when they weren't speaking in their own tongue. When he was cross-examining the union leaders, miners or local politicians that they picked up, Jags would often insist they speak in English. Pablo was quiet for a while, chewing all this over. It was Jags who broke the silence. 'You're right about the weather. Back in Ohio we used to call this kind of cold a *calf-killing cold*. Same thing here I guess.'

Pablo looked out of his window. Sure enough, the few farmers still left in the valley – the dozen or so who had refused to take the mining company's money and go – had all moved their live-stock inside.

'You grow up in Ohio?' In three years, this was the first piece of personal information that Jags had ever volunteered. There had been a few vague mentions of his time in the military, but nothing more than that, not until now.

'Yup, Ohio. The Buckeye State. Right out in the boondocks . . .' He glanced over at Pablo. 'The middle of nowhere. I was born there and raised there. I was stuck there right up until the first day I could drive. Or drive legally. Then I got the fuck out.'

The roadside restaurant that Jags had seen was, in fact, a repur-posed shipping container, planted on scrubland at the side of a

Shell petrol station. It had a large red Coca-Cola sign hanging on the front and was flanked by two tired-looking palm trees. They parked in the petrol station forecourt and walked inside. The deep fat fryer was crackling into life down one end of the counter and the chef stroke waiter stroke restaurant owner pointed them in the direction of a table next to the window. They were the first customers in and as soon as he'd done attaching an orange hose to the twin gas hob at the other end of his work station, the owner hurried over with two laminated menus.

'*Buenas dias, quieres comer?*'

Jags nodded.

'*Un minuto, por favor.*' He took his time studying the handful of items on the menu then glanced up at Pablo.

'What ya going to have?'

'I'm not hungry.'

'You don't want anything to eat? Steak? The stew? It's on me. You should have something.'

Pablo shook his head. He didn't want to explain to Jags why he didn't want any food.

'No thank you, just coffee.' His boss could make him do a lot of things, but he could not make him eat.

'Your call.' He waved the owner over and ordered himself the steak and fried potatoes and coffee for two. He pointed at the fryer. '*Las papas a la Francesa, si?*'

'French fries, *si seño*r.' The owner exchanged a glance with Pablo. Jags saw this look but chose to ignore it. As far as the waiter was concerned he was just another gringo – *consultants* they called themselves – Americans whose work inevitably had something or other to do with the Brochu mine. The locals hated them – hated but tolerated – because the copper mine was all there was and when the mine was gone, there would be nothing. So you had to make a living while you could. The restaurant owner would cut the potatoes into thin strips and fry them the way Jags liked, because if he did that, then maybe more Americans would come? The gringo was probably paid more in a day than the men who worked the mine got paid in a month, but it didn't matter – what mattered was that there was work, not for everyone, but for just enough people to keep the town, the whole region, alive.

Jags worked his way steadily through the three-inch-thick rib eye and French fries; he ate the fat off the steak first and then the chips before starting on the meat. He ate more slowly than usual until a few other customers arrived, whereupon he cleaned the plate, put his cutlery together and raised his hand for the bill. He paid in cash, tipping generously. Outside he suggested they stroll around to the side of the restaurant and smoke another cigarette. It seemed to Pablo that his employer was in no hurry to go anywhere or do anything today and this was both unusual and unsettling. The sun had climbed above the mountains while they were eating, but it was cold still, and windy too. Jags listened to the wind pushing through the dusty palm trees – a dry clacking sound. It was a sound that Jags had come to associate with this place and one that he'd tried to put down in words. He glanced over at Pablo.

'How would you describe that noise? The wind in those palm trees there?' He pointed up at the trees.

'Describe it?' Pablo looked confused. 'I don't understand. It is just the air and the leaves, that's all.'

Jags shook his head.

'You have a poet's name, Pablo. The same name as your great poet, but you've got no poetry in you, have you?' Pablo gave an apologetic shrug and Jags dropped his cigarette and ground it out with the toe of his shoe. There was no need to demean the man, especially now. 'We should go.' They walked to the car, Jags keeping his back to the restaurant windows. He switched on the engine and turned up the heater. It was cold enough that they could see their breath. 'So, how was that coffee?'

'It was good, thank you.'

'No problem. A good cup of coffee is as good as a meal . . . that's what they say, isn't it?'

Pablo looked at Jags.

'In Ohio they say this?'

'Yeah. In Ohio.'

They hit the freeway and Jags drove for twenty minutes, still heading in the opposite direction from Brochu, away from every other job that he had asked Pablo to help him with. So far everything about this day had been different, everything about it had been wrong. Eventually Pablo summoned up the courage to ask.

'Where is the man?'

'Which man?'

'The poor bastard we're going to kill.'

'We're not killing anybody today.'

Pablo felt a wave of relief flood through him. His thoughts turned first to food. The breakfast he could have had but didn't. He kicked himself for not having thought to ask this question earlier. Jags turned and looked at his passenger. 'How many times have we worked together, Pablo? You and me?'

'What?'

'How many have we killed?'

'I have lost the number.' This was a lie. Pablo knew exactly how many. Eight was the number. Eight men shot or beaten to death, their pockets filled with rocks and then rolled down the steep side of the Brochu dam into the filthy waters below. Most nights, unless he was blind drunk, Pablo had nightmares, terrible nightmares. The dream was almost always the same; he was hauling a dead body out of the back of a white Chevy and rolling it over the wall, down into the dam. Then suddenly the roles would reverse and it was Pablo who was in the water, drenched and slowly drowning. He could feel the stones in his trouser pockets rubbing against his legs, but for some reason his hands couldn't reach them. He kicked and flapped around in the water, but it was futile – his body was too heavy to stay afloat. He was sinking. Struggling for just one more breath, he stretched his neck and opened his mouth, but it was too late. He was under. Looking up, he saw the polluted water close over his head. It was at this point in the dream that he would wake, dripping in sweat.

'What are we doing then, Mr Jags?'

'We're meeting someone, a friend of mine, out at the old mine. That place you showed me that time.'

'*Hijo de Dios?*'

'That's the place.'

Hijo had not been mined for many years; it was tapped out and derelict. Occasionally an entrepreneurial local would agree to take a small group of tourists there, to see what mining used to look like back in the old days, but only if they paid handsomely and in advance. It had to be a good amount of money – thirty US dollars per person or more – because the local people were superstitious and *Hijo* was an accursed place. Many hundreds of men and boys had lost their lives there.

Pablo doubted that his boss would even be able to find the old mine again without some help with the directions, but he was wrong. Jags took all the correct turns down an ever-narrowing series of roads and rock-strewn trails until Pablo realised that his employer must have visited the derelict mine without him – maybe more than once.

Jags brought the car to a stop within sight of the entrance. Above a cavernous hole in the rock face was a rectangular wooden sign with thick black lettering painted on it, informing you that you were about to enter *Hijo de Dios*. The white rock around the mouth of the mine was stained a dark brown, a reminder of the many blood sacrifices that had taken place here down the decades. A llama would be slaughtered, its blood smeared around the entrance and its organs removed and left in front of a carved figure that stood guard at the ingress to this and almost every other Chilean mine. These offerings were made by generation after generation of miners, anxious to placate the figure they called *El Tio* – not an uncle, but the devil himself, who they believed held their fate in his hands the moment they entered the mine. Jags had read a lot about this bloody tradition, out of interest but also for professional reasons. The devil was not a metaphor here. Pablo shuffled in the passenger seat.

'Who is it we are meeting here?'

'I told you already – a friend.'

Pablo nodded but he was unconvinced. Nothing about this day made any sense. Everybody knew the old mine was not a place you visited unless you absolutely had to. Only when a lot of money was on offer or, perhaps, if you were an idiot teenager, drunk or high on something and hoping that the many ghosts that haunted the place might scare your girlfriend into doing something she would later regret. Jags jabbed Pablo in the side with his elbow.

'Wake up. Let's walk. I'll bring the flashlight.' After Pablo was out of the car, Jags flipped open the glove compartment and took out a torch and the envelope of photographs, which he stuffed inside his jacket pocket.

A crudely carved tribute to *El Tio* stood just inside the entrance to the mine. The red paint had flaked and fallen away in places, but the devilish figure was no less ugly for that. His black eyes bulged and the twisted horns on his head looked sharp enough to draw blood. At his feet were a few rusted tins of food, bottles of overproof spirits, pouches of tobacco, cigarettes and pornographic magazines. All these gifts were designed to preoccupy the devil for the duration of a miner's shift or, more recently, a sight-seeing visit. If *El Tio* was kept busy there was a better chance he would let you enter and leave the mine unharmed. Jags smiled at the sight of the wooden devil and his pointless tributes, but Pablo looked away. His instinct was to beg one of Jags' cigarettes, light it and place it between *El Tio's* black lips as he had when they'd been here last time, but he knew his boss would only ridicule him.

'Who is this friend that wants to meet you here Mr Jags?'

'He's a mining guy. He thinks there's a seam of copper in here that got missed.'

'A seam? After all this time? It is not possible.'

'We'll see.' The pair left *El Tio* unbribed and walked across the threshold, into the darkness. Jags went first, the torch in his hand, while Pablo trailed reluctantly behind. Soon they had to stoop and then crouch as the tunnel narrowed and the ceiling dropped – first to a height of five and a half feet, then five and lower still. They moved in silence, the only noise was the sound of their breathing and water trickling down the black rock. Pablo let his mind wander. A seam of copper? There had always been stories that at the very centre of this mine, if you managed to dig far enough into the mountain, through the hardest rock and if the mine didn't collapse on top of you, then eventually you would reach a huge ball of solid copper. A ball as big as an office building and worth a fortune. Maybe this was what Mr Jags' friend had found? But this was just a story. They shuffled on; now and again the tunnel would divide and each time Jags took the right-hand turn. Pablo knew where they were heading – it was not far now. The tunnel veered right once more and then, quite suddenly, it opened out into a tall chamber. The space was perhaps three metres high and the same wide, but it felt huge compared to the cramped tunnels they'd been crawling through for the last twenty minutes. Big enough for Jags' purpose.

'Where is your friend?'

'There's no friend Pablo. There's no seam. It's just us.'

'I don't understand.' He glanced around. There was a lit camping lamp placed in each corner of the chamber. The ceiling was criss-crossed with beams of wood. Sitting on top of the thickest beam was a heap of white nylon rope. A jolt of fear shot through Pablo like electricity as the truth dawned. He turned and stared at Jags.

'You're going to kill me here?'

Jags shook his head.

'I'm not going to kill you. You're going to kill yourself.'

'No. Why?'

'It's time.'

Pablo tried to bolt but Jags was too quick. He grabbed hold of his right wrist and held it fast as Pablo wheeled around, first attempting to hit Jags and missing, then straining to break free – pulling and pulling like a fish on a line.

Jags let him tire himself out for a while before throwing his victim against the nearest wall and watching him slump to the floor. 'This'll go a lot easier for us both if you calm down, Pablo.'

The Chilean spat pathetically in Jags' direction, his white spittle travelling no further than his own puffer jacket and jeans.

'Fuck to you.' Pablo slumped forward, his chin on his chest. When he looked up at Jags, there were tears in his lined eyes. 'I do not understand. Why do you need to do this?'

Jags said nothing. 'Please. Help me . . . help me understand, I have done nothing wrong. I have told no one about the work we do. Not a word has come from my mouth. I swear it.' He crossed himself.

Jags looked at him.

'It doesn't matter, you were getting ready to run, Pablo. Or to turn.'

Pablo shook his head. 'No, no. It is not true, I have no such plan. This is wrong. *They* are wrong.'

Both men knew who *they* was.

'They aren't wrong.'

'They don't know me, they cannot read my mind.' His head shaking grew more vigorous, manic. Jags looked away. This conversation was beginning to bore him.

'They don't need to read your mind, you know that. They read your phone, your computer – everything is there.'

'They cannot know me better than *I* know me.'

Jags shook his head. Of course they did. That was the whole point. He pulled the envelope from his pocket and tossed it down to Pablo.

'Look at those.'

Pablo hesitated, then did as he'd been told. He took the photographs from the envelope and flicked through them. It took a moment for him to realise that the blurry photographs had been taken inside his own home. Fragments of furniture, the door to his kids' bedroom and then each of his children, in profile and asleep. He paused at the picture of his youngest son, Claudio – his favourite. The photograph of the boy reminded Pablo of a carved angel that he'd seen, long ago, inside the cathedral in Santiago. Jags pointed at the picture. 'You're doing this for your family Pablo. If you do this then your family will be taken care of.'

'And if I don't?'

'If you don't . . . they won't.'

Pablo stared at the picture of his son. Claudio was too young to know what sort of man his father was and this was why Pablo loved him best. He was still a hero to his youngest boy and if his life ended here, then he would remain heroic. More than a hero in fact – a martyr. One of the most respected in their small community – honoured every November as part of the Day of the Dead commemorations. Jags waited while these thoughts played out in Pablo's mind. He put the photographs back in the envelope and pocketed them before pointing up at the central beam.

'How do you know that this wood will hold my weight? The whole mountain could come down on your head.'

'*You* told me it would hold.'

Pablo remembered now. Towards the end of their previous visit, he had told Jags that this chamber was where the old miners sometimes came to hang themselves and that this beam was the best place for it. When the silicosis had them in its grip and breathing was too hard and getting worse – when every cough brought a mouthful of blood that had to be spat out or swallowed back down. Or when the cancer had almost eaten them away and the pain was too much – then they came here. Partly to save their families from ruinous hospital bills, but also as a favour to their fellow miners. Everyone in these mining communities knew that the flesh that *El Tio* loved more than any other, was human flesh. A human sacrifice, a suicide, had been known to keep the mines accident-free for weeks, months even. Pablo climbed to his feet and stopped, staring past Jags into the tunnel's dark mouth. There were miles of tunnel beyond that. He could walk into that labyrinth and never be found.

'You don't have to do this, I could just go, I can disappear.'

Jags shook his head. 'No you can't, no one can. And anyway, your family—'

'Let me try, let me run, please? Boss?'

'I'm not the boss, Pablo.'

'Who are you then?'

Jags paused. This was a man's final question and he wanted to answer it honestly.

'I am the overseer.'

Pablo repeated the English word and then translated it for himself. The old-fashioned term translated easily into Spanish and now Pablo understood. Jags was the overseer and he didn't need to ask anyone what that made him, he knew what he was. Jags pointed at a sturdy-looking wooden box by the wall.

'Take that and put it underneath the main beam.'

Pablo did as instructed. He wished he'd eaten the last meal Jags had offered him. He wished he'd kissed Claudio goodbye before he'd left that morning. At the end, that was all.

'The company will look after your family. . . a special pension for your wife.'

Pablo stared at Jags.

'A special pension . . .' It was clear he did not believe this, but it wasn't his main concern. 'Just promise me that my family will be safe. My wife, my children. Claudio especially. Tell me he will be safe.'

'We end this now and they will all be safe. I promise you that.'

'Speak it to me in Spanish.'

Jags nodded slowly and looked Pablo square in the eye.

'Tu familia estara a salvo. Now go ahead and haul that rope down.'

Pablo studied Jags as he spoke, then smiled sadly. His face was wet with tears now and he lifted his sweatshirt and wiped it dry. He placed his left foot on the wooden box first and stepped up gingerly. He reached up and pulled the white nylon noose down. He gave it a tug and nodded. It had been well-tied.

'You did a good job.' Leaning forward, he put his head and neck through. He only had one card left to play and so he played it now. 'You know that when you kill a man, you have to carry his soul with you? Carry it on your back – forever. We believe that.' He pointed his finger at Jags' broad back. 'You will have to work not just for one soul, but for two . . .'

'And all the rest.' Jags took a fast step forward and kicked the box away. Pablo's hands reached for the noose, but too late; he clawed uselessly at his skin, trying to get a finger between his neck and the rope, but the more he struggled, the tighter the noose became. Pretty soon his hands dropped limply back to his side, and Jags watched as Pablo twitched and turned on the rope. He watched his jeans darken at the crotch and smelt the sharp stink of piss. This was taking too long. Stepping forward again, he grabbed his victim's leather belt with both hands and pulled. Pablo's stretched neck snapped, a louder sound than Jags had expected. It ricocheted back off the dark stone walls of the cave, then disappeared down into the black tunnel that led deep into the mountain. After that, there was silence.

Sooner or later someone would notice the smell and Pablo Mistral's body would be found. His death would be recorded as suicide, but if the family paid the priest a little extra then the chances were he might still be buried in the Brochu church cemetery. Pablo was right to question Jags' suggestion of a special pension for his wife. Such an arrangement would imply a special connection between the company and this man and there could be no such link. Anyhow, supporting the dead man's family did not suit Jags' purpose. He had done with Pablo Mistral, but he had not finished with his family.

Jags drove, not taking his foot off the floor until he was within sight of Santiago International Airport. His instructions were to return back to base, back to Public Square's headquarters in Cupertino, California. As he drove, Jags searched for answers to the dead man's question: Why him? Why now?

It could have been anything. A word that Pablo had typed into a search engine, something he had bought online or just looked at for too long. Maybe a piece of music he'd listened to had contained the clue, or a conversation with someone on the smartphone that Jags had given him. Perhaps he'd uttered a certain phrase or mentioned one of the trigger words that they listened for. The phone tracker might have told them something about Pablo that even Jags didn't know. It could have been anything.

He steered the Chevy into the short-term parking lot, found a spot he liked and switched off the engine. It could have been anything. But it wasn't – it was the sum total of everything. Every piece of data about this one man, added together and analysed alongside everyone else's. The company Jags worked for had decided that Pablo was unreliable because they knew *everything*. And they were never wrong.

5 Grand Luxe

THE HEADLAND HOTEL, HONG KONG

A grey-toppered doorman in braided uniform and white gloves pulled the heavy glass door open for Patrick and nodded a greeting. Patrick thanked him with one of the dozen or so Cantonese phrases he had memorised. The doorman gave him a look that suggested he appreciated the effort if not the linguistic skill. Patrick reshouldered his kitbag and trudged across the thick carpet in the direction of the nearest empty armchair.

Sitting down in the lobby of the Headland was sweet relief after the tumult of a Hong Kong rush hour. Although the hotel was full – in large part due to the number of hacks who'd checked in in recent days – it didn't feel that way. Almost all of the other wing-backed armchairs distributed around the room were taken, but there was a hush to the place – more like a gentlemen's club than a hotel lobby. An enormous multi-tiered chandelier glistened in the centre of the high ceiling. Underneath this, on a polished mahogany table, was an arrangement of dark red roses and green foliage on a similar scale. Patrick gazed at the display and did a rough count – he could see at least one hundred and fifty large-headed red roses from where he sat. The flower seller outside his local tube station back at home – the place where he sometimes bought flowers for his girlfriend – would probably charge around five hundred quid for that lot.

The Headland was, without doubt, one of the swankiest hotels he'd ever stayed in and he had mixed feelings about the place. If he'd been here in Hong Kong with William Carver, as opposed to John Brandon, then no way would they have booked a room here. Brandon referred to it as the '*Most Luxe of the Grand Luxe hotels*'. Not just the *press* hotel but a *posh press* hotel – Carver would rather have chewed his own arm off. Patrick smiled. Maybe he'd buy a postcard of the hotel from the souvenir shop and send it to him. Although given that his old boss had ignored every email and phone message Patrick had left for the last several months, there was a good chance William would just chuck it straight in the bin.

'Bollocks to him.'

A Chinese man in black suit and tie, who was sitting nearby, lowered the Asian *Wall Street Journal* he'd been pretending to read and glanced across at Patrick. His face was brick-red, his eyes bright. He smiled at Patrick. This man was a permanent fixture in the lobby of the Headland – the least secret secret policeman Patrick had ever seen. But then this man's function wasn't just to watch and listen – his bosses on the mainland had far more subtle ways of doing that – it was to remind everyone that China was here. They weren't going anywhere and, pretty soon, they'd be in charge. Patrick smiled back, then pushed himself up from the armchair and went to look for John Brandon. *First find your reporter, then mix your package and after that – sleep.* He decided a sweep of the hotel would be quicker and more effective than using the phone, since Brandon seldom read messages or used his mobile unless he needed something.

Patrick had been away from home for five of the last six months and for almost that entire time he'd been working with Brandon. He'd heard people refer to him as *John Brandon's bloke* or, even worse, *Brandon's boy*. They'd been together in Egypt as the Arab Spring slowly fizzled out, then Turkey, briefly in Bahrain and Ukraine, and now Hong Kong. Technically Patrick had been promoted – he was producing one of the BBC's most high-profile correspondents – but it didn't feel that way.

He checked the bars first. There were five of these distributed around the hotel, possibly one of the reasons that the place never felt too busy. Brandon was in the third bar Patrick tried.

'Good God Patrick, you look like shit. I'm surprised the doorman let you in.'

Patrick would have liked to respond in kind, but the truth was that Brandon looked fine. Well-slept, freshly shaved and extremely smart in his trademark cream linen suit and blue, open-necked shirt. The sweep of thick white hair was washed and combed and, as Patrick drew closer, he wondered whether Brandon might even be wearing some sort of foundation. The veteran anchorman saw Patrick staring.

'I just did a quick two-way for the news channel . . .' This explained both the make-up and Brandon's good mood. He didn't get asked to do as much television now as he used to and he jumped at every opportunity. 'Updating the Great British public on the latest demos and so on.' Patrick nodded, although he wondered how helpful the viewers would have found this update, given that Brandon clearly hadn't left the hotel all day. His two-way would have been nothing more than a rehash of wire copy and some stuff he'd read on the internet.

'I've got all the voices we need for this radio piece, John. Are you happy to start putting that together?' Brandon nodded. 'My room in twenty minutes if that works for you?'

Brandon looked at his watch.

'Twenty. Absolutely. I'll just finish this . . .' he pointed at the vodka Martini and thimble-sized portion of salted cashew nuts sitting on the bar in front of him, '. . . and I'll be right up. What about this hotel, eh? I bet Carver would never have you staying in a place like this?'

'No, he wouldn't.'

'No. A cut above . . .' He plucked the cocktail stick-skewered olive from his Martini and gobbled it down. 'Especially the bedrooms. Odd isn't it? In Egypt we had to sleep on those dreadful bloody Chinese-made sheets. Here in China – more or less – we get the very best Egyptian cotton. I haven't even had to use my John Lewis mattress topper. Ironic huh?'

'I guess so.'

'Perhaps I should do a *FOOC* on it.'

Patrick hoped that this was a passing fancy. Producing a useable despatch for *From Our Own Correspondent* with Brandon was a tortuous experience.

'So, twenty minutes, in my room?'

'Twenty, yes . . .' Brandon glanced round the bar. A few new faces had wandered in. There was a *'Women in Business'* conference in one of the boardrooms and, by the looks of it, one or two among the group might have recognised him. 'Half an hour tops.'

Up in his room, a maid had turned down the king-size bed. There was a gold-wrapped chocolate on his pillow and a lily of the valley candle flickering on the bedside table. Patrick briefly considered whether a quick nap might not be a good idea, but decided against. If he went to sleep now he might never wake up again. He scoffed the chocolate and tried not to think about the bed. He remembered his last full week off work, back at home in London with his girlfriend. Rebecca had tucked him up in bed on a Sunday afternoon and he'd stayed there, pretty much comatose, until Tuesday. It was the best sleep of his life. He woke at six in the evening to a tray of hot tea and toast slathered in melted butter and Marmite.

'I feel like a new man.'

'You and me both. My current man is obviously broken beyond mending.' He wanted to call Becs; it had been a day or two since they'd spoken and it would be good to hear her voice. He checked the time and did the maths. He couldn't call her now, she'd be teaching a class. But definitely later.

He took a shower, standing under the burning hot water for a full ten minutes, letting it wash a day's worth of sweat and grime from his skin. After that he wrapped himself in a towel and the fluffy hotel dressing gown and stood at the window. From his room he had a clear view down over the harbour and across to Kowloon. Patrick rubbed his blond hair dry and watched the Star Ferry boats shuttle to and fro across the dark water. He pulled on a clean T-shirt and jeans, cleared the dressing table, set up his laptop and tape recorder and got to work.

First he loaded all the audio he'd collected that day onto the laptop and chopped it up into bands. He designated each a different colour and placed one on top of the other. This part of the process always reminded Patrick of his parents and a long-ago holiday on the Isle of Wight. In an Alum Bay gift shop, the eight-year-old Patrick glimpsed a glass lighthouse containing layer upon layer of coloured sand. He'd never wanted anything as much as he wanted that lighthouse; he begged for the souvenir and eventually his mum gave in and bought it, in spite of his father's warning that the ornament would inevitably be broken before the day was out. In fact the Isle of Wight lighthouse survived a year – his most prized possession. It lasted until one long, boring Sunday when curiosity had got the better of him and he removed the cork stopper with his dad's bottle opener to see what might happen.

Patrick crouched over the laptop and studied each jagged layer of sound. He moved things up and down with the mouse, cut the interviews to the right length and arranged the wild track – the rain, the chanting, police loudhailers and the rest – at the bottom of the screen. An hour passed without him noticing, but still no sign of John Brandon. He listened again to his interview with Eric Fung. There was a whole section where Patrick had become rather too technical, asking questions about the way in which the young protestors were organising, the messaging services and apps they were using. It was interesting to him, but the general listener would find it boring. He chopped the section out, but didn't bin it. He moved it to the hard drive, a file where he'd been putting other stuff like this.

Just when Patrick was beginning to think he'd have to go looking for him again, John Brandon tapped on the hotel door.

Once inside he surveyed the room.

'Not bad, not bad at all . . . nice view. Your room's not as big as mine, but you could certainly swing a cat in here – if you had to. That's rare in Hong Kong.' He looked at the clothes and recording equipment strewn across the bed, desk and floor. 'You've rather fucked up the Feng Shui with all this mess though.' Patrick ignored this, clearing a space on the bed so Brandon could sit and record his script. He had written a rough outline already and John went through this, changing a word or two with his Mont Blanc, adding the odd line. 'Right you are, I'm ready when you are squire.' Patrick had to hand it to Brandon, he worked quickly, especially when there was somewhere else he wanted to be. He took the spare duvet from inside the clothes cupboard and draped it over Brandon's head to cancel out the sound of the air conditioning and remove any echo. He handed John the microphone.

'Few words for level?'

'Peter Piper picked a peck of etcetera etcetera . . .'

'Fine.'

There were a few overlaps, but nothing that Patrick couldn't deal with. He set about loading the new audio onto the laptop. At his back, Brandon was getting increasingly fidgety.

'You don't really need me for this next bit, do you Patrick?'

'Don't you want to listen through?'

'No, no. I trust you. Trust you completely.'

'Fine, well then . . .'

'Excellent, good man. I'll see you downstairs. We're in the Purple Bar. Viv, me . . . the usual crowd. Oh, and a new face, this rather charming American fellow. Dan something, he's a big fan of *yours truly*.'

'Yeah, I don't think I'm going to—' But the door had been slammed shut and Brandon was gone. While the audio loaded, Patrick stared across at the lights of Kowloon and at his own reflection in the dark window. Working with William Carver had never been easy, but they'd always rubbed along pretty well – they complemented each other. He checked himself. Maybe he was misremembering? Putting a nostalgic gloss on things? Carver was a perpetual malcontent . . . *mal* most things in fact. Maladapted, malodourous . . . Patrick grinned. Despite this, he missed him. Missed the insight and the intelligence. He even missed the regular bollockings that Carver dished out – sometimes deserved, sometimes not. He was a better journalist when he was working with William Carver.

6 Do No Harm

William watched Jemima McCluskey mount another two-pronged attack on an obstinate prawn ball, spearing it with both sticks before transporting it in the direction of her mouth. She'd tucked one napkin into the neck of her ivory silk blouse and had another across her lap protecting a tweed skirt. Carver had never seen a grown-up so uncomfortable with chopsticks — maybe he should ask the waiter for a fork.

'Not a big fan of Chinese food then, McCluskey?' His lunch companion finished her mouthful.

'Cannae say I have it that often.'

'No kidding?'

'But I know it's one of your favourites and I'm nothing if not game.' She set off in pursuit of another prawn ball. 'How did your lesson go?'

Carver lifted an eyebrow.

'Well, if that's the future of journalism then I think I can safely say . . . we're screwed.' McCluskey smiled a yellow-toothed smile before slurping up a few noodles with water chestnuts.

43

'They cannae all be bad?'

'There's one or two.' Carver took a long draft of his Tsingtao lager. 'One, anyway.'

'No one to lay a glove on your boy Patrick though, eh?'

William hailed a waiter and ordered some more egg-fried rice and another lager. McCluskey was tiptoeing into territory that Carver would prefer to avoid. He'd had a feeling that Patrick would turn out to be the reason for McCluskey's trip up to London. She didn't stray far from her work at the BBC monitoring station at Caversham or her nearby two-up, two-down unless she had a good reason. He ignored the question about Patrick and asked his own instead.

'What about *your* work McCluskey. Overheard anything interesting recently?'

'Oh aye. It's busy, no mistake. This is the first day off I've had in twelve . . . North Africa, the Middle East, Ukraine. Now Hong Kong. It's kicking off all over the place right now.' She glanced up from her food. 'Perhaps you've noticed?' This little dig was to be expected and Carver took it on the chin. He knew how McCluskey felt about his decision to take some time away from front-line reporting in favour of teaching. She thought it was bloody stupid. 'You still read the odd newspaper do yer? Listen to the radio now and again?'

'I do. It looks like you're having some trouble with those chopsticks, do you want me to get you a fork?'

'Me? Nah I'm fine.' She harpooned another prawn ball and held it aloft to prove her point. 'Which reminds me – talking about the radio – is it your boy Patrick that's been producing all of John Brandon's stuff these last few months? Is that who he's with, now that you're . . . doing whatever it is you're doing?' Carver confirmed that this was the case. 'He's doin' a cracking job isn't he? Brandon's been sounding good.' McCluskey really was pushing all of Carver's buttons today.

He poured the dregs of his first lager into the new one and took a swig.

'I don't hear everything.'

'Who does?'

'But the stuff I've heard is a bit mixed.'

'Is that right?'

'Not Patrick's fault necessarily . . . you can only work with what you've got. Can't be easy . . . making a silk purse out of a sow's arse.'

McCluskey grinned; this was more like the Carver she knew and loved.

'Fair point . . .' She paused. 'But it's Patrick that's been with him all along is it? Egypt, Turkey, Ukraine . . . now Hong Kong, all of that?'

'Yes. Why?'

McCluskey put her chopsticks down, one either side of the plate as though they were a knife and fork.

'I've been listening to what's been coming out of those countries these last few months, watching things unfold, and I've noticed something.'

'I see.'

'And I got to wondering whether Patrick has maybe noticed it too.' McCluskey had Carver's complete attention now and she knew it.

'Noticed what?'

'It's hard to explain, it's . . . complex.'

'Complex huh? But you think Patrick might be able to understand it? Even if I can't.' There was an edge to William's voice.

'Like I say. . . maybe. He's there, you're not.' She paused. 'So do you mind if I run some of what I've got by him?'

'Why should I mind? It's none of my business, do what you like. Both of you.' This sounded harsher than Carver had intended.

'Smashing, so will you make the introduction? Phone him or

drop him a wee line? Keep it simple, no names, just ask him if he'll help a pal of yours.'

Carver took a slurp of lager.

'It's probably better if you do it yourself McCluskey. Given that I haven't spoken to him all year and I have no intention of starting now.'

'I've only met him the once and I want the approach to be . . .' She looked for the right word, '. . . subtle. It'd be really helpful if you'd just let him know that a friend of yours needs a favour.'

Carver pushed his plate to one side.

'This is your *first* day off in twelve you said?' She nodded. 'And it *is* a day off is it Jemima? You're not going to be putting this chicken and cashew nuts through on expenses?'

McCluskey's face flushed.

'Me coming here has nothing to do with Caversham.'

'And nothing to do with that *spooky* stuff that goes on upstairs at Caversham either? Up on the top floor?'

She shook her head slowly.

'What exactly are you suggesting William?'

'You know what I'm suggesting.'

McCluskey was on her feet surprisingly fast for a woman of her age.

'We've known each other for twenty plus years William Carver . . .' She put her raincoat on. 'How many favours have I done fer you in that time? I wanted a favour in return . . .' She pulled a black beret down over her white candyfloss hair. '. . . but mainly I wanted to come and jolly you up. Coax you out from underneath that self-pitying shell that you're hiding in.'

'Fuck off Jemima.'

'Don't worry, I will, I've just got one more thing to say to you.' She met his eye and held it. 'What happened back in Cairo wasnae Patrick's fault and you know it.' He shrugged. 'It was *your* fault and the sooner you *man up* and admit that, the sooner ye can start forgiving yourself. You eejit.' She took a £10 and a £20 note from her wallet, pushed them under her water glass and left.

Carver glanced around. Most of the half-full restaurant and all of the waiting staff were glaring at him, wondering what dreadful things he must've said to upset the little old lady. His waiter arrived unbidden and started clearing the table. Carver had to wrestle his lager back from the man's grasp.

'I'm not bloody finished.'

He sat and stared at the flock wallpaper and the tiny vase with a single red carnation – the only other thing apart from his drink that the waiter hadn't removed. McCluskey was *half*-right. Patrick wasn't to blame for what had happened, he knew that. Nevertheless, ignoring his calls, text messages and emails was still the right thing to do. Removing himself from Patrick's life was the biggest favour he could do him. Over the years, too many people had been hurt as a result of his work. Too much collateral damage. The oath he'd taken – Carver's own version of a Hippocratic oath – was the only way to fix that. If McCluskey thought the teaching was a cop out, so be it. If Patrick and the entire press pack thought he'd lost his nerve, that didn't matter either. What mattered was that Carver did *no more harm*.

7 Inside the Square

Jags was met at the airport, even though he'd made no such request nor told anyone when he was arriving or on which flight. Very fucking smooth, just like everything at Public Square Inc. A lean black man in a chauffeur's get-up, complete with peaked cap, picked him out from among the hundreds of faces inside the San Fran arrivals hall – no board with a name on, no mention at all of Jags' name or his employer's either. The driver introduced himself as Eldridge, addressed him as sir, and talked about the fine weather and the gridlocked San Francisco traffic as they walked through the airport and out into the car park. The car was a new model Tesla and Eldridge knew a route that avoided the worst of the rush hour. Jags didn't like being driven, but he guessed that if he had to be driven then it might as well be like this.

Once they were away from the airport and out on the highway, he took in the scenery. The sky was that particular shade of blue that seemed unique to California, decorated here and there with bright dashes of white – not clouds, but contrails. In no time, Eldridge had them beyond the city limits and the scenery started

48

to get greener. The countryside reminded Jags a little of Switzerland, although there were regular reminders of where you *really* were. Groups of prisoners in pink jumpsuits were cleaning up the trash next to the freeway, watched over by armed guards cradling shotguns. They drove past eight or nine of these gangs, most of them clearing rubbish, but some with rakes and trowels, down on their knees, planting pots of bright orange Californian poppies on stretches of ground that had been left blackened by the recent wildfires. The state flower grew wild, but the software company that sponsored this stretch of freeway knew that burnt scrub wasn't a good look and had decided to give mother nature a helping hand. Jags sat back in his seat and closed his eyes. He didn't enjoy being summoned back to base and he needed to be on his mettle when he got there. A few minutes' shut-eye was his plan.

When he woke half an hour later, he felt better, rested. He reached for his notebook and pencil.

A blinding blue sky
Convicts out on day release
Planting wild poppies

He nodded. Not bad. Jags counted the syllables off on his fingers and closed his notepad with a grunt of satisfaction. He was tempted to run the poem by Eldridge, see what he made of it, but he decided against. If Jags read it and received a lukewarm or confused reaction then that would spoil his good mood. The haikus were meant to help keep him calm, he didn't want to screw that up. They were nearly there anyway. A uniformed guard checked a clipboard before waving them through the security gates. Eldridge drove the Tesla at a stately fifteen kilometres per hour up the wide white gravel drive towards their destination.

*

The Public Square headquarters resembled a huge glass egg, balanced on its side. A glass manufacturer in Germany had become very rich as a result of this single order; for two years every curved or flat sheet of reinforced glass the factory made was destined for this building, ten miles outside Cupertino.

Back in the beginning, inside Public Square's first-ever office in downtown San Francisco, the founder and CEO Elizabeth Curepipe had her work station right next to reception – inside a glass box where she could see and be seen. The message was openness, modernity, transparency. Three of her favourite words and this shiny egg was, in part, a nod to that – just a whole lot bigger. Jags counted the five floors of shining glass. At its blunt summit – occupying the entire top floor – was Elizabeth. And her co-founder, Frederick.

'Fucking Fred.'

Eldridge turned his capped head.

'What was that sir?'

'Nothing. Just talking to myself.'

This glass could take twenty rounds from an assault rifle: in the time it took a gunman to fire off that number of shots, he would have been identified and dealt with. Jags had helped with this calculation in his capacity as chief security consultant. He advised on security right across the Curepipe operation – a big job. Big – and also usefully vague.

Over the years Elizabeth Curepipe had come to rely on Jags; she trusted him and when she travelled abroad, a lot of the time he went with her. She ensured that he was well paid – every year another ten or twenty per cent in cash or Public Square shares. She worried out loud that he might leave and other companies and individuals had certainly approached him, offers had been made. But she need not have worried, Jags was loyal. Not to the company – he remembered how much he hated Public Square Inc. every time he was summoned back here to headquarters – but he was loyal to Elizabeth.

Frederick knew this, just as Fred knew everything. It was Fred, not Elizabeth, who had hired Jags, although Jags often wished it was otherwise. Only Fred knew *what* Jags really was and what he did. The full range of responsibilities. Not Elizabeth, never Elizabeth, and while the two men disagreed about many things, they were as one on this. *Protect the Queen* – that was what they used to say, back in the beginning.

Eldridge parked in one of the prime spots in the car park and, opening the boot, handed Jags his bag and then the key to the Tesla as well. Jags was momentarily confused.

'What's this?'

'Mr Curepipe said you should keep hold of the car, sir. In case you want it later.'

'I see.'

There was something about the chauffeur's manner that didn't sit right, but then in this part of California every cab driver was something else – a coder, actor, concert pianist – you never knew.

Walking into the huge glassy atrium of Public Square, Jags noticed a change. There was an empty strip of freshly painted wall where there used to be a long TV screen. The green on black screen was, in fact, a digital ticker tape. It used to feature a rolling, random selection of all the millions of questions that people around America and the world were typing into the Public Square search engine. Now it was gone. Elizabeth had wanted to *let a little light in on the magic* that Public Square made possible. She wanted to be open and transparent. Fred knew that showing the workings was a risk and argued against. Sure enough, it quickly became obvious that the giant screen was not offering visitors a fleeting glimpse into a magician's box of tricks – it was more like chucking a flare down a public sewer. In any half hour a spectator might see searches about *cannibalism, racism, bump stock gun overrides* and pretty much any form of human or animal-related pornography you could imagine . . .

For a while they put a 10-second delay on the live feed and a moderator edited what went out. As a result, only achingly hip and high-minded searches made it to the digital ticker tape. The kid doing the moderating blabbed to someone about the work she was doing and the local then national press found out. They used that stick to beat Public Square even harder. Elizabeth ordered a return to the random and unpasteurised for a while but it was never going to last. The experiment was meant to show how engaged and vibrant America was, how thirsty the people were for knowledge and information and how Public Square was helping quench that thirst. In fact the experiment showed that America – most of the data was home grown – was fundamentally *sad*. A sad, lonely and angry nation; still under God – there were plenty of very strange questions about Jesus – but also preoccupied by thoughts of death and disease, pornography, celebrity and violence. As one of the temporary receptionists at Public Square so eloquently put it, watching the ticker tape all day was *'fucking scary'*. Looking at the gap on the wall above reception, it was clear that Fred had finally persuaded Elizabeth to pull the plug.

The current receptionist, a bright-eyed and bushy-tailed woman who looked like she arrived straight out of college, bestowed on Jags her biggest white-toothed smile. 'A very good morning Mr . . .' Her eyes flicked down at her computer screen, which was embedded in the white Corian work top, '. . . Jags?'

'Hi.'

The girl read something else on her screen and adjusted her expression from friendly welcome to profound regret.

'I'm incredibly sorry sir, but I've just seen that Mr Curepipe's running a little late . . .' Jags nodded. Of course he was. Jags still hadn't got used to Fred's new name, even though it had been a couple of years now since the million-dollar wedding. On marrying Elizabeth, Fred had taken her surname. This had been hailed as an almost heroic act of self-sacrifice and feminism in every quarter.

It seemed like the only person in the world who saw things differently was Jags. Fred hadn't taken Elizabeth's name because he was a feminist – he'd taken it because he was a scheming little shitbag. '. . . but he asked me to give you the trips feedback form to fill in. While you were waiting. Please.' She passed him a sheet of A4 paper. A questionnaire.

'Frederick wants me to fill this thing in?'

'I guess so, sir. He asked me to ask . . .'

'Yeah, yeah.' Jags took the piece of paper and went and sat down on a low white leather sofa. The receptionist called after him.

'Thank you so much. Can I get you cold press coffee? Filtered water?'

'No thanks. What about Elizabeth Curepipe, where's she?' The girl checked her screen.

'He asked me to tell you that she's unavailable . . .' Her face flushed at this mistake. 'I mean, I'm afraid Mrs Curepipe is unavailable.'

Jags read the questionnaire. It seemed strangely low-tech for Fred, but there would be a reason for that. There was always a reason. *Where had the employee travelled to? Purpose of trip. How long was the stay? Hotel or accommodation details. Had the issue been dealt with to the satisfaction of all involved? Possible next steps? Expenses incurred.* He scribbled down some answers to Frederick's dumbass questions.

Jags was kept waiting for a quarter of an hour; after finishing with the form he sat back and watched the people come and go. The average employee age was late twenties to early thirties; they strode in and out in a purposeful manner, most of them holding their laptops open in front of them – just in case they got an urgent email while walking between the water cooler and the crapper, Jags guessed. Eventually the bushy-tailed receptionist strode over and asked if he'd like her to take him up to Mr Curepipe's office.

'I know where it is.'

Fred Curepipe was waiting for Jags outside the elevator, his thin hand outstretched. Forbes Rich List top five, *GQ* Man of the Year, titan of the tech world . . . all of that, standing in front of Jags with that annoying shit-eating grin on his face.

'There you are, I'm sorry to have kept you waiting. Jeez, you look tired Jags, bad flight? Or were you hitting those Pisco sours a little too hard? I hear they're good. Are they good?' Fred Curepipe spoke quickly, especially when a thought or idea excited him. The story was that his engineers and software developers had to record any meetings with their boss that involved him describing a new idea or an improvement to a Public Square product and then play the recording back at half-speed in order to work out what on earth he was talking about.

'They are good. You should go try one someday.'

'I shall, I absolutely shall.'

Jags nodded. One Pisco sour would put Fred on his bony arse. The two men studied one another. Jags noticed that that Fred's mousy brown hair had thinned a little since he'd last seen him. Apart from that, he looked the same as ever. Despite living on the West Coast for over a decade, Fred still wore the same preppy north-eastern wardrobe he'd adopted at college. A blue Oxford button-down shirt open at the neck, khaki chinos, and a bright ribbon belt. His trousers looked an inch too short to Jags, his socks too white and his Italian loafers, just ridiculous. To Jags' eye, he looked like someone who was about to go play lawn tennis or polo or some such sport. And who was probably going to lose. Of course, Fred didn't play any sport, ever. All he did was work.

'Here's that form you asked for.' Jags passed him the piece of paper and watched as Fred ran his eye down the list of wisecracks and obscene suggestions that Jags had made in response to the various questions. Alongside *Purpose of visit?* Jags had written, *To fake a man's suicide on behalf of Public Square.*

'That's very funny Jags, really amusing . . .' Shaking his head, he strode over to a boxy black paper shredder. 'Everyone else at the company has to fill these forms in. You wouldn't believe how much we can ascertain about a person from how they answer a dozen innocent-looking questions. What they write, how they write . . .' Jags watched as, within seconds, the questionnaire was turned into gerbil bedding. 'Not you, of course, you're special. But I thought you might be interested and I didn't want you getting bored while you were sitting down there in reception . . . waiting.' Jags imagined how good it would feel to jam Fredrick's hand down into the shredder and watch the machine eat his fingers, from manicured nail to knuckle.

'Where's Elizabeth?'

'She's busy. You'll have to make do with me for now. Take a seat, make yourself comfortable.' Jags looked around at the options. Fred's office was not short on chairs; his collection mirrored the furniture collection at the Museum of Modern Art in New York although if you gave him the chance, Fred would tell you that his chairs were of a superior quality. Jags chose a Breuer club chair, the one furthest from Fred, who remained standing, one hand on his old oak desk, big as a boat, which Jags remembered him saying used to belong to Washington or Reagan or some crap like that. Once he felt that he'd established his authority, Fred relaxed.

'Elizabeth's in the middle of an *hour-long* meeting with Public Square employee representatives.'

'The company's getting unionised now?'

'Not a union, no, a little less adversarial than that. Hopefully.' He smiled. 'She's calling it the *family council*. It's a dozen representatives across all the various divisions – every arm of the company. It's got no real power, but it's a chance for them to let off some steam, feel like they're being listened to. She's got some real hotheads in the room but she seems to like it that way.' Jags nodded. This sort of thing was right up Lizzie's street. It wasn't enough that Public Square was hugely successful, nor even that it was respected; she needed people inside and outside the company to love Public Square the way she did. Fred was happy for her to look after that sort of thing. It wasn't his strong suit. 'So . . .' he paused. 'Do you need to tell me anything about your trip down to Brochu? Or was it all rather straightforward and dull?'

'I'm not sure dull is the word I'd choose.'

Fred sighed and sat down.

'We had a security problem that needed attending to, Jags, and you're my security guy. All I want is for you to tell me whether you managed to make the problem go away.'

'The problem has gone away.'

'Excellent, so now we . . .'

'I should tell you that the problem made a pretty convincing case for himself. I hope those algorithms of yours were right about him.'

Fred nodded slowly. 'We had more than five thousand different data points on that particular subject, nearly as many as we have on your average American or European. *The sum* wasn't wrong, it was spot on. Does that reassure you?'

'I guess it'll have to.' Jags shuffled in his seat; these things cost tens of thousands of bucks and they weren't even comfortable. 'I sent you those ideas you asked for about what to do with Brochu medium term, too. D'you get a chance to run your eye over those?'

'I did . . .' Fred gazed out across the Public Square campus, straight white paths bisecting neat green lawns – some grass, some Astroturf. Fred preferred Astroturf. 'You want to give every family in Brochu twenty-eight million pesos?'

'I don't want to do anything, you asked me how much it would cost to move the town, Fred – that's how much.'

'Thirty-five grand – approximately. They're expensive peasants, these peasants of yours.'

'They're not my . . .' but Fred ignored him.

'For the sake of argument, let's say we bought the whole town, then that'd be . . . he glanced down at his steepled hands and found the answer there. '. . . around three million dollars.'

'Yep.'

'That's a lot of money, Jags.'

'Depends how you look at it. The last time I heard, the mining part of Public Square was worth fifteen and a half billion dollars. Once you add it all up.'

Fred lifted both eyebrows in a look of exaggerated surprise.

'You've been going through the company accounts in some detail by the sounds of it, Jags. And doing some really big sums too. Bully for you.' All employee searches were monitored; if Jags had looked at the Public Square accounts using any company-owned device, then it would have been red-flagged and Fred would have known about it. These flagged alerts were the first thing Fred Curepipe looked at each morning and the last thing he read at night. Jags shook his head.

'Or maybe I just read about it in the *New York Times*.'

'Nope. The *Times* doesn't have that number. Nor the *Wall Street Journal*. Maybe it was just a lucky guess?' He paused. 'Of course, I'm delighted to see you taking such a keen interest in the company Jags, but I don't see what our internal accounts have got to do with security and security is what you're . . .'

'That's enough Fred. . .' Elizabeth Curepipe was standing at the door. Blond shoulder-length hair, blue eyes, the reddest lipstick Jags had ever seen. 'You know I don't like it when you two fellas fight.'

Her suit jacket and short skirt were charcoal grey and expensive-looking. Jags didn't really like the way she dressed these days. She used to dress different, more casual. Now it was either this kind of thing or the black polo neck and trouser thing, clothes that looked to Jags like some sort of armour. She strode over and, bending from the waist, kissed Jags gently on the cheek.

'Hey Lizzie, good to see you.' He wondered if the lipstick had left a mark, it seemed impossible that it wouldn't have. He glanced at Fred, who was doing a good job of pretending not to have noticed or not to give a shit. Elizabeth went and sat down in an Eames chair by the window and lifted her feet up onto the ottoman, legs crossed at the ankles. Jags noticed that the soles of her black patent shoes were also red, but not as red as that lipstick. It became clear that she must have been standing at the door for a while as she'd clearly heard a good deal of their conversation.

'I read your report too, Jags, and I've been thinking about Brochu. I'm against trying to buy the whole place out. A buyout's not really Public Square's style. *We* do well when *they* do well – remember? And we do well when we're doing *good*.' She smiled; a 100-watt smile that Jags had frequently tried and failed to capture in his battered notebook. 'I want something that feels more like a *win-win*. So I've got a different idea . . .'

8 The Lennon Wall

Patrick finished mixing the radio package, filed it to London and then pulled on some jeans and a shirt and made his way down to the main restaurant. His plan was to eat something decent, drink something non-alcoholic and then straight back upstairs to bed. If he could stay awake until ten p.m. his time then he'd also be able to phone Rebecca during her lunch break.

His drinking had got a little out of hand in recent months. The *one day on, one day off* rule had slipped. First it was *two days on, one day off* and, before he knew it, and for the duration of his time in Ukraine, it was *seven days on and zero days off*. He could make a case for needing a drink at the end of each day in Donetsk, but Hong Kong was different and a bit of discipline was called for.

When the lift doors pinged open at his floor he found himself face to face with one of his colleagues, Vivian Fox, although he almost didn't recognise her. Viv was in charge of the BBC news-gathering operation here in Hong Kong as she had been in Ukraine and Turkey before that. Her main responsibility was TV and

Patrick was a radio man, but they'd spent a lot of time together over the last few months. He'd always respected her, but in recent times he'd come to like her too.

This was the first time he'd seen her wearing anything other than her usual uniform of cargo pants, Bata boots and a dark linen shirt. Instead of this, she was wearing a knee-length, dark green dress, heels and make-up. The most striking change was to her hair, which was having a night off from its usual neat ponytail and was hanging long and dark around her shoulders. Patrick nodded.

'Hey Viv. I thought Brandon said you guys were already in the bar?'

'Yeah, we were . . . I mean they are. I mean I just had to jump back up to my room to get something.'

Patrick smiled at his colleague.

'Like your best dress and a full makeover?'

'What? Shut up.' She paused. 'Have you met him?'

'Who?'

'You know who. The new face. He's called Dan something. He's from Colorado.'

'Dan something from Colorado? No, I've not met him. I've seen him around though. He was at the demo in Central this afternoon . . . it didn't look like he had much of a clue what he was doing. *All the gear, no idea.* You know?'

Viv shot him a look. 'That's a little mean, Patrick. He's probably just new.'

Patrick glanced down at his shoes. Viv was right.

'Sorry, I'm tired. Hungry and tired.'

The lift stopped once more, then sailed down through the floors. As they passed the fifth floor, Viv nudged him.

'Have you noticed how there's no fourth floor in this hotel?'

'What?'

'See how the number 4 above the door never lights up?' Patrick shook his head. 'Try pressing 4.' Patrick tried but the button had no give to it and remained unlit. 'See? One of the cleaning ladies told me all about it earlier today. Weird huh?'

'What's the reason?'

Viv explained that in Cantonese the word *four* sounded virtually the same as the word *death* and was therefore considered unlucky. 'It's a homonym.'

'A homonym? No kidding. You're not just a pretty face.'

'No I'm not, you sexist prick . . .' They'd arrived at the lobby. Viv ran a hand down her front, flattening out a crease in the dress. 'This does look kinda pretty though doesn't it?'

'What? Yeah, Viv, you look great.'

'Cool. So you want to come and help extend the hand of friendship?'

'Tempting, maybe later. I'm gonna go get something to eat first.'

'Okay, I'll see you in there. I'll be the one laughing at absolutely everything Captain Colorado says.'

The chicken Caesar salad in the hotel restaurant did little to lift Patrick's mood. It was the cheapest main course on the menu, but doing the conversion from Hong Kong dollars to pounds Patrick realised he would still have to subsidise his dinner to the tune of fifteen quid. While waiting for his food he got his phone out and did a little digging into Colorado Dan's life story . . . the fellow's name was Dan Staples and he wasn't as green as he'd appeared. His main outlet was an American regional paper called the *Colorado Guardian*; in fact he'd made the front page that same day although the piece read to Patrick like little more than recycled agency copy with a bit of colour thrown in. He was listed as a freelance journalist on LinkedIn and had over ten thousand followers on Twitter, which was nine thousand five hundred more than Patrick had. Dan even had his own Wikipedia page. Patrick scanned it. He'd done a fair amount of work and been a lot of places in a short space of time. Patrick muttered to himself.

'Your own Wiki page? What a vain bastard.'

His food arrived – what looked like a child-size portion. He asked for extra bread and extra dressing and the waiter brought both, although the service became increasingly starchy. He drank tap water with his meal, although what he really wanted was a cold beer. Several cold beers.

On his way back to the lift, he decided to poke his head in at the bar, just to see what was going on. The place was decorated with odd items of chinoiserie, painted screens and the like, and his tribe of hacks and hangers-on filled about half the room. Patrick saw Brandon at the centre, holding court, and Viv deep in conversation with Colorado Dan, busily extending the hand of friendship. Judging by the way Dan was looking at her, anything she decided to extend, this man would take with both hands. He'd swapped his war corps outfit for a blue shirt and chinos and had his arm draped casually across the top of the sofa at Viv's back.

Patrick had to admit that he was a good-looking bloke – a square, stubbled jaw and closely cropped blond hair. The American caught sight of Patrick standing at the door and gave a friendly nod. Patrick pretended not to have noticed and continued to scan the bar, as though looking for a group other than the one right in front of him – the one he belonged to. The most enticing thing he saw was the thick-stemmed, silver Asahi beer pump that sat front and centre of the zinc topped bar. Tears of frozen water at the tap head winked at Patrick and he could feel his resolve weakening. One pint wouldn't hurt. He was rescued by the appearance of the hotel doorman who tapped him on the arm before positioning himself between Patrick and temptation.

'Mr Reid?'

'Er, yeah that's me.' The man had his grey top hat in one gloved hand; in the other was a note.

'A young man was asking for you earlier, but he decided not to wait. He asked me to give you this.' He handed the note to Patrick, who took it and then went to his pockets in search of a tip. He only had the red Hong Kong 100 dollar notes on him. The doorman saw this dilemma play out on Patrick's face and smiled.

'Do not worry.'

'Later, I'll . . .'

'Of course.'

Eric Fung had wasted no time in taking Patrick up on his offer to talk, but it seemed odd that the kid would come all the way to his hotel just to leave a message. If he wanted a face-to-face conversation then surely here was as good a place as any? Patrick found an empty armchair, unfolded the note – a page ripped from a school exercise book – and read. In a neat hand, all capitals, Eric asked Patrick to come and meet him at the Lennon Wall. Eric would be there for the rest of the night, but he asked that Patrick come 'as soon as practicable.'

How soon was practicable? His colleagues were in the bar, he wanted to call Rebecca, he also desperately needed a good night's sleep. Not for the first time that day, for maybe the hundredth time that week, Patrick asked himself what William Carver would do.

There was a row of the distinctive red and white cabs on the street outside the Headland and Patrick took the first one. As he climbed in, he realised that he wasn't sure where the Lennon Wall was. He didn't need to know – his ruddy, round-faced driver was well aware.

'John Lennon out of the Beatles. *Imagine* . . .' He hummed a couple of bars of the anthem, grinning at Patrick in his rear-view mirror. 'Students are making a wall, they are calling it for him. It's at the Government offices.'

'Right. That's where I need to get to. Can you drive me there? Or near there?'

63

'I try yes, but so much traffic. This protests are very bad, bad for reputation, bad for business.'

The cabbie got Patrick within a hundred yards and charged him 200 Hong Kong dollars to do it. Maybe the protests weren't as bad for business as all that. Once out on the street, Patrick had simply to follow the crowd. He'd seen pictures of the Lennon Wall on social media, but they hadn't done it justice. The paper mosaic already reached halfway up the concrete steps to the Central Government Complex and it was growing all the time. It was a rainbow of bought or homemade Post-it notes, each carrying a message of defiance, encouragement or hope. A mix of young activists and tourists were crowded around the wall, reading the messages and adding their own. Patrick read a few of the lemon yellow and dayglo pink notes near the foot of the wall.

Change always appears Impossible – until it is Done

Start where You Are. Use what You have. Do what You can!

He found himself briefly thankful that Carver wasn't there with him. Many of the messages were the sort of banal motivational quotes he remembered seeing on student walls around exam time. If the content hadn't pushed Carver over the edge then the random use of punctuation and capitalised text surely would.

It will not be Easy! But it will be Worth it

He wandered around and soon spotted Eric, deep in conversation with a group of students his age and even younger; these new recruits to *Scholastic* were listening intently as Eric Fung spoke, and nodding vigorously. Patrick wondered how old Eric was? Seventeen or eighteen at most – surely a little young for an oracle or the leader of any revolution worth the name? He waved a greeting, then walked off to read a few more of the messages and check out the crowd. He was annoyed at himself for not bringing his recording machine and collecting a few interviews; some of this audio could have been useful. He got his phone out instead and walked up and down the line, taping overheard conversations, the sound of people reading the messages in English and Cantonese. The quality wasn't great but it could work as wild track. Eric caught up with him at the top of the concrete steps and they gazed down at the crowds, which were continuing to grow, despite it being almost nine p.m. now. The humidity had eased, but it was still warm and most people were in shirtsleeves. Eric pushed the thick glasses back up the bridge of his nose.

'Our protest is becoming a tourist attraction.'

'It certainly looks like it.'

'I have even seen some Chinese tourists here, although they are being careful. They cover their faces.' He pointed at a group of well-dressed Chinese sightseers, all wearing green surgical-style masks. 'You see?'

'I see. So they're worried about facial recognition are they?'

'Yes. They're right to be worried, the Chinese authorities are getting better at that kind of thing all the time. Soon we will all be wearing masks.'

Patrick looked up to his left at a clump of CCTV cameras bolted to a thick grey metal pole, four or five cameras pointing in various directions. Eric shook his head. 'We don't have to worry about those cameras though. One of my comrades climbed up and sprayed black paint over the lenses last week.'

'The authorities haven't sent someone along to clean them?'

Eric shook his head. 'Not yet, I'm sure they want to, but we are always here and we also have cameras. Policemen repairing their CCTV right next to the John Lennon Wall would get lots of YouTube hits I think.'

'I'm sure.'

'Have you read the George Orwell book, *1984*?'

Patrick made a vaguely comical sort of harrumphing sound. 'What? Of course I've read it, I mean not for a while but, yes . . .'

'I have read it several times now. He was English, like you.'

'I know that George Orwell was English, Eric.'

Patrick was beginning to regret coming down here; it had been a long day and Eric was starting to annoy him. There was something unsettling about his direct way of asking questions, something almost accusatory although Patrick had done nothing wrong.

'I came down here because you said you wanted something. So what is it? It's been a long day.'

As thick-skinned as he was, Eric picked up on Patrick's tone.

'I apologise, I understand. It is just two things really, it was one thing but now it is two.' Patrick tried to hide his impatience.

'Right, so item one . . .'

'Item one is your offer to talk about what you saw in Turkey, Egypt, Bahrain and all of the other places. We are particularly interested in communication. The different types of encryption that protestors use to talk to each other.' Patrick noted the switch into first person plural.

'We?'

'*Scholastic*. And the wider movement.'

'Right.' Patrick already felt uncomfortable with the way this conversation was going. The plan was that Eric would be *his* contact and source of information – not the other way around. Having said that, he'd chosen a topic that Patrick was interested in, one that he'd thought a lot about. He had bored on about encryption to various colleagues and even to poor Rebecca often enough in the last few months. 'Encryption's a big subject Eric, it varies a lot from place to place.'

'Okay, say in Turkey for instance?'

Patrick sighed.

'In Turkey, everyone uses encryption apps on their phones now, at least everyone with any brains. At the beginning they were just using their regular mobiles and when you buy a mobile phone in Turkey you have to give them your national ID number.'

Eric shook his head as Patrick continued.

'It was the easiest thing in the world for the authorities to work out who'd been at what demo. When and with who. At the start the students felt safe because of the numbers. There were tens of thousands of them and sure enough the police let them get on with it. The authorities waited until the odds were better. They monitored everything, collected the data and came back and picked off the protestors much later.' He paused. 'This is common know-ledge though Eric, you can read about this.'

The young student nodded again.

'Yes, I know. But what sorts of encryption did they try? What were the names of the apps they used? Which ones worked? This is what we need to know about.'

'Right.' Patrick paused. 'So I'm going to have to think about this Eric.'

'I understand, but you do know about these things, you have seen them, heard them. Maybe you kept a diary?'

Patrick shook his head.

'I don't keep a diary. Not really.' He watched as Eric removed his backpack, opened it and found a school exercise book.

'I have made a list of questions for you, if you could look at them and see which ones you can answer for us? You can take these away with you.' He pulled the middle pages out from under-neath the staples. It was an extensive-looking list of questions, each one written in capital letters and numbered. Patrick turned the page.

'Twenty-eight questions?'

'Yes. These are the sorts of things we will need to know if we are going to succeed . . .' He gave Patrick what was clearly meant to be an encouraging smile, but to him it seemed nothing short of patronising. 'I'm sure that a lot of what you have seen can be helpful for us.'

Patrick folded the list up and put it in his jeans pocket.

'I'll have a read of these and I'll think about it. I'll do what I can.'

Eric held out his right hand and Patrick shook it.

'Thank you.' He paused. 'I was reading some of the messages on the wall earlier and now I remember one message that I think is relevant – *If you're not part of the solution, then you are part of the problem.*'

Patrick nodded; his most pressing problem was that Eric was really starting to piss him off. Sanctimonious little—

'Yeah, I'm familiar with that one too, thanks Eric . . .' He tried to remember where it originated, the US Civil Rights movement maybe? He could look it up later. 'I'll have a think and maybe you message me tomorrow, or come by the hotel if you like.'

Eric shook his head.

'I will message you. We can meet again back here, or somewhere else in the city. But not at your hotel.'

'If you're worried about the secret police then we can always meet in one of the bars, it's too loud in there for anyone to . . .' He stopped. Eric was shaking his head.

'It's not the Chinese police. We know who they are. Where they are.'

'What then?'

A look of concern clouded the young man's face.

'This was the second thing . . . item two. The American newspaper reporter, the one who was at the demonstration with you, he is staying at the same hotel as you. I saw him.'

'So what? There are loads of journalists staying there.'

'He's the reason I left. I do not trust him. He took a mobile phone.'

'What?'

'One of my comrades agreed to be interviewed by him, she was sitting down on the road, her phone was in a rucksack at her feet. She stood up to check some detail that he asked her to check with a colleague. After the interview was finished, she looked for her phone and it was gone.'

Patrick shrugged. 'Anyone could have taken it.'

Eric shook his head.

'She was surrounded by comrades. *He* was the only person there we did not know.'

'Why would he want to take a phone? He's an American news guy, he's probably got at least two or three phones of his own.'

'I don't know. But he took it. Maybe he is an *American news guy*, as you say. But that isn't all he is.'

Back in the Purple Bar at the Headland Hotel the drinks had clearly been flowing. Brandon was stretched out on a chaise longue waving a highball glass around in front of him as he spoke. Viv spotted Patrick, detached herself from the group and walked over – a little unsteady on her high heels.

'Hey radio boy, where'd you disappear to?'

'I had to go back down into the centre, the Lennon Wall.'

'More interviews?'

'Yeah.'

'You work too hard.' She pointed back at the gaggle of hacks. 'We might be moving on soon too.' Apparently Brandon was trying to persuade the group to catch a cab to Lan Kwai Fong. It was not an area that Patrick was familiar with; Viv filled him in. 'It's party central. He keeps going on about meeting *Suzie Wong down in Lan Kwai Fong*.'

'Who's that?'

'She's not an actual person. She's some character in an old film that Brandon's completely obsessed with.'

'Are you gonna go along?'

'Maybe . . .' She glanced back at the group. 'It depends what other people are doing.'

'One person in particular.'

Viv's look slid sidelong into his.

'Yeah. But I'm not sure I'm making much progress in that direction. Colorado Dan seems more interested in talking about you than me. He kept asking where you'd gone to. He says you helped him out at the demo earlier.'

'Not intentionally.'

'He wants to buy you a drink.'

'I dunno Viv, it's been a long day.'

She took hold of Patrick's arm.

'Come on, be a pal. It might count in my favour if I can get you to come say hello. Just *one drink*, I swear.'

Patrick looked at his watch. He'd missed the chance to call Rebecca and one beer might cheer him up, take the edge off the day and he could make his own mind up about Dan: salt of the earth news guy or petty thief and who knew what else? He allowed himself to be pulled across the bar in the direction of the smiling American.

9 Well and Good

Jags quickly realised that the *good things* that Elizabeth Curepipe wanted to do in Brochu were going to mean a whole load of aggravation for him. He listened as she laid it all out.

'From what I read, it's a pretty matriarchal set-up they've got going on down there.' Jags shifted in his seat.

'Well, it's a mining town . . .'

'I know that Brochu is a mining town, Jags . . .' There was a flash of irritation in her voice. 'That's what makes it so interesting. You've got this macho industry – mining – but it looks like it's the women who are running the place. I generalise, but you see what I mean?' Jags stayed silent. Elizabeth didn't understand. Brochu was a copper mining town, the mine was all it had and the vast majority of its menfolk worked in the mines. There were an average of thirty-five accidental deaths each year and if a mining accident didn't kill you then disease would – few miners lived to see fifty. Brochu was matriarchal because the town's men were either dead or dying. 'So I want Public Square to make the most of the fact that we've got all these good, strong Chilean women down there. I want us to build on that.' She smiled that smile. 'I've put together a *one-pager* for you.'

Jags read the one-page summary carefully, word by word. He was only two paragraphs in when Fred piped up.

'Looks good to me, Lizzie . . .' He reached over and fed his copy to the shredder. '. . . really good.' He smiled at his wife. 'Ambitious, exciting, I vote *yes*.' Jags didn't get to vote on the new plan, he was just the sucker who had to put it into practice. He finished reading the summary.

Public Square would build a combined crèche, community centre and museum in Brochu. Elizabeth had identified an old farmhouse that was big enough and well-built enough and could be modified. Jags knew the place that she had in mind, it was overpriced but he could sort that. Her plan was to provide a crèche for the mine-workers' children while turning the barn into a museum. This would tell the history of the region, it would celebrate the contri-bution that mining and thereby the Curepipe family had made to the area, it would also exhibit some of the many petroglyphs that had been found and dug up during the construction of the huge dam. Public Square currently had these ten-thousand-year-old rock paintings crated up and in storage in Santiago. This men-agerie of llamas, pumas, two-headed lizards and flightless birds would be given back to the people of Brochu. The whole project would be staffed by local people, properly paid.

The difference between this new approach and the way Jags had been running things – under Fred's instruction and ever-watchful eye – was the difference between black and white, but Fred appeared unbothered. He chose his battles carefully when it came to Elizabeth and he clearly wasn't interested in fighting this one. Jags finished reading and turned over, in case there was any better news on the other side. There wasn't. He could feel Elizabeth's eyes on him.

'You know Brochu better than anyone Jags . . .' Any of the

three people in this room was what she meant. 'So what d'you think of the plan? Do you think it can work?'

'I guess.'

Elizabeth laughed.

'That's not the most wholehearted endorsement I've ever had, Jags.'

'It can work. With enough time and the right people then yes, it can work.'

'Fabulous, let's fast track it then. Fred will okay any funding you need. Did you tell him about London yet?' Fred shook his head. 'I need to be in London next week for a few meetings, some interesting stuff, a new partnership I've been working on. And I'm giving a speech about my dad. My little team is all coming along, but I'd like you around too. If that's possible?'

Jags nodded. He hated her *little team* just as much as everyone on it loathed him.

'It'd be a pleasure.'

'Have you got a decent raincoat?'

'I've got something waterproof.'

'We'll get you a raincoat, a proper Savile Row raincoat.' She smiled. 'When were you last in London?'

Jags puffed out his cheeks.

'Oh Jeez, long time ago.' This was a lie. Elizabeth looked Jags up and down. He lied well, but Fred decided to intervene anyway to avoid any unwanted supplementary questions about Jags' trips to London and what they might involve.

'Lizzie, I need to take Jags over the road for a half hour or so to show him one or two of these new things we're working on. I've got a few security-related questions I'd like him to ponder.'

Lizzie raised an eyebrow.

'Wow! Jags, Fred's gonna let you take a look inside his *man cave*, you are privileged. I have to make a written application a month in advance to be allowed in there.'

73

Fred laughed.

'What nonsense Lizzie. You know you're welcome pretty much any time.'

'*Pretty much*. You hear that Jags? Don't worry, I've got things I can be doing, you boys run along and have fun.'

The two men rode the elevator down to reception in silence. They didn't speak until they were well outside the glass egg and striding across the campus.

'So that's a fuckin' handbrake turn away from everything we've been doing down in Chile so far.'

Fred nodded.

'I know.'

'You didn't feel like saying something?'

'No point. Once Lizzie makes her mind up about something like this, that's it . . . Brochu is just going to have to tick along a little differently from now.' They walked past a huge white wooden beehive, past the farm-to-table cafeteria, living bike sheds constructed from turf and moss. A couple of Public Square people zipped by on solar-powered scooters. Jags had his own opinions about all this, but he kept them to himself. 'Perhaps she's right, it could be that softly-softly is a better way to run the mining side of things – at least down there in our own back yard. Lizzie's ideas aren't going to help us get more coltan out of the ground in Congo but maybe they'll work in Brochu. She gets to be *humanitarian of the year* or whatever it is she wants, and Brochu becomes more productive . . .' Jags said nothing. 'The price of copper's about to start climbing, so more productive is what we want.'

'What makes you so sure?'

'About what?'

'About the price of copper.'

'Supply and demand. I'm doing a lot of deals right now and we've got several new products in development. We're going to need a lot more copper, coltan, lithium, more silver, rare-earth metals . . . more of everything in fact. First us and then the other big players will follow suit.'

'So you want the mine more productive, but I can't use muscle any more?' Jags had planned to replace Pablo with his eldest son, a slightly thuggish and malleable individual similar to his father. Now he was going to have to think again. 'I don't suppose you've got any thoughts about how this new approach is meant to work?'

Fred shook his head.

'It seems to me that that's a *you* problem, not a *me* problem.' He was grinning that grin again; it was unusual to see Jags appearing unsettled and Fred was enjoying it. 'Find the people who you think can help do things the way Lizzie wants them done. Once you know who they are, send me the names and numbers and I'll run the rule on them.'

'Fine.' They were passing the company crèche. Alongside the bright Comic Sans sign for the *Public Square Nursery School* was a picture of a mobile phone with a diagonal red line through it: *No screens beyond this point*. Jags jutted his chin in the direction of the sign.

'What's that all about.'

Fred shook his head.

'That's just Lizzie's pretend trade union flexing its pretend muscle. They read the last lot of research we did on kids and screens.'

'I must've missed that.'

'If it's correct, then no parent in their right mind's going to let a child under three even see a screen. No kid under twelve should get their hands on a smartphone.'

'I see. I'm guessing Public Square aren't putting a press release out on that right away?'

'Me and Lizzie are discussing it. I'm not sure the research methodology stacks up, I want to run it again.'

'Right.'

Fred's *man cave* was, in fact, a black metal box of a building, hidden by thick lines of mature silver birch trees. He took an *access all areas* pass from his pocket and handed it to Jags.

'So by my reckoning you'll need to head back to Chile tomorrow or the day after, put the wheels in motion down there, then straight to the UK.' Jags nodded. 'The timing of this London trip is fortuitous. There are one or two things over there that I need you to take a look at.'

10 Open Day

The bus was full to bursting by the time Rebecca reached the front of the queue but the driver ushered her on with a hairy hand.

'Got two seats on top if you can fight your way up there.' He glanced up through his periscope. 'One now.' He gave Rebecca an encouraging smile as she edged past the loose knot of people crowded around the door. 'Good luck. Stay alive.' She returned the smile and soldiered on, past a folded buggy and several men with no obvious excuse for not being upstairs and out of everyone's way. She felt eyes on her as she climbed the stairs and regretted her choice of a skirt instead of jeans. The weather forecast on the radio for London that morning had been particularly unhelpful: heavy showers at first, then sunny spells and temperatures climbing into the twenties by the afternoon. How were you supposed to dress for that lot? At the top of the stairs she shuffled out of her red raincoat and tied it round her waist, shouldered her satchel and went in search of the legendary empty seat. It was one row from the back and occupied by a Primark bag belonging to the woman sitting in the window seat. The woman was staring into her phone, headphones in and apparently unaware of Rebecca or anything else going on around her. Rebecca tapped her on the shoulder, gave her the most apologetic smile she could manage and jutted her chin in the direction of the shopping bag. The woman looked around the bus before grudgingly removing the bag and pushing it down between her legs.

'Thank you so much.'

The woman removed one earphone.

'What did you say?'

'I said thank you.'

Rebecca took a scrappy manila envelope from her satchel and looked at the to-do list she'd written on the reverse. She added the words: speak to Mum and then promptly put a line through them – she'd spoken to her mother already that morning. As she did this, she saw Patrick, a sarcastic grin on his face. In recent times, the compulsive list-making habit that her boyfriend had once found so endearing had become annoying. The last time he'd been home – a fleeting visit just before Hong Kong and after . . . where? Ukraine? – he'd decided to raise the matter.

'You make a list and then, straight away, you cross something out. You make a to-do list which includes things you've already done.' Rebecca remembered admitting to this, explaining that it made her feel like she was off to a racing start, but Patrick wouldn't drop it. *'I've worked out what it is. Your lists aren't really to-do lists at all. They're look-what-I've-done lists. In fact, they are look-what-I've-done-compared-to-what-you've-not-done lists.'* She shook the memory from her head; they'd had one stupid argument, that was all. The rest of the time they'd been together had been good. Patrick's mind had been elsewhere and he'd been tired. They would have a full week together pretty soon – her half term and his long-promised leave. They'd sort things out then. The bus accelerated through an amber light then stopped suddenly behind

a van and she felt her stomach lurch. The journey from the flat she and Patrick shared in north London to her school in the south had never been easy, but these last few weeks it seemed to leave her completely rinsed. At least today was a shorter day, no real teaching, just an *inset*. An open day for prospective parents to take a look around the place, meet the friendlier teachers and recce the most presentable classrooms. The headmaster had asked Rebecca to give a short talk to kick things off, meet and greet a few parents and then she could do what she liked with the rest of the day. She'd been asked to perform this role at several open days now and she was happy doing it. The only downside was the resentful looks she got from the head's deputy, who clearly thought the job should be hers. Rebecca had suggested this herself, but the head was emphatic. 'I prefer to save Mrs Shepard for the parents who look like they *want* their children to be beaten on a regular basis'. Rebecca had done this presentation often enough not to be worried about it and at the forefront of her mind this morning was how best to spend a precious free weekday afternoon. The British Museum maybe? Or the National Portrait Gallery, she hadn't been there in ages. She took her phone out and googled the opening hours.

The bus took her within half a mile of her school. Walking her usual shortcut through the old red-brick council estate, Rebecca was vaguely aware of someone, a woman, walking not far behind and drawing slowly closer. Chances were she was lost; it was easy to lose your bearings around here, she'd done it herself many times during her first few weeks working at the school. On reaching the side gate Rebecca paused and waited for the woman to catch her up.

'Hello.' Rebecca checked the woman out. She wore a grey business suit and had a tote bag slung over one shoulder. A mass of unruly red hair framed a friendly-looking face.

'Hi, sorry, I'm . . .'

'Lost? I'm guessing you're here for the open day?'

The woman laughed.

'I am. But I think I've fallen at the first hurdle, I can't find the bloody school. I thought that maybe you were another – parent? One with a better sense of direction than me.'

'No, but you're close . . .' Rebecca reached into her satchel and pulled out a school lanyard and security fob. 'I'm one of the teachers, Miss Black.'

'Pleased to meet you.'

'But I'm afraid I can't let you in through this gate. You'll have to walk around to the main entrance . . .' She pointed in that direction. '. . . they're registering all the parents at the reception round there.'

The red-haired woman nodded.

'Brilliant, thank you so much.'

'No problem. I'll see you inside.'

'Absolutely.'

11 Naz

Carver stewed and sulked for a full twenty-four hours after his falling out with McCluskey in the Chinese restaurant. Righteous indignation and anger slowly dissipated, making way first for a few shadows of doubt and then the slow realisation that he had behaved like a complete ass. This revelation came coupled with the knowledge that he didn't have that many friends. Certainly not so many that he could afford to lose McCluskey over some small matter. She'd helped him on more occasions than he cared to recall and this was the first time he could remember her asking for anything in return. She'd asked him if he'd phone Patrick on her behalf and he'd not just refused, but also accused her of being up to something. He'd been an idiot and he woke up that morning determined to make amends. An email or phone call was insufficient, he would take a train out to Caversham and apologise in person.

Before that he had a half-day's teaching to get through, but this did not dent his mood either. Today's class was a practical and he was a lot happier teaching those than the theoreticals. He also had to talk to them about the last piece of homework he'd set – a straightforward task, which pretty much every kid in the class had failed at.

William bought a large latte and an egg and cress sandwich from the canteen before catching the lift up to his classroom. As the students arrived, they dutifully switched off their phones and placed them in the fire bucket by the door.

'Today we're going to start trying to find out if you've got the basic equipment to do the job of a radio reporter. Namely – ears.'

He instructed the students to gather together at the front of the classroom, two-deep around his desk. He found a long list of audio files on his laptop, highlighted one and pressed play. The sound was a little tinny, but loud enough. The young people craned their necks to hear; they were waiting for a voice, for speech but there was none, just wild track. He let it play for a minute or so then turned to the class.

'What do you think that is you're listening to?'

There was a nervous silence, then Naz spoke.

'A river, cars, some birds.'

'Not a bad start, you go first then Naz. I'll play it to you through my cans. . .' He plugged his favourite pair of Bakelite headphones into the laptop and passed them to her. '. . . be careful with those.' Carver pressed play and watched Naz concentrate; she closed her eyes and listened.

'I can hear water, maybe not a river though. Some street sounds, cars, birds I think.'

'Better. So where do you think you are?'

'I am . . . in a small town.'

'Good. And the water?'

'Definitely not a river. The water is . . . controlled somehow. Maybe it's a fountain?'

'Maybe. And what time of day do you think it is?'

A few of the class laughed, but not Naz. She was getting the hang of this now.

'I can't hear a church bell or anything like that.'

'No, but maybe you don't need one. Listen.' She listened.

'I think it's the morning, early morning, like six or seven. But I don't know why I think that.' Carver nodded and paused the tape.

'I recorded that at six thirty in the morning, outside a café in a little public square in a place called Vejer in the south of Spain. You get a sense of the time because of the birdsong – it has a particular sound at that time of day and we're programmed to know that. The water is a fountain, you were right.'

'I nailed it.'

'You did okay. We're all walking around with a huge sound bank in our brains, it's just we don't use it like we should.' Naz handed the headphones back.

'Your café and that fountain? They're up at the top of a hill aren't they? Maybe at the top of some kind of steep narrow street?' Carver studied Naz.

'What makes you think that?'

'I can hear it in the noise those cars make, the sound of the engines and the gears.'

William nodded. Naz had painted an almost perfect picture of the spot where he'd made the recording.

'Not bad.'

The next hour was spent teaching close microphone technique – a way of recording the voice with such clarity that listening back to the interviews you could hear the lipstick on a woman's lips, the cigarette in the mouth. Carver let the class mess about with this idea and they were the most engaged he'd ever seen them – recording each other and themselves and listening back, their hands hard against their heads and straining to listen. It was Naz who lost interest first and came over to his desk, tape recorder in hand.

'Is it just the physical things you can hear do you think sir?'

'As opposed to?' Carver knew what she was thinking about, he'd wondered the same thing when he was training. He'd wondered it many times since.

'Can you tell the difference between real and faked emotion? Fear? Love?'

'Some people think so.'

'What about a lie? Can you tell the truth from a lie?'

Carver had set aside the second half of the lesson for something he knew the students would find less pleasant than the practical. After they'd packed away the recording equipment he got them to sit back down behind their desks.

'Last week I asked each of you to send me an example of the sort of news that you read or listen to or watch and that you respect. Newspapers, radio, TV. . . I didn't care what form it took . . .' The students' heads nodded. '. . . but I wanted news. What most of you sent me was *not* news, it was *opinion*.'

Getting his students to understand that there was a difference, and what that difference was, took the rest of the lesson. First he went through the stuff he'd been sent.

'This isn't fact-based journalism; we can argue about objectivity and whether it exists . . .'

Naz stuck her hand up and the two of them batted that backwards and forwards until Carver sensed that he was losing the rest of the class.

'There is room for opinion in journalism, of course there is. But to quote one of the old fellows, "*Comment is free, facts are sacred.*" Also, it seems to me like you're reading and watching stuff that just reinforces your own opinion. You should be actively looking for things that challenge your existing opinion.' He looked at the class. Derek's studded face wore a look of puzzlement.

'Why?'

'Because that's how you learn. And, it's how we learn to live with each other.' He paused. 'Try and find and listen to the other side of the argument, whether it's party politics, international politics . . . identity politics especially.'

'You do that do you, sir?'

'Yes Naz, I'm not a complete dinosaur, I try and stay current when it comes to things like LGBT rights and the rest.' William was rather pleased with this answer. Then he saw that Naz had her hand up again. 'Yes?'

'LGBTQIA+'

'Eh?'

'It's LGBTQIA+ now, sir.'

'Really? They added more letters? What are those ones for. . . actually, never mind. Tell me after the lesson. My point is that if you want to campaign, go be a campaigner. You want to be a journalist? I can teach you that.'

12 Department Eight

Fred's idea of organising Public Square's research centre in the same way as a typical American middle school had won Public Square plenty of column inches. The seven subject areas were maths, English, biology, chemistry, physics, social studies and health and wellness. Each team worked out of its own *classroom* but the different disciplines were encouraged to mix and swap ideas, especially during *recess*, which was what was taking place as Fred showed Jags around. Milling about and lounging around in small groups were scores of young people of various nationalities, assorted colours and creeds, all wearing casual and colourful clothes. The scene reminded Jags of the old billboard ads for the United Colours of Benetton, except that this lot all had laptop computers, tablets or phones with them at all times. They walked through the cafeteria . . . 'That's all organic food, completely free, twenty-four hours a day. They can work whatever hours they want to work, complete flexibility.' Jags saw a knot of kids all wearing the same T-shirts with the same slogan on them: *90 Hours a Week and Loving It.*

It was a whistle-stop tour, taking in all of Fred's subject areas, but at speed. His summary of what was going on in each computer-stuffed classroom or white-tiled lab was cryptic bordering on the unfathomable. The maths team was *'focussing on predictive modelling, algorithms and super algorithms.'* His English students were on *'speech patterns, rhythm and such.'* Biology was *'all about pig brains right now.'* Chemistry *'dopamine, real and synthetic.'* Physics *'bending different stuff.'* Fred stopped outside the social studies classroom. *'This is interesting. You see how I've got some of the math guys in there with them?'* Jags gave a non-committal nod of the head. One geek looked much like another as far as he was concerned.

'So what're they doing?'

Fred glanced at Jags.

'It's complex. It's about what you can do once you've got the predictive stuff right – *tuning, herding,* stuff like that.'

'Tuning and herding what?' But Fred had moved on; either he didn't think Jags was smart enough to understand or he didn't care to say. They moved past the health and wellness class without stopping. 'They're researching the original old chestnut – *how not to die.* People are always keen to spend their money on that ticklish little problem . . .' Jags had heard Elizabeth tease Fred about his tendency to start talking like a phoney English aristocrat when he was showing off. '. . . we need to take the lift . . .' The basement was where they were headed. 'This is Department 8.' The steel-sided goods elevator opened out onto another classroom, but there were no computers in sight. Behind these glass windows were seven individuals in white open-neck shirts and black slacks, each sitting behind a desk, taking what appeared to be some sort of multiple-choice test.

'These guys don't look like your usual common or garden geek. Who're they?'

'I thought you might recognise them Jags . . .' Fred smiled.

'They're like you, or what you used to be.' Sure enough, the four men and three women in the room had a former military or maybe intelligence agency look about them. Not just American either, but a mix of nationalities: north European, Chinese or Chinese-American, Middle Eastern.

'If you're looking to replace me, Fred, then please – be my guest.' Fred shook his head.

'I don't want to replace you . . .' He paused. 'Even if I did, Lizzie wouldn't let me, you know that. In fact, I need a few more like you. They do look like you, don't they?' Jags ignored him.

'What do you need them to do?'

'New stuff – new for us, anyway. Public Square is going to start offering a little . . . I guess you could call it *aftercare.*' This made no sense. There was no money in aftercare, nothing sufficiently difficult or interesting to appeal to Fred either.

'I thought you said we don't do aftercare? It's just aggro.'

'It can be, but I've realised that it depends on the kind of after-care you're offering. It depends on what you're attempting to fix.'

Jags examined Fred's face; he was being deliberately, annoyingly cryptic.

'Fix? So it's repairs you're talking about? What's broken?'

'A lot of things, in a lot of different places. Lots of stuff that a company like us can help with.'

Jags looked again at the new recruits; they had finished the test and several were staring back in his direction now too.

'So what's the idea? You want me to talk to these new recruits of yours, is that it?'

'No, I told you. I just wanted you to take a little look at them, tell me what you think.'

'They look like ex-military, they look . . . committed.' Fred smiled.

'They do, don't they?'

'Are they the first lot of whatever the fuck they are?' Fred shook his head.

'Second wave. Two point zero. The first little crew has been up and running for a while, but I underestimated demand. Hence – these fellows.'

13 Heads & Tails

THE NATIONAL PORTRAIT GALLERY, LONDON

The rain-rinsed pavement outside the National Portrait Gallery shone like rose gold in the autumn sun. Rebecca stood on the opposite side of the road for a while and watched the people and their reflections rush by; it was good to be reminded how much she loved living in London. Inside the beautiful old building, up on the third floor, a hassled-looking teacher in a creased suit was trying to shepherd a large group of kids out of the Tudor gallery.

'Twentieth-Century photography, then home. Come on guys, we can do this.' He had a soft Yorkshire accent. Leeds, Rebecca guessed. She stood aside to let them pass and gave the man an encouraging smile. He paused.

'Somebody shoot me. You're a teacher as well are you?' Rebecca confirmed that she was,

'Where are your kids?'

'I gave them the slip on the Piccadilly Line.'

'Smart.' He looked back at the group of thirty or more twelve-year-olds, which was subdividing in an alarming manner. 'Onwards and upwards.' He walked off in a sideward direction and set about trying to sheepdog a loose knot of children back towards the Twentieth Century.

Rebecca wasn't sure if she was pleased or mildly pissed off at being so easily picked out as a fellow teacher. It happened a lot these days. No teacher wore a uniform, they weren't always trailing around after school parties, but it seemed the longer she did the job, the easier it was both to identify other teachers and be identified. Maybe it was just one of those professions? Army types always seemed to be able to spot each other. Farmers and doctors as well, she'd heard. She remembered asking Patrick if he thought he could pick a fellow journalist out in a crowd. She couldn't remember the answer he'd given.

Rebecca strolled around the rooms in no particular order, stopping when she felt like it, taking her time. She walked past long lines of heavily framed forgotten men, punctuated by the occasional long-locked Pre-Raphaelite. The men were almost all beetle-browed, austere or just plain tortured-looking. The women, serene and other-worldly. Eventually she ended up in front of her favourite picture, on display inside a special cabinet: Jane Austen, in pencil and watercolour, by her sister Cassandra. If you waved your hand or moved your head in front of the display cabinet then the light inside switched on and off.

'It's Jane at the disco.'

Rebecca grinned. This was how Patrick had described the picture when Rebecca first took him to see it. The gallery had been the first stop during what proved to be a definitive early date. The strobing effect had kept the pair amused for some time. Rebecca wondered whether Jane might have preferred Voguing to the endless quadrilles, but then again maybe her bonnet would've got in the way. Eventually the moustachioed gallery guard, who was sitting on a folding chair just next to Lord Byron, cleared his throat. When this didn't work he stood up and wandered over.

'I think you've had your fun. Go on, shove off.' They shoved off happily, grateful to have been gifted the first of their many shared jokes and stupid catchphrases. 'Go on, shove off' soon became the only way they could say goodbye to each other. Increasingly annoying for all their friends, but endlessly funny as far as they were concerned. It felt like a long time ago now. Rebecca circled the cabinet then moved on.

Back at the start of their relationship, and for a long time afterwards, everything seemed in sync. Their personalities were similarly sunny, but not identical. They liked the same stuff or embraced each other's particular passions with ease: Monday night curry, Sunday morning netball, Quentin Tarantino, Janet Evanovich, and all the other things that constitute the raw material of a relationship. Most importantly, the plans they had for how life might work out seemed to match up too. Highbury was beyond their means, so before long they would move, closer to Rebecca's school and far enough away from anywhere fashionable so that they might be able to buy a place instead of renting. If that was still the plan then they needed to do it soon. The rising tide of gentrification was already lapping at the lower end of Peckham High Street. Patrick had been away so much, he'd missed most of it, but Rebecca gave him regular updates. A fancy coffee bar-cum-bookshop had opened, a dog-friendly gastropub. If they waited too much longer then there'd be a Planet Organic or a hot yoga studio and then it would be too bloody late. They'd have to go further south or a lot further east.

Halfway into the revolving doors at the gallery exit, Rebecca decided she'd go back and buy Patrick a postcard of Jane at the disco. She ignored the exit and kept walking, completing a full circle and stepping out back inside the high-ceilinged lobby. She stopped. Standing there in front of her, wearing a countenance that hovered somewhere between surprise and anger, was the lost parent she'd met outside the school that morning. Rebecca hadn't seen the woman in the hall during her new parents presentation, but here she was now. She'd swapped her grey suit for a blue jumper and jeans and the red hair had been tucked up inside a black beret, but it was the same person. Rebecca gave a quizzical smile.

'Goodness, how about this? Small world . . .'

'Yeah. How are you?'

'Er . . . how did you enjoy the open day?'

'Oh, it was good, really good. Impressive school you've got there. I'm sorry I didn't get to see you again. I guess it must've been someone else's classroom they showed me.'

Rebecca gave a non-committal nod.

'I guess so. I'm glad you liked the school though . . .' She paused. 'Do you think it might suit your . . . your . . .'

'Son, my son. Yes I think it might, I got a really good feeling about the place.'

'That's good. Where does he go now. . . your son?'

The woman's hand went to her head and she pushed a strand of loose hair back beneath the beret.

'Oh he's at a place not far from there. A nursery just down the road in fact . . .' She hesitated, looking slightly flustered.

'Little Angels?'

'That's it. Little Angels, that's the one.'

They exchanged a few more pleasantries. Rebecca wished her and her son well and said a brief goodbye before entering the gallery shop.

The red-headed woman turned right outside the Portrait Gallery and walked briskly down towards Trafalgar Square. Outside the South African High Commission, she looked back across her shoulder before heading east down the Strand. In the courtyard of Somerset House she sat down on an empty bench and got her phone out. She went to her search engine and typed in *Little Angels*. Then . . . *Little Angel*. Then . . . *The Little Angels*. There was no such nursery anywhere near Rebecca's school. Not in

Peckham, nor anywhere else in the borough of Southwark. Not the neighbouring boroughs either.

'Shit.'

She waited for a handful of Japanese tourists to complete a circuit of the courtyard, then dialled a phone number she knew by heart. An answering machine clicked in, but there were no words, just a tone. When it finished, she typed in a code. A man's voice answered.

'Problem?'

'I'll file you the photos and my report in a couple of hours. If you decide you want to keep a tail on, then you're going to have to sub someone else in.' There was a mirthless laugh from the other end of the line.

'Right, so I'm guessing the pretty primary school teacher isn't as dumb as you thought she was?'

'Something like that.'

14 Pelmanism

The range of flowers on offer at the M&S on Paddington station was uninspiring. Carver loitered a while in front of the black buckets of cellophane-wrapped red or yellow roses, the chrysanthemums and lilies before deciding not to buy anything. They reminded him too much of the sad-looking flowers that his father used to bring home for his mother. *Petrol station offerings* she called them. Or *doghouse daffodils* – because that was what William's father would be attempting to avoid by showing up with a bunch of flowers that had either blossomed long ago or never would.

On the train from London to Reading, Carver rehearsed his apology. He would tell McCluskey that he'd been an idiot. It was best to put it as strongly as that. He doubted she'd want to hear an explanation for his behaviour the last time they'd met, but if she did then he would tell her why he was so reluctant to talk about or to Patrick. He would tell her about his version of a Hippocratic oath, his attempt to avoid harming anyone else that he cared about.

95

He arrived well ahead of the usual commuter rush home and the taxi rank at Reading station was overflowing. A long line of bored-looking drivers flicking through newspapers or watching Lord knows what on their telephones. Usually Carver took the pink-painted, single-decker bus out to Caversham, but he decided to spoil himself with a cab this afternoon. He'd been on his feet teaching for most of the day and the bunion on his right foot was throbbing. The driver was mercifully monosyllabic and speedy too; in no time they were out of town and flying past fields and allotments and, just beyond that, the grand iron gates to BBC Caversham itself. There was a chance that McCluskey was still there, and if so William would have to find somewhere to wait, but he had a feeling that Jemima's current obsession was more likely to be a freelance operation and, therefore, one that she worked on at home. The Italian baroque-inspired stately home went by in a flash and before Carver knew it they were turning off the main road and into the small estate where McCluskey's red-brick two-up, two-down was to be found.

'Nothing wrong with your local knowledge is there? I thought this place was a bit tucked away.' The cabby made eye contact in the rear-view.

'Not just your London blokes got knowledge mate . . .' He smiled

'Right.' Carver saw lights on in McCluskey's living room and up on the floor above and so, having paid the fare and tipped him a quid, he let the cabby go.

Jemima's house was situated right by a golf course and closest of all to the eighteenth green. She'd had many run-ins with the club management as a result and when they refused to pay for a broken bathroom window, she stopped returning the dozens of golf balls that ended up in her front and back gardens. Closing the gate on the low flint wall, Carver saw a ball bobbing about in the goldfish pond and retrieved it. He glanced up. The ball must have just cleared the top of the house then bounced down off the roof. The Caversham Golf Club was lucky that no visible damage had been done to McCluskey's collection of short-wave radio aerials that were sprinkled around the chimney stack and eaves. If it had, she'd probably have set fire to their club house.

He rang the doorbell and heard movement inside, a door closing. Through the small stained-glass window he saw the door closest to the front door open. McCluskey appeared, looking a little flustered.

'Carver. What you doin' here?' Her Glasgow accent sounded particularly thick.

'I've come to apologise, you know? To say sorry for . . .'

'For being such a cunt when I saw you in London?'

'Er, yes. I guess.'

'What's that you've got there?' She held her hand out for the golf ball, which Carver handed over. 'Nike One Tour. Lovely, those are worth a coupla quid.' There was still no obvious sign that McCluskey intended to let Carver in through the door.

'So anyway, I wanted to say sorry, try and put us back on terms . . .'

'Right, and you thought just turning up unannounced would do it, did ye?'

'Well.' Carver shuffled his feet. 'I nearly bought you flowers.' McCluskey laughed.

'You nearly did? Right. Carver – you're unique. Well, I suppose it's the thought that counts.' She pulled the door wider and stepped aside. 'You better come on in, now you've come all this way.'

She walked him past the closed door to the living room and on into the kitchen. 'If you decide to go the whole hog next time and actually buy the flowers then I like freesias. And lilies. I like a geranium too, but in the garden not in the house – they smell a bit like shite.'

'Right.' Carver made a mental note. There was a faint smell of tobacco in the room. 'Have you started smoking, McCluskey?'

'Wha? No. That'll be all the bonfires down at the allotments you're smelling.' A tortoiseshell cat entered and began to stalk the kitchen.

'Is this yours?'

'Nah. Mine died years back, but I've still got the cat flap and this young lady likes to pay me a visit every now and then.' The tortoiseshell cat was circling Carver's chair. 'Don't let her up on you, she's a chest sitter.' It was too late. The cat was on Carver's lap in one bound and already high-stepping her way up the north face of Carver's belly in the direction of his chest, where she planted herself. William stretched his neck and leaned back as far as he could in the chair.

'Can you get her off?'

'Too late. She'll scratch you to ribbons if I try an' move her now. Just keep still, she'll tire of you soon enough.' The cat appeared to be snuggling in. 'She likes you right enough. Likes your smell.' The feeling was not mutual. The cat smelt like offal and piss, but Carver kept this thought to himself and concentrated on breathing through his mouth and not his nose. 'So, you've come to apologise, I get that. What else?'

'What do you mean?'

'You wouldn't have come if there wasn't at least a wee chance of you being willing to help me out. I asked you to call Patrick, you don't really want to. What d'ye need to hear for that situation to change?' Carver lifted his head; he was starting to feel a little wheezy.

'Why don't you show me what you're working on and then I'll see if I can help.'

'Excellent, let me take you up to *command and control*. Cat. Off.' The animal leapt down as requested and Carver glared at McCluskey.

The command and control centre was McCluskey's spare bedroom but with the bed, wardrobe and any other home comforts shoved against the windowed wall to make room for . . . well, Carver wasn't quite sure what it was he was looking at. The whole of the back wall and most of the floor had been given over to some sort of investigation; Carver picked his way past the box files and headed for the wall, which had been divided into sections. Each section included newspaper headlines and stories cut out with serrated dressmaking scissors. These headlines had been harvested from many different news sources and came in a variety of languages – McCluskey spoke at least seven. Most of the headlines were in English, but Russian, Arabic, German and Greek were also well represented. As well as these, there were paragraphs clipped from recent reports by Amnesty International and Human Rights Watch people in Egypt, Bahrain, UAE, Turkey, Russia and China. As well as all the printed material, there were scraps of conversation that McCluskey had heard and transcribed in her spidery handwriting. Certain words were high-lighted and appeared in several different areas across the wall. Carver picked one.

'So what does "*maslih*" mean?'

McCluskey snorted.

'Funny you should land right on that one, Carver. That's my *word of the week*.' She joined him at that section of the wall. 'It usually translates as *reform* or *restoration* or something like that. But it's being used in a slightly different way . . .' She pointed. '. . . here and here.'

'Reform? Just in Arabic?'

'Not just Arabic, I've heard words and phrases that mean more or less the same thing in Russian and Greek, Spanish and, more recently, in Mandarin and Cantonese.'

'Heard them where?'

'Here and there.'

Carver stared at his old friend.

'This obviously isn't BBC monitoring business you're doing here, is it?' She shook her head. 'You're wandering a little off reservation with all this stuff aren't you McCluskey?' She laughed.

'I haven't seen my wigwam in months.'

'Go on then, walk me through it.'

McCluskey pointed at the lines of thick blue marker pen that linked certain stories.

'It's connections I'm looking for. . . like the toughest game of Pelmanism you've ever played.'

'Pelmanism?'

'Pairs . . . but you're pairing small parts of each picture, not the whole thing. Then you have to pair the pairs and so on. There are definite patterns, but it's confused; every time I think I have it in my hand, it slips away. I'm beginning to think that confusion and contradiction is part of the strategy. Do ye get me?'

'Not really.'

'No. I don't get me either. It's starting to send me a little mad. I'll end up in the funny farm.'

Carver looked again at his old friend.

'Are you getting enough sleep, McCluskey? You look knackered.'

'How much is enough these days?'

'I don't know. Five hours? Six maybe?'

'Then no. Not much. I'm having to pay attention to stuff across a fair few time zones . . .' She stifled a yawn. 'But anyways, I got to thinking, maybe I can't see it because it's just too abstract. I'm too far from the places where this shite's actually going down.' Carver nodded. 'An' so I got to thinking about your boy Patrick.'

'I see.' Carver paused. 'I'll call him for you, I'll call him now.'

'Thank you William.'

McCluskey insisted that they make the call some distance from the house.

'I'll walk you to the end of the close, I've been sitting in that room fer too long, I need to loosen my legs.' She left the door on the latch and they walked a hundred yards, up to the corner where cars turned in off the main road. McCluskey stopped next to a recently painted red postbox. 'This should do us.' She watched as William got his phone out and scrolled through contacts. 'Were you going to call him on that?' He nodded. 'Is it your BBC phone?'

'Yeah.'

'Do me a favour and use mine instead.'

'Why?'

'I dinnae like those BBC-issue phones. They're no' very secure as it is . . .' She paused. '. . . and from what I hear, there's a good chance they're going to get a lot less secure very soon.'

'How come?'

'There's an intriguing commercial partnership coming down the pipe. I shan't spoil the surprise. In the meantime, use this . . .' She handed William a blue Nokia.

'You're using burner phones now McCluskey?'

'I am. If you don't like the blue I've got other colours.'

McCluskey briefed Carver before he made the call. No details over the phone, just a simple question: would Patrick be happy to help a friend? That plus confirmation of the hotel where he was staying and his room number were all she needed for now. Carver sighed.

'You're aware how unhinged this all seems, are you McCluskey? No names, burner phones, bugs in your own house, all of it?' Jemima nodded.

'I am, yes. But you've only seen a fraction of what I've seen, Billy Carver. Take the most batshit crazy paranoid stuff you can think of . . .' McCluskey paused. '. . . then double it. Go on, please, make the call.'

15 Crossed Lines

Rebecca was at first confused and then genuinely disturbed by the strange encounter inside the entrance to the Portrait Gallery. She walked into the gallery shop as she'd intended but then straight out again with no memory of what it was she'd meant to buy there. She considered heading home, but what if the red-haired woman was waiting outside? Her legs felt weak, she needed to sit down – quickly – before she fell down.

She took the stairs down to the café and bought a pot of tea. She carried it to the far end of the catacomb-style restaurant with the teacup shaking on its saucer and found an empty table facing the bare brick wall. She slumped into the seat and used the paper napkin to wipe a film of nervous sweat from her forehead and the back of her neck. She breathed in through her nose and out of her mouth as slowly and fully as she could until she managed to get her breathing back on track. She needed to think. Why would some weird woman want to follow her around London? She definitely hadn't been at the school open day, Rebecca would have seen her. And she hadn't been hanging around afterwards either, so how did she know to find Rebecca at the Portrait Gallery? Who the hell was she? Not a prospective parent, that was for sure, but why tell a lie like that? She looked at her watch – after five p.m. in London would be the early hours of the morning in Hong Kong. Patrick might be asleep and an unexpected call from home might panic him. Rebecca wondered whether she should wait, but her heart was still thumping in her ears. She needed to calm down and at the moment, the only voice she knew would help was Patrick's. She could talk it through with him and work out what just happened. Rebecca poured three sachets of sugar into her tea and stirred it well before gulping half the cup down. She didn't want to sound like a complete mad woman when he picked up. She took a couple more breaths then dialled Patrick's number. The strange slowed-down ringtone chirruped half a dozen times before he picked up.

'Patrick?'

'Becs, hey how are you? I was going to call but . . .'

'Patrick, something really strange just happened . . .' She talked him through the last half hour and the earlier encounter with the woman, too. She could feel him trying to focus, to make some sense of it all, although he was *ah-ha-ing* and *umming* a little too much. 'Where are you Patrick?'

'I'm . . . you know. In the hotel.'

'In your room?'

'Not yet, just heading there now.'

'That's a late night.'

'Yeah, I just needed a drink, to help me sleep, you know?'

Several other questions occurred, but Rebecca didn't ask them.

'I'm a bit freaked out, Patrick. Have you *any* idea what all this could be about?'

He paused.

'There'll be an explanation, Becs.'

'Like what?'

'Well . . . like . . .' she could hear the booze in his voice now. '. . . maybe she just fancied you, maybe . . .'

'Fancied me? Don't patronise me Patrick, do you think I'm an idiot?'

'Course not, listen Becs, you're upset, I get it. It is weird, I'll give you that . . .'

'You'll give me that?'

'I mean yes, it's definitely weird, but there'll be a simple explanation, like . . .'

'It couldn't have anything to do with anything you're doing?'

'What? No, nah . . .'

'You've been followed before.'

'Yeah, but in places like Turkey and Egypt, Bahrain . . .'

'Or there.'

'Sure, maybe here in Hong Kong too, but not back in London. Not where you are. Like I say, it'll just be some kind of mis—' Rebecca heard a beeping sound at the other end of the line. Another call coming through on Patrick's phone, at . . . nearly two in the morning.

'I'm sorry Becs, let me just get shot of this other call. It'll be London, some kinda problem with the package. I'll call you right back, I promise.'

16 Maslih

McCluskey listened carefully to Carver's phone call, nodding her approval as he stuck to her suggested script and kept it short.

'Nice job.'

Carver made a harrumphing sound and handed the phone back.

'Hardly the toughest assignment, making a bloody phone call . . .'

'Course, no offence. Come on back to the house and have a quick cuppa before you go. I've got some of those Fondant Fancies.' Carver nodded and followed McCluskey back towards the house. Tousled clouds zipped across the fast-darkening blue sky, heading west. The truth was that it had felt good hearing Patrick's voice after so long, even if only a handful of words had been exchanged. He'd sounded okay, perhaps a little the worse for drink, which was unlike Patrick. Then again, it was the middle of the night in Hong Kong, maybe he'd woken him. Either way, Patrick wasn't a kid any more, he didn't need anyone worrying about him, least of all Carver. Whatever it was that McCluskey wanted Patrick to do, Carver was sure he could handle it.

*

'Yellow or pink?'

'Huh?'

'What flavour Fondant Fancy d'you want?' They sat in the living room, surrounded by McCluskey's collection of snow globes featuring landmarks from every corner of the world – many of them gifts from Carver himself. She saw him staring. 'I've not had a new one for a while now.'

'Ask Patrick, I'm sure he'll sort you out.'

'I'd rather be asking you.'

'Yeah well . . .' he looked at his watch. 'I need to be going.'

'Okey dokey, wait one minute though will you?' McCluskey disappeared up the stairs and Carver listened to the floorboards above his head creak as she moved around. When she reappeared she had a bundle of papers with her. 'How about a wee bit of light reading for the train? I gathered up all the bits and pieces I've got on that word that caught your eye . . . *maslih*.' Carver was tempted, he thought about it. But then he shook his head. He had a bundle of student essays in his bag that he had to mark and anyway, he'd done his bit.

'I can't. I'm sorry. I made a promise to myself McCluskey – just to focus on the teaching for a while. It's better for me, better for everyone.'

'Okay. I understand. I don't agree but I understand. I just thought I'd see if I could push my luck that wee bit further. If you change your mind, well, you know where I live.'

The train back into London was quiet, a few youngsters dolled up for a night out in the West End up at one end of the carriage, but Carver had the other half to himself. He tried marking essays for a while, but his concentration kept slipping. He stared out of the window at dark furrowed fields and let his mind wander. *Maslih* – meaning reform or restoration. It meant something else as well, though. Carver was sure of it.

17 Soledad

Jags sat in his Chevy, watching the dogs.

'A real fifty-seven fuckin' varieties, aren't you boys?' The dogs wandered around Brochu in packs of various sizes; a couple wore collars, but most were stray. There were some odd mixes, like this one – a bulldog head on a border collie body. They were the complete opposite of the dogs he saw back in California. Those were pure breeds with hefty price tags and they were treated more like children than animals by their owners. The mutt in question lifted its head and sniffed the air; three hundred million odd odour receptors had caught a whiff of something new. Jags recalled that one of the projects Fred was working on back in his lab was a computer that could smell. Humans had a pathetic number of odour receptors compared to a dog, but still millions more than any digital device anyone had come up with. At the last annual hackathon that Public Square organised – a day-long event where everyone in the company came together to eat hot dogs, drink beer and fix a problem that had so far eluded the rest of the world – the staff had been asked to pick something that humans *can do* that tech still *couldn't*.

Suggestions had included *joke, feel, smell* and *cry*. Crying was ruled out first of all, since no one could think of a reason why you'd need a computer that could cry. Joking and feeling were put on the back burner and the combined might of the Public Square brain set about inventing a computer capable of smell.

The bull-collie or whatever the hell it was made a low growling sound and the rest of the dogs turned in his direction and set off after him up the road towards the graveyard. They were digging a hole for Pablo Mistral up there and Jags guessed that they might have dug up something that the dogs liked the smell of.

He hadn't gone to the little dark stone church for the ceremony and he wouldn't go to the grave either, at least not until the funeral party had moved on. It could be another hour or two yet, Catholics took their sweet time about these things and Chilean Catholics seemed to take even longer than your average. Jags yawned and shunted his seat back; the flight from Los Angeles had been a bumpy one, he hadn't slept. He pulled his mesh-back baseball cap down over his eyes, folded his thick arms across his chest and tried to sleep.

A peal of bells woke him and he saw that an hour had passed. People were drifting back from the cemetery, past the church and towards a nearby bar or home. It looked like most of the mourners had done their mourning and it wasn't a bad-sized crowd. He saw Pablo's wife and sons walk by with the priest in close attendance. Jags waited a little longer, then climbed out of the car, locked it and headed up by the church and towards the graveyard.

He'd been up here before, more than once, paying his respects. One grave stood taller than the rest and looked better tended than most. It belonged to an English missionary who'd spent the last years of his life trying to spread the good word to the indigenous people in this part of Chile in the early 1900s. Jags read the dedication and did the math: the man was in his late forties when he died – he probably didn't intend to die out here. Edward Butler was his name and the dedication claimed that Mr Butler had 'Closed a Useful Life' in this unlovely corner of the world.

'What a crock.'

Jags guessed that a useful life was something to aspire to, but how would you go about measuring a thing like that? Many people had made use of Jags' time and talents. Did that mean he'd led a useful life? He walked on up the hill. 'Up to the cheap seats.'

Soledad was standing at her father's grave, though her thoughts were far away.

'I'm guessing you're Pablo's daughter?' Soledad turned at the sound of the stranger's voice, but she did not appear startled. She looked Jags square in the eye and then glanced at his baseball cap. He removed it and held it out in front of him. 'I've come to pay my respects.'

'The mining company sent a representative.' Her English was good, he'd heard that it was. Top of her class, she would've gone to university if there'd been money.

'Right. I knew the mine were sending a rep, but I'm different. I'm Jags.' He held out his right hand for her to shake, but the young woman ignored it. 'I knew your father, he did some work for me. Now and then.' Still no response. 'Odd jobs. Stuff around the copper mine. But not mining.' Nothing. Jags glanced around. The shadows were lengthening, the sun was beginning to set. 'A lot of graves here, aren't there? Filled, unfilled.' He was starting to get impatient. In order to negotiate with Soledad he needed her to talk to him. 'I guess one of these will be yours one day, won't it?' She shrugged. 'Where'd you reckon it'll be?' She heard everything, understood everything, but as yet Pablo's daughter showed no sign of being interested. 'Halfway up that hill would be my guess. Give or take a few yards.' She looked up at the rocky ground and nodded. Unmoved. Indifferent. 'I guess that's not your main worry right now though, is it?' He paused. 'Nope, your prime concern right now is how the fuck to pay for this grave here, the one your father's lying down dead in.' They stared down at the freshly turned, red-hued earth and Jags kept on talking. 'Yeah, you gotta pay for that and for the headstone . . . and for the priest.' He sucked at his teeth. 'That can't have been cheap, getting that priest of yours to bury a suicide. Catholic priests don't care for suicide.'

Soledad turned and waved a hand in the direction of the dark little church.

'The man in there is more a thief than a priest.' Jags nodded. It seemed that anger was the way to reach her.

'How much did he charge you? For everything I mean.' Soledad looked at the American. There was no reason not to tell him. She could not burden anyone in her family with the information and she felt a strong need to tell someone.

'Four hundred and fifty dollars.'

'American?'

She nodded.

'Four hundred and fifty bucks?' Jags whistled. He could have taken a few notes from his fat black wallet and paid the debt right now, but this did not suit his purpose. For Soledad and her family, four hundred and fifty dollars was an astronomical sum. It might as well have been a million. 'How much money have you got?'

'Twenty.'

'Twenty? Wow. Perhaps you should have gone for a cheaper funeral.'

'My mother wanted him to have the best.'

'I see. That figures.'

Jags kept quiet for a while. He let the seriousness of Soledad's situation sink in some more. 'So your family's got a big ol' debt, but you've got no breadwinner.'

She turned and glared at him.

'What is this to you, American? What do you want?'

'Like I say, I knew your father.' Soledad looked him over

properly now. He didn't look like the other consultants that she'd seen, but who knew?

'You said that already. And you work *around* the mine, whatever that means.'

'That's right and so I came to pay my respects.'

'And now you have. So, goodbye.'

'But not just that. I came 'cos I've got a proposal for you and your family.'

'A proposal?'

Jags glanced up at the mountains. The sky was darkening fast.

'Yep. But I don't much like to talk here and it looks to me like there's a storm coming. Are you hungry? You look hungry.' Soledad was grey-faced. Underneath a long black coat that Jags guessed was her mother's, she was stick-thin. He knew how things worked in her house. Pablo Mistral and his three boys were served first and given the most, then Soledad served her mother, and only after all those mouths were fed would Soledad take what was left. 'I can talk while you eat.'

'Eat where?'

'The American place, the diner.'

'They will not let me eat in there.'

'Yes they will.'

They did, although the waiter sat Jags and his ashen-faced guest right at the rear of the restaurant close to the toilets. This suited Jags fine and Soledad did not notice, she was too overwhelmed simply at being *inside* the restaurant to care where she was sitting. As a child, she and her friends would hang around at the back of this building, torturing themselves, filling their nostrils with the smell of good beef being cooked over charcoal. Fresh fish, lemon, whole roasted onions and peppers and potatoes slow-baked in hot coal. In the past, some of this food had been farmed locally, but now almost everything came from elsewhere

– freighted in from all over Chile or, in the case of the beef, flown in from Argentina or the United States. The waiter arrived with a basket of warm bread rolls, salted butter and a bottle of mineral water. He filled their glasses and Soledad wolfed down a bread roll and drank.

'What is this water?'

Jags took a sip of his.

'It's just water. Still water.'

'It tastes . . . sweet.'

Jags ordered for both of them – all the starters, the steak, the swordfish and every side dish on the menu too. He picked a Pinot Noir from the Casablanca Valley that he'd had before and liked well enough. It was way too much food for two people, but Soledad could take the rest home for her brothers and mother and deliver that along with Jags' proposal.

'How's your mother holding up?'

'Most of the time she is in bed. She has fallen in love with her grief. She loves it as much as she loved my father. More.'

Jags nodded. He wasn't great at conversations like this, but he needed to get her talking.

'Your father was a good man.' Soledad pulled a face; she considered putting her cutlery down then decided against it.

'I thought you said you knew him?'

'I did.' He paused. 'Sure, he made mistakes.'

'Mistakes were all he made. Mistakes and children.'

Jags laughed. As Soledad ate, the colour returned to her face and with it the confidence and the attitude that he hoped was going to make her useful. 'My father was a *mujeriego*. What is that word in English?'

Jags hesitated a second.

'Mujeriego? It means . . . a *womaniser*.'

'Yes . . .' she paused. 'A *womaniser*. I think I like it better in English, it sounds too pretty in Spanish. Too poetic.' She was

112

right. 'If he had not killed himself, he would have left us. He was getting ready to leave my mother for his other woman.'

'I see.' It seemed that when it came to a match-up between Fred's algorithms and Soledad's instinct, it was a tie. While she ate and occasionally drank – she sipped while Jags gulped – Soledad recounted the many wrongs her father had done to her mother.

'He would return from work filthy and wash in the kitchen sink. You know the mine, you know that the men can shower there but he would never do that. He would wash in front of us, dirtying everything in sight. Then he would watch her while she cleaned it.'

Jags looked at Soledad.

'I've seen men do worse.' He'd seen this girl's father do much, much worse, Jags thought. But then, on reflection, perhaps not. All the murderous acts Pablo Mistral had been involved in had been done under Jags' instruction. This regular humiliation of his wife was something he'd thought of all by himself.

'What kind of work did my father do for you?'

It seemed that Soledad had an ability for reading minds.

'He helped me run errands. Move stuff around.'

'Was he good at it?'

'He was pretty good, he was reliable.'

'And I suppose you think one of my brothers will be good at this too, you think this is a job that runs in the family? I am guessing that this is your idea?' Jags grinned. Her mind reading ability was not without limit. She had guessed at his old plan, but not the new one.

'No, Soledad, I'm not interested in your brothers. It's you that I want to offer a job to.' He washed a mouthful of steak down with a swallow of red wine. 'And I'm not asking you to do the work your father did, not at all. This would be different work, better work . . .' He filled her wine glass, though she had scarcely drunk. 'And not just for you, there would be work for your mother as well. Francesca isn't it?'

Soledad stared at the stranger.

'My mother could work again?'

Jags nodded. She didn't trust him, he knew that. But then she didn't need to trust him, she just had to want what it was he had to offer. To want it a lot. 'My mother hasn't worked in . . . a long time.'

'I assumed not. I bet she was a different person when she did work.' Soledad could not argue with this. Her memories of her mother from back when she was working were fond ones. Life had worn her down, her husband had worn her down, diminished her. But now he was gone.

Jags explained to Soledad about the museum, how the company he worked for was planning to buy up an old farm not far outside Brochu. Soledad knew the place Jags was talking about. The plan was for a nursery for the miners' kids, a community centre of some sort and a museum. The museum would celebrate the miners and mining, tell the story of Brochu and the Americans would return some of the petroglyphs they had dug up and taken away during the construction of the dam.

'What would my mother do?'

Jags explained that she could take her pick, she could either choose to work in the nursery or the museum and that either way she would be paid a starting salary of four hundred American dollars a month. Soledad took a sip of wine. This was incredible. Her mother would choose the nursery job, of course, and she would be good at it. Having a job like that could simultaneously save her mother's life and put food in her brothers' mouths. It would leave Soledad free to do what she wanted. Jags saw this thought process at work.

'But you gotta remember this is a package deal, Soledad. Your mom only gets the gig if you take a job too. This is one of those non-transferable, non-negotiable deals, you understand?'

'What would my work be?'

Jags finished his wine in one swallow.

'The thing about people, Soledad, is they need leadership. They need it like they need water. The men who represent the miners here in Brochu are a bunch of fuck-ups – excuse my language – they have been for years.' This was true; what Jags didn't bother mentioning was all the work he'd done in the past to make sure it stayed that way. All those bodies buried in mud at the bottom of the dam. Now that Elizabeth Curepipe was going to take a more direct interest in Brochu, things were going to have to change. A new approach was called for and Jags had a feeling that Soledad was the key to that.

'You already have a leadership role in your community.'

'That is only for the . . . I do not have the English word . . . *ceremonia*.'

'It's pretty much the same word . . . your role is ceremonial.'

'Yes, ceremonial.'

'And people respect you because of that.' Soledad stared at Jags.

'Maybe.' They both knew that it was more wariness or fear than respect that the people of Brochu felt towards Soledad. On the one night each year when she performed her ceremonial role – the same role as her mother and grandmother and great-grandmother before her – locals showered her with tokens of appreciation and kind words. The rest of the time they kept their distance. Soledad had no problem with that.

'It's All Souls' Night soon and that is good timing for us. It will remind people who you are. Show them your *leadership qualities*.' Soledad was getting an idea now of what it was this Jags was asking.

'I am not a community leader. Certainly not a miners' leader, the men who work in the mine would not accept me as their spokesman.'

Jags refilled his glass.

'You're right there might be some resistance at the start . . .' He took another swallow of wine. 'But they'd come round to the idea. How about you speak to your mother, see what she says?'

115

18 The Watching Man

Fred stared at the screen on his desk. It was similar in size to a large television, but longer and thinner, landscape and concave. He placed his thumb and forefinger on the black pad at the centre of his keyboard and pulled his fingers together, as though picking something up. On the screen, the map of America's West Coast became more detailed and he could see a sprinkle of silver lights, seven of them, gathered closely together. But not too close; separated by several feet, by walls and windows, each in a separate room, but all staying in a beachside hotel down in Santa Monica. The trip was sold as forty-eight hours rest and relaxation, before they headed off on their various assignments. Of course, every one of them knew that this was really just the last stage of the recruitment process. A chance to check that they weren't screwing around, or fucking each other or meeting anyone they shouldn't be meeting. The new recruits knew full well they were being monitored, just as surely as they knew that there were cameras inside the fire alarms and behind the bathroom mirrors. Why else did one of the women prance around so much, practically putting on a floor show for Fred every time she got out of the shower? It wasn't really his kind of thing, but he liked the thought of her knowing that he was watching.

He spread his fingers and it was all of the Americas he saw. Then again and it was the world, or most of it. The same silvery dots that were gathered together on the Pacific coast were sprinkled elsewhere, but individually. Down in South America, one dot. A couple in Europe, a few in North Africa and around the Middle East. Even China, or at the fringes of it anyway. All of them working for an assortment of masters, but all of them watched over by one man. He heard Elizabeth's heels ricocheting down the hall and stowed the map away behind a complicated-looking spreadsheet.

'Hey husband of mine, I've lost that speech I give when people want to hear about Dad, don't suppose you've got a copy?' Fred's right hand skipped across the keyboard, his fingers scarcely seeming to touch the keys.

'*The high-tech hippies*, yes?'

'You're a genius.'

'It's in your in tray . . . now.'

'Thank you. The people in London want me to talk about the old man as part of this exhibition they've got going on . . . *The Fathers and Mothers of Our Technological Future* they're calling it.'

'Oh yeah?'

'Guess how many men they're celebrating and how many women?'

Fred knew better than to guess.

'Tell me.'

'Ten guys. Two gals. How'd you like that?'

'About as much as you do Lizzie.'

'No.' She shook her head. 'No one could be more pissed about crap like that than me. I'm gonna tell them so too . . . right around the time they ask if I want to sponsor a lecture theatre or a scholarship or whatever it is they end up asking for.'

Fred looked back across his shoulder at his wife. 'I could come to London with you, you know? Instead of Jags.' Elizabeth walked closer and placed her hands on his shoulders.

'I'd love that.' Here came the *but* . . . 'But I don't think now's the right time, you've already got too much on your plate and most of the stuff I've got to do over there is boring. Let's fly back, just the two of us, later in the year. Do London and Scotland, a proper vacation?'

'Sure.' Elizabeth felt bad. She didn't want to leave Fred disappointed; she ran her bright red nails though his hair and offered a consolation.

'How about you wander over later on, when you're done with work? I'll stay up.'

Fred and Elizabeth lived in separate halves of this house, known locally as Big Mac. The outskirts of Cupertino boasted plenty of extravagant and ridiculously expensive mansions and McMansions. The Curepipes' house was bigger, better-located and more securely guarded than any. Its design was a copy of, or in Elizabeth's words a tribute to, Frank Lloyd Wright's Fallingwater House. Cut into the hills behind, it looked at first sight like half a dozen enormous, square-sided sandstone trays hovering above each other at irregular angles. These trays were separated by air and connected at the centre by a broad stone chimney. There were no natural waterfalls available in this part of California, so the falling water for the new Fallingwater House was pumped in a never-ending cycle, up the back of the house through hidden pipes before being released to cascade down over a rock façade at the front. For hygiene's sake the waterfall was chlorinated, but after a while you stopped noticing the smell. Fred smiled and looked up from his screen, craning his neck to gaze up at her.

'Sure that'd be great. I'll just finish with this then I'll stroll on over.' Elizabeth matched his smile and headed back to her half of the house. She'd expected Fred to refuse her offer; he looked tired and she was tired herself. The chances were that he'd forget or get distracted, but she changed into a black silk slip just in case. She didn't want to fuck, but these days some passionless kissing and a little *tug and cuddle* was usually enough to send Fred back to his side of the house happy enough.

Fred waited until the sound of his wife's high heels had receded before he opened the map up again. Down on the south-eastern tip of China one of the silver dots was on the move, crossing water and travelling, by the looks of it, at a considerable rate of knots.

19 Chinese Rules

The late-night call from Carver had asked more questions than it answered, but Patrick remembered that it was often this way with William. It had been good to hear his voice. Even better was the knowledge that Carver was actually willing to talk to him – after months of radio silence, Patrick had begun to think he might have been shut out forever. Less encouraging was the content of the call. A brief hello and how are you and then that cryptic message, which was obviously the point of the call: *Are you in a position to help a friend of mine with something?* It was as vague as that. No clue as to what this help might involve or who it was for but, of course, he'd agreed without hesitation because it was William doing the asking. That was pretty much it. *Where are you staying? Room number? Someone will be in touch.* Thinking about it now, he wasn't even sure that William had bothered with a goodbye, maybe he'd just hung up. Patrick spent a while replaying the conversation and trying to see if there was more to it. The call had come from a number Patrick had never seen before and it was brief and deliberately vague. Carver was obviously working on the assumption that the telephone might be tapped or listened to in some way and Patrick wondered about that for a while. Eventually this train of thought led him back to Rebecca, her urgent phone call, the weird story about being followed and how worried she'd sounded. He'd promised to call her straight back. He looked at his watch. 'Oh fuck.' Almost an hour had passed since he'd made that promise. He called her number and it rang until eventually her answerphone message clicked in. He hung up and tried again, but the same thing happened. He left a message – a rambling apology and a plea that she call him back when she could. Any time she liked. He fell asleep with the phone on the pillow next to him, although he suspected there was very little hope of Rebecca returning his call.

Patrick had a fitful night's sleep, punctuated by at least one trip to the toilet and brought to an abrupt end by the deafening ring of the hotel room phone, not a foot from his ear.

'Hello? Becs?'

'No. This is the telephone call you were told to expect.' The accent was unmistakeable.

'That's McCluskey isn't it? Are you the friend William was talking about?'

He heard a sharp tutting sound down the other end of the line.

'That's a cracking start son, brilliant. I was about to say *no names* and there you went telling everyone mine. So, now I'll say *no more names*. You understand? We're playing Chinese rules from now. You get me?'

'Yes, sorry.' Patrick understood what Chinese rules meant; working with Carver he had learnt about the particular precautions you needed to take depending on which corner of the world you were trying to report from. Nowhere were the rules stricter than when trying to do any investigative reporting from China. In the past, Hong Kong had been different, the rules more relaxed, but from what McCluskey was telling him, that was no longer the case. 'I dinnae know that this phone line's tapped, but we're going tae assume that either it is, or it soon will be. You and me have to find a reliable way of communicating.'

'I understand.'

'Wi' that in mind I'm going to start us off a little bit *old school*. Just until we come up with a better idea.' She talked him through the plan. Patrick rubbed at his eyes with his free hand and tried to concentrate, but McCluskey's accent seemed to be thickening by the minute. He wondered whether this was deliberate; either way he wasn't sure he'd fully understood what she was telling him.

'Did you say you're going to try and *fax* me through some of these documents?'

'Aye.'

Patrick stifled a laugh. 'It's 2014, Mc—' He stopped himself. 'It's 2014, no one's got a fax machine any more.'

'I have son. More importantly, so has the Headland Hotel, I checked. So how's about you go and find out where they keep it, switch it on and make sure you've got plenty of paper tae hand. Stand across it and dinnae let anyone else take a look at what I'm sending you. Naebody, d'you understand me?'

'I understand.'

'Fab.' The phone went dead.

'You're welcome.' Patrick heaved a sigh and fell back on to his bed. 'Careful what you wish for.' It was exactly like working for William Carver again, just a female version with an impenetrable Glaswegian accent.

20 The Devil's Work

Even when Soledad did not love her mother, she loved her hair. Ink black and heavy with natural curls, it fell in calligraphic swirls from the cheap scrunchie she used to keep it out of the way. In the past, she had loved to kneel behind her mother on the double bed and brush out her hair. Francesca would hum or sometimes sing a few words of old Chilean folk songs as Soledad ran the antique silver-backed brush through her mother's hair again and again. It had been a long time since they had done this together.

'Augusto says you were seen with an American man in the American restaurant, so I suppose you have decided to become a prostitute now?' This was her mother's invitation to embark on the latest of their loud and bitter fights. Soledad held her tongue.

'You have just buried your husband.'

'Yes.' Francesca's hand went to the Catholic cross, glittering on her neck. 'And you see how that woman – his whore – she could not even find the time to attend the funeral?' Soledad nodded. The other woman was stupid enough to have got involved with her father, but not so dumb as to turn up at the funeral. If she had, Soledad was pretty sure her mother would have killed her with her bare hands. This too, she left unsaid, staring instead at the flowered wallpaper next to her mother's bed, sample sheets each with different flowers, in different colours, stapled together and stuck to one wall. Francesca saw her looking. 'God loves the empty more than the full, Soledad.' Her daughter smiled.

'In that case Mother, he must really, really love us.' She paused. 'Father used to work for this American. He ran errands for him. That was why he was there, that was why he wanted to talk to me.'

Francesca's eyes brightened.

'He has a job for one of the boys? For Augusto?'

'I thought you wanted Augusto to be a priest?' This was a cheap shot, but one that Soledad could not resist. Her eldest brother was constantly getting into trouble these days. Augusto was more likely to end up in prison than the priesthood the way things were going and both women had expended considerable energy and called in many favours trying to delay the inevitable.

'The American doesn't want to offer one of the boys a job. He wants to offer *you* a job. And me.'

'A job for me?' Francesca checked her daughter's face for signs that this might be some kind of cruel joke. Soledad was more than capable. 'What kind of job?'

Francesca had been tempted to simply accept the American's offer on the spot, but her pride and a commitment to the proper way of doing things dictated otherwise. Instead Jags had been invited to visit to discuss the proposal properly, formally.

'What do we have to give this man to eat, Soledad?'

Her daughter shook her head.

'He won't have time to eat.' It had been difficult enough persuading the American to come and meet with her mother at all. There was no way he was going to sit down for dinner.

'We must give him something.' She dug around in her purse

and handed Soledad a folded note. 'Tell Augusto to run and get some empanadas and a bottle of beer.' Soledad did as she was told, although she was quite sure that once she gave Augusto this money, they would not see him again until tomorrow or the day after. Her mother had her silver mirror in one hand and a lipstick in the other. She caught her daughter's eye in the mirror.

'When we are both working, maybe we could buy another goat.'

'A nanny this time.' The two women smiled at a shared memory from several years ago. The nanny goat that Pablo bought and brought home that turned out to be male not female. After his horns had grown in, the billy goat made life miserable for Soledad and her brothers, bullying and butting them without provocation. The day they killed and ate the animal was a happy day as far as she was concerned.

Soledad left her mother to get dressed for their visitor and went to take a look inside the fridge. She saw a bottle of water and two opened tin cans, one half full of tuna and the other of beans. It wasn't much to work with, but she could fry it up into a something that the American could dip potato chips in if he wanted to. It would have to do, there was no way that Augusto was coming back with empanadas, beer or anything else. She had just finished preparing this food when there was a loud rap on the door. Soledad opened it to find an impatient-looking Jags standing outside.

'This had better be quick Soledad, I've got a plane to catch, where's your mother?' A door at the end of the hall opened with a creak and Francesca appeared, wearing a cornflower blue-coloured dress that Soledad hadn't seen in . . . how long? It was a dress from a happier time and she wasn't even sure where her mother could have been keeping it. Not on the clothes rail next to the damp wall, that was for sure, because the dress both looked and smelt fresh. Her mother arrived at her side and extended her hand in a way that suggested she was nervous to give it to the American.

'Ma'am.'

Francesca instructed her daughter to go and fetch the food while she encouraged their guest to take a seat at the small family table. Soledad disappeared briefly behind the screen that separated dining room and kitchen and returned with a patterned tray. Jags hesitated a beat too long before taking a chip and dipping it in whatever the fuck that sauce was. Francesca noticed this.

'I am sorry, this is not very much. Usually I would offer you chicken and watermelon . . .' Soledad glanced at her mother; she couldn't recall them ever eating a meal like that. '. . . But we had so little time.' Jags shook his head and smiled.

'Nope, this is great, just what I wanted Mrs Mistral. So do you want me to tell you a little more about this proposal? I'm sure Soledad has talked you through it but maybe you have questions?'

She had many questions. She wanted to know when the nursery would open, how many children it would have, what ages, what facilities . . .? Jags talked a lot of bullshit, made some stuff up until eventually the woman seemed satisfied.

'Soledad told me that you used to work with my husband?'

'That's right ma'am.'

'He was a good worker.'

It was a statement not a question, but Jags knew it required something from him.

'He was. A very good worker. And a good man as well.' Jags could feel Soledad's eyes on him. 'He spoke about you all the time.' He pointed a friendly finger at Francesca 'You mainly. but the children too of course.'

She nodded slowly. Of course, yes.

'When did you last see him Mr Jags? How long before the accident I mean.'

The accident. Cute. Jags gave his cheek a thoughtful scratch. It was a passable impression of a man attempting to remember something that was difficult to remember.

'Far as I recall, it was ten days or maybe a fortnight before the accident Mrs Mistral.'

'I see. And how did Pablo seem to you? People say he had depression.'

Jags noticed she used the Spanish word *el abatimiento*, which was closer to melancholy than depression.

'I can't say that I saw that in him ma'am. He was . . . tired I guess.' She nodded. 'But he had a good family and a steady job, it was a shock to me, what happened. A complete tragedy.' Jags watched the woman's eyes fill with tears. He tried not to think of the last time he'd actually seen her husband – hanging from a thick wooden beam, his neck stretched, legs twitching, a look of absolute terror in his eyes. Soledad passed her mother a handkerchief and she blew her nose loudly.

'Soledad says that you plan to come and visit next All Souls' Night?'

'I certainly hope to ma'am.'

'For the ceremony?'

'That's right.'

She smiled.

'I am proud of my daughter, of course, but I wish that you were able to have been there when I fulfilled the role. Soledad speaks the words well . . .' she looked over at her daughter. 'But you have to feel the words, you have to believe them.'

'I would've liked to have seen you do that, Mrs Mistral. I have heard how good you were from other people in town.' He had heard no such thing. Jags glanced at his watch. 'I'm really sorry but I have to get going. Will you have a think about my offer? Your daughter can let me know what you decide tomorrow.'

Soledad walked him to the car.

'Where do you go now? America?'

'I'm going to London.'

'England? The Queen? The Houses of Parliament?'

'Yeah, that one.' He could feel his stomach starting to churn, and got to his feet. Jags had a strong stomach but that godawful dip was too much even for his gut. If he left now he could drive out of town a mile then stop and stick his fingers down his throat. 'I'm gonna arrange a meeting between you and the local union guys over at the mine.'

'My mother hasn't said yes yet. I think we—'

'She will Soledad. We both know she will. She needs this job and so I want you to start thinking about *your* job. I'll arrange the meeting, for now all those idiots know is that you're going to be playing a role. So go meet them and try to be nice.' Soledad nodded.

'What if it turns out that I am not the right person? What if this arrangement does not work?'

They were at the Chevy. He pulled open the driver's side door and climbed in, rolled down the window.

'We go our separate ways. No big deal.'

Jags was pleased with this answer and Soledad seemed satisfied too. She nodded. It was reassuring. And obviously convincing enough, at least for now. He waved a brief goodbye and put the car in reverse. The only problem with Jags' answer was that it bore absolutely no relation to the truth. He swung the car round, kicking up a fair amount of dust as he did so. The truth was that if this arrangement didn't work out, if Lizzie Curepipe's plan wouldn't fly, then it would be back to Plan A. Under that plan, Soledad, and possibly her whole family, would wind up dead at the bottom of the Brochu dam – fish food for whatever fucked-up kind of fish still managed to survive in that water.

Soledad walked back into the little house and back into her mother's bedroom. She stood behind her and helped unzip her best dress. Francesca turned and put her hand on her daughter's hand.

'You have to be careful, Soledad. I smell the devil on that man.'

'I know Mother, I smell it too.'

PART TWO

It often happens that, if a lie be believed only for an hour, it has done its work, and there is no further occasion for it.

Jonathan Swift

PART TWO

21 Sammy

A thunderstorm burst over central Hong Kong. Eric Fung stood shivering, drenched to his bones but, nevertheless, grateful for the rain. A downpour like this helped lessen the effect of the tear gas, washing the billowing clouds away and flushing the noxious-smelling gas down the storm drains. The police still had the canisters of pepper spray, of course, and Eric watched from a distance as his fellow protestors pressed again against the police lines, shielding themselves against the eye-blinding spray with a combination of plastic umbrellas and cling film. It worked, but not particularly well. He pushed the thick glasses back up his nose – he guessed the same could be said about much of what he and his comrades had managed to achieve in the last few days. On the face of it, their achievements were many and obvious: Harcourt Road, a major freeway running east to west across the Admiralty area of Hong Kong, was now *Harcourt Village* – a sea of brightly coloured tents and basic wood and tarpaulin structures that ran the entire length of the occupied road. There were stalls serving fish balls, rice and stinky tofu. A group of green-fingered protestors had turned a grass verge into a vegetable garden. True to their name, the *Scholastic* volunteers were setting up home-working zones and students were encouraged to take time away from the front line, to learn. The standard school subjects were taught, as well as an eclectic mix of craft skills – weaving, wood and leather working and origami.

From this vantage point, standing on a plank of wood balanced between two sets of stepladders, Eric could see half a dozen junior school-age children folding powder-blue airmail paper into origami umbrellas. The food stalls, shops and makeshift school rooms were all powered by portable generators and the thrum of these had temporarily replaced the din of Hong Kong traffic. Still Eric felt nervous; the police were holding their line, biding their time rather than pushing back and Eric remembered what the BBC radio man had told him about what he saw happen in Turkey. The authorities would wait until the novelty of these protests wore off, until some among their number got tired of living in tents or standing in the rain or being tear-gassed. Most importantly they would wait until the world's media got bored with this story and moved on.

Eric had watched Harcourt Village grow and grow in just a few days, but he knew that the authorities could sweep it all away just as quickly unless he and his fellow protestors remained vigilant. Already there were worrying signs; the previous night a group of well-organised thugs had set upon a bunch of students in Mong Kok and beaten the living daylights out of them. Three of his comrades were in hospital, one with serious head injuries, but they'd urged him to come back here to tell anyone who would listen what had happened to them. The consensus was that the gang were triad members, doing someone a favour – the Hong Kong authorities or the Chinese State being the most obvious suspects. The degree of violence used was a wake-up call, but what really worried Eric was how the gang of thugs had found out when and where the students were going to be. It was a *pop-up demo*, the details of which were known only to him and one trusted comrade. This young man had met the twenty plus students at one train station and escorted them on a magical mystery tour via several others before arriving at the Chinese-owned travel agency they planned to disrupt. The gang of thugs had been waiting for them, armed with baseball bats and knuckle dusters. Eric knew that there were bound to be infiltrators among the protestors, that was inevitable, but that could not explain this. He had complete trust in the boy he'd put in charge of shepherding the students last night. And even if he hadn't trusted him *then*, he had to trust him *now*. The boy was currently lying in a hospital bed with two broken knees and a fractured skull.

Eric took the brick-like black phone from his pocket and gave it an accusatory stare. He would have to change phones again, the third time this week. He'd begun to wonder whether the only way to organise and coordinate securely might be by using no technology whatsoever. He'd read how protestors had rallied and organised in the old days: posters and flyers and word of mouth. It seemed impossible to imagine. The rain had eased and from behind police lines he heard a familiar popping sound – more tear gas. He climbed a step higher up one of the two ladders and looked around for a competent volunteer. His gaze settled on a skinny kid in a black tracksuit, a green surgical mask covering half his face. He was holding an old-fashioned wooden tennis racquet. Eric recognised him; he'd been hassling him and others for a couple of days now, begging to be given a job to do. Some real responsibility. Eric watched as the boy ran through the crowd, picked up a spinning tear gas canister with a gloved hand, dropped it onto his racquet and deftly lobbed it right back into the middle of police lines. The cops scattered. Eric climbed down from the ladder and went to talk to him.

*

The sunken-cheeked hotel receptionist had politely but firmly denied that the Headland had anything as outdated as a fax machine. He suggested the computers, printers and scanners in the business suite as an alternative and Patrick was wondering whether to try up there when the top-hatted doorman waved him over.

'There is a fax machine in the room at the back of the hotel gift shop.'

'Great, thanks. I didn't think anyone had them any more.'

'Sometimes it's useful.'

A female shop assistant wearing a suit in the same light grey as the doorman, and with short, bleached-blond hair, was dusting unsold souvenirs. The gift shop at the Headland didn't get a lot of action and she seemed excited to have a customer, especially one with such an unconventional request. The boxy beige fax machine was right at the back of the storeroom, switched off at the plug but otherwise, she assured him, fully functioning. She was studying for a business qualification at a college over in Kowloon and was keen to show off her English. This involved telling Patrick quite a lot that she possibly shouldn't. She explained that some of the staff used the fax to place bets with a friendly bookkeeper up at the Happy Valley racecourse. She switched the fax on and they waited for it to warm up. Off-course betting was illegal, but this guy doctored the faxes he received to look like regular betting slips and told anyone who asked that they'd been laid in person. As he listened to her make a full confession on behalf of her colleagues, Patrick saw the fax machine's green eye blinking into life. There was a grinding of plastic cogs then a smoother whirring sound as the fax sucked in and printed out one page of A4. Patrick picked it up and read McCluskey's scribbled capitals.

'Initial this and send it back if everything's kosher.'

He did this and before long the fax was fully employed, printing out five, ten, eventually forty-eight pages of photocopied news-paper articles, typed notes and scribbled addendums. There was a PS at the end of the last page. *'No phone calls from now. Read all this then Skype me from the busiest internet café you can find.'*

Beneath that was a jumble of letters that Patrick assumed must be a Skype address. No *thank you*, no sign off and although McCluskey clearly thought this the safest form of communication, she still hadn't used his name or hers. Still, there were plenty of other names and dates and details in this stack of single-sided A4. Enough to keep him busy reading for a good long time. The question was when he would have the time to do that alongside all his BBC commitments. The shop attendant sold him a brown envelope to put the papers in and charged him fifty cents a page for the use of the fax.

'It is cheap yes?'

'Yes, thanks.'

'This is a pleasure . . .' She paused, obviously nervous. 'But I am not really sure that I should have told you about the horse racing.' She wore a worried smile.

'Don't worry, I'm not going to tell anyone.' He watched her eyes flick in the direction of the hotel entrance.

'Especially not Mr Kip?'

'Especially not him.'

She looked relieved.

'Thank you, my name is Ada.'

'I'm Patrick.'

'Pleased to meet you. If other fax messages arrive for you then I will let you know.'

'It's a deal.' He held out his hand, which Ada took and briefly held, rather than shook, the colour rising in her cheeks as she did so.

Patrick would have liked to start reading the intriguing pile of documents right away, but he had another radio piece to make first. He thought about taking the faxes back up to his room and locking them away inside the safe, but a familiar voice in his head suggested otherwise. Better to keep them with him. He tucked them down at the bottom of his canvas and leather grab bag and headed for the hotel door.

Eric was briefing the boy about what he needed him to do. 'How is your memory Sammy?'

'It is good, I remember everything – all my brothers' and sisters' birthdays, they all ask me when the birthdays are. My mother's birthday I never forget. I know all the names of all the streets here. And in Kowloon—'

'Fine, good. You know Hing Yip?'

'The Commercial Centre? Yes . . .' He scratched his head. 'So I would go down Connaught Road, past—'

'That's fine. Take this . . .' He handed him his phone. 'Put it somewhere safe and here's what you do . . .'

Sammy was determined to complete the task Eric had entrusted to him in double-quick time; he took a shortcut he knew between two tower blocks and was almost at the Hing Yip when a confused-looking tourist, wearing a green anorak and backpack and with a lost look on his face, waved him down. The man was after directions. He was trying to find a street that was just a couple of hundred yards from where they were standing, but he seemed baffled by what Sammy thought were very easy-to-understand instructions. The young Hongkonger checked his watch before deciding that it would be easier just to walk the man to where he needed to be. He led him another hundred yards down the main road, then up a side street, walking quickly in the hope that the westerner would follow suit. Halfway up the side street, Sammy felt a hand on his tracksuit collar. At first he thought the tourist must have stumbled and he turned ready to help. The man hit him hard in the face with the heel of his hand, breaking his nose with one blow. Sammy tried to scream but the westerner's hand was quickly across his mouth, muffling the sound. The man threw him hard against a nearby garage door then swept his legs away and pushed him flat down onto the floor, placing a boot on his chest to hold him there. Sammy tried to yell again, but there was blood in his nose and mouth. The man looked back over his shoulder, then knelt down, pinning Sammy to the ground with one knee on each arm. He took a canister of pepper spray from his backpack, the same type the Hong Kong cops used, and sprayed a blast of the pepper directly into Sammy's eyes. When the boy opened his mouth to scream again, he put a longer blast of pepper spray straight down his throat. Placing the canister to one side, he clamped one hand over Sammy's mouth and pinched his nose closed with the other. The boy's eyes were red and tear-filled, they darted about, looking for rescue but finding none. When eventually he realised that he was not being robbed or assaulted, but that this man meant simply to kill him, Sammy stared at the westerner – confused, scared. Looking for an answer to a question that he could not ask. The man stared back, interested but unmoved.

It took less than a minute for Sammy Kwok to die. His assailant propped his dead body against the metal garage door in a pose that might suggest sleep, or drunkenness. He took both the phones that Sammy had on him, his bank card and student ID. The kid was dumb to have been walking around with things like this on him. He would strip the phones and send the dead boy's details to a Dropbox address he knew by heart. They would take care of the rest.

22 Content Provider

As far as Carver was concerned, the worst part of being seconded to the School of Journalism, by a country mile, was having to go to the monthly BBC management meetings. They took place in a big glass box on the ground floor of the even bigger glass box that was New Broadcasting House and every significant department in BBC News was expected to attend.

William arrived early, partly because he preferred to be early for everything, but also to make sure he got his spot on a low purple sofa in a corner of the room furthest from the action. Most of the endless to and fro took place around a long white table in the middle of the room, where the Head of News, Head of Newsgathering, Head of the rolling TV news and all the other Heads of stuff sat. The BBC bosses' meeting was of great interest to everyone apart from anyone who'd had the misfortune of having to sit through it. Carver's very keen student, Naz, had recently asked him what the fabled meeting was about.

'It's about an hour of my life that I'll never, ever get back.'

It was an eight a.m. start and William arrived at quarter to. The large room was empty apart from Naomi Holder, editor of the *Today* programme and his old boss. She looked her usual smart self in flat shoes, a dark green sweater and black cigarette pants. Naomi was given special dispensation to say what she needed to say early in the meeting and then run back upstairs so she could catch the best part of the 8.10 interview on her own programme. Not that there was a best part these days – in Carver's humble opinion. A bunch of mediocre Tory and Lib Dem MPs who, for some unfathomable reason, were being introduced to the listening nation as Secretaries of State for this and that.

'Hey William. How you doing?'

Carver nodded. 'Fine thanks Naomi.'

'Good, you look well, I like your corduroy jacket.' William chose to ignore this and, having hung his jacket on a coat stand by the door, took his usual seat. He'd nicked a few of the broadsheets on his way through the newsroom – no one else seemed to read the papers these days – and he laid these down on his lap; at least he'd have something to read during the meeting. 'How's the teaching going? Have you got a good bunch of kids?'

'There are a few good ones, a couple.'

'Excellent. Let me know if you want to send any of them my way for a try-out at some point.' Carver nodded. This was a generous offer and typical of Naomi; it was a pain in the arse taking a BBC sponsored trainee on and most of the bosses did everything they could to avoid it.

'Thanks, I appreciate that. There might be someone, a little further down the line.'

'Cool, let's stay in touch.'

He and Naomi got along a lot better now that she no longer had to try to manage him day to day. When he'd asked her for some time away from reporting she'd been supportive, and the Head of News had described the reference she'd written for Carver when he went for the School of Journalism secondment as *'not so much glowing as incandescent'*.

'So have you heard about today's special guest?' Carver shook his head. 'Elizabeth Curepipe is supposed to be paying us a visit.'

'No shit? Curepipe as in Public Square and all of that stuff?'

'The one and only. Expect lots of fresh haircuts and aftershave from the boss class.'

'Bugger.' He looked around. 'This room is going to be heaving, isn't it?' Naomi nodded. 'Are you still planning to leave early?' Maybe he could have her seat, nearer the door and a source of ventilation?

'Are you joking? I'm here for the duration this time. I want to see this show, start to finish.'

'What's she doing here?'

'There's gonna be some kind of announcement. A partnership between us and them is what some people are saying. Very hush-hush. Your old friend Julian Drice is the warm-up act.' Carver racked his brains and from out of the fog he saw a small man in a blue tailored suit with steel-rimmed glasses and a damp hand-shake.

'That tosser?' Drice had held a senior position at the BBC for a while, in between working for various prestigious PR companies and a fizzy drink manufacturer. One of his jobs at the BBC was to chuck out the dead wood. He'd tried unsuccessfully to persuade Carver to take redundancy. 'What's he doing at Public Square?'

'He's their head of press and public affairs these days.'

'You're joking? Incredible.' It never ceased to amaze Carver how infinitesimally small the correlation between ability and career advancement seemed to be these days.

'Well, he's moved around a lot. I'm guessing his CV looks pretty impressive by now.'

'But it doesn't include successfully sacking me.'

'That's true . . .' Naomi smiled. 'Now you mention it, that's probably why the poor guy's having to struggle by on three hundred and fifty thousand pounds a year working for the world's biggest tech company.'

Carver pulled a face. 'Public Square is the third or fourth biggest I think.'

Naomi laughed. A clump of BBC bigwigs was gathering outside the door and there was a palpable sense of excitement. Carver shuffled through his blanket of newspapers before picking up the *Financial Times* and disappearing behind it.

By eight a.m. as he feared, the meeting room was standing room only, with just one seat left empty, a brand-new black ergonomic number placed in between the Head of News and his deputy and anticipating the arrival of the star turn.

But first they had to put up with a full fifteen minutes of Julian Drice. Public Square's press man was still sporting the tailored blue suits, but he'd swapped the steel-rimmed glasses for contact lenses and the Oxford brogues for a soft loafer the same colour as the suit. He'd decided to experiment with his facial hair as well, with mixed results. Underneath the well-tended salt-and-pepper beard, the weak chin was still clearly visible – to Carver at least.

Drice began by extolling the many virtues of his employer, Public Square's *mission to connect the world,* its *unprecedented reach* and *influence.* For several minutes he blethered on about *clicks* and *hits* and *memes,* which to Carver's inattentive ear made Drice sound like a malfunctioning machine. Still, pretty much everyone else in the room was listening intently and there was lots of nodding and it was all going swimmingly for Drice until, in the time it took for him to look down at his notes and back up again, he saw that he had lost his entire audience. Every pair of eyes was now looking past him and out of the glass room at a tall, impeccably dressed woman with shoulder-length blond hair and red lipstick. She smiled in a somewhat self-effacing-looking fashion and motioned to Drice to keep going. But it was pointless and he galloped through the last page of his notes before beginning a well-rehearsed introduction for his *'friend and boss – mainly my boss'* . . . pause for laughter, of which there was some . . . *'Elizabeth Curepipe'*. The crowd around the door parted and she walked into the room with a measured stride, heading for the empty chair. She stopped to shake a few hands and exchange a few words with several senior people as she went. On reaching her seat, she stayed standing and smiled, properly now. This smile swept the room like a follow spot. Each face it lighted upon smiled back, a few people blushed and glanced away, others managed to hold her gaze. About a quarter of the room started to give serious thought to having their teeth whitened. A couple of women who were sitting near to Carver were whispering brand names that meant little to him.

'Is that Max Mara or Armani?'

'Mara top, Mugler skirt.'

'Right. Of course.' She paused. 'I would sell one of my children to look like that.' Elizabeth Curepipe took her seat and folded her hands on the table in front of her. She sat, smiling and nodding and laughing in all the appropriate places, as the Head of News told everyone how excited he was about this partnership with Public Square. How excited he was to have Elizabeth and her team here today and how exciting the future looked. When he'd finished being excited, he invited Elizabeth to say a few words. Drice hastened to her side with a handful of cue cards, but she waved him away. This felt rehearsed to Carver, but maybe it wasn't. He was racking his brains, trying to remember the details of a recent newspaper story about Public Square. It was back in the spring – something to do with how much tax the London-based part of this tech giant had paid the previous financial year – a paltry sum, he seemed to recall. He patted at his trouser pockets and felt his wallet but no phone. He must have left it in the corduroy jacket. Carver nudged his neighbour and pointed at his mobile, which the young man was holding out in front of him like a hymnal. He glanced at Carver before grudgingly handing it over.

Curepipe's presentation was designed to impress more than inform, but a few facts leaked out. She wanted the BBC's help with a new mission – improving the service Public Square provided for the benefit of all: she wanted to educate and enrich her millions of customers as well as entertaining them. With that in mind she wanted to *news-ify* Public Square. Carver winced.

What Elizabeth Curepipe wanted was *content* – although for most of her pitch she remembered to talk about this in terms of *stories* and *news*, unlike Drice, who had repeatedly referred to journalists as *content providers*. Carver loathed this reductive description of his chosen trade and he wasn't alone. The proposed partnership between Public Square and the BBC was a *win-win*. It quickly became clear that many things in Elizabeth Curepipe's world were a *win-win* and a lot of other things were *no-brainers*. In return for helping to make Public Square feel more *newsy*, the commercial arm of the BBC would receive a percentage of the ad revenue that could be ploughed back into local journalism. '*We want to help you make a bigger BBC splash globally and then reinvest it locally.*' Heads were nodding, faces smiling. '*What's more we'll all get to learn a lot more about what audiences want to read and listen to and watch.*'

It took him a while but eventually Carver found the figure he was looking for; he held the phone up for his neighbour to see, pointing at the number. The man shrugged.

'Can I have my phone back?'

Sure.' Carver handed it over and watched while the bloke selected his settings and pressed firmly on *clear search history*. Carver nudged him in the ribs again.

'That doesn't work. They hold your whole search history on record for years. For forever, some say.' The guy shook his head and pocketed the phone.

Curepipe was talking about *'leveraging the power of data and technology to raise us all up.'* Looking around the room, Carver remembered the recent *Thought for The Day* that he'd heard: *'All flowers bend towards the sun'.* Whenever it seemed like the energy in the room was in danger of falling away, she would smile. Elizabeth Curepipe was a businesswoman, but her smile was a movie star smile.

'I've taken too much of your time already, I know . . .' Heads shook. 'But I'm aware that up 'til now I've only been making a *business case* for this partnership.' She paused. 'I would be remiss if I didn't tell y'all that there is a personal side to this project too. The BBC means a lot to me and the truth is that this project would also be a way for me to honour my old man. My dad . . .' her eyes flicked in the direction of the ceiling and other eyes followed, as though they might find Curepipe Senior hovering around up there. 'My dad used to love listening to the BBC news when it popped up on our local NPR station. He'd tune in on his old shortwave wireless wherever he was in the world. He told me that it was the only news service that you could *really* trust. I remember that cheesy old theme tune you guys used to use, it's burnt into my memory in fact – Libbybolero is it?' Several voices piped up with the correct title. The BBC Head of News went one step further and attempted to hum the opening bars of Lilliburlero.

'Da de da de da de da . . .' A warm nostalgic feeling filled the room and Elizabeth Curepipe smiled again before finishing her pitch and asking, in a rather unassuming way, whether anyone might be interested in asking a question? Two thirds of the hands in the room went up and she picked a few. Carver got the impression that most of the people asking questions were doing so in order to get a few seconds of her undivided attention or so they could say afterwards that they'd spoken to Elizabeth Curepipe. The questions were dull and without challenge. *Tell us more about*

*your father, tell us a little about those new headquarters of yours, can
you tell us how you got started as an entrepreneur?*

'Well . . .' Curepipe paused, creating the impression that this
was a question she hadn't been asked a thousand times before,
'. . . I remember my mom and dad telling me from a very early
age that I really could be *anything* I wanted to be . . .'

'Big mistake.'

Carver's muttered remark carried further than he'd intended. It
reached the ears of their guest, who responded with a taut smile;
the people sitting either side of William shuffled away from him.
To her credit, Elizabeth Curepipe regained her composure in an
instant and won the room back round in no time.

'Well, I know I'm bored of hearing me speak so I'm pretty sure
you must be . . .' It was now or never, so therefore it had to be
now. Carver put his hand on his neighbour's shoulder and pushed
himself up on to his feet.

'Three point five million pounds.'

Elizabeth Curepipe raised her eyebrows and located William at
the far end of the room.

'I'm sorry?'

'Your UK operation paid three point five million pounds in tax
last year. That's nought point three per cent of profits.' He paused.
'It's not very much is it?' In an instant, Drice was at her side,
doing his human shield impression.

'That tax settlement was agreed by the revenue and is absolutely
above board.'

'I'm not accusing you of tax evasion, Mr Drice. I'm just pointing
out that it's not very much money, is it? And I was asking the
organ grinder. Not you.'

'How dare . . .'

'It's okay Julian.' Elizabeth Curepipe pushed Drice gently
aside. 'It doesn't sound like very much, you're absolutely right
Mr Carver . . .' William felt himself temporarily thrown – how

come she knew his name? Had she memorised the name of every person in the room? '. . . so I think I'm going to take a look at that and see what's going on there.'

'Er . . . you're going to take a look?' was the best he could manage.

'Yes, I will. The BBC is one of the most respected news organisations in the world, as far as I'm concerned, if we want to work with you, we have to match that standard, not just meet the minimum legal requirement. That will apply to everything we do, for as long as we're working together. You have my word on that, is that okay with you?'

Carver nodded.

'I suppose so.'

She turned her attention back to the whole room.

'I think what we're proposing here will be pretty darn good for everyone involved. But of course . . .' Another smile. '. . . it will be up to you to decide. For my part, I hope we *can* make it work, because I just can't wait to be working with such a committed and talented bunch of Brits.' There was laughter, then enthusiastic applause. Quite a few among the audience would undoubtedly have laid down palm fronds, if they'd happened to have them on them. Elizabeth Curepipe shook some more hands on her way out before pausing at the door and nodding graciously before Drice and the rest of her entourage ushered her away.

Carver was the last out of the room. The glass box had felt like a sauna for the last half of the meeting and William's hair was stuck to his head with sweat, his glasses slightly misted. Naomi was waiting for him outside.

'That was quite a performance.'

Carver looked slightly abashed.

'Well, I felt someone had to say something.'

Naomi smiled.

'Not you, William. Her.'

'Oh yeah, I mean, she's impressive and all that.'

'She certainly is.' His old boss paused. 'Interesting that she knows your name – don't you think?' Carver turned and glanced at Naomi.

'Yeah, have you got any idea what that might mean?'

'Well, I guess it means that you're very lucky.' Naomi patted Carver on the arm. 'Either that . . . or you're toast.'

23 Partners

The number and size of different demonstrations taking place simultaneously across Hong Kong was growing fast. Admiralty, Causeway Bay and Mong Kok had all been affected, and as the scale of the protests grew, so the story had moved up the international news agenda, from mid table to headline news. Running the BBC operation in Hong Kong was like being in charge of a three-ring circus and Vivian Fox was the ringmaster. Her work schedule was punishing and she'd had to call on John Brandon to do more telly work. It meant that Patrick had to spend more time than he wanted down near the harbour, hanging around by the growing line of TV broadcast points waiting for Brandon. The row of arc lit, smart-suited anchor men and women from every corner of the developed world, talking earnestly into the camera in a dozen different languages, was something to see, but it wasn't where the story was. His editor, Naomi, had called from London asking Patrick to look into these rumours that triad gangs were being hired or bribed to beat up groups of student protestors. He also needed some time to read through the bundle of faxed documents that McCluskey had sent him and he wanted to do it in the privacy of his hotel room. He checked his watch and waved again in Viv's direction.

She'd got a good-sized spot for the BBC gantry, sandwiched in between Al Jazeera and CNN. He watched her talking John Brandon and a burly-looking local cameraman through a list of times and broadcasting commitments. When the camera guy tried and completely failed to repeat what he'd just been told, Viv lifted up her red clipboard and pretended to bash him on the head.

'Let's go through it once more, then John you can do the World Service hit solo while I go find out how much of your time *radio boy* needs and when.' She went through the complicated grid of two-ways and bulletin pieces once more and left them staring at the clipboard while she came bouncing down the gantry steps and striding over to Patrick. She was wearing her professional get-up of boots, cargo pants and a blue linen shirt and had an apologetic look on her face. 'I'm going to need Brandon a while longer, Patrick. I'm really sorry.'

'Don't worry, I understand. I can make do without him for a while longer.'

'They're flying another reporter out late today. Thanks for being such a sweetheart about this.'

Patrick shook his head.

'I actually get more done when he's not with me. People talk to me more easily than they do when I'm with him.'

Viv smiled.

'That's because you're a bee charmer . . .' she glanced back in Brandon's direction and gave him the thumbs up, '. . . whereas John's an insufferable bore.'

'I hope he can't lip read.'

'I wouldn't worry. He has trouble hearing what I'm saying when I'm standing right in front of him, talking straight at him. He told

149

me yesterday that he thinks it's got something to do with the pitch of my voice.'

'Ah, yes. Your high lady-voice.'

'Exactly.'

'You're in a good mood. Given the general chaos, I mean.'

She grinned and pushed a strand of dark hair back behind her ear.

'That'll be because I've got *a date*.'

'A date?'

'Yeah. Don't judge. The only other date I've had this year came stuffed with almond paste.'

'Morocco?'

'Yep.'

'I had some of those, they were delicious.'

'They were fine as far as they went.'

'So, who's your date with . . .' Patrick shook his head, '. . . not Colorado Dan?'

She frowned.

'Yes Dan, why not Dan? It's Dan Staples by the way.'

'I know. I checked him out.'

Viv laughed.

'Me too. He's got his own Wikipedia page!'

'Yeah, I think I was a little less impressed with that than you appear to be . . .' Patrick shrugged. 'But he seems like an okay enough guy.'

'He does, doesn't he?'

'He's keen to please, that's for sure.'

'You know, I think it's only us Brits who consider that to be a character fault.'

Patrick smiled. It was a fair point. Colorado Dan had done everything he could to get along and fit in with what could be a rather closed and cosy circle. 'Anyway, he asked me out and I thought *why not?* I've been hanging out with you lot so long, pretending to be one of the lads. Most of the time I think you actually forget I'm a woman.'

'You're a what?'

'Shut up.' She punched Patrick on the arm and smiled. 'Anyway I'm going out with him later . . .' She paused. '. . . but you've got him first.'

'I've got him? What're you talking about?'

'BBC security have raised the risk level after those kids got beaten up in Mong Kok. If you're going to go cover the demos then you need to travel in pairs.'

'And Dan is my pair?'

'Well, you can't have Brandon and Dan offered. He worked as a nightclub bouncer to make some money when he was back in college and he's . . . well . . .'

'A bit bigger than me.'

Viv gave a broad smile.

'Just a little bit. You've got the brains and he's got the brawn. You've got to admit, partnering you two up does make sense.' *Partnering up* sounded more like Dan's language than Viv's 'And the truth is I don't have anyone else to give you.' Patrick mulled it over. There were advantages to Viv's plan, the most attractive being that he could gather the material more quickly and finish earlier if he went with Dan. Viv watched him weigh it up. 'You can go solo and I'll pretend we never spoke if you want . . . but you'd be doing me a favour too.'

'How's that?'

'You can do a little investigative work on my behalf.' She poked at Patrick's chest with her finger. 'Make sure his intentions are honourable. Or. . . honourable-ish.'

Patrick smiled.

'Fine. Where is he?'

'Good question. He seems to have gone *AWOL*, I'll message him again now.'

It had been raining on and off for most of the day. One of Eric Fung's more practical comrades had attached a bright bouquet of long-handled golfing umbrellas to the stepladders that he was standing on. He had a megaphone in his hand and was taking his turn at leading the crowd in the now-familiar series of *call and response* chants. Alternating between English and Cantonese, Eric would ask his fellow protestors what they wanted and the students would reply with a variety of demands – *universal suffrage, the sacking of the Chief Executive, an end to police brutality* and so on. Now and then the riot gear-clad cops on the other side of the barricades would try to drown out this noise with announcements of their own, warning of more tear gas or mass arrests unless the demonstrators dispersed. These warnings had little effect; both sides were well dug in and Eric simply waited for the police commander to finish barking his threats before leading the crowd again in another round of chanting. He was beginning to lose his voice and when one of his fellow protestors offered to take over, Eric passed her the megaphone willingly. He stepped down gingerly from the rain-soaked ladder and looked skywards; the clouds were clearing and there were even a few patches of blue. This was good news, but Eric wasn't in the right mood to take much comfort; his mind was elsewhere. Sammy had been gone too long; he'd set off like a greyhound out of the traps and the address where Eric had sent him to fetch the new phone was only half an hour's walk at a steady pace. It was almost three hours since he'd left. Friends had messaged him on Eric's behalf but so far nothing . . .

Viv arranged for Patrick to rendezvous with Colorado Dan at an internet café on the Lung Wo Road. They could walk from there to Harcourt Road and the heart of the demo. Dan arrived bang on time, showered and shaved, wearing what looked like freshly ironed camo pants and white shirt along with his black Kevlar press jacket. He had a neat little backpack slung casually over his shoulder. Patrick was reminded of the Action Man dolls he used to get at birthdays and Christmases. Dan looked like he'd stepped straight out of the box.

'Hello Dan, you all right? I thought Viv said you'd been out and about already?'

'Hey Patrick, I was, but I got a little too close to the action – a few flares and some tear gas – I didn't want to turn up to see you looking like a bum so I decided to run back to the Headland and switch clothes.' Patrick nodded. When Dan said he'd run back to the hotel he probably meant it. 'I really 'preciate you letting me tag along.'

'There's no need . . . I mean it's fine, it'll be useful.'

And it was. Dan turned out to be both willing and extremely able, while at the same time more than happy to let Patrick take the lead.

'You're the old hand here buddy, I'm a newbie compared to you. Tell me what to do and I'll do it.'

They gathered interviews, asking a succession of people whether they knew the students who'd been beaten up over in Mong Kok. Several did; one had even been allowed in to visit his friend in hospital. While Patrick recorded an interview, Dan watched his back and vice versa.

Several of the people Patrick spoke to suggested he talk to Eric. He hadn't been in Mong Kok when the students were attacked, but he knew everyone who had been and Patrick got the strong impression that it was Eric who'd organised the pop-up protest. He left Dan and worked his way down the edge of Harcourt Road to the point where the front of the protest came face to face with the police line. Eric was standing on a Heath Robinson-like arrangement of stepladders, umbrellas and planks of wood.

'Hey there Eric, me again.'

'Yes.' His voice sounded croaky.

'Sorry I haven't got around to looking at those questions of yours quite yet. I've been crazy busy. You too I guess?' Eric nodded. 'I wanted to talk to you about what happened over in Mong Kok. That business with the students being beaten up?'

'That business?'

'Well . . .'

Eric pointed down at the strange arrangements of planks and ladders.

'I can see a lot from up here.'

'Right.'

'We talked when we last met about problems and solutions. I think that you have decided *not* to be part of the solution . . .'

'I don't know what you're talking about.'

Eric pointed in Dan's direction.

'You have chosen your side.'

'I'm a journalist Eric, I don't have a side.'

'Everybody has a side. There is no choice. Not here, not now . . .' Nearby, a group of students who'd been standing, leading the crowd in a singalong, bellowing out the words to a Cantonese pop song, suddenly went silent and sat down. A mobile phone was being passed from hand to hand. '. . . so I don't see that there is any point in us talking.' Eric stepped down from the ladder and edged past Patrick. 'Goodbye.'

Patrick worked his way back through the crowd. He found Dan sitting on one of the white water-filled crash barriers.

'He doesn't want to speak.'

'How come? I thought you guys were buddies?'

'Yeah, well . . .' Patrick was uncertain how to explain. 'The thing is, Eric saw that I was here with you and . . .' another awkward pause. 'Basically he thinks you might've taken someone's phone.'

The American laughed.

'Oh, is that it? I geddit, but I think you're being all English and polite with me Patrick. Not *might've taken – deliberately freakin'* stolen. This girl I interviewed started jumping up and down just afterwards – telling everyone I'd lifted her phone. Like I need another phone . . .' He found his own two phones in the pockets of his camo pants and held them out for Patrick to see.

'I know, it's probably just some kind of mix-up.'

'Must be. But I'm sorry that's gone and screwed things up for you buddy. Do you want me to go tell Eric we hardly know each other?'

Patrick shook his head.

'Nah, no. Thanks though . . . I appreciate the offer. Listen I've got enough material to make this piece without Eric. How about we call it a day?'

'Suits me, back to the ranch then?'

'Back to the ranch.'

The photograph on the phone that was being passed from hand to hand was of Sammy, slumped against a garage door with his nose bloodied, his eyes open but emptied of light and his face a sickening grey. There followed a number of instant tributes from people who claimed to vaguely know him. These were followed by a flood of other posts from dozens of different social media accounts. Accounts with names like: *HK The Truth*, *ThePeople@HK*, *Cantoprotest* . . . none of the accounts were ones that Eric was familiar with, he'd not heard of any of them until now, but all claimed first-hand knowledge of what had happened to Sammy Kwok.

Some asserted that he'd had an allergic reaction to the pepper spray, stumbled off and suffocated. They pointed to the blood on his face and someone claiming to be a junior doctor at a central Hong Kong hospital said that this pattern of bleeding often happened as a result of a violent allergic reaction. Other social media accounts suggested that the boy had committed suicide and his friends had decided to make it look like he was a victim of police brutality. The picture was a fake – if you looked carefully you'd see the dead boy's head was out of proportion with his body, someone had grafted Sammy's head onto a different body. Others weighed in; they'd seen this boy elsewhere in Hong Kong –nowhere near the Connaught Road – others reported a recent sighting across the water in Kowloon – Sammy Kwok wasn't dead at all, much less murdered. So it went on. A seemingly endless wave of speculation and misinformation that left you not knowing who or what to believe. Eventually, this deluge of lies, conspiracy theories and nonsense became too much for Eric to bear. He gave the mobile phone back to the student who'd lent it to him, together with a health warning.

'We're going to find out what happened to Sammy. But we're not going to find it in there.'

Fred Curepipe pushed his laptop shut and pressed his forefinger hard against the centre of his forehead. Sometimes this worked. The migraine that had been building slowly behind one eye or the other would beat a slow retreat. At other times not. Fred glanced at his watch and realised that he must have been staring at the screen – coding, typing, reading – for four hours solid. No wonder his peripheral vision had started to go, replaced by a blurred rainbow of colours and, soon after that, head-splitting pain. He pressed his finger harder against his forehead and closed his eyes. He needed a break. He'd done enough, more than anyone else could have managed with the modest amount of data he'd been sent. The various hares he'd set running would run on without him.

24 Wishful Thinkers

SERGIO'S, GREAT TITCHFIELD STREET, LONDON

It was Carver's custom to reward himself for sitting through the godawful monthly BBC management meeting with a second breakfast. A cheese toastie and large cappuccino from the Italian café just round the corner from Broadcasting House. Today was no exception, although as he worked his way steadily through the warm focaccia and mozzarella sandwich, he was aware that he wasn't enjoying it as much as he usually did. It was Elizabeth Curepipe's fault. Certain parts of her presentation kept popping into Carver's head. How the BBC would help provide a quality news service to Public Square's millions of users. *Newsifying* the site she had said – Carver winced again. In return the BBC would receive cash to invest in local journalism; it was impossible to object to that. And both the BBC and Public Square would learn more about their audiences. *Win-win*. That was the other rather annoying thing she kept saying.

Carver could feel a familiar sensation in the pit of his stomach. It was a feeling unrelated to the quantity of cheese-slathered bread he'd eaten. This was a fluttering sensation, a premonitory feeling that he'd experienced throughout his career. It had rarely steered him wrong.

'Bollocks.'

He finished eating, paid the bill and headed back to Broadcasting House.

He caught the lift heading down, down as far as it would go, past the canteen and lower ground, all the way to the basement level. He was looking for Donnie – a colleague, a contact and, as far as William was concerned, one of the best-kept secrets in the BBC. Usually, locating Donnie would involve wandering the building in the hope of seeing the familiar sight of a round-shouldered man in a beanie, headphones on, pulling a red roll-along vacuum cleaner down one of the many long corridors. Carver had tried phoning him, but Donnie changed his number frequently and rarely answered his phone, even if you did have the right number. Face to face was the best way and it turned out that today Carver was lucky; when he knocked on the black metal door marked *Maintenance*, Donnie answered.

'I'm on my break, fuck off.'

'Hey Donnie, it's me . . .' Carver pushed the door open. 'Lucky for you I'm not management.'

'I thought you *was* management.' He folded away the companies section of the *FT* that he'd been looking at and squinted over the top of his spectacles at William. 'What d'ya want Carver? I thought you'd retired.'

'No. Who said that?'

'Don't recall, a fellow wishful thinker I guess.'

'Good to see you too.' Carver looked around. Donnie was sitting in the centre of a tatty brown sofa; the only other furniture in the room was a wooden folding chair and a row of battered green lockers. Assorted cleaning equipment was scattered around the poured concrete floor – the roll-along vacuum cleaner with its unconvincing smile, a mop standing in a metal bucket. 'I like what you've done with the place.'

'Yeah, I had that Marie Kondo lady come in. You heard of her?' Carver shook his head.

'Thought not. I refer you to my previous question . . . what d'ya want?' He unpeeled the lid of the Tupperware box that was sitting on his lap and sniffed the contents – a meaty stew of some sort. The more Carver thought about Elizabeth Curepipe's impressive pitch to the BBC bosses, the more uneasy he felt about it. He wanted to know what Donnie thought.

'I'm guessing you've already heard about this proposed partnership between us and Public Square?'

Donnie laughed.

'Course I heard about it Carver. But it's no proposal man, it's a done deal.'

'Not yet . . . not according to the meet and greet she did with the management team this morning anyway.'

Donnie shook his head.

'Window dressing. From everything I hear . . . the deal's already done. They just need to do the paperwork.' He glanced up from his Tupperware lunch. 'Cross some i's, dot some t's. How come you care?'

'I don't know. There's something about it just doesn't feel quite right.'

Donnie waved a plastic fork in William's direction.

'Millions of people get to listen to and read BBC stuff – your stuff. Public Square ploughs a few million back into local journalism. I thought all that would be right up your street?' Donnie was smiling now. Carver got the feeling he was being tested.

'You're not sure about this thing either. Are you?'

'I haven't given it too much thought.'

'Why not? You work for the BBC.'

'I work for a cleaning company that works for the BBC. Big difference.'

'Come on Donnie. Tell me what you think's going on?'

Donnie put his food to one side.

'All I know is that if Public Square want to work with the BBC then it'll be because one way or another, they're gonna make a shitload of money out of it.'

'How?'

'Not sure. Not off the top of my head but there'll be a way. Public Square talk all that philanthropic talk – just like all those big tech companies, but underneath that they still adhere to their one true God.'

'Eh?'

'Shareholder value. That's all that matters. That plus paying your execs a big pile of money. Everybody's so dazzled by these guys, the whole world seems to think they're performing some kinda magic trick – they're not. It's the same old wine, just shiny new bottles: squeeze costs, put your production somewhere cheap, automate where you can and don't pay tax. Same. Old. Shit.'

'Elizabeth Curepipe is offering to pay more tax.'

'She is? She said that at this meeting you were at did she?'

'Yeah.'

Donnie pondered this new piece of information.

'Maybe she thinks she's got to. To seal the deal.'

'Or maybe she's different?'

Donnie laughed.

'Maybe. Hey, while we're thinking along those lines, maybe Beyoncé lost my phone number?' Donnie put the lid back on his Tupperware. 'So you're telling me the UK arm of Public Square's about to cough up some real tax?'

'She gave her word.'

Donnie nodded.

'Okay, that's interesting. I might have to look at my portfolio. Limit my exposure a little.'

'You've got shares?'

'Sure.' Donnie got his phone out and started tapping away. Carver watched.

'So, Donnie, the thing is . . . you're good with numbers . . .' Donnie looked up. '. . . you're better than good. I wondered if you might take a proper look at Public Square's accounts for me, see what you can see?'

'What would I be looking for? Lemme guess. Something that might suggest a partnership between them and the BBC isn't such a great idea? That pretty much amounts to you investigating your own employer. Isn't that . . .' Donnie paused. '. . . a little disloyal?'

Carver shook his head.

'It's the opposite.'

Donnie laughed.

'Okay, I'll do it.'

'Great, thanks Donnie.' William reached into his jacket pocket and pulled out a tatty-looking chequebook.

'Don't worry about money right now Carver. I can do a few hours on this in return for that information you just *didn't* give me.' He stood and stretched. 'Also . . . it's not actually so bad seeing you again. Things got a bit boring around here while you were away.'

25 Favours for Friends

THE HEADLAND HOTEL, HONG KONG

Back at the ranch Dan persuaded Patrick to have one beer, just to take the edge off the day. They found two seats in a reasonably quiet corner of the bar, most of which was given over to the *Women in Business* social event. Standing amongst the tasselled lamps and hand-painted Chinese screens were groups of smartly suited women, each holding a champagne cocktail, a cube of brown sugar fizzing and falling slowly apart at the bottom of each tall glass. Dan pointed at the drink.

'How about I rustle us up a couple of those?'

Patrick shook his head.

'Just a beer for me please man, I need to work.'

'Course yes, understood.'

He worked his way across the room, in the direction of the long bar, generating a fair amount of comment as he went. Patrick checked his bag, first making sure that his digital recorder was switched off and then giving the stack of faxes that McCluskey had sent him a reassuring pat. A quick drink, cut and mix the radio package with Brandon and then he could spend the rest of the evening taking a proper look at what she'd sent and try to figure out why she thought *he* might be able to help. He'd order room service and hole up in his bedroom. He also needed to speak to Rebecca. She'd sent the tersest of replies to his many apologetic text messages and he knew that only a proper, uninterrupted conversation was going to do if he was going to get them back on the right track. He also wanted to know if Rebecca had seen or heard anything more from the mysterious woman who she believed had been tailing her. Dan returned with Patrick's beer in one hand and a Long Island iced tea in the other; he tilted his head in the direction of the women.

'I reckon it's just as well you're only havin' the one drink . . .' Patrick gave him a quizzical look. 'The cougars are circling. I think they've got you in their sights.'

'I don't think it's me they're interested in.'

'It's you those fine-dressed ladies at the bar were talking about.' Patrick could feel himself beginning to redden. He took a long swig of beer.

'I'm taken.' He paused. 'You are too I think? Viv told me that the pair of you are out on a date later?'

Dan grinned.

'Is that what she said?' Patrick nodded. 'Then I guess that's what's happening. What d'you think we should do? What does she like?' Patrick suggested a couple of places that he remembered Viv mentioning. She hadn't had the time to ride the Star Ferry yet and he knew she'd wanted to do that. Dan listened attentively. 'Viv's your boss, right?'

'Well, not really.'

'She's in charge of the whole BBC operation out here isn't she?'

'Sure.'

'Then she's head honcho for everyone. You included.'

'I suppose so, but it's never really felt that way.'

'More like a friend?'

'Yeah, more like a friend.' He took a gulp of his drink. 'She comes across as very confident most of the time, Viv. But she's actually pretty sensitive.'

'I see that.' Dan smiled. 'I'll bear it in mind. You sure you don't want to stay, have one more?'

Patrick shook his head.

'I need to get this package done and then I've got some other stuff I need to do too.'

'Anything interesting?'

'Nah, not really. Just a favour for a friend.'

'Another friend? You've got lots of friends.'

'Yeah, well . . .' Patrick drained the dregs of his lager and stood, picked up his bag. 'Have a nice time with Viv.'

'We will. I 'preciate those pointers.'

'I'll see you tomorrow.'

Bet on it . . . and thanks for today bud. I mean it. I learnt a lot – hanging out with you. Maybe we can do it again sometime?'

'Yeah, maybe. Good night Dan.'

26 Playing the Slots

Fred stood and walked to his office window. Lines of Public Square employees were queuing, waiting for the private coaches that would take them home to their poky little apartments down in the Bay Area. Elizabeth was in London, even his most dedicated employees were packing up and heading home. He looked at his watch. He'd worked most of the previous night and all day with only a couple of hours' sleep on his office couch in between. But he wasn't tired. He deserved a break. More than a break in fact – Fred deserved a treat.

In the executive bathroom down the hall from his office he brushed his teeth and gargled several times with a strong peppermint mouthwash. Behind one of the floor-to-ceiling mirrors was a concealed cupboard; from inside he took a new button-down blue shirt from one of the drawers, shook it out and changed into it, binning the used shirt. He picked a striped tie from a wooden rail of almost identical striped ties, put it on, rebuttoned the shirt collar and then stood in front of the mirror for a while, staring at himself. His *treat* would be a trip to the Cherrywood Hotel. To *play the slots* as Elizabeth used to call it. Walking back down the hall past his office and towards the lift, Fred kept his eyes on the floor and tried not to think about the computer on his desk. Nor the laptop. He could check the red-flagged searches later, at home. He knew that if he sat back down in front of a screen now then he would be there for the duration. A few hours at the Cherrywood Hotel would be *fun*.

He walked slowly across the Public Square campus. Fred preferred it at night when there were fewer people about. The huge beehive shone brightly in the moonlight and walking past, Fred slowed, then stopped. The dull murmur of bees that had been so loud when the hive and a million plus bees first arrived from Mexico was quieter now, almost inaudible. He moved closer and put his ear, rather nervously, alongside the wooden slats. Nothing. Or almost nothing. He took his phone out and called his secretary. She picked up immediately.

'Speak to the bee guy and get him to come check the new hive. Mrs Curepipe will be pissed if all her bees disappear or die while she's away.' He ended the call before she could respond, but his secretary texted straight back – this was Fred's preferred method of communication. She confirmed that she'd call the *apiarist* and have him check the bees first thing. *Apiarist*. Fred was unfamiliar with that word; he wondered if his secretary knew it already or had looked it up. He'd check that later.

His silver Tesla was in the second spot at the front of the Public Square car park; he drove slowly down the long gravel drive and was waved respectfully through the security gates and out onto the freeway. It was only a fifteen-minute drive to the Cherrywood at this time of night and Fred left his car with a valet at the front of the hotel. He gave the kid ten bucks and told him to park it and plug it in. The car had plenty of charge on it, more than enough to get him back home, but he liked to keep it topped up around full. Same with his phone and laptop. He waited and watched as the kid drove it twenty yards and parked it at the end of a long line of similar cars, reversing into the space with exaggerated care.

Inside the lobby, the receptionist greeted him by name and asked if he was planning to eat with them that evening, Fred shook his head.

'Just a drink tonight, I think.'

'The main bar or the Comma Club, Mr Curepipe?'

The Three Comma Club was a separate bar and dining room reserved for the richest of the rich: the men and women that the Forbes Rich List named as billionaires rather than plain old multi-millionaires.

'Main bar's fine.'

He walked down the thick-carpeted corridor, past the hotel boutiques with their glittering display cabinets of jewellery, watches, Chanel dresses and objets d'art. Halfway down, he passed a smoked glass door with a trinity of chunky Helvetica Bold commas painted on it in gold leaf, but Fred walked on. Elizabeth Curepipe hated the exclusive club and regularly poked fun at it. Fred understood why. With more than two thousand billionaires knocking around the planet these days, it no longer felt like a very interesting thing to be. What's more, whether they'd made their stack of money selling plasterboard or chicken parts, in property or tech, members of the Three Comma Club were – generally speaking – not very good company. The Club's only redeeming feature was that it remained an excellent way to impress the impressionable.

The main bar at the Cherrywood Hotel was a venture capitalist or VC hang-out where money came to meet good ideas. Elizabeth's phrase – *playing the slots* – summed the place up nicely. Idealistic young entrepreneurs wanted to get funded, the middle-aged multi-millionaires wanted to feel alive. The VCs would bet anything from fifty thousand dollars to a few million on a start-up they thought might turn into the next big thing – the next Twitter or Facebook or Public Square. Sometimes they won big, sometimes they lost the lot, but the fear of losing a few hundred thousand was less of a concern to these men than the fear of missing out. The bar was busy, heads turned in his direction and he was pleased he'd decided to come. The first person to approach Fred was an old business associate who had invested in Public Square early and sold his shares for a handsome profit, but in retrospect, too early and unwisely.

'Hey! Your old lady letting you out on your own now then Mr Curepipe?' The man had a long face, a sharp nose and an unconvincing toupee.

'Hello there Ferdy.'

'How come you're all on your lonesome? Where's America's sweetheart?'

'She's in London.'

'What's she—? Oh I know, I read something about that. You two are doing some kinda *news thing* with the Brits aren't you?' Fred nodded.

'I don't see that working.'

'You don't see a lot of things Ferdy, that's probably why you fell out of the Forbes top two hundred.'

'Very good . . .' He grinned. '*I'll be back* . . . as our old Governor used to say. In the meantime, I've still got just about enough left to buy you a drink. What'll you have?'

Fred asked for a Jack and Coke and walked outside to get some fresh air while Ferdy went to fetch it. On the terrace, casually dressed VCs stood around in open-necked shirts and blue blazers, drinking thirty-dollar cocktails and talking about money. Fred found a quiet spot at the rail; darkness had rubbed out most of the view but he could still see the outline of the mountains against a clear starlit sky and in the centre of the Cherrywood's impeccable gardens, a turquoise swimming pool shining brightly in the gloom.

Beneath him, stooped figures shuffled around in the dark, working to keep the perfect gardens perfect. They wore torches strapped to their heads and work belts round their waists; the shift had just begun and would see them working right through to five a.m. All of the gardening and maintenance work at the Cherrywood took place at night, so as not to spoil the look of the place during daylight hours. Ferdy returned with the whiskey and a creamy looking cocktail of his own, and the two men drank and chewed the fat. Ferdy was after information, tips or useful gossip and the longer the conversation went on, the more obvious the interrogation became. Fred tired of it and his restless attention turned in the direction of a young couple at the far end of the terrace.

'You want to know who you should invest in? How about them? They look like a good bet.'

Ferdy brightened.

'You know about them?'

'Sure.'

Fred knew nothing. Nothing other than what his eyes could tell him. Handsome, square-faced, fair-haired – unmistakeably American. If you were looking to populate a new planet then you might well start with these two. There were several men standing on the terrace who were interested in doing exactly that, while the other VCs who were buzzing around them just wanted to make some money.

'You think I should go check them out?'

'I think you absolutely should. Let me know how it goes.' Ferdy strolled off, cocktail in hand, and soon he was at the front of the civilised scrum that had developed around the two blond entrepreneurs. The pair were wearing sky blue sweatshirts, the logo of their so-far non-existent company emblazoned on the front.

Fred returned to the bar and ordered another Jack and Coke. He could allow himself one more drink and still drive home. The other people at the bar were talking Silicon Valley talk: *convertible notes, preferential shares* . . . somebody was calling somebody else *a sandbagging son of a* blah blah blah. He was about to down his second drink, cut his losses and leave when he felt an arm brush his. The young woman had extricated herself from her group of potential investors and was standing next to him. The barman was there in an instant and Fred listened as she wondered out loud about a few drinks before ordering a bottled beer, the cheapest thing on the menu. She had a good voice – clear but not too high. She glanced over at Fred.

'How about you sir? Are you interested in Artificial Intelligence?' Fred looked at her.

'I'd take any form of intelligence right now.'

She laughed.

'Maybe you should come over and talk to me and my business partner?' Fred glanced back at the crowd of VCs gathered around her partner. They were talking to him but they were waiting for her.

'I'm fine here, thanks. I like your sweatshirt.'

'Do you? I can get you one of these, they only cost fifty thousand bucks.'

'Is that right? I'm going to guess that you've sold quite a few of those tonight?'

'I have . . . I mean *we* have.'

'Good for you.' He gestured at the logo on her blue sweatshirt, the company name.

'Cloud Chancer. What does that mean then?'

'It's AI related.'

'You said that already.'

The woman blushed.

'Sorry, yes. Well it's a little complicated, although I'm sure you . . .'

'How about you try me? Give me your elevator pitch.' He smiled; 'I'll concentrate really hard.' Fred didn't need to concentrate; her idea was straightforward. Not uninteresting, but hardly revolutionary. It was the sort of idea that would attract a lot of funding. It involved AI and voice recognition, an area that Fred had explored himself, although with different objectives in mind. He nodded in all the right places and waited for her to finish. 'I see . . .' Fred smiled. 'So I'm interested, but I've got some questions. Maybe we should talk later, when you've finished selling sweatshirts?'

'I can just stop now if now's better for you?'

He shook his head.

'No . . .' He looked back at the group of men gathered around her business partner. 'You've got them on the hook. The thing to do when you've got something hooked is reel it in, not walk away.'

'Right, yes.'

'Can I ask your name?'

'Christy . . . Christina Newmark.' He watched her wonder whether she should ask his name in return and decide against. The right decision. She knew who he was, everyone here knew.

'Okay, Christy. So, I wonder, have you ever eaten at the Three Comma Club?'

She scratched at her arm through the sweatshirt.

'As it happens, I haven't yet.'

'Then we'll go there.'

27 The Pushback

THE HEADLAND HOTEL, HONG KONG

Patrick counted the seconds. The rumble of thunder had shaken the window in its metal frame – the lightning couldn't be far behind. One, two, thr— *crrr-ashh*. The noise seemed to simultaneously crush Patrick's chest and lift his bed. His hotel room was twenty-three floors up and right now it felt like he was inside the storm. A blinding bolt of pure white light lit the room. And then another. Patrick sat up in bed. He'd been terrified of thunderstorms as a small boy and he didn't much like them now. The third bolt lit the floor, strewn with the documents that McCluskey had asked him to read. He'd read them, several times and in various orders and arrangements, and because of this and the difficulties he'd had finishing and filing Brandon's latest radio report to London, he hadn't got to bed until after one. The storm had woken him a few hours later and now he would not sleep. Patrick wrapped the duvet around himself like a cape and slid out of bed and onto the floor. He picked up one of the sheets of paper and read it for the third or fourth time. Increasingly he found his eye going not to the main body of the text – stories cut from a range of international newspapers or the chunks of transcribed conversation that McCluskey had acquired from God knows where – but to the notes that she'd written in the margins. Here, next to a story about a recent massacre in Myanmar, she'd scribbled *'mention of restoration again but restoring what unclear as per maslih.'* Patrick shuffled across the floor and placed this piece of paper next to one that featured a recent story from the *South China Morning Post* about the protests in Hong Kong and underneath that, two blocks of untranslated Chinese text. McCluskey had underlined a handful of different characters that cropped up several times. In the margin she had scribbled *'similar to maslih maybe? Check.'*

It was not obvious whether this was a note McCluskey had made to herself or an instruction aimed at Patrick. Better safe than sorry. He took a new notebook and carefully copied down the Chinese characters.

He sat with his back against the bed and stared at the paper-strewn floor. He had spent months . . . no, not months, years now, since the first days of the Arab Spring, watching people across the Middle East, North Africa and now Hong Kong challenging the old order. He had seen half a dozen different revolutions spark and burn – brightly often, briefly always. He had spoken to hundreds of young revolutionaries about why they wanted change and how they planned to make it happen. Here, in front of him, was the other side of the story. Here was *the pushback*.

He moved some more of the papers around on the floor. Protestors in one country tried to learn lessons from other protests elsewhere, that was obvious. The regimes in question did the same, just as you would expect. But that wasn't what McCluskey was suggesting here. It was more than that. The pushback wasn't just similar from country to country. *It was the same.* The thunderous section of the storm had moved away, but not the rain; it pounded at the window, like applause.

Patrick made himself a cup of instant coffee using the neat little kettle and tea-making set that was stowed away behind one of the wardrobe doors. He drank it in bed, watching the uncurtained window slowly whiten as the day dawned. He picked up his phone and tried Rebecca's number again. She picked up on the second ring.

'Hello useless.'

'It's Mr Useless to you.'

'You found a spare five minutes to phone the love of your life then did you?'

'I've got ten minutes actually.'

'Lucky me.'

'I've actually got all night. Or is it all day? Whatever it is where *you* are . . . I've got all of it.'

They fell easily back into their old pattern of conversation. Joking and teasing while at the same time avoiding anything that might come across as too sincere-sounding or corny. For instance, telling the other person that you loved them and missed them every single day.

'How's your class? Did what's his name get excluded?'

'Barry? No.'

'How come?'

'He got himself a pretty shit hot lawyer.'

'Really?'

'No, of course not really, you idiot. I decided to give him a second chance.'

'If I remember right, that was Barry's seventh or eighth chance.'

'Everyone deserves an eighth chance.'

Patrick paused.

'Even me?'

'Even you.'

Patrick apologised again for not calling her back to talk through what had happened at the National Portrait Gallery.

'Never mind, I don't know why it freaked me out so much. Perhaps it *was* just some kind of mix-up. It just seemed weird, running into her twice in one day. And why lie about the nursery school you send your kid to?'

'I don't know. I wish I'd been there though Becs.'

'I wish that too but . . .'

'But I wasn't.'

'No. And you're still not but let's look on the bright side.'

'What's the bright side?'

'Life is long and no one, not even you, can be a workaholic idiot forever.'

They ended the conversation in a much better place than when they'd started. Happier and more sure of each other than they had been for a long time. Patrick made himself another cup of instant coffee. McCluskey had told him to Skype her when he was ready to talk and he was ready now. The information she'd sent him was fresh in his mind and it made sense to do it before the day got going and his own programme and other parts of the BBC started to hassle him. He reached for his laptop and dialled the Skype address she'd given him. The saccharine little ditty that signified Patrick's line attempting to find another sang out for a few seconds and then he heard McCluskey's voice, or rather the loud clearing of a throat and then her voice.

'Internet cafés open early where you are.'

'Yeah, well actually I thought it'd be easier if I just called you from here.'

There was a pause.

'Here being?'

'Well . . . my room.'

'Christ alive. Are you an idiot?'

'I know you suggested I use an internet caf—'

'I didn't *suggest* that. I *instructed* you tae do it. I told you we

175

needed to be careful and the next thing I hear is you calling me on your *own* laptop from your *own* bloody bedroom. I despair.'

'I'm sorry, I thought . . .'

'No you didn't. You didn't think at all and now you've compromised my bloody Skype address as well as your own . . . so it's back to square one.' She sighed. 'I'll fax you a new address.'

'What? When?'

'Now, you eejit. So go an' fetch it, get your arse down to a nearby internet café and we'll try again.'

A digital plopping sound confirmed that the line had been dropped.

'Shit.'

Patrick closed his laptop and frisbeed it down the bed, shrugged off the duvet and got up. He wondered briefly about a shower, but decided against; better to throw on some clothes and head down to the souvenir shop and the fax machine sharpish. He didn't want to make McCluskey any more furious than she already was.

28 God mode

In a locked stall in the marbled hotel bathroom, Fred sat down on the toilet lid and got his phone out. He went to the Public Square site and typed in *Christina Christy Newmark*. There she was: long-time member, regular poster. Reading her resumé, Fred saw that she'd actually worked for Public Square for a year straight out of college. Their paths had never crossed; if they had then Fred would have remembered. If she'd left under a cloud then he would have known that too. He went to the search box and tapped in a long series of numbers and letters, a password that increased his access rights to Public Square data past and present. *God Mode* was what Elizabeth called it back at the beginning and only she and Fred had access. He used it often, Lizzie hardly ever. There was nothing in Christina's data to concern him; he scrolled through the last eight years of her life, well-documented in messages and photos, *likes* and sad face emoticons. He went to her deleted posts and looked through those for a while. Nothing out of the ordinary. There was leverage if he should ever need it – embarrassing family members, some dodgy friends, druggy stuff, several interesting photographs from her high school and college days. Not pornographic but . . . provocative. Fred dug a little further into the dustbin of Christina's life. You learnt so much more about someone from what they deleted than from what they chose to keep or display.

He'd told the maître d'e at the Three Comma Club that he was expecting a guest and so by the time he'd finished his research and freshened up, Christina was already sitting at a corner table in the almost empty club dining room. She'd changed out of the sweatshirt and into a dress with some sort of floral print on it. She had both hands out in front of her and seemed to be testing the weight of the silverware. He walked up behind her, his Italian loafers silent on the plush carpet.

'The silver's real . . .' She jumped at the sound of his voice. 'As far as I know, I guess it could be silver plate.'

Christy smiled.

'I'm sorry, not very classy, checking out the cutlery.'

'It's fine by me. I think it's good to be interested in things. In everything in fact.'

His guest nodded as though he'd said something very profound. He sat down opposite her and paused while the waiter made a show of removing the starched white napkin from its ring and unfurling it for her. 'I like your dress, I had wondered whether you might only have that sweatshirt to wear. I suppose we could've bought you something from the hotel boutique, but I guess that's not ideal?' Christy shook her head and silently cursed her luck. The man sitting opposite her would have bought the black Chanel dress she'd seen in the shop window without batting an eyelid. He probably would've bought the necklace as well, if she'd shown the slightest interest in it. She took a sip of the iced water and tried to focus. This was a big opportunity – for her, for her new company –and she didn't want to blow it. The trick was, like always, to just pretend like you belonged. She picked the menu up and ran an eye down it.

'So . . . what's good here?'

Fred smiled.

'It's all pretty good, most of the time anyway. It depends what kind of thing you like. If there's something you want that's not on the menu, I can ask them to make that too, it just might take a little longer.'

'I'm in no hurry. Are you in a hurry?'

Fred shook his head. He hadn't planned to stay for dinner, he needed to get back and do some work at some point, but not immediately.

'No more than usual.' He looked up from the menu. 'Maybe a little less than usual.'

'Good. So how about we start with wine?'

Fred laughed.

'Good plan.'

They ordered wine and food and talked shop. Christy made the running.

'So you said that you like our idea?'

'I said I found it interesting. Not completely original, but interesting nonetheless.'

'Nothing's *completely* original is it? Everything builds on what came before.'

Fred gave this some thought.

'That's broadly correct, but there are revolutionary moments . . .' He had a hard-baked breadstick in his hand and was waving it like a baton. 'I think the great leaps forward come when someone realises that you can use the existing technology for a different purpose.' He was talking quickly now, as he did when an idea excited him. His examples of *great leaps forward* included the ways in which space race technology changed the home, how calculators became computers that became laptops and now phones, how the internet itself had been designed with rather airy-fairy ideals in mind, but taken and used in ways that its inventors had never imagined, generating trillions of dollars and creating millions of jobs along the way. It was a history lesson that Lizzie would have found tiresome – she and her mom and dad had lived it, they defined it – but Christy Newmark hung on Fred's every word. When he paused she jumped in.

'And AI is the next thing isn't it? The next great leap?'

He nodded.

'It can be. It depends what we do with it. Artificial Intelligence is just a different way of saying computer programmes. You, me and everyone else are developing computer programmes that *imitate* human intelligence, yes?' She nodded. 'First we *imitate* it and then we seek to improve on it.'

'Right.'

'But why stop there? If computers can understand and imitate human intelligence, then why wouldn't they be able to imitate *other human qualities* as well?'

For the first time, Christy looked confused.

'Like what?'

'Human emotion. With enough computational power and the right data, computers can understand and imitate a range of different human emotions – happiness, sadness, fear, disgust etc.'

'And then . . . what? *Improve?*'

'Change.'

29 Date Night

In his eagerness to try to make amends for screwing up McCluskey's plan, Patrick rushed down to the lobby before checking whether the souvenir shop was actually open at half past five in the morning. Not surprisingly, it wasn't. He looked at the opening hours, stencilled on the shop window, and decided to get a take-away coffee from the restaurant and wait until someone, hopefully Ada, came to open up at six.

He was sitting, flicking through the Asian *Wall Street Journal* and drinking a watery machine-made Americano when he saw Viv. She was standing outside, pulling and pulling on the heavy glass front door before eventually realising that she needed to do the opposite. She put her shoulder to the door and ended up almost falling in. She was wearing her green dress again, underneath a long blue coat and with high heels. She made her way slowly across the lobby, looking down at her feet and concentrating on every step. She only noticed Patrick once she was practically standing next to him. She gave a lopsided smile.

'Good morning you.'

'Morning. I'm guessing the date went well? It certainly went long.'

Viv put her hand on the top of the tall wing-backed chair to steady herself and sighed.

'Best. Date. Ever. We just went backwards and forwards on the Star Ferry for most of the night. From here to Kowloon, Kowloon back to here . . . talking and eating and drinking.'

'Especially drinking.'

'Especially drinkin'. We made tock-cails. No . . . wait. Cocktails! Weird word *cocktails*, isn't it?'

'Very.' Patrick looked at his watch. 'Do you want me to help you back up to your room?'

She shook her head vigorously.

'Don't patronise me Patrick.' Viv grinned. 'That's not *extremely easy* to say either is it? Don't Patrick-nise me.' She laughed. 'Funny, huh?' Viv paused. 'Dan laughs at all of my jokes.'

'I'm glad.'

'I know very well exactly where my room is . . .' she checked the pockets of her coat. 'I even have a key. Good night, good friend.' She leant over and pecked him on the cheek, then set off towards the lift, walking in a reasonably straight line. Patrick called after her.

'Drink some water.'

'Yeah, your mother drinks water!'

'What?'

'Nothing . . .' She waved a hand. 'I was trying to be funny, but I think it came out rude. Sorry 'bout that.' The lift doors opened and she disappeared inside.

Colorado Dan arrived a couple of minutes later, less rumpled than Viv but also rather red in the face, not from drink, but by the looks of his stormy countenance, more out of anger.

'Hey there Patrick, good morning.'

'Morning, you okay?'

'Me? Yeah. Just pissed off. That taxi driver was being a dick, driving us round in circles for half an hour, then trying to rip us off at the end of it. I had to set him straight.' He looked around the empty lobby. 'Where'd Viv go?'

Patrick pointed at the lift.

'Up to her room.'

'Glad to hear it, she's a little liquored up. Sleep and water is what she needs. What you doing up at . . .' He took a phone from his jacket pocket to check the time, then tutted at himself and put it back. But not before Patrick had noticed the familiar looking case.

'Isn't that Viv's phone?'

'Yeah, she left it back in the cab . . . like I said, she's a bit booze high.' He got his own phone from the other pocket. 'It's a quarter off six, what are you doin' down here?'

'I have to get a couple of things at the shop.'

Dan glanced over at the gift shop. Its lights were off and the windows dark, but you could still make out the carousel of post-cards, a selection of yesterday's newspapers, assorted souvenirs.

'Gotta send an urgent postcard?'

'Toothpaste, some ibuprofen.'

'I got both of those in my room, if you wanna come up?'

Patrick shook his head.

'Thanks, but it's okay. I'm here now.'

Dan nodded.

'Yes you are . . .' He clapped Patrick on the back. 'Well then buddy, I guess I'll catch you later.'

'Sure, sleep well.'

'I always do.'

At one minute to six, Ada hurried into the hotel and across the lobby, the key to the souvenir shop in her hand. She nodded at Patrick and unlocked the door.

'I'm sorry to be late sir.'

'You're not late at all Ada, you're bang on time.'

He perused the postcards, spinning the carousel slowly while she went into the storeroom to change out of her coat and track-suit and into her grey uniform.

The beige fax machine took its time to warm up, but once it had and the green light started blinking, it wasn't long before it pulled in and spat out a sheet of paper with McCluskey's familiar scribbled capitals on it.

'INITIAL AND SEND BACK.'

Even her faxes came across as angry. He did as instructed and Ada stayed and watched. Patrick opened his new notebook and under-neath the Chinese characters that he'd painstakingly transcribed, scribbled the fax number that McCluskey had sent this message through from, just in case there was a problem with the Skype later. There was an awkward silence while he and Ada sat waiting for the second message. He turned and smiled at the young woman.

'Thanks again for your help. Er. . . you said you were on a business course I think? How's it going?'

'Good, really well . . .' She talked him through her most recent class on bookkeeping. She was planning to specialise in business and hospitality because that was where the jobs were – jobs and the possibility of travel. They heard the grinding sound of plastic cogs as McCluskey's second message made its way six thousand miles across land and under sea.

'HERE YOU GO – DON'T FUCK UP.'

She'd written the Skype address out and underlined it. Next to that was a note reminding him to shred the fax. She really didn't trust him at all. Patrick copied the Skype address down onto his pad, then tore the page out, folded it up and tucked it away in his wallet. He ripped the fax with its identifying phone number up into small pieces and stuffed them in his pocket. He would flush those down the loo when he got back to his room. He stuffed the notepad in his jacket pocket and was checking he hadn't forgotten anything when Ada cleared her throat.

'Is that all?'

'Er, yes.'

'I thought maybe you wanted to talk about something that is broken?'

'Sorry?'

'Perhaps you have a problem with your room, a broken thing?'

'No, the room's all fine.'

'Oh, well good . . .' She paused then gestured at his jacket. 'Then I am sorry I was being rude. Nosy.'

Patrick smiled.

'Nosy? What do you mean?' Ada pointed at his jacket pocket.

'In your book.'

'My notepad?'

'Yes . . . in the notepad, in Cantonese slang – you wrote that you require a repairman.'

30 The Influencers

THE CHERRYWOOD HOTEL, CUPERTINO, CALIFORNIA

Christy asked questions. Good questions, smart. Maybe because of that, maybe because he'd drunk two Jack Daniels and half a bottle of Chardonnay, Fred found that he had soon told her as much about the project he was currently working on as anyone. More.

'We've known for ages that we can sell people zit cream on a Friday afternoon because they're thinking about Friday night, we know they'll buy trainers and cycling gear on a Sunday morning, we know that if they're a member of the golf club or the gun club that they'll like this policy or that kind of politician . . . all that sort of thing goes without saying.' Christy was nodding. Fred was used to being listened to, but not quite like this, he was enjoying it. 'But we've got around five thousand different data points for almost every single American right now. Soon we'll have more. The more we have, the more we'll know.'

'And the more you'll be able to predict?'

Fred's hand went to the knot of his tie.

'Predict yes. But not just predict.'

'What then? Influence?'

He smiled.

'*Influence* is a good way of putting it. I've been talking about *tuning*. But *influencing* is better. Gentler.'

He paused and refilled her glass.

'You see the potential in what I'm talking about, don't you?'

'Yeah, absolutely.'

Fred took another sip of wine.

'And do any of these things that we're talking about . . . does any of it make you feel . . . *queasy*?'

'Queasy as in sick?'

'Yes. Someone I know said the sort of developments that I'm talking about . . . the future that I'm imagining . . . made her feel queasy.'

Christy shook her head.

'Not at all. We'll just know a whole lot more about what people want. We'll be able to offer it to them before they even know they want it. It'll be cool. It'll feel modern.'

'I think that's true . . . but there will come a point, a little further down the line, when people will start to worry about things like *free will*.'

Christy nodded.

'What kind of people?'

Fred shook his head. 'Mainly old people I bet. What's that quote about freedom and happiness, how, given the choice, most people would pick happiness? I can't remember who said it, I read it back in high school, but I remember thinking *"yeah, of course. Who doesn't want to be happy?"* She reminded him of Elizabeth, back at the beginning, when as well as the confidence that came from a good upbringing and real confidence in the rightness of her ideas, she had that invincible confidence of youth. She smiled at Fred. 'You shouldn't worry about that. Even the people who don't like it straight away, they'll get used to it. People are really good at getting used to stuff.'

PART THREE

They sicken of the calm, who knew the storm.

Dorothy Parker

PART THREE

31 Oaths

STOCKWELL ROAD, LONDON

To say that the microwaveable Indian *banquet for one* had been a disappointment was an understatement. The curry was bland, the rice starchy and the naan bread tasted like cardboard. Carver cleaned the debris from the dining room table and went to rinse it off in the kitchen sink. He had a dishwasher – a good one – but it rarely saw service. It wasn't worth it when most of the time you were talking about one plate, a knife and a fork. Back in the living room, he pushed the sash window open wide to try to get rid of the curry smell. It was raining stair rods outside, but as a result the air felt as fresh as the air on the Stockwell Road ever did. Carver billowed the curtains a bit and soon the smell was gone. At the bus stop on the other side of the road, a mum and her buggied toddler were taking cover from the rain, the mother chatting away on her phone, the toddler in the buggy whining and waving her little fat hands around. As William watched, the mother finished her call, bent down and handed the child her phone. The bubble-haired toddler gave her mother a brief questioning look, then turned her attention to the screen. Carver pulled the curtains shut and glanced at his watch. He'd marked all the latest essays that his students had handed in, he'd prepared tomorrow's lesson, he'd even laid out his bloody clothes for the next day. He thought about calling Donnie and asking whether he'd managed to dig up anything interesting on Public Square yet, but he quickly changed his mind. Donnie liked to do things his own way and in his own time; hassling him this soon after asking him to do the work would only piss him off. William went and switched the radio on instead – he could listen to the news bulletin while he finished the crossword.

Hong Kong was still leading the summary. The newsreader read a late-breaking statement from the Hong Kong government before cuing in the latest report from John Brandon. Carver tuned his ear and listened. It was bad – William was never slow to find fault with Brandon's delivery, but that wasn't what was wrong with this piece. It was poorly constructed, badly scripted and the whole thing sounded like it had been bolted together rather than professionally edited. William put his newspaper to one side. Maybe it wasn't Patrick who'd produced the piece? It didn't sound like his work – nothing like. He walked over to the radio and switched it off before the report had even finished. It was really none of his business who'd produced the package. If it had been a piece of work that he'd set his students to do, then William would have a stake, an interest. But it wasn't and, therefore, he didn't.

The radio he listened to when he was in the living room was part of an integrated music system that Carver had put together over the years and that lived inside a smoked glass cabinet in the corner. He switched the amp from *Tuner* to *Phono* and picked up a nearby pile of records. It didn't take him long to find what he was looking for: the Choir of King's College singing Faure's Requiem. He removed the heavy circle of black vinyl from its sleeve and hesitated, briefly undecided whether to go for side one or two.

'Pie Jesu.'

He blew a few spots of dust from side one, placed the record down gently on the turntable and lifted the stylus into place. Once done, he hurried back to his most comfortable armchair and plonked himself down. He liked to be sitting when that first booming note from the King's College organ reverberated around the living room. He closed his eyes and the music transported him – but not as far or as wholeheartedly as it usually did. If Patrick wasn't producing John Brandon, then what *was* he doing? The obvious answer was that he was doing whatever secret squirrel stuff it was that McCluskey had asked him to do. The King's College Choir were doing their collective best, but it wasn't enough. Carver opened his eyes. His gaze fell upon his trusty leather and canvas grab bag, stuffed next to the front door in the hall. He still hadn't got around to sticking it in a cupboard or up in the loft and staring at it now, he knew that he would not. The personalised oath that he'd promised himself he would observe – his pledge to *do no harm* – was laudable, but if you had something to offer and did not offer it? Wasn't that even worse than risking some future, accidental harm? The familiar, long first note of 'Pie Jesu' stopped Carver's thought process. Stopped everything. For the duration of the song he was aware of nothing apart from the treble's voice and Faure's genius.

. . .grant them rest, grant them everlasting rest.

If a person had the wherewithal to do something, yet opted to do nothing. Could that ever be the correct choice? Carver gazed up at the ceiling but the answer was not there.

32 No Hay Problema

Soledad was nervous about this meeting with the miners and her mother wasn't helping.

'Remind them who your father was . . . who your mother is.'

'I'm not sure that the people in Brochu have as large a place in their hearts for you and my father as you think they have.'

'They prefer *us* to *you* . . .' There was no arguing with this. The townspeople thought Soledad a strange young woman, aloof and arrogant. 'People think you believe yourself *too good* for Brochu.'

'They're right.' She tightened the belt on her jeans and zipped up her blue tracksuit top. 'I am too good for Brochu. And so are they, so is every poor bastard unlucky enough to have been born here and too foolish to leave.'

'You are right to be worried if this is how you intend to talk to the men at the mine.'

'I won't talk to them like this. I know what I am going to say. I'm going to tell them that it doesn't have to be like this, not any more.'

Jags had arranged for Soledad to meet with the miners'

representatives. He'd also sent her a summary of what Public Square hoped to do in Brochu. A *one-pager* he'd called it. She had tried to work some of this into the speech that she had written, but the language was odd and slippery to translate. Phrases that Soledad guessed must sound catchy and inspiring to an English ear – *win-win, driving change* – sounded at best *odd* and at worst just stupid once translated into Spanish. Her speech would stick to the simple facts of what Public Square planned to build for the town and then talk about Soledad's belief that if the whole community got together, then this could be the start of something big for Brochu. Her ambition stretched far beyond a nursery and a small museum; she imagined a model mining community, run by and for the miners and their families – running profitably, of course, but also safely and for the benefit of all. The summary that Jags sent through hadn't said *exactly* this, but it had talked a lot about *doing well while doing good*. That was another hard-to-translate phrase, but one which squared absolutely with everything that Soledad had in mind.

As well as sending the *one-pager*, Jags had arranged for four hundred and fifty dollars to be deposited into her bank account – an advance on her first month's salary. This money had allowed her mother to pay the priest what was owed for her father's funeral with a little left over. Father Victor was visiting that morning, to thank them for the money and no doubt to find out whether there might be some more where that came from. Soledad was keen to be gone before the priest arrived. Her mother looked her up and down.

'Are you really going to make your speech dressed like that?'

'I really am. I'm meeting these men outside the mine, they're in the middle of their working day. I don't need to look smart.'

Her mother sighed.

'At least, *please God*, brush your hair.' She put her hands together as though in prayer. 'Do it for me?' Soledad went to look for her mother's hairbrush. She heard Father Victor arrive while she was in the bedroom and decided to stay there. She listened to the priest's cursory thank you for the money her mother had paid him and then . . .

'Of course, as soon as our little church receives some piece of money, so I have to write a dozen more cheques . . . especially with the *ceremonia* happening so soon.'

'Of course Father, although I think you will agree that our family has always contributed more than most to the ceremony. In every sense.' Soledad heard her mother's vain little laugh and winced. The priest was undeterred.

'Of course, of course. But as the parable tells us – Mateo Thirteen Twelve I believe it is: "*Whoever Hath Shall Give More*". Soledad shook her head; this didn't sound quite right. 'And as I say, the collection box has been very light in recent months.'

'Yes well these are difficult times for—'

'Which reminds me, I have not seen you or your family at our Sunday mass for some time now.' Soledad silently cursed the priest and listened as her mother made her excuses. Her leg had been troubling her, the pain beyond agony. It made movement impossible. Father Victor responded by explaining how regular church visits, attending mass in particular, would ease the pain. Soledad decided to leave them lying to each other and go. It was time. She put the hairbrush down and hurried through the living room and out of the front door with the briefest and least respectful farewell she could manage.

She began walking and then changed her mind and decided to take her eldest brother's bike. If Augusto had a problem with that then he could take it up with their mother – Soledad was the breadwinner now. She cycled slowly down the street and up the hill that led out of town. This route to the mine took her out to the north of Brochu and up and around the dam. Soledad did not cycle regularly and the hill soon grew uncomfortably steep. It was hard going, even with the bike in its highest gear. Her legs began to ache and she could feel her hair starting to stick to her forehead with sweat in spite of the cool morning air. She didn't want to look too neat in front of the miners, but nor did she want to look like she had been pulled through a field by a horse. She got off and walked the bike up the steepest stretch of the road.

At the top, a small group of workmen in orange fluorescent tabards was working its way along a stretch of the dam wall, patching up leaks with buckets of sand and gravel. Soledad stopped.

'The wall is leaking worse than usual?'

The oldest of the workmen stubbed his cigarette out and hauled himself up. He was shaking his head and smiling.

'No more than usual.' By the look of him, this man was the foreman, self-appointed perhaps. Soledad wheeled her bike closer and studied the tiny hairline cracks in the dam; thin trickles of water dribbled from some and zigzagged down the wall, pooling on the floor. There were more cracks in the dam wall than when last she'd been up here. More than she'd ever seen. The foreman stood beside her. 'No need to worry your head girl.' He gave the side of the dam a firm kick with his steel capped boots. 'This wall is as solid as a rock. It's not going anywhere.' He proceeded to explain exactly why Soledad needn't worry. This dam was a *tailings* dam, formed from the sludge-like mining waste known as tailings. There were scores of them all across South America and they were one of the safest types of dam there was. 'The waste material – metal and mud and rock – it sticks together to make a wall you see . . .' he kicked again, '. . . and solidifies. Now and then there's the odd little leak, but we plug those. No problem.'

Soledad checked the time on her phone. She didn't have time to debate with this old man right now.

'Be sure to fix it well then. You guys don't live in Brochu. We do.' She pointed at one of the men. 'What's he doing?' The workman in question was attaching a small black plastic box to the base of the dam wall.

'That's one of the new water pressure monitors.' He grinned. 'More safeguards for you good people of Brochu. Courtesy of the company.'

'Does it work?'

The man fitting it turned and looked up at Soledad, grinning. 'Sure.'

Soledad climbed back onto the bike, wished the workmen a good day and left. She knew more about this dam than these men, she knew very well how a tailings dam worked. And what happened when it didn't. Her father had been obsessed by the dam, he dreamt about it when he slept and talked about it often when awake, especially when drunk. The only bedtime stories Soledad remembered her father ever telling her or her eldest brother, Augusto, were horror stories about the Brochu dam.

How the semi-solid waste that held the dam in place would suddenly *liquefy*, for no apparent reason and with no warning. The consequences of such a collapse were so horrific that most locals preferred not to think about it. Soledad had never had that luxury.

The crowd of men waiting to hear Soledad speak outside the mine was much larger than she'd expected. Perhaps the company had ordered them to be here? It seemed unlikely that so many would voluntarily give up their half hour lunch break to listen to her. The miners had placed a wooden pallet, reinforced with planks of wood, next to the mine entrance for her to stand on and gave her a pair of oversized white rubber boots and a battered yellow helmet to wear as the safety regulations required. The men stood and stared and waited for her to begin. Fearful of losing her nerve, and with it her words, Soledad had written some notes on a piece of paper and she held this in her shaking hand. Looking down she saw that she had at least *one ally* – a small stray dog with wiry hair and a blunt muzzle had taken a liking to her and was standing sentry alongside the wooden pallet as Soledad began to speak.

'I am not very old, but I remember when the water in our river was as clear as glass. It would shine in the sun . . . and the fish we caught there . . .' She let the men fill in the rest. The people of Brochu had been proud of their river in the past and particularly proud of the plump, perfect trout that swam and splashed around in it. 'Now it is different, our river is dirty, if you walk down there today you will see fish that have jumped onto the bank, leapt clean out of the water because there isn't enough oxygen in the river for them to breathe.' She paused and looked up from her piece of paper. The men were listening, standing as still as stone, their faces the colour of the copper they mined.

33 The Collection

There was a ballet school upstairs from the internet café in Central where Patrick went to Skype McCluskey. Patrick had noticed a sign for the place on the street outside and now he could hear the rapid tap of tiptoeing feet as the first class of the morning got underway. Staring out past the computer terminal that he'd rented for the next half hour, Patrick looked up at the building opposite and saw a fat man standing in the second-floor window, a pair of binoculars in his hand.

'Ah yes, that gentleman over there is a big fan of the ballet.' The café manager handed Patrick his change. 'Sometimes the police come and take his binoculars away or him away, but he will not stop.' Patrick took the money.

'Thanks, am I good to go then?'

'All good.'

Patrick got the piece of paper with McCluskey's new Skype address out from inside his wallet. He knew it was important not to mess this call up. He hadn't exactly covered himself in glory so far and he had to assume that an account of his general incompetence would reach William Carver sooner or later. This thought stung Patrick; it was time to start acting like he knew what he was doing. He plugged his headphones into the back of the machine and dialled the Skype address. The tinny theme tune had barely begun before it was replaced by the sound of a deep hacking cough.

"Scuse me, I'm a bit bunged up. So . . . do me a favour son and tell me you're sat in the middle of Hong Kong's busiest internet café.'

'I am. You can see for yourself if you like . . .' He moved his head out of the way of the pinhole-sized camera at the top of his screen.

'No thanks, no cameras.'

'How come?'

'I'm not too happy with my make-up. Sweet Jesus, son, did Billy Carver teach you nothing? We don't *need* the cameras so we're not using them. Cover yours up will you?'

'I'm switching it off.'

'Not good enough. Cover it up.'

'With what?'

'Whatever you've got, William generally uses whatever food he happens to be eating. Use what you like, just cover it.'

Patrick reached into his jeans pocket for his wallet. Tucked among his collection of old receipts was a book of second-class stamps. He peeled the Queen's familiar profile from its backing and stuck it over the camera's eye.

'Done.'

'Excellent.'

'So we're okay to talk openly now?'

'We're as okay as I can make us, given the circumstances . . .' She paused. '. . . that's assuming you've not got any dodgy-looking individuals hanging around earwigging where you are?'

Patrick leant back in his chair and glanced at his neighbours. A boy with a bowl cut hairdo two chairs down was machine-gunning zombies; on the other side and also two seats away, a teenage girl with pink hair was hurling whispered abuse at a surly-looking kid in a leather jacket. Outside the café window in front of him, the people rushed by in the rain and a blur of headlights and brake lights glistened in the early morning gloom. Everything was in motion and no one showed any interest in giving this nervous-looking westerner a first glance, never mind a second one. The only dodgy-looking individual was the large man up on the second floor in his string vest and pyjama bottoms, but his binoculars were trained firmly on the ballet class and nothing else.

'I think I'm good.'

'Belter. Let's try and keep this as short and sweet as possible. So what did you make of that little library of information I sent you yesterday?'

'It's complicated.'

'Aye, it is.'

'So many different things happening in so many different places.'

'Yep.' Patrick could sense that he was already trying McCluskey's patience.

'But I read through it a few times last night and it seems to me that all this stuff you've found and the material I've been collecting are two sides of the same coin.' There was silence at the other end of the line. 'Hello?'

'I'm here. All the material *you've* been collecting? What's that exactly? Do you mean the pieces I hear on the radio?'

'No, there's much more than that. Hours more. Some of it's the more technical stuff. A bit boring.' Patrick told McCluskey about the scores of interviews he'd done with individuals at the forefront of various protest movements across the Middle East, North Africa and now Hong Kong. Interviews dating back nearly three years now. He explained how he'd seen protest leaders in one country attempting to learn lessons from what worked and didn't work elsewhere. 'And obviously the regimes they're trying to remove, they do the same.'

'Right.'

'But I don't think that's quite what your collection . . . your investigation is saying. Is it?'

'What do *you* think it's saying son?'

'It suggests to me that the *pushback* in all these places . . . it isn't just *similar*. It's practically the *same*. It's almost like there's some kind of playbook.' There was a throaty laugh at the other end of the line. 'Am I making any kind of sense?'

'As much sense as there is to be made out of all this, you're making it son. What's more, you've helped persuade me that I'm not losing my mind. If the camera was on, I'd kiss ya. So count your lucky stars it isn't.'

Patrick looked again at the piece of paper with McCluskey's Skype on it and at the Chinese characters he'd transcribed above it.

'There's one more thing.'

'Go on.'

'That note you wrote, next to those chunks of untranslated Chinese text. You asked me to check if it was similar to the Arabic word, er, *maslih*?'

'Oh, aye, good old *maslih*. That was more a *note to self*, but go ahead. It means something like *reform* does it? Or *restoration*? I've seen it mentioned all over the shop, in Arabic, Turkish, Russian . . .'

'It's not as vague as that, at least not in those bits of Cantonese and Mandarin conversation you sent through. It's not vague at all, it's a straightforward request.'

'Fer what?'

'For the *repairman*.'

34 Red Flags

SAND HILL ROAD, CALIFORNIA

Fred left the keys for the Tesla at the hotel reception with an instruction that a member of Public Square staff would come and pick the car up first thing the following morning. He was driven home by one of the Cherrywood's drivers in a car almost identical to his own.

'The New Fallingwater House, sir, is that right?'

'Yes.'

Fred didn't want to talk, he'd talked enough for one evening. He wanted to get back home, do the work he needed to do on the computer and then rest. It was often this way; he'd be at a social engagement of one sort or another, either with Elizabeth or by himself and appearing to be having a good time. Until suddenly he wasn't. Just like tonight; halfway through the main course it became clear to Fred that Christy had said everything that she had to say. Everything that he found interesting anyway. He could feel his restless attention turning to other matters – more pressing matters – and there was no point pretending otherwise. She agreed to stay and finish eating, he had paid the bill and left.

She'd insisted on giving him a hug before he went, a long and close embrace. More would surely have followed if he'd chosen to stay, but he had to go.

Nevertheless, he would see her again. He'd offered to take a proper look at her company's prospectus and its projected growth figures. If he liked what he saw there, then maybe he'd invest in Cloud Chancer. Fred had offered this not because he thought Christy and her partner's new company was something special – the chances were it was just another over-hyped flash in the pan. The company might well be a waste of time, but *Christy Newmark* wasn't. She had absorbed and understood everything Fred had told her. She understood the work he was doing in a way that neither his clients, nor even Lizzie could understand. She understood it instinctively. So if a twenty-something-year-old kid could get it, then why couldn't the people he was working with? Working *for*, technically speaking. All that his current slate of clients were interested in was Fred's help to do the same things they'd always done: bugging and burgling. Rounding up the usual suspects, just using slightly more sophisticated techniques. Once they'd identified these suspects . . . again they did the only thing they knew how to do; stuck them on watch lists, chucked them in prison. He glanced out of the window at the glittering lights of the McMansions all along Sand Hill Road. Fred didn't need to know what else they did, he didn't want to. None of his clients could see the real potential that the technology had to offer. The prize was so much bigger. Fred's phone buzzed in his pocket and he took it out and glanced at the screen. It was his secretary.

'Yes?'

'Hello sir, the bee guy . . .'

'The *apiarist*?'

'Yeah . . .' she paused, '. . . the apiarist. So he's had a quick look at the hive already, he went straight over there, he says he thinks he knows what the problem is. He wants to check things over once more in daylight, then he'll write something up. He says whatever happens he'll get the problem sorted in the next couple of days – before Mrs Curepipe gets back.'

'Fine.'

The drive back to Fallingwater did not take long. Fred told the driver to drop him just outside the perimeter so he could walk the last few hundred yards for the exercise. The jagged arrangement of square-sided stone trays looked particularly dramatic at night, lit subtly and surrounded on all sides by thick dark trees. Fred was proud of the house; he enjoyed it even more when Elizabeth was travelling and he had the place to himself. It also meant that he didn't have to listen to her complain about the stink of chlorine wafting from the waterfall, which was particularly strong tonight. He let himself in, flicked on a couple of lights and walked directly to his office and the main computer. This machine was linked to the computer that sat on the desk at Public Square headquarters, the twin in fact, as any activity undertaken on one of the computers was visible on the other. Fred clicked on the black pad next to the keypad and the screen lit up. He checked *recent activity* to confirm that no one had touched either machine since he'd logged off at headquarters. No one had.

Fred checked the *red flags* first, although there weren't many to check. Over a dozen employees had accessed a variety of porn sites during the day on their laptops or phones, but that was standard. A few had been looking at political material, but again it was pretty harmless stuff. Half a dozen Public Square employees had spent more than an hour reading or sending messages that had been identified as non-work-related. All of these individuals would receive a warning. Reoffending was rare since most people at Public Square knew that a second warning usually resulted in dismissal.

Fred switched from the list of red-flagged employees to the Public Square home page and typed in Christy's name again. In the half hour since he'd seen her, she'd changed her profile picture to a photograph taken that evening. She was sitting at the table where they'd sat together. She must have asked the waiter to take the photo just after he'd left. There were no obvious clues as to where she was sitting and she made no mention of the Comma Club or of Fred in her latest posts. The last entry was only one line long:

'The most inspiring, exciting evening since ... Ever. @TheCherrywood'

Subtle, Fred liked this. He liked her. He typed in the password needed to increase his access rights and went again to her deleted posts. Christy had been busy, binning several dozen old posts in the last half hour. Most of them related to past relationships or included photos of her with a variety of square shouldered boys, sporty types, on romantic breaks in and around California. Fred dug deeper, back to the college and high school photographs that he'd seen earlier. He selected a few and put them somewhere safe. He unbuttoned his shirt collar and loosened his tie. It was late and he should sleep, just one last chore. He clicked on a non-descript looking icon in the centre of a screen full of similar icons. A map of the world appeared, stretching the entire length of the oversized monitor. He pinched his thumb and forefinger on the pad at the centre of his keyboard, focussing first on the several dots of light distributed across his own continent, then China, Myanmar, across to North Africa and the Arabian peninsula, Southern Europe. Finally to the UK – he zoomed in closer. And closer still. Central London, then a few miles west. Fred leant forward and studied the screen for a time before panning back, way back, until once more the entire world filled his screen. The sprinkle of silver dots that spanned the map looked like stars in the night sky – constellations, visible only to him.

35 Being Careful

McCluskey checked the time; this Skype call with Patrick had already taken longer than she'd intended. The longer they talked, the more likely that anyone scouring the lines looking for them might get lucky.

'I'm going tae go back to my command and control centre and try to work out what these *repairmen* of yours are all about. Where else in the world they pop up. If we can work out *who's* asking for them, then mebbe we can figure out why.'

'Sure, that makes sense . . .' He hesitated. '. . . what do you want me to do?'

'You've done well enough for now. Get on with the day job and I'll be in touch when I've got something, but listen. . .' She was silent for a moment. '. . . you need tae start being more careful.'

'I thought we were being careful?'

'Not careful enough. Where've you put this collection of yours? These interviews?'

'They're all on my laptop . . . but hard to find, I've buried them pretty deep.'

'The people we're dealing with like digging. Move them, put them somewhere else, somewhere safer, 'til we know what it is we're dealing with.'

'Okay.'

'You've not noticed anything particularly odd going on out there have you?'

'Odd? The whole place is in turmoil.'

'Sure, but anything *specific* to you? Emails that don't look quite right? Funny noises on the phone? No one following you?'

'Following me? Not here no, I had a bit of that in . . .' He stopped. His thoughts switched suddenly to Rebecca. '. . . I don't think anyone's been tailing me here in Hong Kong, but if it's weird stuff we're watching out for, then I need to tell you something else . . .'

He recounted every detail that he could remember of Rebecca's recent experience. Her original conversation with the woman outside her school and then the odd encounter at the National Portrait Gallery. Patrick had dismissed it as a coincidence or some strange mix-up and he'd managed to convince Rebecca of this too. Now he wasn't so sure. 'What do you think?'

'I think that given what we know already, it'd be wise to assume that there are *no such thing* as coincidences. At least for the foreseeable. What do you want to do about her? You want me to go and talk to her?'

Patrick gave it some thought.

'Thanks, but I think that might just upset her all over again. She doesn't know you.' He paused. 'She knows. . . out mutual friend though. She's always liked him. Do you think he might agree to go and talk to her, find out exactly what happened and figure out whether it's connected?'

'I'm pretty sure I can persuade him. Leave that one with me. We've been talking too long, take care you and well done son, you've redeemed yerself.'

A musical plop confirmed to Patrick that McCluskey was done with him and the line had been dropped. He gazed out of the window; the sky was lightening now and the traffic getting busy. Above his head, Patrick could hear the muffled tap and shuffle of ballet shoes continue. The fat man in the building opposite was no longer standing, but kneeling down on the floor. All he could see of him now was a balding head and a pair of binoculars.

McCluskey powered down her spare laptop and unplugged the new modem from the socket. She went downstairs to make a fresh pot of tea. The tortoiseshell cat was sitting in the middle of the kitchen floor, a haughty look on her face. McCluskey saw that the food bowl was empty.

'I'm terribly sorry, has madam been waiting long?' She filled the bowl with the stupidly expensive dry food that the cat seemed to prefer and put the kettle on. She stood at the kitchen sink, staring at the window, out past her reflection out into the pitch-black night, deep in thought. McCluskey hadn't had a full night's sleep in a long time, she wouldn't sleep much tonight either. The plan was to take her tea back up to the spare room and get to work. First she would gather every mention of *repair* and *repairmen* together on one wall; once she'd done that, she could . . . McCluskey frowned, her train of thought derailed by a movement in the garden, hard to discern but definitely something. She leant closer to the window and squinted past her reflection into the dark. The cat stopped crunching at its food and looked up, tilting its head in the direction of the door. 'Dinnae mind that, it's just the foxes. You stay in here 'til after they've gone. You're safe in here.' When she looked back up, a woman was staring straight at her. Standing just the other side of the glass, a few feet away. McCluskey screamed and grabbed for the counter to stop herself from falling. The cat arched itself into a horseshoe and then bolted, out through the cat flap and into the night. The white-faced stranger on the other side of the glass glanced at the cat, then back at McCluskey. No facial expression, no words, just a stare. A look that froze McCluskey's blood. The ghostlike form took half a step forward and for a second she feared the woman was going to walk right through the glass, through the wall and into the kitchen. Instead she stopped, just inches from the window, and stood there, still staring. She lifted a leather-gloved hand and pointed at McCluskey, then turned and walked slowly back down the garden, the darkness swallowing her before she had taken more than a dozen steps. McCluskey could hear her heart pounding in her ears. She needed to sit down but when she let go of her grip on the counter her legs would not turn or lift. She fell, collapsing in a strange slow motion, down onto the linoleum floor. The cat returned and sat down next to her, licking tentatively at her hand.

36 Secrets

RULES RESTAURANT, LONDON W1

Elizabeth pushed her food around the plate, creating the impression she'd eaten more than she actually had. She looked around the restaurant. Faces gawped back in her direction and she acknowledged this attention with a nod and a polite smile, directed at no one in particular. She could put up with some staring, she would rather do that than buy out the entire restaurant as was Fred's preferred option. Not only was it stupidly expensive to do this, it was also bad PR. Elizabeth's main objection, however, was that eating in an otherwise empty restaurant just felt odd. Her dad had drummed into her that when it came to restaurants, busier was better. *'I don't always hold with that wisdom of crowds stuff, Lizzie, but when it comes to the wisdom of people's bellies – I'll buy that every time.'* She changed the angle of her chair by a few degrees, moving her gaze away from the gawpers and towards her dinner companion.

'How's your food Jags?'

'It's good . . .' He waved his fork in the direction of their fellow diners. 'D'you want me to go and tell this lot to stare at the people they're eating with instead of you?' Elizabeth shook her head. 'You sure? I'll ask them very politely.'

She smiled. A real one this time.

'I'm actually not sure it's *me* they're looking at, I think it might be you.'

Jags smiled.

'Well, I did shave.'

'That'll be it.' She filled Jags' wine glass and then her own. 'How'd you find time to shave? I thought you'd been tearing around all day?'

'I was. Tearing around after you.'

'Not all the time. My team said you kept disappearing . . . running some errands, you told them.'

Jags sucked at his teeth. God, how he hated her little team of sycophants and squealers.

'I had to do one or two other things.'

'Like what?'

'Just company stuff.'

'It's my company. Remember?'

'I remember.' Jags was starting to worry that the unexpected dinner invitation was, in fact, an ambush. 'Is this gonna turn into some kinda inquisition Elizabeth?' She looked at him.

'No, not at all . . .' She leant across the table. 'I just wanted to give you that new raincoat I'd promised.' She gestured at the new purchase, which was sitting wrapped in tissue paper in a smart Savile Row bag next to Jags' chair. 'And I wanted to buy you a fancy meal. Go ahead and eat.' Jags ate and Elizabeth watched. She had never known anyone for whom eating was so obviously a straightforward refuelling job. Jags ate quickly and without care or comment. He didn't seem to have the vocabulary to describe what he was eating; she suspected that he didn't have the taste buds to fully appreciate it. 'How's that pork?'

'It's good.'

'It's glazed with honey and single malt whisky.'

'Is that right?' Jags could feel her studying him. 'You want some?' He chiselled off some meat and crackling and handed her the fork.

'Thank you.'

She took a tiny bite; it was – as he'd said – *good*. She passed the fork back. 'You know this meal will probably cost the best part of six hundred bucks?'

Jags lifted an eyebrow.

'Are you short? How about we do a runner? I'll make a fuss, you hit the door, I'll follow. I bet you're pretty fast in bare feet, you just need to push those heels off.'

'I've never run from a restaurant.'

'Never? You should, it's good for the digestion. I bet your old man would've approved.'

Elizabeth smiled.

'He probably would.' She paused. 'I wanted to ask you about Chile . . . did you make some progress with this new plan of mine?'

Jags looked at her.

'I think I might've found the right girl to front up what it is you want Public Square to do.'

Elizabeth frowned.

'Girl?'

'Beg your pardon . . . woman. Young woman. She and her mom are both on board and they fit the bill – pillars of the community, smart, all that stuff.'

'Sounds good. And you think they get how ambitious we want to be about all this? I want it to be a model for how we can do things. . . going forward.'

'Yeah, I reckon so. I think you'll like 'em, 'specially Soledad.'

'Soledad? Is that the daughter?' Jags nodded. 'That's a beautiful name.'

He realised now just what the blue colour of Elizabeth's eyes reminded him of. It was the perfect shade of faded denim. Like your best pair, those few months when they're just right, before they fade right out, beyond blue. Jags wanted to go write this down. He didn't want the thought to slip his mind, but nor did he want to leave the table. He repeated the thought to himself several times while half listening to Elizabeth describe her day. She'd said something about the meeting she'd had with MPs at the Palace of Westminster. Jags picked up the thread.

'Oh yeah, I meant to ask how things went with the politicians?'

'Things went fine, I bamboozled them with technical terms like *mobile phone app* and *advertising model* . . . spent most of the meeting explaining how the internet works.'

'You promise a couple of dozen jobs and a million bucks for that Silicon Roundabout of theirs and they're doing cartwheels, was that it?'

'It was a little trickier than that . . .' She stared at Jags over the rim of her wine glass. '. . . if you'd been there you'd have seen. I was pretty impressive.'

'I don't need to have been there to know that you were impressive.' He wiped the plate clean with a scrap of brown bread and munched it down. Elizabeth shook her head.

'You know that taking you out for a meal feels a lot like taking a car to the gas station for a fill-up.'

'Is that right?'

'I'm not sure how rewarding an experience it is.'

'For you? Or for the car?'

She laughed.

'Let's start with the car . . .'

'Well, I think maybe the older cars 'preciate it. I used to have a Buick that would gurgle like a baby when you put gas in her. She ran way better on a full tank. I'd always buy her the good stuff mind, top notch gas and oil.'

'That's touching.'

'I knew you'd understand . . .' There was a silence. 'I'm sorry I didn't get to see you *wow* those political folk over at Westminster. Those errands, all that other stuff I need to do, it's nothing secret, it's just . . .' Jags took a moment to find the right word, a word that was neither the whole truth nor an absolute lie '. . . it's just *mundane*. You carry a big old load on your shoulders Lizzie. Too much. So when there's some stuff I can do, I do it.'

'At Fred's instruction?'

Jags nodded grudgingly.

'A fair 'mount of the time, yeah.'

'Okay. But I wanted to tell you that if there's ever anything that Fred asks you to do that you're *not* okay with, you can bring that to me. You know that, don't you?'

'I do now.'

'Good, good . . .' She paused. '. . .so nothing he's got you involved in right now makes you . . . uncomfortable?'

Jags shook his head.

'No.'

And this was true. None of the dreadful things he'd done left him feeling uncomfortable. No matter how wrong, illegal, unjust . . . pick an adjective. Pick an atrocity. Jags didn't feel uncomfortable with any of it. He didn't feel *anything* in fact. He glanced up and saw Elizabeth smiling at him. Hardly anything.

'Good, I'm glad to hear that. I was . . . concerned.'

'Don't be.'

'I won't. But remember, you can talk to me. Any time.'

Jags looked around for a change of subject.

'You've never run from a restaurant huh? Maybe tonight's the night.'

'We should finish the wine first.'

'It's good.'

'It's Château Lafite.'

'Cool, cheers . . .' He lifted his glass and clinked it against hers. 'Here's to your good day.'

'Pretty good . . . the only downside is that Public Square is probably going to have to pay a shade more tax . . . I promised to look at it.'

'Why?'

'I got interrogated about it by this old radio guy after my speech at the BBC. It was clever, doing it in front of a roomful of journalists.' She paused. 'Paying a shade more tax over here is no bad thing. It'll be good PR – and it's the right thing to do too, I reckon we've been getting away with nought point three per cent of profit for long enough.'

Jags shrugged.

'Fred's not gonna like it much.'

Elizabeth put her unfinished wine back down.

'Now and again, I have to do things that Fred won't like.' She smiled. 'If only to stay sane.'

She stared at Jags' empty plate. 'It's been a long day Jags. I think I might head back to the hotel.'

He nodded. 'Sure, good idea.'

She reached down for the white silk clutch bag that was propped against her chair leg. She tipped the contents onto the table. Inside was her mobile phone, a credit card, a red lipstick and a small pale pink envelope with the crest of her hotel embossed on the front. She was reaching for the envelope when her phone began to buzz. The blue screen lit up and the caller's name appeared then quickly disappeared as Elizabeth pressed reject.

'Poor Fred. His ears must have been burning.' She smiled at Jags. 'I'll call him back later.' She put the mobile back in her purse then slowly removed one of two key cards from inside the envelope. Elizabeth palmed the card across the table before pushing it underneath Jags' crumpled napkin with one painted fingernail.

'So . . . I think I'll take the car. If that's okay with you?'

'Like you said before . . . it's your company. Your car.'

'Right.' She stood. 'You stay and have a coffee, dessert or something.'

'Okay.'

She paused.

'But maybe I'll see you later?'

'There's no maybe about it.'

Jags ordered a double espresso and drank it then called for the bill, only to be told that it had been taken care of. The maître d' informed him that Elizabeth had paid not just for their dinner, but also for the dinners of everyone else still eating in the restaurant.

'She is a remarkable woman, Mrs Curepipe . . .'

Jags nodded. Good for public relations he guessed, although looking around it seemed blindingly obvious that no one eating in this restaurant needed their meals buying for them.

Out on the street it was raining that particular London rain that soaks you to the skin without you really noticing. He had his new coat in its smart bag, but he decided to leave it there and wait and smoke a cigarette beneath the restaurant canopy instead. He lit a Marlboro, got the notepad and pencil from inside his coat jacket and wrote.

A wet London wind
Pushes down a Soho street
Blue eyes wait for me

He read it through a couple of times before tucking the notebook away with a satisfied grunt. It was unusual for him to be happy with his first try, no crossings out or corrections. Maybe he'd read it to her? Through the restaurant window he saw the waiter clearing their table. The grey-haired man stacked the plates carefully and wrapped the cutlery up in a dirty napkin before placing that bundle on top, then he stopped. He picked up Elizabeth's glass and, after checking back over his shoulder, drank the inch of red wine she'd left undrunk in her glass. He held the wine in his mouth a moment and closed his eyes. Jags looked away, pulled up the collar on his old coat and stepped out into the rain. The only thing that was bothering him was the phone call. The caller's name had appeared so fleetingly, for a tiny fraction of a second – but Jags had seen it anyway. It wasn't Fred who'd called Elizabeth. The name on the screen was *Eldridge*. Jags thrust his hands in his pockets and walked faster; he didn't want to wonder what that call meant right now. *'Blue eyes wait for me.'*

Maybe it meant nothing.

37 A Refresher Course

THE COLLEGE OF JOURNALISM, ELEPHANT & CASTLE, LONDON

Carver put the red metal fire bucket back in the corner and checked the room. The lesson had gone fine – better than fine in fact, despite his mind being elsewhere. Naz had been helpful. Carver's plan was to give the class a quick introduction to digital editing and then let them practise, but she was already proficient enough that most of the students ended up standing around her desk and watching her do it. She was slow compared to Carver, but better than him at explaining things in a language they understood.

He was in the corridor stooping down and struggling to lock the classroom door, when the sudden sound of someone clearing their throat startled him. He dropped both the keys and his brief-case.

'What the . . .?'

He turned to see McCluskey; she was wearing a canary yellow mac and a flowery headscarf. She looked him up and down.

'Well, blow me if it isnae *Mr Chips*. I've said it before and I'll say it again, that cord jacket of yours really is a fright.'

'You almost gave me a bloody heart attack McCluskey. What do you want?'

'I've come fae a journalism refresher.'

'Is that right? Well then you need to go and sign up at reception.'

'Not a journalism refresher for *me*. A journalism refresher for *you*.'

'Very funny.'

'Glad you think so. Have you time for a wee cup of tea?'

'Have I got a choice?'

'Nope.'

They took the lift down to the canteen. Lunch was just finished and a solitary cleaner was pushing a mop around and packing up the tables. He agreed to leave one of the pull-down tables with button seats out for them to sit at and McCluskey went to get a cup of tea and a hot chocolate from the drinks dispenser. She put the tea down in front of William and took the seat opposite.

'Feck, these seats are uncomfortable. Which buttock are you s'posed to sit on?'

'I usually go for the right-hand one.'

'Got it.'

She was about to say her piece when she noticed a young Asian kid in jeans and a green Adidas tracksuit top loitering at the canteen entrance, staring at her and Carver.

'Is that one of yours?'

William turned.

'Christ on a bike. Yeah, that's Naz.'

He waved her over.

'Hello Mr Carver . . .' She glanced at McCluskey, a sheepish smile on her face. 'I'm terribly sorry to interrupt.' Carver shook his head.

'Don't worry about it. Just be quick. What do you want?'

Naz explained what she wanted. In short, an extension to an essay deadline.

'Why do you need more time?'

'Well, I've been offered a couple of extra shifts at the local paper. Some junior sub-editing. It's holiday cover but I thought . . .'

'Which paper?'

'The *Hounslow Chronicle*.'

'You didn't tell me you did shifts at a local paper.'

'Well . . . you didn't ask.'

'I guess not. Sure, you can have an extension, will one week do it?'

'Awesome.'

'Awesome?'

'Well, yeah.'

'Have you seen the Sistine Chapel, Naz?'

'Er, no.'

'The Grand Canyon?' She shook her head. 'How about St Paul's Cathedral?'

She nodded vigorously.

'I went there on a school trip.'

'Right . . . so St Paul's Cathedral is awesome, like the Vatican, like the Grand Canyon. Me giving you an extra week to finish your essay isn't awesome.'

'Okay. But it means a lot to me. That's what I meant to say.'

'Fine. Now bugger off.'

McCluskey waited until Naz was out of earshot before talking.

'She seems like a smart one.'

'She's the best of the bunch.'

'You're enjoying the teaching then are ye?'

'Most of the time.'

'I'm glad fer ye.' She paused. 'Don't miss your old life at all then?'

'I wouldn't say that. I miss it sometimes.'

'Of course you do.' She glanced around the empty canteen; there was a whiff of bleach in the air. 'What you're doing here Billy is

222

'. . . you're grazing and *you're* not the grazing sort.' Carver shrugged. 'You're the type of horse that's meant to die in harness.'

William laughed.

'If that's your idea of a motivational speech, McCluskey, then it needs work.'

'Perhaps I'm not putting it quite right, but the point is y*ou* need to be working.'

'Teaching is working.'

'You're teaching part time. What do you do the rest of the time?'

'Plan classes. Attend pointless BBC management meetings. Shout at the radio. That kind of thing.'

'You need to be doing the work that you're good at . . .' She hesitated, '. . . and other people need for you to be doing that work as well. You want an example of why you need to pull yer finger out?' She didn't wait for a response. 'I was *assaulted* last night.'

'What?'

Carver coughed; a mouthful of tea had gone down the wrong way. 'Assaulted? Christ almighty Jemima, why didn't you say so at the beginning? I'm so sorry. Assaulted by who?'

'I don't know for sure.' She paused. 'And it wasn't exactly *assaulted* . . . but some strange woman showed up in the garden last night, trying to scare the shite out of me.'

Carver relaxed.

'Good luck to her with that.'

'Shut up. I'm assuming you know what this means?'

'No, but I'm absolutely certain you're going to tell me.'

'It means we're on the right track.'

'By "*we*", you mean you and Patrick?'

'For now, aye. Patrick is the reason I'm here. He needs a favour.'

'A favour? From me?'

'Of course from you, you eejit. Who else?'

38 A New Tradition

BROCHU, CHILE, SOUTH AMERICA

Soledad told the men about Public Square's plans for a nursery, a community centre and a museum. She explained that the missing petroglyphs – the ten-thousand-year-old rock paintings removed during the building of the dam – would be returned and properly displayed.

'But this isn't all that we need to get back, is it? Our ancestral paintings of llamas and pumas and lizards are one thing. Our self-respect and dignity is the other. First and foremost . . . our safety.' Soledad had tucked the notes away in her jeans pocket now, she was speaking from the heart and every person there was listening. One of the miners was even taking photos or filming her with his phone.

She spoke about the dam, about the leaks in the wall that everyone knew about, but preferred not to dwell on, she talked about the early warning system that did not work. The siren that was supposed to alert the entire district was barely loud enough that the houses nearest to the dam wall could hear it. At the last test, the sirens had failed completely, and the mine managers had sounded the alarm using their car horns. She saw some in her audience shuffling their feet, arms being crossed. 'The first step to changing something is to talk about it honestly. No matter how uncomfortable that might make us feel.' Heads nodded. Looking down to the side she saw that her friend, the stray mutt, had fallen asleep in the sun, his flank gently rising and falling. Soledad smiled. 'I have bored even this poor dog to sleep.' There was laughter. 'I will finish, I promise, but please remember . . . the company tell us that they want to do something new here in Brochu. We need to help them be ambitious, we have to show them how revolutionary this *new thing* could be.' Nods and even a smattering of applause. She acknowledged this and applauded the miners in return. Stepping down from the platform, she turned to the knot of miners closest to her. 'Now, please, I would like to see inside the mine.' The applause stopped and faces turned away from her and in the direction of a pouchy-eyed man standing on the edge of the crowd. He shook his head.

'No.'

'If I am going to properly represent you, as I would like to, then I need to see the work that you do. I need to understand that work.'

'It's not possible.'

Soledad had expected this. No women were allowed inside the mine, a superstition rooted in these miners' belief in *Pachamama* or the earth mother who resided deep inside the mine and was prone to fits of jealousy. If a woman on her period or, God forbid, a pregnant woman entered the mine then Pachamama, in a fit of fury, would hide the ore, bury the seam beneath tons of useless rock. The devilish *El Tio*, too, was believed to have strong opinions about allowing women underground. Soledad saw several of the miners casting a wary look in the direction of their resident icon. The cartoonish representation of *El Tio* that stood outside the entrance to this mine was particularly macabre. Made from clay and the size of a toddler or small child, this devil sat with a black-toothed grin on his face, his arms outstretched, welcoming the miners into his domain. A cigarette was jammed between every finger, a half-smoked cigar in his mouth. Sticking out from in between his legs, his most noteworthy feature – a foot-long, bright red penis. The year that the tailings dam officially opened, the Curepipe company had invited a government minister to attend the ceremony and Santiago had sent the mining minister, a woman. The minister was only allowed to set foot inside the mine after agreeing to plant a kiss on *El Tio's* member.

Soledad knew that to back down now would be to lose all of the ground she had managed to win with her speech.

'I do not see why it wouldn't be possible for a woman to walk into this mine. Let's see . . .'

The pouchy-eyed man moved towards her, yelling now.

'It's the tradition.'

'Get a new tradition.'

Soledad strode towards the mine, the dog following.

'Girl, girl stop! At the very least you must do what the politician did. Before you cross the threshold you must kiss *El Tio's* . . .' Soledad turned suddenly and stared the man down.

'No!' She glared at him. 'Things need to be different, you all know that. We need a lot of things to change – so here's the first thing.' She shot *El Tio* a look. 'Let the devil suck his own dick.'

Some of the men laughed, albeit nervously. They were scared, but also impressed. This scrawny young girl had no fear. Not of man, nor the devil. She was strange but she was also brave and smart and maybe that was what they needed now. They'd been outwitted and outmanoeuvred all their lives. Why not let her see what she could do?

39 Short Legs

From a distance the Lennon Wall looked like some sort of strange animal, its pelt rustling in the light breeze. Only as you drew closer could you see that the animal's skin was made up of thousands – perhaps it was now hundreds of thousands – of hand-written notes, messages of support and solace. Patrick found a space among the scores of people crowded around the wall and read:

> Thousands of candles can be lighted from a single candle,
> and the life of the candle will not be shortened.

The note was signed *Chris from Canada*, although Patrick was pretty sure that Buddha had come up with this idea some time before Chris had. There were words of wisdom from Shakespeare, Maya Angelou, Gandhi and many others . . . Patrick had remembered to bring his recording equipment this time and he taped people reading the quotes and their various reactions. There were rumours that the police were planning to come en masse and rip the Lennon Wall down before long and if that was the case then this audio would be useful. But that wasn't the main reason for Patrick's visit. He was here to see Eric. McCluskey had told him to get on with the day job and let her check out exactly where else in the world these so-called *repairmen* cropped up and who was asking for them. It made sense for her to do that *big-picture* stuff, it was her investigation. But it also made sense for Patrick to do some digging at his end too. He was at the coal face after all.

Eric Fung was sitting at the centre of a group of fellow *Scholastic* supporters, halfway up the concrete steps that led to the Hong Kong Government Complex. Patrick worked his way through the crowd until he was standing at the edge of the group. He felt somewhat apprehensive; their last encounter had ended badly, with Eric accusing Patrick of having chosen the wrong side in Hong Kong's increasingly fractious political battle. Judging by the hostile looks on the faces of Eric's fellow students, he had been categorised as a Hong Kong Government lackey or worse.

'Hello there Eric.'

'Hello Mr BBC.'

The group eyed him suspiciously.

'I was hoping we might talk.'

'About what?'

'I had some more questions about how the authorities here are responding to the protests . . .' He held up his kitbag, inside which, along with his recording equipment, were the faxes McCluskey had sent him. '. . . also, I had some documents I hoped you might take a look at.'

'Information that will be useful to us?'

'That wouldn't be the purpose of me showing them to you Eric . . .' He paused. '. . . I can't do that. But if you read them and for some reason find them helpful, then I don't have a problem with that.'

Eric glanced at Patrick's bag.

'And you think that is possible?'

'It's worth a punt, isn't it? What have you got to lose?' Patrick stared at the young student. His face was pale, almost grey and behind the thick, black-rimmed spectacles, his eyes were red and puffy. He looked knackered. 'How about we go and get something to eat? My treat. Noodles or some milk tea. You look like you could use a break.'

They sat at a wooden fold-out table next to one of the many food stalls that had set up shop near to the Lennon Wall and ate noodles in hot oil and sesame sauce. As he ate, some of the colour returned to Eric's face, but he was still strangely quiet and considerably less cocksure than usual.

'Are you all right Eric?'

'I am tired, I haven't had much sleep this week.'

'Where do you sleep. I mean where are you living?'

The young Hongkonger glared at Patrick.

'Why do you want to know?'

'I'm not asking for your address Eric, I'm just interested in how you . . . keep going, avoid arrest, stuff like that.'

'I move around. I stay with comrades in different parts of the city. Every night a different place.' He attempted a smile. 'Sofa-surfing, people call it.'

Patrick shook his head.

'Sofa-surfing is meant to be fun. What you are doing doesn't sound much like fun.'

'It is necessary. I do not mind. I am not the important thing, it isn't me that I'm worried about.'

'Okay, I've heard rumours that the Hong Kong police are about to try and take the Lennon Wall down. Is that it?'

Eric shrugged.

'If they try, they try, we are ready for that. My worry is a bigger worry than just the Wall.'

'Tell me.'

'If you watch the international news right now, or read the papers, you might think that our protests are succeeding.'

'Well, the numbers are growing . . .'

'Yes, but so are the number of reversals. The number of protestors under arrest . . .' He met Patrick's eye. '. . . or having accidents of one sort or another.'

'Accidents?'

Eric nodded. He lifted his bowl and slurped down the last of his food.

'Did you hear about Sammy Kwok?'

Patrick racked his brains; the name rang a bell.

'Sammy . . . was he the kid who had the asthma attack? An allergic reaction to the pepper spray. Er . . . he died I think.' Patrick paused. 'I'm sorry, I know he was part of the protests, was he a friend of yours?'

'Not a friend. He was a fellow student, a comrade. But Sammy wasn't allergic to pepper spray, he didn't have asthma. The only part of what you just told me that's true is that Sammy Kwok is dead.'

'Right, so why do . . .'

'Why do *you* and most other people think it was an accident?'

'Yes.'

'Because the truth is, he was murdered and whoever murdered him is good at lying.' He balanced his chopsticks on top of the empty bowl. 'Better at lying than the rest of us are at telling the truth. My grandmother used to tell me that lies only had very *short legs* and so they can't travel far . . .' Eric looked across at Patrick. '. . . this is not true any more.'

He told Patrick about Sammy; he knew far more about him now than he had when he'd asked him to run what had seemed like a simple errand. 'If you search his name now, you will read horrible things . . . not just inaccurate information about allergies and asthma. Malicious things. People claiming that he was spying for the Americans, spying for the Chinese, that he was a common thief, even a prostitute. I have been to visit Sammy's mother. She told me that the people who killed him killed him not just once. With the lies they tell about him, they murder him again and again. Sammy was her eldest, his brothers and sisters cannot persuade her to eat. She is slowly starving herself to death.'

'I'm sorry Eric. I can look into this? I'd be happy to.'

'Thank you.' He took a sip of his milk tea, making eye contact with Patrick over the top of the polystyrene cup. 'I sent Sammy to run the errand that got him killed. It was my fault.'

'What? No. The only person to blame for this is . . .'

'I told no one else about it. Not about Sammy or the job I needed him to do. No one. Do you see?'

'I see.'

'I knew that the authorities would try and infiltrate our organisation, I knew that there would be spies and that they would hack into the phones and computers. But now I'm beginning to think that they are somehow . . .' Eric hesitated. '. . . inside our heads.'

40 Small Fires

Jags woke early, just after dawn. He disentangled himself from the sheets and rolled out of the side of the four-poster bed with Elizabeth still sleeping. He knew from the previous and only other time that such an invitation had been extended that this was how she preferred it. He used the emergency stairs and went out through the back of the hotel using the fire door. The only camera he saw was situated above the holding bay. He avoided that by jumping down next to a laundry lorry and shuffling around the side before marching swiftly out onto the empty street. He kept his collar up and his head down during the twenty-minute walk back to his own hotel and he waited until he was sitting on the bed in his room before putting the SIM card back in his mobile phone and switching it on. There were several messages but none that demanded an immediate response so he decided to take a bath. He ran the hot tap only right up until the flow started to cool and then added just enough cold water that he could bear to lower his naked frame in through the thick layer of bubbles. He kept the lighting down low and before long he was asleep again and dreaming of what he'd hoped to dream of. The phone call jerked him back to an unwelcome state of consciousness; the number was unknown, which most of the time meant it was Fred.

'Yeah?'

'It's me.'

'Yep.'

'You've been offline for quite a while.'

'I've been sleeping,'

'With your phone off?'

'Yep.'

'Too much sleep can kill you, did you know that? Just the same as too little.'

'Is that right? What d'you want Fred?' Using a real name on an unsecured line was absolutely against protocol and completely deliberate. He hoped it might encourage Fred to keep the call short and then fuck off so he could get back to his daydream.

'I've been sent something from a friend in South America. A video.'

'Okay.'

'Your job is to make problems go away, not invite them in through the front door.'

Jags sighed.

'Most likely it's nothing, she was giving a speech and she just got a little over-excited.'

'Well then you better go unexcite her. Put her straight. We need her back on script . . .' He stopped. '. . . before anybody suggestible flies down there.'

'I understand.'

'Good. There are a couple more London-related matters I need you to sort out, I've FedExed the details.'

'Fine.'

'The envelope's at the hotel reception. *Your hotel.*'

'I'll go down and get it.'

'Okay. You're sure you're up to this are you? I could always send someone else, one of the new guys, to help you out.'

'I don't need any help.' Jags hung up. He skimmed the phone in the direction of a towel that he'd left lying on the bathroom floor, but it overshot and ricocheted off the skirting board. He heard the plastic case crack. 'Fuck. And fuck you Fred.' The water had begun to cool and the dream he'd been enjoying had slipped beyond his reach. He pushed himself angrily out of the bath, sending a wave of suds out over the edge and onto the floor. He would ask reception to bring the envelope up and deal with Fred's latest to-do list. After that he would book himself on the next direct flight from London to Santiago. He thought about calling Elizabeth, or texting her to tell her what was going on. To thank her for the meal. For saying that he could talk to her if he needed to. To thank her for everything. He quickly dismissed the idea as too risky. Not just risky in fact, positively reckless. He went to his jacket and found his notebook. He would write to her instead and have a bellhop at reception run it over. He checked the idea for flaws but found none; he started writing and for once the words came easily.

Fred sat behind his desk and stared at the computer screen. Elizabeth had sent him a couple of emails, asking that he call her on a secure line. He knew what she wanted to talk about, he'd already done the *little research job* that she'd requested, albeit against his better judgement. He'd let her wait a little longer before he called her.

His thin fingers danced across the keyboard and the map of the world filled with silver lights appeared before him. In certain locations there were clumps of brighter light – three or four pin pricks gathered close together, working together. And soon there would be more. Fred leant back in his seat and stared.

41 The Play

THE LENNON WALL, CENTRAL GOVERNMENT COMPLEX,
HONG KONG

Patrick listened patiently to Eric's somewhat paranoid-sounding account of the last few days.

'We take every precaution, we use the latest encryption, we change phones all the time or pass messages by hand, but still they have some way of working out what it is we'll do next, where we'll be.'

'The police are always going to guess right some of the time.'

'It's not some of the time these last several days, it's all of the time. And I am no longer sure that this *is* the police.'

'Who then?'

'I do not know.'

Patrick reached into his canvas and leather kitbag and found the faxes that McCluskey had sent through. He'd left the sheets that he wanted Eric to look at and try to make sense of on top.

'Have a read of these for me will you?'

Eric cleaned his spectacles on the tail of his T-shirt and started to read. It took a good while for him to work his way through the blocks of untranslated Chinese text.

'What is this?'

'What does it read like to you?'

'It reads like it is a play. . .' He pointed at the pages. '. . . a very odd play.'

Patrick nodded.

'You're not far wrong. It's a transcription of a conversation, something that a colleague of mine in England sent me.'

Eric nodded.

'It is incomplete.'

'Yes. I think this is the only section of the conversation she managed to hear.'

'To hear? I see.'

'So what do you think?'

'I think she overheard an extremely boring conversation.'

Patrick smiled.

'Right, but what is it about?'

Eric tried to summarise. The two people were talking about an exchange of information of some sort.

'One person is telling the other that no piece of information should be considered insignificant. They're asking for *every item of information* from *every source* available. They say that even the smallest dot or scrap of information is significant when placed alongside another. That is why they need everything.' Eric pushed his glasses back up his nose. 'Maybe they are talking about a scientific study of some sort?'

'Maybe.'

'Then at the end it gets simpler. The person who has been doing most of the listening just asks the other for an update, about the *repairmen?* He or she wants to know where they are? It reads like a request.'

Patrick nodded.

'Yes, we'd figured that part out already. Nothing else?'

Eric shook his head.

'As I said. It is incomplete. If you got hold of the rest then I could probably tell you more.'

'Yes. My colleague back in England, she's working on it.'

42 Promises

William was sitting on the park bench outside Rebecca and Patrick's flat on Highbury Fields. He'd laid an old newspaper down on the bench; the air felt more crisp than cold and he had his anorak on anyway so he was fine. He checked the time. Rebecca taught down in south London somewhere and it would take her a while to get back, even if she got to leave when school finished and he knew that was rarely the case with teachers. He had a book to read plus a few notes about Public Square's accounts that Donnie had messaged him, although he hated reading anything like that on his phone. He'd wait until he got home. But he was happy to wait, more than happy in fact. He guessed that every person had one place where the memories were strongest. Either you'd spent so long somewhere that there was plenty to remember. Or the handful of things that happened there were so significant. A single event in some cases – a choice made or a defining event. This patch of London was his place. The long straight line of plane trees shone in the early evening light. Autumn had taken a toll, the footpath was mulchy with fallen leaves, but there were still enough clinging to the dark branches to make the scene spectacular. At least to Carver's eye. He stared and sighed.

'Bollocks to New England in the fall.'

When he'd first started out as a cub reporter on a local newspaper, this had been his patch. He'd bored Patrick stupid with stories about Highbury's colourful past – before the estate agents moved in and pushed the proper good old-fashioned gangsters out. Carver wondered whether Patrick had told Rebecca any of these stories. If not then maybe she'd appreciate a tale or two? He enjoyed telling them. He was wondering which of the various horror stories he'd reported on might be most appropriate to tell Rebecca when a neckless young man in a blue quilted jacket, grey tracksuit bottoms and trainers strode up, an apologetic look on his face.

'Hey there boss, sorry to bother you. I don't suppose you've seen a dog wandering around near here have you? Looking a bit lost?'

'No 'fraid not.'

'Ah, no problem.' The man glanced across the road in the direction of the houses. 'Perhaps he's headed back home.'

'Perhaps. What type of dog?'

'What? Oh, he's a cross. A mutt really. Medium-sized, brown.'

'Okay, I'll keep an eye out.'

'Thanks, appreciate it.'

Carver nodded and studied the man. 'You lost the leash too?'

'What?'

'You don't have a dog *or* a dog lead.'

'Right . . . he ran off wearing it. Slipped out of my hand . . .'

Carver nodded.

'That explains it.'

The man tried to smile, but it wouldn't stick. He moved away, up the footpath towards the clock tower at the top of the Fields.

As soon as he was out of sight, Carver reached into his briefcase for his notepad and scribbled down a brief description of the man and beneath that, a sketch. It wasn't bad. He was wondering about the possible significance of this encounter when, glancing up, he saw Rebecca outside the door to her house She was digging around inside her satchel for the door keys. He shouted her name and she turned to see where the call had come from. Seeing Carver, she smiled, before a sudden look of panic crossed her face.

'Is he all right?'

Carver stood.

'What? Yeah, he's fine. Absolutely fine.' He put his notepad back in his briefcase, clicked it shut and crossed the road to her side. 'I was in the area, thought I'd come say hi . . .' He paused. '. . . and actually Patrick asked if I'd come talk to you, reassure you about stuff you know? Tell you he's okay and, er . . .' One reason he'd decided that a visit would be better than a phone call was that he wasn't sure how to start a conversation like this. Now he was here, he realised that doing it face to face was going to be just as tricky. More so perhaps. He wasn't good at things like this, whatever this thing was. 'Any chance of a cup of tea?'

'Of course William, sorry. Come on up.'

They sat side by side on a worn grey sofa, a tray of tea and chocolate digestives on a low table in front of them. The sitting room looked out onto the Fields and the autumn sun filled it with light. There was a richly coloured rug on the floor that William remembered Patrick buying in Casablanca. He pointed at it.

'He was desperate to get that rug for you, spent ages haggling over it. He drank about ten cups of mint tea and still got fleeced as I recall.'

Rebecca smiled.

'He's a rubbish haggler.'

There were various interesting knick-knacks around the room and on the mantelpiece, as well as framed photos of the two of them on holiday, at a family wedding, both dressed up to the nines. It was a good room. Carver had munched his way through several chocolate digestives before he noticed that Rebecca hadn't touched them. 'You don't want a biscuit?'

'No, thanks. I'm not feeling great today . . .' Carver nodded; now she mentioned it, she did look a little green around the gills. '. . . I think maybe I ate something that didn't agree with me.'

'Like an Ofsted inspector?'

Rebecca grinned. They talked about her school for a while, then about Carver's teaching before eventually working their way back to the purpose of his visit.

'So Patrick asked you to come speak to me?'

'Yes.'

'How come?'

'He said that you'd been followed by someone.'

'I thought I had . . . last week. Some woman pretending to be a parent. I don't know why it freaked me out so much. It just seemed weird, running into her twice in one day. Patrick figured it was some kind of misunderstanding or mix-up.'

'If he thought that then, I'm pretty sure he doesn't think it now.'

'Why, what's changed?'

'It's not a one-off, it's part of a pattern of – as you say – *weird things*. Something similar happened to a colleague of mine, a friend really, McCluskey. Maybe Patrick's mentioned her to you?'

'Oh yes, at length.' Rebecca paused. 'I'm sorry to hear that, is she all right?'

'Yeah, she's fine. McCluskey's bullet-proof. So can you tell me what happened with you?'

Rebecca talked Carver through it; several times he asked her to slow down or repeat something, he wanted every detail.

'How come you decided on the Portrait Gallery?'

'I hadn't been for a while, I couldn't remember the opening hours so I checked those.'

'On your phone?'

'Sure.'

When eventually he felt like he'd got the story straight in his head, Carver sat back on the sofa. He glanced up at the ceiling.

'Clever.'

'Huh? The woman who was following me?'

'No, not her. You. Engaging her in conversation, testing her with a fictitious nursery name. Really smart.'

Rebecca smiled.

'Thank you William.'

'But it won't put them off, they'll just have someone else keep an eye on you instead.' He considered telling her about the stocky fellow with the missing dog, but decided against. Rebecca stared down at her feet.

'So does all this have something to do with what Patrick's working on?'

'Well . . . I can't think of any other explanation. Can you?'

'No.' She paused. 'That's great, just what I need.'

'Eh?'

'More reasons to be angry with Patrick.'

'Are you two not getting along?'

Rebecca laughed.

'I've seen him for five days in the last forty-five William.'

'Right, I see.'

'And he slept for most of that. He's so wrapped up in the work he's got no room for anything else. These last few months, even when he's back . . .' She shook her head. '. . . he's not completely back. Do you know what I mean?'

'I do.'

Having not wanted to start talking about Patrick, Rebecca was now finding it difficult to stop.

'I know that the idiot I fell for is in there somewhere, I'm just having a hard time finding him right now . . .' She smiled.

'. . . geographically, emotionally, in every way.' She paused. 'We had our annual *auction of promises* at the school last night.' She laughed and looked over at William. 'Sorry that must sound like the non sequitur to end all non sequiturs.'

'It's definitely up there.'

She grinned.

'Soon after I started at this school – my first term – they had the auction of promises. I made a complete fool of myself. I tried to deal with how nervous I was by drinking a couple of glasses of white wine. Then a couple more. Patrick had come along to lend some moral support and he tried to slow me down, but I was flying and towards the end of the night, the last few lots were being auctioned – a week in Malta, the VIP experience at Charlton Athletic Football Club, that kind of thing – and I staggered up and said that I would cook my famous Chinese stir-fry, in fact a whole meal at the home of whoever bid the highest.' Carver shook his head. 'There was this deathly silence. Nothing. I was standing up there next to the auctioneer, staring at this hall, filled with people staring back at me. All my colleagues, the parents of every kid in my class and all the other parents too. Just silence. I was about to walk back to my chair when Patrick stuck his hand up and shouted that he'd pay twenty pounds and a couple of people laughed. Then he bid thirty. Then he moved seats and bid forty . . .' Carver glanced up at Rebecca, her eyes were damp. '. . . moved back again and bid eighty and the whole room was laughing now. The auctioneer joined in and by the end he'd paid one hundred and fifty quid, just bidding against himself and everyone in the hall was in hysterics. My stir-fry raised more than the VIP trip to Charlton Athletic.'

Carver nodded.

'He'll be back before long, er, and you two will sort it out. I'm sure.'

'Right. I wish I was sure. He's not the same man at all, not right now anyway.'

'There'll be reasons.'

'Sure, I know that. He isn't sleeping enough, I think he's drinking too much. He just isn't looking after himself properly – everything is about the work. He loves his job and I know that what he's doing is important, but so is what I'm doing. And so's our future. I'm worried that he's going to end up—' She stopped.

William smiled.

'End up like me?'

'Sorry, I didn't mean . . .'

'Don't worry, I understand.' He paused. 'It's the right thing to worry about. I didn't intend to end up like me either. It just kind of happened, over time – the way things do.'

Rebecca put her hand on Carver's arm.

'I think with you – it's different. I mean, you're brilliant. Patrick always says you're brilliant.'

He shook his head.

'No, I've met a few brilliant people down the years, I'm not one of them. I'm . . . *dogged*, I suppose.' He took another biscuit and dunked it in his tea. 'I've been trying to persuade myself that I could live a *different kind of life*.' He looked around Rebecca and Patrick's living room. 'That it would be better for me, for everyone if I did that. But I'm beginning to think that maybe I was wrong.'

Walking back down the side of the Fields, Carver stopped and retied his shoe. There was no sign of the man with the missing dog. Best-case scenario was that the guy had been following him – this was possible but unlikely. The lost dog story was just a ham-fisted attempt to find out why Carver was where he was. They weren't that interested in him, they were watching the house, watching Rebecca. The question was why?

43 Harm

Patrick took a taxi back to the Headland Hotel; the prickly stink of tear gas was in the air and he was starting to worry that repeated exposure to the gas was affecting his breathing. As the cab got closer to the harbour, he opened the window and gulped air. Eric had promised to keep his ears open for any mention of *repairs* or *repairmen* and to read anything else that Patrick found that he thought he might be able to help with. In return Patrick was going to look into the killing of Sammy Kwok and make sure that at least the BBC's account of what had happened was accurate. He wondered quite when he was going to get the chance to do this, alongside everything else. Perhaps if Viv could spare some more of John Brandon's time?

He knew something was up the moment he opened his hotel room door, but it took him a while to figure out what it was. Someone had been in the room – not housekeeping, the bed was still unmade, the curtains closed. Not the maid, but someone, he was sure of it. He went first to the window and kneeling down on the carpet ran his fingers along the hem of the curtain. He heaved a sigh of relief; the memory stick he'd hidden inside the lining – one of Carver's old tricks – was still there. He opened the curtains so he had some more light to work with and checked the drawers and cupboards; all his clothes and spare kit were as he'd left them as far as he could tell. He'd taken his laptop and the tape recorder with him to the Lennon Wall in his grab bag along with the faxes from McCluskey, so there was nothing to worry about there. Perhaps he was imagining things? He went and stood back by the door and studied the room again. Something was different but what? Then he saw it. The new reporter's notepad, which he was certain he'd had next to him on the bedside table, was now sitting underneath the wall mounted TV. He picked it up and flicked through the pages. It was blank.

'No harm, no foul.'

He tossed it back onto the bed, but as he did so, he noticed something. On the top page, pressed into the paper, a scribble, indented only, but . . . He tore the page out and held it sideways to the light. He traced the indented words and letters with his finger, as clear now as if it had been written in ink – the Chinese characters he'd copied out and underneath that, McCluskey's fax number and her new Skype address.

'Fuck.'

44 Search History

Fred was sitting on the toilet, scrolling through messages on his mobile phone. One of his development teams wanted a supplementary meeting, they weren't sure they'd fully understood his last briefing on microtargeting. He sighed, but agreed both to this meeting and to a face-to-face with the bee guy who'd come up with a plan to save Lizzie's precious bees. Fred had briefly considered letting the hive die, but decided against this. He was interested in what the guy had to say. A Beijing-based client was chasing up a recent request – '*user data relating to recently received messaging application information*'. He mumbled something under his breath – not just impatient, but verbose with it. He texted back that his team was scraping the data right now and he should have something for them soon.

He scrolled through his contacts – down through the As and Bs to C and *Christy Newmark*. He had her personal and work mobile numbers, home address, Twitter, Facebook, Skype, her Public Square log-in of course. He knew where she was at any moment in time and had even added her tracking information to

247

the map on the mainframe computer where he kept everyone else. He had every piece of information necessary for the moment he decided to contact her. But the time wasn't right, not yet. He wanted to watch her from a distance for a little longer.

He put the phone down on the edge of the bath, tore off a couple of squares of toilet paper and leant forward. Opening his legs as wide as his trousers would allow he reached his right hand between his thin, hairless thighs and caught the stool before it could touch water. He brought it back and raised it to eye level for a closer look. Shiny and brown as a polished shoe. Solid as a shoe too – it looked and smelt healthy. He dropped it back down into the toilet bowl and reached for the hand sanitiser and a nail brush. Once he'd washed thoroughly and changed into a new shirt, *then* he'd call Elizabeth. He'd made her wait long enough.

'Hey Fred, what's going on over there? Too busy to talk to your wife?'

'Never too busy for that, Lizzie. I've just been trying to make sure that the information you want is properly sourced . . . all present and correct.'

'Cool, thank you.' She paused. 'I know you probably don't approve.'

'You're right . . . I don't. But when does that ever stop you?'

'Most of the time Freddy, but I've got a good feeling about this thing.'

He sighed.

'From what you tell me, this guy's already cost us over a hundred million bucks. I think we should just write that off and move on.'

'We would've had to pay that tax sooner or later, other people would've asked questions.'

'Maybe.'

'But my main point is that engaging with people like this is good for Public Square. If we can persuade a few of these folk who *really* don't like us that we're not all bad, then it looks good to the outside world. *Turning nay-sayers into yay-sayers.*'

'God, that's an ugly phrase. Who came up with that?'

'Julian Drice.'

'He's drunk *all* the Kool-Aid hasn't he? I wouldn't use that if I were you.'

'You might be right. But doing this kinda thing is useful Fred, it's educational. You know how my dad loved stress-testing his ideas like this.'

'I understand that Lizzie. But things like this, the Public Square pretend trade union or whatever it is – it all takes time, energy.'

'My time Freddie, not yours. Come on, tell me what we know about this Carver guy.' Fred already had the file open on his computer screen, a mystifying list of characters and symbols – complete gobbledegook until, with a few key-strokes, he removed the encryption and started reading.

'So Carver's data set is sub-optimal.' He scrolled down some more. 'Sub, sub-optimal.'

'Give me what you got.'

'He doesn't use much tech. His digital footprint is – small.'

'Like how small?'

'Like baby-bootee small. He's not with Public Square.'

'Of course not. When do we ever get that lucky Fred?'

'He's not on Facebook, Twitter or any other social media platform either.'

'Right, I worked out he wasn't now . . . but never?'

'Never.'

'Shopping?'

'Looks like he's a physical shopper.'

'For everything?'

'Almost, he bought one thing from Amazon once.'

'What was it?'

'A poetry book, some poet I've never heard of. I'll send you the details.'

'Thanks.' She paused. 'How about his search history then Fred? What jumps out?'

'What jumps out is that you're trying to make nice with the most boring man in the world. It's almost all *news searches*, some classical music stuff . . .' He read some more. 'A device with proximity to his device was looking for news stories about Public Square's UK tax liability at the same time as you were making your pitch at the BBC, I'm guessing that was something to do with him. There really isn't much else Lizzie. Nothing interesting, certainly nothing compromising. Not on his own devices anyway, maybe he uses a white computer we don't know about, I can get my team to keep looking if you want?'

'Nah. I just wondered if there was something that might give me an inside track, but I'll go with what's public knowledge.'

'Public knowledge is he's a pain in the ass. Disruptive – not in a good way. Hostile.'

'I think you're underestimating how charming I can be when I want to, Fred.'

'I never underestimate that, Lizzie.' He paused. 'How is Jags by the way?'

Elizabeth switched the phone from one ear to the other.

'Fine, as far as I know, Fred. You talk to him a lot more than I do. I bought him that new raincoat yesterday, like I promised I would . . .' The chances were that Fred would know this already. '. . . and I asked him to join me for some dinner. He was looking so hangdog, I took pity.' Fred would know this too. She had to hope that the fact that he was fishing meant that this was all Fred knew. Jags certainly wouldn't have said anything. 'I kind of wish I hadn't asked him to join me, it was like eating with some kind of animal.'

'Yes, I've seen him eat, it isn't pleasant.' Fred paused. 'Try and sweet-talk this old journalist guy if you want to Lizzie, finish what you need to finish and then hurry back to civilisation will you?'

'I will Fred. Thank you for your help.'

'You're welcome.'

Fred steepled his hands on the desk in front of him. Let Lizzie do what she wanted to do, perhaps she *could* make a convert of William Carver, Fred had learnt never to bet against her. He took another look at the unencrypted file on the screen in front of him. There were a couple of things that he hadn't mentioned to Elizabeth. Nothing that would help with her foolish proselytising mission, but *all information* was important and there were one or two things there in the data of particular interest. Carver wasn't a worry – a busted flush by all accounts. But some of the company he kept *did* interest Fred. He checked the time; Jags would have read the FedExed letter by now and contacted the people Fred needed him to contact. The chances were that what needed to happen was happening already.

45 Crows

McCluskey was washing up after having finished breakfast: a boiled egg and soldiers, half a dozen rashers of bacon and a pot of tea. She liked to clean the teapot straight after using it as the tannin stained quickly and it was a family heirloom of sorts. It had been a clear, cold night and out in the garden a pair of black crows were pecking at the frozen grass, circling the gardening fork that she'd left jammed in the middle of the lawn. The crows strode about in that strange high-stepped way they had. McCluskey noticed that she'd left her gardening gloves outside too; they were draped over the handle of the garden fork. They'd be frozen stiff. She took a sip of tea.

'*No.*'

That was wrong, her gardening gloves were on the dresser in the hall. She'd seen them there earlier. She opened the back door and walked out.

The cat had been cut in half lengthways and gutted. The animal's skin had been left draped over the handle of the garden fork. Its insides were on the grass – carrion for crows. As McCluskey walked closer, the birds shuffled reluctantly away then took flight, but only as far as the tarpaper roof of the shed. They hadn't finished this meal. McCluskey lifted the cat gently from the handle of the fork and held it in her arms, cradling it. The animal's blood stained her blouse and she could taste vomit rising in her throat, but it was not fear she felt. Only anger. She laid the cat's body down on her kitchen table and sat down. Carver was coming to see her later, primarily to report back on his meeting with Patrick's girlfriend, but he'd also asked McCluskey if he could have a proper look at what she and Patrick were working on. Carver was back in the game and she could not allow anything to distract him from that. She would bury the cat at the foot of the garden. And when she got her hands on whoever it was that had done this . . . McCluskey would bury them there too.

PART FOUR

Once a new technology starts rolling, if you're not part of the steamroller, you're part of the road

Stewart Brand

46 Persuasion

Carver drank one thoughtful pint and then another. He was considering whether to chance a third when someone tapped him lightly on the shoulder and he nearly jumped out of his skin.

'Arghhh . . .' He shuffled round on the stool and stared. 'What the f—? I mean, what're you doing here?' Carver glanced around the pub. 'Are you lost?'

Elizabeth Curepipe smiled.

'Not lost, no. I'm sorry, I didn't mean to startle you. I wanted to talk and your manager . . . Naomi?' Carver nodded. 'Naomi said that you like to hang out here now and again when you aren't teaching.'

It was delicately put.

'Talk about what?'

'Well . . . can I buy you a drink?'

She bought a pint of London Pride for Carver and, after some umming and aahing, a half of cider for herself. They found an empty table at the back of the pub and Carver sat down in the

257

heavy wooden chair, facing the wall. When he looked up, he saw that his surprise drinking companion was still standing.

'Would you mind if I sat in that seat?' She wore an apologetic smile. 'It's just that if I'm facing away from the rest of the room then I think there's less chance we'll be disturbed.' Carver mumbled an apology and swapped chairs.

'I should've thought. You do seem to attract quite a lot of attention.' Elizabeth nodded. She had already had to endure an *arm around the shoulder*, *thumbs-up* selfie with Norman the land-lord, as well as signing several beer mats.

'Way too much attention.'

As soon as he was sitting where she'd asked him to, Carver spoke.

'So what can I do for you, Mrs Curepipe?'

Elizabeth had her glass halfway to her lips, but she put it back down on the table.

'Right, of course. Well I wanted to let you know that we've done what I said we'd do. I looked into how much tax Public Square UK paid to the Treasury last year. In my view it was ungenerous. We're already talking to the revenue and in the next day or two I'll be writing a cheque.'

'For how much?'

'Well . . .' She lowered her voice. '. . . this is market sensitive information of course, but between you and me I guess it'll be a little north of one hundred and thirty million.'

'Pounds?'

'That's right.'

Carver did the sum in his head; if Public Square's profits were as reported then this was around about the right amount.

'Fine. Well I'm sure the Chancellor of the Exchequer will be grateful.' He drank the foam off his new pint. 'You're not expecting *me* to say thank you or something are you? I mean all you're doing here is paying the tax that by rights, you should be paying.'

'No, of course, I get that. No need for thank yous. But I wanted you to know first . . .' She took a sip of the cider and winced. 'Interesting drink.'

'That's dry cider. Maybe you're used to the sweet? I'm sure Norman will swap it for you if you ask him.' He was pretty sure Norman would do the hokey-cokey stark naked if Elizabeth Curepipe asked him.

'No, it's growing on me.' She took another sip. 'See? The thing is, there was something else I wanted to talk to you about.'

'I see.'

'I got taken on a tour of Broadcasting House after the news meeting . . .' She took another sip of cider. '. . . saw the studios, George the something's old microphone.'

'George the Sixth.'

'That's the fellow.' She smiled but got nothing from Carver in return. 'So . . . I was shown all around the old building, upstairs where all the bosses live. That's a lot of oak panelling they've got going on up there.'

'Yeah, I've seen it. Usually when they're trying to fire me.'

'Why would they want to do that?'

Carver shrugged.

'I'm not to everyone's taste.'

'I see. Well, anyway, the Director General showed me round his trophy cabinet . . .' William was almost beginning to feel sorry for the poor woman, what a bore. '. . . and I couldn't help notice that quite a few of those statues and certificates in there had your name on them.'

'Right.'

'He'd just gotten hold of a new one, looks kinda like the bonnet ornament on a Rolls Royce car. She's pretty cute.' Carver knew the award she was referring to although he hadn't seen it yet.

'That's some French prize. I'd not heard of it . . . not until we won it anyway.'

'Your boss had certainly heard of it.'

'Then I guess it makes sense for it to stay there in his trophy cabinet.' He doubted that this feigned indifference was fooling the woman sitting opposite. He certainly wasn't fooling himself. The truth was that the longer he'd been away from front-line reporting, the more he found himself thinking about the various awards he'd won. This small silvery harvest was distributed around several trophy cabinets inside Broadcasting House and recently he'd wondered whether it might be nice to have one or two of the prizes on show at home. There wasn't anyone there to show them to, but nonetheless . . . Regardless of this, Carver realised he'd quite like to take a look at the new statue and at the certificate that went with it. Hopefully it credited Patrick as well as himself – they'd both done the work. 'Maybe I'll take a look next time I'm in the building.'

Elizabeth Curepipe nodded.

'You absolutely should. Anyway Mr Carver, here's the thing . . . there's gonna be a letter published in all the main British newspapers tomorrow morning.'

'I see.'

'It'll welcome this whole BBC and Public Square partnership and it's gonna to be signed by a bunch of very obvious people . . . me, your Director General, the Head of News. But I want for us to have the names of a few *super respected* journalists on that list too.'

'And *they're* all on holiday, so you thought you'd ask me?'

She laughed.

'That'll be some of that famous ol' English self-deprecation in action I'm guessing?'

Carver shrugged.

'I'm not really a *letter-signing* kind of person Mrs Curepipe.'

She nodded slowly.

'Any kind of letter?'

'Well, this sort of letter in particular . . .' He took another swig of his bitter. '. . . in fact, to be perfectly honest, this letter specifically, *your letter*, I would never, ever sign.'

Her smile, which had been in place pretty much from the moment she'd walked into the pub, now slipped.

'I see. So I'm guessing that you don't think this partnership is a good idea?'

'That's right.'

'Well, how about this . . . how about I have a go at persuading you otherwise?'

Carver looked down at his pint. It was still three quarters full.

'It's a free country. More or less.'

The case Elizabeth Curepipe made, sitting here in front of Carver in the corner of the Yorkshire Grey, was significantly different from the pitch she'd made to his bosses down the road at Broadcasting House.

'I think that you and I are more alike than you might think Mr Carver. We're both after the same thing.'

'Which is?'

'People's attention.'

'Right, but it's not just about *wanting* the same thing. *Why* you want it matters too. I want people's attention so we can tell them what's going on in the world – things they should be interested in, things that they might want to think about, worry about.' He looked at Curepipe. '*You*, or rather, *your company* . . . you want their attention so you can sell them stuff they don't need.'

She shook her head.

'No, that's where you're wrong about us. There's more to us than that. I want to run a profitable business, sure . . .' Carver made a harrumphing sound. '. . . and I believe we should pay the proper amount of tax on that profit. But more important than that, I want people to *read* and *see* and *listen* to the good stuff – good journalism most of all.' She took a sip of cider. Over the top of the glass, her eyes found Carver's and she smiled another one of those movie star smiles. 'You know, I've always thought there was a sort of *poetry* to good journalism.'

'A poetry?'

'Yes. Just like there's a poetry in good prose . . . same with the best kind of journalism. You don't agree?'

Of course he agreed, he agreed completely. But he wasn't about to tell her that.

'Most of the time it's just hard work, *hack work. Shoe leather and good luck* was how one of my first bosses put it. But yes, now and again something vaguely poetic might happen – if you're lucky.'

'Yes. And that's the sort of thing we can help with. We have *a billion people* using Public Square. That's a thousand million.'

'I know what a billion is.'

'Yes, I'm sorry. But the point is that there are a billion people there – eager to read and learn and share. And the *best stuff* spreads.'

Carver shrugged.

'You're sure about that?'

'Absolutely. Plus we can help identify the real niche groups who get ignored and give them something too.' She was motoring now. 'Foreign news junkies like you. Or birdwatchers, trainspotters . . .'

'Holocaust deniers.'

The smile slipped again.

'We monitor that kind of thing. We're getting better at filtering that crap out, we really are . . .' She paused. '. . . and I'm not sure it's fair to put all the blame for that kind of stuff on us. In Rwanda, the bad guys used radio to whip people up and encourage genocide . . . we don't react to that by *banning all radio*.'

Carver shook his head.

'I was in Rwanda.'

'I know you were. I've listened to your dispatches from there. That's why I chose that particular example.'

He stared at Curepipe; again she had surprised him. He took a gulp of beer.

'I'm sure there are loads of people falling over themselves to sign your letter Mrs Curepipe . . .'

'Please, Elizabeth. Or Lizzie?'

'Elizabeth. You don't need me to sign the letter.'

'Don't need you, no. But I'd really like it if you did.'

'Why?'

'We want to turn *nay* . . .' She stopped.

'Huh?'

'Nothing. My dad always thought that the best way to test a new idea was to find the toughest audience you could and run it by them.'

'I can see why that would make sense.'

'You'd have liked my dad and mom. When they got started – back in the seventies – it wasn't about money, not at all. It was about connecting the whole world, bringing people together like never before, sharing the products you made. *Peyote parties* in the desert . . . all of that.'

'Sounds like fun.'

'Doesn't it?'

'How much of that do you remember?'

She paused.

'Not as much as I'd like. But a lot of us still hold to the same principles. It's just that everything's got faster, a lot faster. What's happening in Silicon Valley right now, it's a complete revolution and if you want to survive a revolution you have to *move fast and break things.*'

William put his beer down with a clunk.

'Spare me.'

'What?'

'That line . . . that's not your line is it?'

'No, that's Zuck's, but —'

263

'But that's what you believe.' He picked his drink back up, swilling the last of his beer around in the base of the glass and swallowing it.

'Well . . .'

'And I don't. I'm more of a *"move slowly and try not to break anything"* kind of guy. That's why I can't sign your letter.'

Elizabeth smiled again. She finished her cider.

'I understand. I'm disappointed but I understand.'

They took their empty glasses back to the bar. Out on the street, Elizabeth's entourage was waiting. A couple of shiny black Mercedes were parked at the kerb and half a dozen smart-suited men and women were striding up and down, impatiently texting other people and trying to look busy. Elizabeth gestured in their direction.

'That's one of the downsides of being me. I need this crowd of people.'

'But you can't face them day to day?'

'Exactly.' Carver stifled a laugh. Elizabeth shot him a look. 'Did I say something funny?'

'Not particularly. Those are lines from an old song. A song I used to listen to a lot, I haven't heard it for a while.'

'What's it called?'

Carver opened his mouth to tell her. Then changed his mind.

'I don't think I'll tell you.' Elizabeth gave him a puzzled look and reached for her phone. He put his hand out to stop her, briefly touching her arm, then quickly removing it. 'Sorry, but don't do that. Please.'

'What? I'm just going to . . .'

'I know what you're going to do. I'm asking you not to, not now anyway.' He paused. 'Why don't you try asking around? Ask some people if they know that line, if they remember the song?'

'I just asked you.'

'And I couldn't help.'

'Fine, fine. I get it . . .' She put the phone back in her pocket. '. . . how about a clue?'

Carver nodded.

'Okay. It's the kind of song that your father and mother might have liked. From what you tell me, it could've been their kind of thing.'

'The Grateful Dead?'

'Not a bad guess. But no.'

'I feel I should tell you, Mr Carver, that this has been – by some margin – the *least successful* meeting I've had while I've been here in the UK.'

'Right. Well, *you win some, you lose some*.'

'Yeah . . .' She smiled '. . . I've heard people say that.' She held out her hand and William shook it. 'It's a shame, I'm a good person to have in your corner, Mr Carver, ask anyone.'

'I'm sure. But my corner's just fine.'

47 Memory Sticks

THE HEADLAND HOTEL, HONG KONG

Patrick found an empty seat at the far end of the hotel lobby. He put his laptop and notebook down on the coffee table in front of him and stared at the wall. He needed to collect his thoughts. And quick.

'Concentrate . . .'

He'd written a note to McCluskey warning her that both her fax number and the Skype address she'd given him might've been seen by someone else. He told her that the same someone had broken into his bedroom, but that nothing had been taken – everything she'd sent him and all his interviews were safe. He didn't want her to panic, although he had known as he was writing the hurried note that it was *him* who was doing the panicking. He turned in his seat and saw the red-faced Chinese cop who met his eye and smiled before disappearing back inside the pages of the *Wall Street Journal*. Patrick wondered whether it was this guy who'd searched his room? It seemed unlikely – the black-suited secret policeman never appeared to do much of anything. His function was ornamental, not operational. Who then? Patrick glanced over at the hotel gift shop and checked the time again. He'd planned to fax McCluskey straight away, but the horses were running up at the Happy Valley Racecourse today and so the fax machine was in use. Ada had been very apologetic, but she'd made it clear that he wasn't allowed anywhere near the stockroom, much less the fax machine until there was a break in racing. They'd agreed that he should wait in the lobby and she'd come find him. So he waited. He had his laptop and the memory stick, although now he came to think about it, perhaps this would have been safer left in the lining of the curtains. Whoever had searched the room had searched it once and not found the stick; logic suggested that they were unlikely to search again. At least not right away. He considered running back up to the bedroom and putting it back in its original hiding place, then changed his mind. The priority had to be sending McCluskey the fax.

'Hey there bud!' A thick hand clapped him hard on the shoulder. 'I thought I recognised those crappy old sneakers.'

'Oh, hey Dan. How're you doing?'

'I'm good. Real good. What ya doing hiding away here in a corner of the lobby?'

Patrick shrugged.

'Oh, you know, the usual, editing.' He pointed at the laptop. 'I came down here for a change of scene, I was going a little stir crazy in my room.'

Dan nodded.

'I can understand that . . .' He glanced across at the gift shop. 'Perhaps you could use some company? I could go grab us both a beer . . .'

Patrick was tempted, but he shook his head.

'No, thanks Dan, but I should push on.' He reached for the laptop. 'Maybe later?'

'Sure buddy. Hey, how about this . . . I promised Viv I'd fetch us some food from this cool takeaway place I found down in

Admiralty. How's about the three of us get together later and have a meal in one of the rooms? It's better food than the restaurant here does and way cheaper. We could get us a pitcher of those dragon cocktails and some beers to wash it down with?'

Patrick wanted to be left alone. It seemed like the quickest way of achieving that was to agree.

'That sounds fine Dan.'

'So you're in?'

'I'm in.'

'Cool. Let's make it . . . your room at eight p.m?'

'My room?'

'Yeah. We'll come to you. Don't worry bud, we'll bring everything . . .' He clapped Patrick on the shoulder. 'See you at eight.'

48 All Souls

Jags woke with a start and reached instinctively for the open glovebox. He had his hand on the pistol butt when he realised that the voice that had roused him was a recording, not a real person. A tannoy announcement he'd heard before. In a low voice, American-accented and slow, first in English, then Spanish, came the familiar alert:

This is a test message. The Brochu dam warning system is operational. This message is being broadcast on all channels. We repeat, this is a test.

He wound the window down and squinted, staring beyond the green metal Brochu sign, in the direction of the dam. It looked like it always looked. They played the recording a couple more times, then the basso voice announced that the test was over and there was silence. One day it would not be a test. Jags opened the door and climbed out of the Chevy. He walked around the car a couple of times to stretch his legs. Soledad's mother had invited him to the family house for some food in half an hour. Then, later that evening, Soledad was on parade,

albeit rather reluctantly, at the All Souls' ceremony. The unburying. Jags lifted the front of his shirt and took a sniff; he had
the smell of airports and travel on him but there wasn't time
to shower. He climbed back into the car on the passenger side
and dug around in the glove compartment again. He pushed
the gun to the back; it was the deodorant he was looking for
– that and the brand-new phone that Fred had sent him. Jags
sprayed a couple of blasts of the sandalwoody-smelling
deodorant under each arm and billowed his shirt a little before
having another sniff. It was an improvement. His thoughts
turned to Elizabeth, to London and their night together. Or
half a night anyway. He would like to call her, say hello. More
than hello. But it was out of the question; Fred would know.
One way or another, Fred always knew. He opened the plastic
bag containing his assorted burner phones and took out the box
containing the new mobile. Latest model, all the bells and whis-
tles. Boxed up and cellophane wrapped, no way on earth of
knowing that Fred and his geeks had been crawling all over it
adding who knew what? He had to persuade Soledad to use
this phone from now on.

'Get her to swap her old mobile for this one and, more importantly,
get her back on script. No more rabble-rousing speeches. Remind her
who she's working for. A forceful reminder if necessary.'

Fred had offered to send one of the *new guys* down to help him
out. The second time he'd made this offer. Jags told Fred that
he'd handle it.

He put the box in his jacket pocket, walked back around to the
driver's side, started the Chevy and drove down the hill, parking
in front of Soledad's family home. There was a nanny goat teth-
ered to a metal pole in the front yard, a new addition. The animal
was eyeing up a few heads of lettuce that were growing from a
compost bag in front of the house, but the blue nylon rope she
was tied to wouldn't reach that far. Jags gave the goat a tentative

pat and strode on up to the door. He knocked and heard voices from inside the house; Soledad's mother Francesca answered, greeting him with a polite if rather nervous smile and some well-rehearsed English.

'Hello, you are most welcome here today.' She slipped back into Spanish in order to tell him that Soledad was getting ready and that he should sit at the table. The chicken stew she'd hoped to give him last time he visited was on the menu this time, and sure enough the small house was filled with the smell of garlic and seared chicken.

Soledad soon appeared, wearing what looked like her father's old tracksuit, but with her face fully made-up and her hair piled high on her head. He had never seen her with any kind of make-up before and it was quite a transformation. To Jags she looked like a teenage kid playing Liz Taylor playing Queen Cleopatra.

'Well, that's something different. . .'

Soledad said nothing. She got her backpack from behind the front door and sat across from him at the dinner table. He tried to engage her again. 'You must be excited? It's your big night. Star of the show . . .'

She gave a non-committal nod of the head. Soledad had the backpack open in front of her and was looking for something.

'So you know the *one-page* thing from Public Square that you gave me?'

'Yup.'

'We have written one too.'

'Who's we?'

'The people of Brochu. I wrote it – but on their behalf. I have spoken to quite a few people now, it reflects the general opinion I think, but we can always alter it.'

Jags nodded. Sure . . . either they could alter it, or alternatively how about burning it and never speaking of it again? She passed the piece of paper over and he skim read from the top. It was just

271

as bad as he'd feared. Possibly worse. The one-pager called for a commitment to use local labour to build the museum, community centre and nursery. It wanted local people put in charge of repairs to the dam as well, plus regular safety inspections carried out, independent of the mining company, not commissioned by them. It called for an end to a number of things, including something called *veinicuatrear*.

'What's *veinicuatrear*?'

Soledad's brow furrowed as she considered how best to translate the word.

'It means . . . *to twenty-four hour*. To work twenty-four hours in a row.'

'How often does that happen?'

She shook her head.

'All the time.'

The paper called for statistics to be kept on the number of mining-related injuries, for compensation for these injuries etc, etc. A large part of the list related to safety, but down near the bottom it got round to pay. Jags read the first line and laughed.

'Am I reading this right? You want Public Square to pay the equivalent of the Californian minimum wage?'

'In Chilean pesos, yes.'

'Eight bucks an hour? You're dreaming.'

'It goes up to nine dollars soon.'

Jags shook his head.

'No kidding?'

'Yes. So in fact you should take eight while it's on the table.'

He laughed again, then stopped. Something occurred to him.

'Where've you been finding all this stuff out? You talked to someone?'

'I looked it up myself. Trade union websites, other websites.'

'Right.'

'You don't think I'm capable?'

Jags shook his head.

'I know you're capable.' The trouble was that he knew what other people were capable of as well.

49 Questions

McCluskey watched Carver work his way around the room, reading as he went.

'So we're working on the basis that *maslih* and all the other similar words in all these other languages refer to *repairs* now?'

McCluskey nodded, noting with approval his use of *we* as opposed to *you*.

'That's right. *Repairs* and *repairmen*. It was thanks to Patrick that we managed to unpick that particular knot.'

'Right. I knew the word *maslih* rang a bell, I just couldn't place it.' He scratched at his chin. 'But looking at your wall here, it seems like that has *raised* as many questions as it's *answered*?' The wall looked even more confusing than when William had last seen it. McCluskey shook her head.

'The way I look at it, we've got one or two main questions that need answering now – what is it they're repairing? And fer who? It only looks more confusing because we've got a few more places in play now.'

Carver nodded.

'Myanmar, Manila, Chile . . . those are new aren't they?'

'Yep.'

'And Xinjiang? I should probably know, but where the hell's Xinjiang?'

'Way up in the north-west of China. The arse end of nowhere. It's where the Chinese army have been doing all sorts to those Uighurs.'

'Oh yeah.'

He moved closer and saw that chunks of untranslated Mandarin text in this section were connected by thick blue marker pen to similar-looking chunks over in the Hong Kong section. He stepped back again and tried to get some perspective. 'I'm not sure how much these lines are helping me McCluskey. It looks more like a huge bowl of blue spaghetti than a game of . . . what did you call it before?'

'Pelmanism. Pairs.'

'Right . . .' The three pints he'd had at lunch, the last one courtesy of Elizabeth Curepipe, had slowed his thinking, but maybe that was no bad thing. 'So how about we focus on just one thing for a moment? One location and one person. Let's take Hong Kong . . .'

'And Patrick.'

'Yes.'

McCluskey had put her collection of Hong Kong-related material right in the centre of the wall with Patrick's name underneath.

'So Patrick is helping you, he solves one part of the puzzle.'

'Yep.'

'Even supposing that *someone, somehow* knows that. One of these *repairmen* . . . whatever the hell they are . . . there's got to be more to it than that. Patrick has to have something that somebody wants. That's the only way to explain things like Rebecca being followed and strange women turning up outside your kitchen window.' He glanced at McCluskey. 'You've not had anything else like that happen have you? No more odd threats? Attempted break-ins?'

She shook her head. Her eyes firmly on the wall.

'Nah. I've got this place locked up like Fort Knox.'

'Good . . .' Carver homed in on the Hong Kong section of wall. 'Help me while I walk myself slowly through this McCluskey. So they think that Patrick's got something, but they're not sure either what it is, or whether he's shared it with anyone else – *you, Rebecca, whoever*. For now, they're guessing. Does that make sense to you?'

'It does.'

'So what do we know that they don't? What is it that Patrick's got? D'you know?'

'I think so.'

She told William about the dozens of interviews that Patrick had collected with individuals in the front line of the protests across the Middle East, North Africa and now Hong Kong. 'He said he thought they were all too technical to be of much interest to anyone, but I'm not sure he's right about that. It sounded to me like quite the collection.'

'Where's he put them?'

'I told him it was too risky to send them my way. I advised him tae put them somewhere safe.'

'I hope he was listening.'

'Aye, me too.' She paused. 'He's a good lad Patrick, I can see why you two got on so well . . .' Carver made a harrumphing sound. '. . . and you obviously taught him plenty, but I'm not sure you taught him enough about how to be *careful* . . .' She put a hand on Carver's arm. '. . . and he really needs to be careful right now.'

McCluskey left Carver to navigate his way around the rest of her painstakingly put together investigation and went down to the kitchen to make some food. She was peeling potatoes at the sink when he joined her.

'That blue spaghetti of yours has given me a headache.'

'I know the feeling.' She pointed the potato peeler at a nearby cupboard. 'There's a packet of paracetamol in there, next to the tea.' McCluskey broke away from peeling the spuds to pour him a glass of water. He sat down at the kitchen table, swallowed the pills and glanced looked around, something was missing.

'Where's that cat of yours?'

'Eh?'

'That tortoiseshell cat? The one that likes sitting on people? Her bowl's gone.'

'Oh aye, you're right . . .' McCluskey kept peeling although she already had more potatoes than she needed. '. . . I think she must've found someone else to pester. It's probably just as well, I wasn't so good at looking after her.'

Carver frowned.

'Really? It didn't look that way to me.' He finished his glass of water. 'Shame, I was starting to like her.'

'Aye. Me too.'

50 Good Fortune

'I can just sell you a new queen, Mr Curepipe, it'll take a little while to bed in but that should fix things for you.'

Fred hadn't offered the bee guy a chair; if visitors stood and he stayed sitting behind his desk then meetings like this went off a lot quicker. He could have simply said yes to this suggestion and sent the man on his way, but he was interested.

'Tell me how that works. Briefly.'

'You betcha.' It was a story of larvae and frames and cages and careful feeding. He gave the guy the go-ahead, dismissed him and turned his attention back to other matters. One of his Beijing-based clients had been in touch thanking him for the *'user data relating to the messaging application address'*. Fred shook his head. Why not just say *Skype*? One of his data scraper guys had done a good job in double-quick time. He'd found a list of calls to and from the address, duration and origin – or a pretty accurate idea of origin. The client wanted more – they wanted to know the content of the most recent call. Fred emailed back, warning them that this was a tall order, but offering some guidance on how it might be done. It was a case of old-fashioned, on-the-ground legwork rather than anything computer related. He signed off with *Zhu hao yun* – good luck or good fortune – and he meant it. Fred was as interested as they were in the content of that call.

51 We & They

BROCHU, CHILE, SOUTH AMERICA

'What we've got here, Soledad, is a bad case of miscommunication . . .' Jags handed the piece of paper back to her. '. . . this here looks a lot like a list of demands.'

'It is a list of demands.'

'That's not the way this is going to work. You need to remember who you work for.'

'I work for the people of Brochu.'

'No you don't. Take another look at your payslip. It isn't the people of Brochu putting the big bucks into your bank account. They didn't pay for that goat out there or any other of these other little home improvements. It's us paying for all that and you need to remember that and stop fooling around.' He didn't like talking to her like this, but it was for her own benefit. Her mother had retreated to the bedroom as soon as Jags started to raise his voice, but Soledad didn't move.

'I see. So what happened to *doing well by doing good*?'

'We are gonna do good. We're going to give you a nursery and a community centre and a museum for your freakin' fossils.

What they're not going to give you is some kinda communist collective.'

'They? Or we?'

'What?'

'You said *we* and then you said *they*.'

'I meant *we* . . .' He reached into the pocket of his bomber jacket.
'. . . we got you this too.'

'A new phone?' Jags nodded. 'I've already got a phone.'

'Think of it as a free upgrade. You'll use this from now on.'

'Why?'

'Because *we* say so.'

52 The Hunt

He'd walked up and down the aisles a couple of times already, staring over the shoulders of the King Chung café's customers. A mix of gamers, people from the Chinese mainland chatting to family back home, and assorted oddballs who got nervous whenever he moved close. One of them was using the machine that he was looking for; the question was, which one? He walked once more around the café, formulating a plan. He would start at the back and work forward, up and down the desks of computer terminals, paying for the minimum fifteen-minute slot on each and switching after he'd checked each machine and the next nearest one came free. It would take a freaking age, but there was no alternative. The first thing was to draw a sketch of the place so he could cross off each terminal after he'd checked it. Sitting down at an empty terminal in the window, he saw something. Stuck to the side of the computer next to him, currently being used by a kid playing *Mario Cart*, was a stamp, a blue British second-class stamp with the Queen's profile on it. He paid the boy twenty bucks to swap, logged in and attached an external hard drive. Now he'd found the right machine, the next part was easy.

53 Fair Weather

Carver agreed to stay for dinner. McCluskey had made enough shepherd's pie to feed an army and he liked shepherd's pie. She opened a bottle of red wine too. They ate the dinner in the living room, from trays on their knees. McCluskey had the TV on and kept half an eye on it, while at the same time chatting away to Carver. As a concession to her guest, she kept the volume down low. First there was McCluskey's favourite soap opera, then something about a middle-aged female detective based in a picturesque part of Scotland, followed by an American cop show. All of these seemed to revolve around issues of abuse of one sort or another.

'Do you ever watch a TV programme that doesn't offer the viewers a helpline number at the end?'

McCluskey shot him a look.

'I like gritty telly, so sue me. It looked to me like you were enjoying it.'

He was enjoying it. She'd asked him to light the fire and after much fiddling around with twists of newspaper, kindling and logs, it was now burning strongly; he could see the flames reflecting from McCluskey's collection of snow globes and the room felt cosy and warm. As different as it was from Rebecca and Patrick's living room, it still seemed to William that the two rooms had something in common. McCluskey appeared to read his mind.

'You never said how it went with Patrick's wee girlfriend?'

'Oh yeah, fine.' He told her about his meeting with Rebecca, how well she'd dealt with the tail they'd tried to put on her. 'She's still being watched, some idiot approached me when I was waiting outside her flat. Her main concern is Patrick – how he is, when he's coming home, what state he's going to be in once he gets there. The usual stuff. She's worried he might end up . . . well, like me.'

'I see. Did she ask you to have a chat with him?'

'Not in so many words.'

'How many words would you need?'

'Eh?'

'Are you not seeing a theme developing here Billy? All the people that you're wanting to protect – Rebecca, Patrick . . . me. We're all saying the same thing. I understand this whole Hippocratic oath thing, I get where it's coming from, but the truth is we'd all be better off if you were away doing what it is you're good at. You included.'

The television was still on, but the sound was turned down. The fire crackled in the grate and they sat in silence for a while.

'Even if I wanted to . . .'

'You do *want* to go. I've known you long enough to know that . . . *they sicken of the calm, who knew the storm.*'

'Who's that?'

McCluskey pushed a hand through her candyfloss hair.

'Nope. I cannae remember. I remember the lines, but not the folks that wrote them these days.'

Carver nodded.

'Even if I did decide to go. I can't just up and leave . . .' He put his glass down on one of McCluskey's many occasional tables. '. . . I'd need my boss to sign off on it for starters. I'd need to find someone to cover my classes . . .'

'Who's your boss?'

'Naomi.'

'The *Today* programme woman? Well that's not a problem then, is it? She'll say yes in a heartbeat.'

'Maybe.'

'How about you sleep on it tonight, see how you feel in the morning?'

'Nah, I don't want to put you to any . . .'

'Stay the night Carver. There's already a bed made in the spare room and . . .' She gazed out of the sitting room windows; she'd neglected to draw the curtains and her reflection stared back at her. '. . . anyway, I'd like it if you stayed.'

Carver nodded.

'Sure.'

'Good man. Now what kind of nightcap shall we have? I've got Ovaltine, hot chocolate or there's a twenty-five-year-old Glenlivet.'

'Are you joking?'

54 Ultimate Glory

THE HEADLAND HOTEL, HONG KONG

The last race of the day at Happy Valley was a close one. A horse called Ultimate Glory won by a nose and judging by the smile on the face of the top-hatted doorman, Mr Kip, this was a favourable outcome. It was Mr Kip who came to tell Patrick that the staff had completed their stocktaking work and Ada, the souvenir shop attendant, would be happy to help him now.

Ripped-up facsimiles of Hong Kong Jockey Club betting slips littered the stockroom floor like confetti. The fax machine had been working overtime and it clanked and complained as it slowly ingested Patrick's message to McCluskey and sent it on its way. The scribbled note, warning her that both the fax number and the Skype address that she'd given him might've been seen by someone else, seemed to take an age to send. He sat down at an old wooden school desk to wait for the confirmation note, telling him that it had arrived safely on the other side of the world. Once it had, Patrick relaxed a little. It was peaceful in the stockroom, fusty with the smell of old cardboard boxes and dust, but a good place to sit undisturbed. He glanced over at Ada, who was sweeping the old betting slips into a metal dustpan.

'Excuse me Ada but do you think I could stay here and work for a while? Just half an hour or so?'

She studied the Englishman; he looked tired. Mr Kip was in too good a mood to tell her off for any minor infraction of the hotel rules.

'It is fine, yes. Half an hour.'

She went back to work, leaving the door to the stockroom slightly ajar in case Patrick needed anything. He got his laptop out, connected to the hotel Wi-Fi and typed in the name *Sammy Kwok*. Now he'd done what he could to warn McCluskey, Patrick's next priority was the promise he'd made to Eric. If he was going to persuade John Brandon to spend some time on this story – the real story of what had happened to Sammy and the tsunami of misinformation that had followed his death – then he needed to make sure that everything Eric had told him about the boy's killing and what had happened afterwards was true.

In the end he spent over an hour reading about Sammy. It was, in equal parts, a confusing and depressing experience. The truth about Sammy's death was not just hard to find, it was impossible, buried somewhere beneath layer upon layer of falsehood, ill-informed speculation and half-arsed reporting. Patrick was disappointed to find that the handful of BBC reports that mentioned Sammy had fallen into exactly the same traps as everyone else.

He messaged Viv, who as luck would have it was still in the hotel, sitting in the lobby surrounded by camera equipment and waiting for John Brandon.

'I seem to spend most of my waking life either waiting for Brandon or wishing he'd go away.'

'I know the feeling. When's a good time for me to have him work on a radio piece for me today?'

Viv checked her clipboard and shuffled some of the television two-ways around. She had one more reporter now and there was a little more slack. They agreed that Brandon could be ring-fenced for radio early evening.

'Are you taking him back down to Harcourt to get tear gassed?'

'There's actually another story I'm hoping to get him interested in.'

'I see. You want to tell me what it is? Me being the boss and all?'

'It's about this kid that got killed, Sammy Kwok?'

'That poor boy who had the asthma attack?'

'Yeah. Or rather – no. There's more to it than that.'

'Is it something that telly need to know about?'

'Probably not yet. I just want Brandon to do a sort of *anatomy of a story* piece. It's gonna be mainly script and a little archive this time. It should work for you once I find the time to do some proper work on it. I need to speak to his mum and his mates and stuff like that.'

'Okay. Well Brandon's all yours this evening, but don't forget you've got me and Dan coming over to yours for dinner later. You remember?'

'Oh bollocks. Dan mentioned that did he?'

'He mentioned little else. Eight p.m. Try not to forget, he'll be devastated if it turns out to be just me he's eating noodles with.'

'I'll do my best. Is that green dress of yours getting another outing?'

'You betcha.'

55 The Unburying

Tradition had it that the young woman overseeing the ceremony should be transported through the streets of Brochu to the unburying by carriage. This tradition had to be updated when the barn where the carriage was kept burnt down. For the last twenty years the woman had been collected from her home and taken to the ceremony at the graveyard in the back of a white Oldsmobile convertible. Soledad sat alone and unsmiling on the back seat, her long white gown pooled around her. The role she was required to play demanded a certain solemnity, but Soledad's stony face was no act. She considered the ceremony an anachronism and her role in it an embarrassment. Although perhaps this year it might perform a useful function, if she could remember the lines she'd learnt and hold her nerve. Jags followed the crowd, walking at the very back of the parade of people who were marching behind the slow-moving Oldsmobile. He found himself wondering what this car could be used for when it wasn't being some sort of Chilean Popemobile. He had read about the unburying, but this was the first time he would get to see it. Each All Souls' Night, the people of Brochu would gather outside the town graveyard. Inside, a group of volunteers had been busy for most of the day, supervised by Father Victor and the head gravedigger. Half a dozen corpses had been disinterred, studied and, if deemed suitable, wrapped in fresh white shrouds. Each year different bodies were selected and the families of the dead were invited to take the body and carry it around the town. The idea was that loved ones and ancestors – some buried for mere decades, others for centuries – should be shown the scraps of land that were still being farmed and the modest homes in order to convince them that everything was well. That the place they had left was still being properly looked after. This unburying drew a crowd. The entire town was there, of course, but in addition several dozen outsiders. Not tourists exactly, but guests, sprinkled in among the people of Brochu. Some of these were anthropology students from America or Europe, whose colleges or parents had agreed to pay the priest or the local council leader enough money that they were invited to attend. It was a cold evening; most of the spectators were wearing several layers and, as she climbed from the back of the car outside the dark little church, Soledad looked freezing. She was escorted to the top of the graveyard and up onto a small podium covered with the same fake grass the diggers used to flank the unfilled graves. The wind was stronger here and her long white gown fluttered at the hem. The moon was bright. Her voice shook slightly as she started to speak.

We are here
Standing with our forefathers and our mothers
Be silent and hear it
The songs of the ancients

Her mother was gesturing to her daughter to raise her voice. The belief was that both the words spoken now at the beginning and the music that was played later needed to be loud enough to waken the ancestors and call them back. She spoke again, louder now.

> We are here
> Here with a sincere and tender heart
> We take them like the bride and hold them near
> We are one in two ways

The unburying was a well-choreographed affair.

Violetta Rojas

The first family moved to the front of the crowd and to the first open grave. A middle-aged man and woman lifted the shroud-covered corpse that was lying alongside the hole and the woman took the long bundle in her arms and held it rather as you might hold a small child. The crowd parted for her as she walked back down the path, past the church and in the direction of the dead woman's old home. A group of musicians began to play, quietly at first, then with more confidence and volume. They were a three-piece outfit, brothers by the look of them. One played a handheld wooden and leather bass drum, the second a lute-like stringed instrument that Jags had seen played a lot in this part of Chile, a *charango* they called it. The back of the thing was often made from armadillo skin. This one thankfully was not – the sight of the skinned animal being plucked and played had a strange effect on Jags – it sickened him. The third and oldest member of the band blew through his grey handlebar moustache into a long, rather wheezy-sounding flute. They were not good musicians, but the music they were making was profoundly, almost unbearably, sad. More names were read, more families came forward and carried or in some cases slowly danced their ancestors away down the path. When the first woman returned, Soledad spoke again.

Sleep peacefully with serenity
We leave you with a flower, to thank you for your kindness

The corpse was placed back alongside the grave and Father Victor strode forward and crossed himself somewhat theatrically before placing a single añañuca flower on top of the shrouded bundle. Most of the families had returned and the ceremony was reaching its close when Soledad suddenly went off script. The first thing Jags noticed was the perplexed look on her mother's face as she stepped down from the podium and began pointing at individual, unopened graves. First she named the occupant: '*Joaquin Martinez*' and then, more loudly, the cause of death: '*accidente de dinamita*'. Next: *Gerardo Bustos . . . roca cayendo . . .* and so it went on. Buried by rockfall . . . dynamite accident . . . mine shaft fall . . . grinding machine . . . silicosis, silicosis, dynamite. Circling the crowd, her voice becoming hoarse, but still loud, she named a dozen names before moving back past the podium, in the direction of a recently dug grave. Jags saw Soledad's mother shaking her head slowly, begging under her breath but Soledad was undeterred.

'*Mi padre. Pablo Mistral. Depresión. Suicidio.*' She paused. '*All these men here . . . and many of our women too . . . they have died too young. They deserved longer lives. And a different death.*'

Jags looked at his feet; he could feel Soledad's eyes on him. He kept staring down until he was sure she'd turned away, then he glanced around the crowd. Several of the anthropology students had their phones out; some held them surreptitiously at their sides, others were more blatant. It didn't matter, all of them had been filming everything. He shook his head.

'Now we're screwed.'

56 An Invitation

Fred studied the brown paper package, tied together not with tape or ribbon, but old-fashioned white cotton string. He liked how she'd done it. The package had been opened already, of course. Opened and poked and prodded and scanned, but once they'd told him who it was from, he'd ordered that it be rewrapped and sent up. He read the card first, which she'd signed *Christy*. Her surname was underneath in closed brackets and next to that a kiss. The parcel contained one of the blue Cloud Chancer sweatshirts. It was a large and Fred was more like a medium, but it didn't matter, there was no way on earth he would ever wear the thing. He hated everything about it, apart from the fact that it was her who had sent it. She'd written her personal mobile on the card – one of the several contacts of hers that he had already. But now he had a reason to call it. More than a reason – an invitation. Cloud Chancer were demo-ing the latest version of their voice recognition software to new investors soon and Christy would *absolutely adore it* if Fred could come.

The electronic mail also brought good news, with an encrypted message from Beijing letting Fred know that they had successfully managed to retrieve one half of the Skype conversation from local storage. They thanked him for his advice and complemented him on his team's professionalism. They wondered whether he might be interested in hearing the material too? He responded immediately – congratulating them on their good fortune, thanking them for their courtesy and confirming that he would indeed like them to send him the material.

57 The Moonlit Flit

CAVERSHAM, ENGLAND

Carver managed to get up off the lumpy single bed on his second try. His head hurt, the result of one glass too many of unwatered whisky. He moved stiff-legged to the window and looked out onto the street. The car didn't leave second gear; it drove slowly down the narrow road that began at the postbox on the corner to just outside McCluskey's front door, where it slowed to a virtual standstill, then drove on. A minute later it was back, doing the same slow loop. Twice could have been a taxi driver looking for a fare, but three times? He doubted it. Carver pulled the bedroom curtains all the way back and stood in the centre of the first-floor window, watching. It was still early, still dark and whoever was driving had the headlights off, so it was difficult to be sure, but it looked like a Mercedes, one of the boxy old models. He liked this kind of car – generally speaking – but not this one, this one had woken him up and now it was pissing him off.

His feet were cold against the bare floorboards and he was only half dressed, white shirt and boxer shorts. He took off his glasses and cleaned them on his shirt tail and when the car came by again, he squinted. It was an odd registration number – three numbers, one letter then three more numbers: 269 D 700 maybe? Or 268? He stepped back from the window, got his notepad and pen from next to the bed and wrote these possible combinations down. When he resumed his watch, the car was making another pass, definitely an old model Merc, but well-kept and black as wet coal. This time the car practically stopped outside the house. Carver muttered under his breath.

'Idiot.' It was the worst surveillance job he'd ever seen. So then the chances were it wasn't a surveillance job.

He took his trousers from the back of the folding chair and pulled them on. He would go down and confront the driver, stand in the road if necessary. He couldn't leave McCluskey when there was this sort of rubbish going on. First some weird woman hanging around outside her kitchen window and now strange cars with D plates driving up and down.

By the time he'd made his way downstairs and out into the street the Merc was gone. He waited a while, but it seemed that whatever message the driver had wanted to send had been sent. Back in the hall, McCluskey was waiting for him, wearing tartan slippers and a floral nightie.

'You woke me up you eejit, all that shuggling about.'

'I'm not going to Hong Kong or anywhere else while these idiots are staking out your house.'

McCluskey shrugged.

'I appreciate the thought Billy, but don't worry yourself.'

'I mean it Jemima, I'm not going anywhere until I know you're going to be all right.'

She paused.

'I've got a sister I can go stay with. She lives down in Brighton. I'll pack up the war room tomorrow, throw some things in a suitcase and do a moonlit flit in the evening. I want you to do what you need to do. You don't have tae worry about me.'

Carver was halfway through slathering the buttered crumpets with a layer of marmalade when McCluskey walked into the kitchen.

'You found yourself some breakfast then?'

'Yes, sorry 'bout that, do you mind?'

'Not a bit. Unless you've eaten the last crumpet in which case I'm going tae gut you like a fish.'

'I think there's one or two left.'

'Super.'

Most days McCluskey listened to World Service dawn 'til dusk, but this morning, as a concession to Carver, she retuned to Radio 4. During the eight o'clock bulletin they both stopped chatting and listened. Hong Kong continued to dominate the news, both the protests and the international response, then there were a few mundane domestic stories. At the end of the bulletin, the *and finally* story was about a letter that had been published in several newspapers this morning, announcing an ambitious partnership between BBC News and the American technology giant Public Square. McCluskey tutted.

'I don't like it when the BBC does stories about itself. Especially not *this* story.' The newsreader read into a clip of Elizabeth Curepipe extolling the virtues of the new arrangement. Carver tried to listen above the sound of McCluskey's tutting. 'That wee girl could sell a bag of *party ice* to an Eskimo.'

He smiled.

'You think this partnership's a bad idea too?'

'Giving away your journalism for nothing? To them? Course it's a bad bloody idea. Public Square want tae eat our lunch and we're running around laying the table for them.'

Carver paused.

'I never told you, she came to see me.'

'She? Curepipe?'

'Yeah.'

'How come?'

'About this letter of hers. She wanted journalists from right across the board to sign it.'

'And?'

Carver looked up from his breakfast and saw the mischievous grin on McCluskey's face.

'Very funny.'

'I hope you told her where to stick it. What did you say?'

'I said *no* of course.'

'Glad to hear it.' She passed him another toasted crumpet. 'It's good to know that your *bullshit detector* is still fully functioning.' McCluskey pulled herself to her feet. 'You should warn your woman Naomi off this whole Public Square thing when you see her – though it sounds like it's already too late.'

'It might not be.'

'How come?'

'I'm going to see someone else up at Broadcasting House at the same time as I see Naomi. You know?'

'Your numbers fellow?'

'Yeah. I asked him to have a little look at Public Square's accounts for me. He messaged me to say he's got some stuff for me to read.'

Carver ate another mouthful of hot buttered crumpet. The whisky hangover was gone and despite the early morning interruption from that black Mercedes, he felt well-slept. The day ahead would be busy in a way his days had not been for quite some time. But he felt fine about that.

58 The Fourth Floor

THE HEADLAND HOTEL, HONG KONG

Viv heard her phone buzz. She picked it up and checked the message. Dan was sitting on the floor opposite her, separated by a coffee table piled high with half eaten takeaway.

'Don't tell me, lemme guess . . . That's our buddy Patrick saying he's not going to join us after all?'

Viv nodded. Patrick had cried off the drinks before this takeaway meal, then said that he'd rather Viv and Dan ate elsewhere since he was still working. Now he wasn't coming at all.

'He's got more work to do, he says he's really sorry.'

'Sure.' Dan took a slug from one of the miniatures they had lined up next to the tin foil takeaway cartons. 'His loss. Shame though, I was hoping he might drop by. You want some more food?'

Viv shook her head.

'I'm stuffed.'

'What's he working on? You never said.'

'He's got Brandon doing something a little left-field. That's

300

probably why it's taking so long. I'm not sure John knows where left field is.'

'What kind of a thing?'

Viv poured the remains of the miniature vodka into the purplish-coloured concoction in her plastic cup.

'Do you remember that kid, Sammy Kwok? We all reported that he died from an asthma attack.'

'Vaguely.'

'Apparently there's more to it than that.'

'I see.' Dan glanced around his room. 'We've kinda trashed this place. Here's an idea – how about you have that bath you've been dreamin' about having while I do the clearing up?'

Viv smiled. She was slightly fuzzy-headed from the Long Island iced tea that they'd made by mixing the contents of Dan's minibar together. She'd mentioned several times how much she missed having a bath. Her room was significantly smaller than his and shower only.

'Really? You're sure you don't mind?'

'I insist. There's new towels in there. And I promise I won't come peek.'

Viv ran the bath almost to full and used half a bottle of bubble bath to get it as foamy as possible before pulling off her tights and green dress. She was about to finish undressing and climb in when she remembered that she had a hairband in her coat pocket. She wrapped a towel around herself, opened the door and stepped back into the bedroom. Dan was sitting cross-legged on the bed, her laptop open in front of him. She stopped.

'What are you doing?' He ignored her. 'Hey, I asked you a question. What're you doing with my computer?' There was still a slight lightness to her voice, incredulity rather than anger.

'I'm just checking a couple of things out.'

'Like what?'

'Some stories I was interested in, some other stuff. It's not a big deal Viv. You go have your bath.'

'I don't want the bath.'

'Have another drink then.' He waved at the row of miniature bottles lined up on the coffee table.

'I don't want a drink either Dan, I want . . .' She took a quick step forward and grabbed the laptop from underneath Dan's hands, '. . . my computer back. This has got BBC stuff on it, confidential stuff.'

Dan sighed.

'You shouldn't have done that Viv.'

'Why?' She glanced down at the screen and saw why. 'How come you're looking at . . .?'

Behind her, in the bathroom, a phone started ringing, her mobile. She clasped the laptop to her chest with one hand and stepped backwards, picking up the phone from beside the sink with her other hand. 'Hello?' She paused. 'Hey there Patrick, how're you?' She took another step back, putting some more distance between her and Dan, who had moved off the bed and was walking towards her. 'Yeah, I'm okay . . .' She paused. 'I'm still here in Dan's room. What can I do for you?' The American was edging closer, staring at her. 'Sure, Paddy you can have Brandon for the rest of the night, he's all yours . . .' Dan had stopped at the bathroom door.

'Finish the call.' The words were whispered. *'Just tell him goodbye. You and I need to talk . . .'* She edged further back, past the sink, the back, of her legs against the side of the bath. She needed to think.

'. . . was there anything else Patrick?' She paused, long enough that a question could have been asked. 'Oh yeah, that new gear you've been talking about? I think it might be down on the fourth floor, Patrick. I, er . . . I don't know.'

Dan stepped forward and grabbed the phone, switching it off

before throwing it behind him, back onto the bed. Viv stared at him, incredulous.

'That's it. Get out of this bathroom Dan, I'm going to get dressed, get my stuff and go.'

'You don't need to do that Viv. We were having a good time, weren't we? How about we just press reset?'

'How about you tell me why you were logged in as me, Dan? How do you know my password? Why were you looking at those shared files?'

The American shook his head.

'I was curious, it's not a big deal.'

'It's a big deal to me Dan . . .' She grabbed her dress and tights. 'Please, step out of my way.'

Dan sighed and stepped aside to let her pass.

'Ah, Viv.' He smiled. 'I want you to know, I really hoped it wasn't going to play out this way.'

59 Departures

Carver nodded at the security guard on reception at Broadcasting House and swished himself in through the tall glass revolving doors. Down in the main newsroom – *the pit* as most of the hacks here at the BBC called it – it was business as usual. Dozens of journalists sitting closely together in a space-saving pattern of white desks and black computer monitors. Carver stared at the large screen that listed the most recent radio and TV despatches filed by BBC correspondents elsewhere in the world: Washington, Tokyo, Sydney. The city and then the name of the reporter and the time the story was sent. At the top of the list were several *HongKongBrandons*. He sniffed and headed for the lift.

As McCluskey had predicted, Naomi was delighted to hear about Carver's travel plans.

'I thought I'd lost you to teaching for good to be honest William, and your timing is excellent. Patrick's exhausted, every time I talk to him these last few days he sounds worse. You'll be just the tonic he needs.' She told Carver she'd help the School of Journalism find a replacement to sub in for him for a few weeks and asked if he needed any new equipment. He shook his head. He had his own stuff, plus a couple of bits of kit that McCluskey had insisted he take with him.

'Nah, the MiniDisc and Marantz are fine and I've still got one of the office laptops.'

Naomi lifted an eyebrow.

'That must be seven or eight years old by now. I assumed all of those were in landfill in China. It still works okay?'

'It's slow, but it's fine.'

She opened her mouth to say something, then thought better of it.

'Sounds like you're all set. When are you planning to go?'

Carver thought about this. He needed to book a flight, pack his stuff and see or at least speak to McCluskey and Rebecca once more. He wanted to make sure that McCluskey's sister had agreed that she could go stay with her and also suggest to Rebecca that she moved somewhere else for a week or two. Perhaps her parents could put her up?

'Tomorrow. I'll book a seat on the first flight out of Heathrow. I reckon I can do everything I need to do between now and then.'

Naomi offered to buy Carver a quick lunch down in the canteen, but he refused; he was due to meet Donnie shortly and he needed to get a wiggle on.

They'd arranged to meet at the coffee shop just outside New Broadcasting House. It was a sunny late autumn day and having looked around inside the café, Carver took a table outside. It was quieter out on the piazza and there was less chance of being over-heard. Donnie appeared outside the glass revolving doors carrying a blue Ikea reusable bag in each hand, both stuffed almost to overflowing with documents. Carver watched him waddle his way over and waited while he unburdened himself.

'What the hell is all that?'

'That's one hundred and eighty quid's worth of photocopying

and printing is what that is.' He sat down heavily and pushed his beanie hat back away from his forehead; he was sweating. 'It's also five years' worth of Public Square accounts . . .' He pushed the bags back towards the wall with his boot. '. . . and all their shareholder reports too.' He stared at the empty table. 'Where's my coffee?'

'I've not bought anything yet. There's a queue.'

'Well you better go stand in it. I'll have a gingerbread latte and a blueberry muffin.'

'Fine.'

'Chocolate sprinkles on the latte.'

When Carver got back, Donnie had a handful of the many hundreds of documents he'd printed off fanned out in front of him on the table. He took a slurp of his sugary coffee and cleared his throat.

'So Public Square is quite a company. It's like an octopus with about a billion tentacles. It's here, there – every fuckin' where.'

'You told me you were a shareholder.'

'I am.'

'So surely you had an idea about the kind of stuff it does?'

'I had a vague idea – tech, phones, mining. I knew a bit about it, like just about every other shareholder I reckon. But that stuff isn't even the half of it. Way less than half.'

'Can you give me the headlines?'

Donnie talked Carver through some of what he'd found, but it soon became too detailed for William to make much sense of it.

'What's the most interesting thing Donnie?'

'The most interesting? Okay, so Public Square's research spend is something incredible.'

'Like big?'

'Like the GDP of a medium-sized country big. And the income streams that fund the research flow straight into that bit of the business – they don't go anywhere near the main company.'

'And that's unusual?'

'Yep.'

'Why would somebody want to do things that way?'

'Well, it looks to me like some of that money's coming from interesting old places: Philippines, Myanmar, China . . . all via the usual offshore favourites – Cayman, Panama, Channel Islands and the rest.' Donnie pointed at the Ikea bags, stuffed with documents. 'It's all in here, that and much more I'll bet. I've only skimmed the surface.'

'Right, so you've not finished?'

Donnie laughed.

'I've got a full-time job here at the BBC and several other full-time jobs in other places too. I haven't got time to go through all this for you line by line. You're lucky I found the time to do what I did.'

'Sure. I'm sorry Donnie, I'm grateful. But what am I supposed to do with all this? I'm flying to Hong Kong first thing tomorrow.'

Donnie shrugged.

'Where's that lanky blond kid who used to do all the work you didn't want to do?'

'Patrick?'

'That's him.'

'He's in Hong Kong already.'

'Well then, I guess you're either going to have to find yourself a new sucker or . . .' He waved a hand at the Ikea bags again. '. . . you're going to have to shell out for some serious excess baggage.'

Carver thought for a moment.

'Now you mention it, there might be someone.'

60 Video Nasties

Jags threw the Chilean burner phone back in the glove and slammed it shut. He took the notepad from inside his jacket pocket and read a few of the poems he'd written in recent weeks. The haikus were crap, he knew that, but they helped to calm him and right now he needed some of that.

> Through a car window
> A moonlit mining town, hills
> One man awake, me

He remembered sitting almost exactly here and scribbling that down – not so long ago either. He'd written it just before going to hang Soledad's father. No moonlight now, hardly any light at all in fact, despite it being mid-afternoon. A leaden sky and the steady drizzling rain meant he could barely see the pockmarked metal Brochu sign that he was parked next to, let alone the town or hills or dam.

'Shit.'

He got the burner phone back out of the glove and re-read the recent exchange of text messages between him and Fred.

'*Another day, another video nasty featuring your new recruit. I'm sending help.*'

Jags had messaged straight back.

'*I don't want help.*'

'*I'm not asking you any more. I'm telling you. He'll arrive tomorrow. He'll tell you what needs to be done. No more messages.*'

So that was that. Soledad had texted him too, asking to meet, possibly to apologise or explain what her performance at the unburying had been meant to achieve. Although Jags doubted it. There was no point in a meeting now anyway, not yet. He had to wait and meet this guy that Fred was sending and work out what his function was. It would be a recent graduate from Fred's school for former military or intelligence agency people. It might even be one of the individuals that Jags had watched taking that test during his tour of Department Eight. Sending one of his most recent recruits to put Jags back in line would appeal to Fred's sense of humour. The more he thought about it, the more convinced Jags was that the man being sent to straighten things out *would* be someone he'd seen in that room. He ran through what he remembered of each of them. It turned out to be a fair amount.

They were all younger than Jags, that almost went without saying. No doubt some were stronger and one or two were probably quicker. But none were more experienced. Experience sometimes gave you half a second's advantage and in Jags' line of work, half a second was usually enough. If it came to it – then he would kill Soledad himself. He'd do it before they could. Jags could do it quick and kind – which Fred's man might not. He pulled a pack of cigarettes from his bomber jacket and lit one. He took a deep draw and opened the car window a couple of inches to let some fresh air in.

He remembered something that Soledad's father had said, just before he'd died. Some old Chilean superstition about having to carry the soul of the man you kill around with you, carry it on your back. Jags shook his head. The burden he'd been chosen to carry wasn't a dead man's soul; it was his daughter's life. He got his notebook and pencil back out and turned to a fresh page.

Fuck fuck fuck fuck fuck
Fuck fuck fuck fuck fuck fuck fuck
Fuck fuck fuck fuck fuck

Elizabeth had asked him to promise that he would go to her if he was ever unhappy with one of Fred's orders. He smoked some more of the Marlboro, pulling so hard on the filter that his head felt dizzy. He was unhappy now.

'*You can talk to me . . . any time.*' That was what she'd said. He'd bought a new phone, unregistered with Public Square, the number unknown to anyone but him. Him *and* Elizabeth, if he decided to take a chance and call or message her. If the risk had been his alone, then he almost certainly would have called her already. But it was not. Such a move risked putting Elizabeth in harm's way and he could not countenance that.

61 Slow Journalism

PORTLAND PLACE, LONDON, W1

Naz answered on the second ring.

'Yeah?'

'Hello, is that . . .'

'Whatever it is you're selling bruv, I'm not buying.'

'Er, okay. It's William Carver here, Naz. Your journalism teacher?'

'Oh shit. I mean, sorry sir, I thought you were some random man.'

'I see. Well . . .'

'What can I do for you Mr Carver?' She paused. 'Is this about the essay deadline?' There was a slight nervousness in her voice.

'What? No, you can take as long as you like with that.'

'Ah, cool.'

'It's something else. What're you doing right now Naz?'

'Right now? I'm doing a little karaoke.'

'Karaoke? In the middle of the day?'

'Yeah, just practising. I'm pretty serious about my karaoke. I can do this any time though, what d'you need?'

'I've got a job for you, a journalistic job. How long will it take you to get into town, Oxford Circus?'

It took Naz forty minutes. Carver stayed where he was, sitting outside the café on the BBC piazza; there was no way he was going to lug those Ikea bags around if he didn't have to. He read through a few copies of Public Square's shareholder reports and ate a disappointing tuna sandwich while he waited. When Naz arrived, wearing her usual jeans and tracksuit top and looking like she'd run from the tube station, Carver let her catch her breath and then gave her the background.

'You've heard of Elizabeth Curepipe? Public Square?'

'Sure.'

'I'm doing a little investigative work.'

'Investigating her, why?'

'Well, partly because she has shown an interest in me and I figure it would be rude not to return the favour. But also she's pitching this partnership between Public Square and the BBC and I'm not so sure about it.'

'Why not? She's amazing, it'll be brilliant.'

'Okay. Well, you might be right, but I prefer it if you tried to keep an open mind while you're doing this job I need you to do . . .'

Carver explained what he needed Naz to do; he removed a few more of the documents and went through them with her.

'The key to doing something like this Naz – I probably said this to you in class – is that you need to *turn every page* . . .'

Naz looked at the Ikea bags.

'That's a lot of pages.'

'I hadn't finished . . . *Turn every page, read every word*.'

'Right.' She nodded knowingly. 'I get what you're talking about Mr Carver. You mean, like, *slow journalism*.'

Carver pulled a face.

'I suppose so. But it didn't used to be called slow journalism.'

'What was it called?'

'Just journalism.'

'Okay . . .' She sucked at her teeth. '. . . you said this is a job, right Mr Carver?'

'Right. I'll pay you . . .' He paused. '. . . the minimum wage is around six quid an hour these days I think.'

'The London living wage is more like twelve.'

'I'll give you seven.'

Naz sucked at her teeth some more.

'Even the *Hounslow Chronicle* pays ten.' This was smart.

Carver nodded.

'Okay, I'll pay bloody ten . . . but keep a proper account of the hours and read quickly.'

'I'll do my best Mr Carver, but I need to *turn every page, read every . . .*'

'Yeah, yeah. Very good.' He looked at his watch. 'I need to get going.' He stood up from the table. 'This is a bit of proper journalism I'm giving you to do here Naz. And a test of your initiative too.'

'Right.' She looked at the Ikea bags. 'How am I supposed to get this lot back home to Hounslow?'

'There's the first initiative test right there. I'll message you as soon as I've got a Hong Kong mobile. Good luck.'

62 The Common Denominator

Halfway across the Public Square campus, Fred stopped briefly to admire the elaborate sprinkler system that was watering a tennis court-sized patch of plastic grass. The Astroturf didn't need water of course, but Fred enjoyed the sight and, in particular, the sound the sprinklers made; they brought back a childhood memory that he was fond of – hence the pointless, pretty sprinkling.

Up inside his office, Elizabeth was waiting. She'd left for work even earlier than him that morning, which was unusual.

'Hey husband of mine, how're things?'

'Everything's good thank you . . .' He sat down behind his desk and switched on his computer; the machine whirred quietly into life. The screen, almost as long as the desk itself, flickered. '. . . are you well?'

'Very well.'

It was obvious that Elizabeth had something she wanted to ask him, but in the meantime, he needed to work. Everything was *not* good. As Elizabeth watched, Fred's eyes assumed that glazed, lifeless look they got when he was concentrating hard on something. He moved the mouse around, a frown clouding his face.

'What's the problem Fred?'

He looked up from the screen.

'I never asked you how that meeting with the old BBC guy went. What's his name again?'

Elizabeth looked at him.

'I'm pretty sure you remember what his name is Fred, let's not play games. My meeting with William Carver was interesting but ultimately unsuccessful.'

'Right . . .' He paused. '. . . are you familiar with that old piece of folkloric advice about how best to deal with a sleeping dog, Lizzie?'

She laughed.

'Don't patronise me Fred. What's the problem? What's Carver done that's upset you?'

'Nothing serious, not yet but . . .'

'Let me guess . . . you're in the *nipping in the bud* business?'

'That's right.'

'I can talk to him again . . . if you like.'

'I don't like.' He sighed. 'Don't worry Lizzie, I shouldn't have mentioned it, it's fine. I'll sort it . . .' He looked up from his screen again and smiled. '. . . it's really not that big a deal.'

'Okay.'

'Now what was it you wanted?'

'I wanted to ask if you knew where Jags was at?'

'He's in Chile. Checking that everything's the way we need it to be before you fly down there.' Fred paused. 'You knew that was the plan, how come you're asking?'

'No reason. I'm just really keen to make that trip, I wondered if you'd heard from him?'

Fred lied easily.

''Fraid not.'

They arranged to have lunch together in the Public Square canteen. Fred never particularly enjoyed doing this, but he did it anyway. Once a month was usually enough to send a message to the staff that they were all in it together.

After Elizabeth had left, Fred went back to work. He'd been wrong about William Carver and that annoyed him. Carver wasn't a major problem but nor was he a *busted flush*. More an inconvenience. Fred had the right people in all the right places to deal with him and his associates – people Fred could rely on. You needed to be able to rely on people and the only way you could do that was if you knew all about them. *Secrecy equalled unpredictability*. He glanced up from his screen and out across the glass-walled offices. Elizabeth was nowhere to be seen.

He typed in the password that allowed him complete access rights to Public Square data past and present. *God Mode*. An alert would notify Elizabeth that he'd looked at her file, but that wasn't unusual. Fred liked to check her diary. She wouldn't know why he was looking at it, or for what. On the other side of his screen he pulled up every piece of data he had on Jags – travel records, phone records, search history, Public Square . . . everything. A new piece of code he had would run across both files simultaneously – again and again and again. Until it found something it considered interesting – a coincidence, a common denominator, a clue. Fred sat back and let it run.

63 Ringing True

Viv was missing. The only people who knew it so far were Patrick, John Brandon and a handful of bosses back in London. The instruction from that end was not to push the panic button, not yet. They'd spoken to her parents, in part to check that she hadn't been in touch, but also to reassure them that they were doing everything they could to find her. It had only been fourteen hours since she'd last been seen, Dan had said goodbye to her at the door to his room just shy of midnight as far as he remembered – she was heading in the direction of the lifts and her bedroom. Patrick had one of the hotel security guards open the door using a master key and found the bed still made and no sign either of her or any of her kit – phone, laptop or anything else that she'd had with her earlier in the evening. Dan suggested they check through the CCTV to see if she might have left the hotel for some reason, but it seemed she hadn't, at least not by the front entrance and why would she use any other? The CCTV confirmed that she'd left Dan's room at three minutes to twelve; it showed her in the lift and then walking into her own bedroom a few minutes

317

later. After that, nothing. Patrick kept ringing her phone and leaving increasingly worried-sounding messages, despite the fact that her mobile was obviously switched off.

'*Where the hell are you Viv?*'

He tossed the phone onto the bed and paced his room. He reran the last conversation he'd had with her in his head – or as much of it as he could remember. He'd been checking he could keep hold of Brandon for the rest of the evening and apologising again for not being able to join her and Dan in his room. She'd interrupted him to say something odd about some new kit that had arrived and that he could go collect it. He had no clue what it was she was talking about and she'd hung up on him before he could get it straight. He remembered thinking that if it was a big deal then she'd call him back, he was busy. Now, however, it seemed significant, or potentially significant anyway. He retrieved the phone and scrolled down through his contacts until he came to *Colorado Dan*. The American picked up on the second ring.

'Patrick. How you doin'?'

'I'm okay. But still no news from this end. You?'

'Me neither buddy. I'm sorry . . .'

'Dan, were you in the room with her when I rang last night?'

There was a pause.

'Yeah, I was in the room, but I wasn't really tuned in. I was sending some copy back to the paper right around then, I seem to recall.'

'Viv said something I didn't really understand. Something about going to collect some kit. You don't have any idea what she was talking about do you?'

'No clue, sorry.'

'Her voice sounded . . . odd.'

'She was fine, she was having a good time. It could've been she was a little drunk? We were both pretty liquored up last night.'

'Right. I see. Maybe that was it.' Patrick paused. '. . . and you're sure she didn't leave anything in your room? Her phone, laptop, purse, nothing?'

'Not a thing. You saw the CCTV, she took everything back to her room with her.'

'Right.'

64 Negative Treatment

Jags' instructions were to pick the guy up from Santiago International and drive to Brochu together, but he was damned if he was going to hang about in arrivals with a board held up. He parked the Chevy on the top floor of the short stay car park and messaged to say where he was. He wound his window down and watched planes take off and land until he caught sight of a well-built young man in sunglasses, white T-shirt and camo pants who could only be looking for him. The fellow looked tall when Jags noticed him in the wing mirror and even taller by the time he reached the car.

'Hi.'

'Hi.'

'I'm Nate . . . Nathan.'

'You're not sure?'

The guy smiled. A real-looking smile, he was nervous.

'Let's go with Nathan.'

'Right, glad we got that sorted. Do you want to get in, or do you want to run after the car while I drive?' Nathan looked like

320

he could run a good part of the way from here to Brochu without drawing sweat, but he decided to get in the car anyway, pushing his kitbag down into the footwell. Jags noticed that he'd placed it zip end up and not by accident. His own gun he'd moved from the glove compartment to the map holder on the driver's side door. Nathan was a lefty from what Jags had seen so far and Jags was right-handed; this would leave him at a slight disadvantage. Hopefully they wouldn't have to try to shoot each other straight away. 'Where to?'

'Er, Brochu I guess.'

'You guess? I was told you were the man with the plan. That you were going to tell me what was going to happen.'

'I'll tell you on the way.'

'Okay.'

They drove in silence for a while, Nathan drinking in the scenery and trying to get the measure of the man sitting next to him.

'You saw me back in Cupertino, I was taking a test. Maybe you remember?'

'My memory's not great.'

Nathan smiled.

'You saw me. And I saw you back.'

Jags nodded. The kid was beginning to find his feet.

'How did you do? In the test?'

'Aced it. Aced all of it. *Summa cum laude* and all that crap.' Jags nodded. If he had to guess he'd say this boy was a farm boy, Midwest like him and clever, like him. And itchy-footed.

'So how come you quit the army?'

Nathan sniffed. Jags had guessed right.

'Other opportunities presented themselves. Like you I guess.'

'Right decision so far?'

'So far, great decision. Too many meatheads in the army, I'm not one of those.'

'No . . .' He glanced across at his passenger. '. . . I bet you're not.'

The road started to get steep, and Jags shifted down a gear. 'Get us, shooting the breeze. We could probably talk all day, but you know what? I think I'd like you to tell me what the fuck the plan is now, Nathan. If you don't mind.'

The young man nodded.

'We're going to offer her a scholarship. Somewhere in the States, anywhere she likes. Get her out of the way.'

He set it out at some length – memorised perhaps, as Jags could hear Fred's voice in much of what he told him. Soledad would be given a fully funded scholarship to any American University she chose – Harvard, Yale, MIT, New York if she wanted to go to New York – her choice. The objective was to get her the hell away from Brochu, out of the country, until things were working the way the company wanted them to work. They could leave open the option for her to come back later and play a role. Public Square had provided this sort of opportunity many times before and the kids who took the scholarships were often a lot more employable, more useful to the company after the scholarship than before. Jags listened carefully.

'And the mother gets to keep her job here?'

'We don't give a shit about the mother.'

'Okay. And if Soledad says no.'

'We don't think she will.'

'Is that right? But if she does . . .?'

The young man glanced around the car, scanning the dash and the sills above the windows. Jags shook his head and smiled.

'Don't worry Nathan. This is a very old Chevy, the only thing listening to you in *here*, is *me*.'

He nodded.

'If it should come to that, then we'd be authorised to use *negative treatment* . . .' He turned and looked at Jags. '. . . you understand?'

'I understand what *negative treatment* means, yes. I just thought it was only Mossad who called it that.'

'Well . . .'

'So let me get this straight, Nate – either she says yes to the scholarship, or else Fred wants us to kill her.'

65 Letters

STOCKWELL ROAD, LONDON

Carver had bought a block of slow-release goldfish food, although it looked to him like it was releasing too much food, too fast. His fish couldn't believe their luck.

'Slow down you idiots, that has to last you a fortnight at least.' He scooped the block of food back out with a wooden spoon – he'd drop it back in just before he left – and went to check his luggage one more time.

Packing had taken longer than he thought it would. Most of yesterday evening, in fact, and much longer than it used to. He'd recovered his grab bag from behind the door, dusted it down and checked the contents. Unsurprisingly, the three sets of clothes that had been stuffed in there for over a year smelt a little musty, but he could live with that, he'd air them when he arrived. He'd checked that both passports were still in date and counted the money and he did the same again now. He had more euros and American dollars than he would need and not enough Hong Kong dollars, but he could sort that at the airport. His washbag contained everything that a washbag should, although the toothpaste had dried in the tube so he'd made a mental note to buy some of that at Heathrow too. Most importantly his recording equipment – the MiniDisc recorder and the Marantz – were in full working order. After checking them, he had wrapped them back up inside their yellow plastic bag along with the bit of kit that McCluskey had given him. What took the longest amount of time was deciding what he should wear to travel in, not something that he ever remembered having thought about before. He'd got quite attached to his brown corduroy jacket, but that seemed like the wrong choice, as did the brogues and briefcase. In the end he decided on his favourite pair of Farah trousers, black Doc Marten shoes and an old blue blazer that had gone a little glacé at the elbows, but was otherwise fine. It wasn't until this morning, when he put these clothes on, that he realised this was exactly what he'd been wearing the day he returned home from Egypt – his last foreign assignment.

He put the bag by the door and went to make himself a quick tea and a slice of buttered toast. He wanted to call McCluskey and find out whether she'd made it down to her sister's yet. He suspected not, since her packing job was considerably more daunting than his. He checked the time. He'd have to call her from the airport, since more pressing now was the arrangement he'd made with Rebecca to meet at Paddington station. She wanted to give him a letter to take to Patrick and she'd arranged a later-than-usual start at her school in order to do it. Carver would meet her at the statue of the bear and then jump onto the Heathrow Express.

Carver wondered what the station staff did with all the jars of marmalade that children and Japanese tourists left next to the Paddington statue. Most likely they'd have to bin them for health and safety reasons. It was a shame, there was a jar of perfectly good Dundee orange thick-cut with its seal still on. He moved to a nearby bench and sat down; Rebecca was late but the underground was horrible this morning and the trains to Heathrow left every fifteen minutes or so – he had time. He was about to use that time to call McCluskey, when he saw Rebecca frantically circling the statue. With her blond bob and wearing a red raincoat with a brown satchel on her back, she looked like a character from a children's book herself. He waved, picked up his bag and walked over. She was apologising before he was even within earshot.

'. . . and that change at King's Cross is such a nightmare, I'd forgotten, I'm so sorry. I was absolutely certain that I'd missed you . . .' Her forehead was damp with sweat and she looked pale.

'It's fine, I've got time. Are you all right? Do you want to sit down? I can go grab you a tea if you like?'

She shook her head and pushed her hand back through her hair then glanced at her wet palm.

'No, I'm fine. I mean I'm sure I look a fright, but I'm generally fine. Let me give you this letter and then you can run. I need to get off to school anyway.' She unshouldered her bag, opened it and pulled out a long cream-coloured envelope. She'd written Patrick's name on it in bright blue ink and underlined it. 'Here it is . . .' She held it briefly in both hands before passing it over. '. . . thank you so much for agreeing to take it.'

'It's nothing.' He stuck it in his inside pocket, next to his passport. 'Have you thought about what I suggested? Moving in with a friend or your parents for a week or two?'

She nodded.

'Yes, I did. My mum and dad are back from holiday in a couple of days. I can go stay with them, if you think that's a good idea?'

'I do.'

'Fine. Consider it done.' She attempted a smile but it wouldn't quite stick. 'I hope you have a good trip William. Or a safe trip anyway. Say hello to Patrick for me, say . . .' No words came. '. . . well maybe just give him the letter.'

'I will.'

The floor interested both of them equally. Neither seemed sure how best to bring the encounter to a close. Carver didn't know whether he should try to give her a consoling hug? Or shake her hand? Or what? The moment passed – Rebecca put her satchel back on and, with a brief wave, turned and left. Carver watched until he lost sight of her among the crowds of commuters streaming back down into the underground. He picked up his bag and was about to head for the train when the jar of Dundee thick-cut caught his eye again. He reached down and picked it up. A tourist – French by the sound of her accent – was watching him and tutted.

'What is it you are doing?'

'I'm taking this marmalade.'

'It is not yours.'

'No, that's true. But realistically . . .' Carver pointed at Paddington's stony countenance. '. . . he's not going to eat it, is he?' He stuck it in his blazer pocket and walked purposefully in the direction of his platform.

66 The Good News

Soledad knew trouble when she saw it. As Jags and his fellow American pulled up outside the house she called her youngest brother in from out of the yard where he'd been playing keepy-uppy with a battered-looking leather football. She gave him a handful of change and sent him off in the direction of the shop. Jags overheard the instruction she gave him as she was zipping up his jacket.

'Buy whatever you like, but don't come back until you see that this car has gone.'

With Claudio gone, she was alone in the house. She invited the two men into the front room and sat them down at the small dining table. She directed her attention at Jags only, scarcely acknowledging the other American's presence.

'I left you messages – after the ceremony – you ignored me.'

'I was busy.'

'Busy waiting for your bosses to tell you what you should do about me?'

Jags smiled.

'It was quite a performance Soledad, nobody who was at the unburying this year will forget it in a hurry.'

'I called you because I wanted to explain.'

'Explain? Or apologise?'

She shook her head.

'I have nothing to apologise for. I did what I did for a reason.'

'Which was?'

'By reminding everyone how bad things *have been* here in Brochu, people are more united than ever around the idea of changing the town.' Nathan sighed heavily and Soledad shot him a look before resuming her conversation with Jags. 'That one-page document you gave me said that Public Square wanted to *take the people with you.*'

'Right.'

'So now they're with you.' Jags nodded slowly. He had no doubt that Soledad had persuaded Brochu to back her. The problem was that the changes she imagined and the change that Public Square was offering were two very different things. She jutted her chin in Nathan's direction while still addressing Jags. 'And this man? What is this man here for?'

'Ask him.'

She looked at Nathan now, who to his credit managed to hold her stare.

'Have you read my list of proposals for Brochu?'

The young American nodded.

'Oh, yeah. Yeah I took a look at that.'

'Good. So what happens now? We negotiate?'

'Negotiate? No, what we do is . . .'

Jags interrupted.

'This is Nathan, I picked him up from the airport in Santiago, he's just flown in from California. He had some good news to give you and we thought we'd do that face to face.'

'Good news?'

'Yup. You remember how, when we first met, you told me you wanted to get your mother and brothers all set up so you could get away, see some new places?'

Soledad nodded.

'Sure.'

'Well, it looks like we might be able to make that happen sooner rather than later.'

Jags sold the offer of the scholarship as persuasively as he could. He did a better job than Nathan would have done – emphasising the fact that her mother would work, her family would be looked after, holding out the possibility of her returning with a bunch of qualifications and better able to help Brochu in the long term. He saw the occasional flicker of interest but no more than that. When he'd done, Soledad stood up from the table.

'I realise that I've not offered you anything to eat or drink. My mother would be angry with me.'

Jags shook his head.

'It's not necessary.'

'It is necessary. At least let me get you a drink of water.' Soledad disappeared behind the wooden screen that separated the living area from the kitchen. Jags and Nathan listened. They heard the fridge door open and close again, but that didn't mean the water they were about to be offered was bottled; more likely the family just kept a jug of tap water in the fridge. Nathan had read the briefing notes on Brochu, most likely memorised them too. He knew not to drink the water, he probably knew exactly how much manganese, mercury and iron there was in every glass. Jags watched all this play out on his face. Soledad returned holding three mugs. Nathan sat, arms folded as she put one of these down in front of him.

'You ain't got water glasses?'

'I'm afraid not.' She slid the other mug across to Jags and then raised her own. 'Cheers.' She took a gulp. Nathan picked the mug up, but did not drink. The fact that *she* was drinking the water counted for nothing. She was local, she'd been drinking this shit for years, she'd probably got used to it. He hadn't.

'I'm not thirsty.'

'No?' Soledad laughed. 'Don't worry, I don't blame you. I won't consider you rude Mr Nathan. And I hope you won't consider me rude when I say I am not interested in your scholarship. So I suppose that means this meeting is over. You came all the way from California for nothing.'

'We'll see.' Nathan stood, his chair scraping against the floor noisily as he did so. He looked down at Jags. 'Let's go.'

'Be patient . . .' He took a gulp from his mug of water and looked at Soledad. '. . . maybe you need a little time to think about this? Talk to your mother? Your brothers?'

She shook her head.

'Thank you, but I have thought about it. I want to stay and make the project Public Square have proposed work for the people here in Brochu. I'm happy to talk about that, but I don't want to hear any more about scholarships.'

They were ten kilometres outside Brochu, heading for the guest-house where Jags liked to stay, before either man spoke. Nathan gave a mirthless laugh and turned to look at Jags.

'How the fuck d'you explain a thing like that?'

'Like what?'

'We're offering that girl a ticket out of this shithole, a proper well-paid job further down the line. She should have been down on her knees, kissing our feet.'

'I guess she didn't see it that way.'

Nathan made the laughing sound again.

'I guess not.' They drove in silence for several more kilometres before Nathan spoke again. 'So how d'you want to proceed with Plan B?'

'Plan B? I'm not sure.' Jags paused. 'What did Fred suggest we do?'

Nathan shrugged.

'He told me *you'd* know what to do. He said you'd probably want to play it the same way you did with all the others.'

Jags nodded slowly.

'*All the others*. Of course. So I killed all those men . . .' He paused. '. . . men and some boys – I killed them in various out-of-the-way places. Somewhere well outside town. I shot or stabbed them . . .' He paused. '. . . strangled one of them too, now I remember. And then we pushed their bodies down into the tailings dam late at night. Soledad's old man and me. Weighed them down with rocks so they'd sink quicker.' Jags glanced across at Nathan to see what he made of this.

'Fine. Let's do that then, if that's what works.' The young American hadn't heard Jags' confession. All he'd heard was a plan.

67 Priorities

The express train to Heathrow was extortionately expensive but swift, which was just as well since the rest of the process took an age. There were long queues at the bag drop, passport control and especially going through security where no one was having a good time. While he was removing his shoes and belt for X-ray, someone dropped their roll-along suitcase with a loud gunshot sound, shredding the passengers' already frayed nerves. It seemed that air travel – once one of William's great pleasures – was no longer fun, not even a tiresome chore. It was *an ordeal*. Carver made it to the gate with just a few minutes to spare. He sat where he could keep an eye on the queue for boarding, got his phone out and dialled McCluskey's landline.

'Yes?'

'You're still at home then?'

'For someone who's supposed to have given up the journalism, you're still bloody nosy. Are you my mother?'

'No.'

'I thought not. You're uglier than her. . . not much, but a

333

wee bit. I'm leaving in a couple of hours, the suitcase is in the hall.'

'You managed to get all those papers in one suitcase?'

'One case and a carpet bag. Don't worry about me, it's all in hand. Worry about yourself, they should be calling your flight around now, no?'

'It's boarding now.' He paused. 'So, I'll be in touch once I meet up with Patrick. I'll get a new chuck away phone and message you the number.'

'Smashing.'

'Anything you'd like bringing back from Hong Kong?'

McCluskey sucked at her teeth.

'Now you mention it, that snow globe you got me last time you and the boy were there, the one with the harbour in it?'

'Yes.'

'It was shite. If they've got anything better – glass, no plastic. Then I'd take that.'

'I'll make it a priority.'

'You do that Billy, an'. . . take care.'

'Sure. And you too Jemi—' But she'd hung up.

McCluskey unplugged the phone at the socket and walked back towards the hall. There was no suitcase there. If Carver or Patrick wanted her help, then everything she needed to provide that help was here in this house. She could hardly transport her entire house to her sister's in Brighton. Especially as she didn't have a sister in Brighton. She didn't have a sister at all. But there was no need to worry Carver with these sorts of details right now, he had enough on his plate.

68 Hackathon

PUBLIC SQUARE HQ, CUPERTINO, CALIFORNIA

The weather was so good that weekend that Elizabeth decided to hold the annual hackathon outside in the grounds around Public Square HQ instead of inside the Zaha Hadid-designed auditorium as was usual. The previous year, Fred had asked the team to work on inventing a computer that could smell and the results had been interesting. But it was Elizabeth's turn to set the task this year and she'd decided to choose something more obviously useful and, she believed, worthwhile.

By nine a.m. the entire staff of Public Square was sitting in neat lines of white folding chairs on the great lawn in front of the glass egg. The scene resembled a graduation ceremony or a huge wedding and at the front, on a raised platform standing behind a clear plastic lectern with Fred sitting nearby, was Elizabeth. She wore a knee-length, lemon yellow dress and black Nike high tops and the massed ranks of Public Square employees gazed up at her and waited while she shuffled her cue cards around and readied herself to speak. She tapped a red-painted nail on the microphone and surveyed the crowd. She still sometimes got a little nervous addressing larger gatherings like this.

'Good morning.' There was a chorus of *good mornings* in response and she smiled her hundred-watt smile. 'So I know you guys have heard my old *Mom and Pop's semiconductor shop* story about a billion times . . .'

A wise ass at the back couldn't resist.

'But we're 'bout to hear it again . . .'

Elizabeth laughed.

'Maybe. And you, Mawhinney . . .' she pointed at the heckler '. . . are on a warning.' There was laughter and applause. She knew his name. She knew the names of every person that worked here at Public Square, close on three hundred and eighty people. No one knew how she did it, but she did. 'In actual fact, Mawhinney, I'm not going to tell that story again. I'm going to tell you a new story, but it's one that I hope might become as important to me as that hoary old tale. So make yourselves comfortable . . .'

The preamble to this year's hackathon was nothing less than a new mission statement.

'Thanks to your incredible hard work and your cleverness, in less than ten years Public Square has helped transform our under-standing of what humans are capable of. Along the way, we have also grown into one of the world's most successful and respected companies.' There were whoops and cheers, which Elizabeth lifted a hand to calm. 'Every aspect of the *human experience* . . . or, as my brilliant husband prefers to call it, *behavioural data* . . .' More laughter. '. . . every aspect is of interest to us and we learn more every day. But this year I wanted us to remind ourselves *why* we are interested.' She paused. 'It's not about making money. We have enough money . . .' She spotted her heckler again, stage whispering to his neighbours. 'I promise you, Mawhinney, I will can your ass. I know exactly how much I paid you last year and trust me, it's enough money – way too much in fact.' Elizabeth wanted silence for what she was about to say and so she waited.

'For me, this company of ours only has *one* purpose.' Three hundred and eighty people sat in silence, waiting to find out what this was. 'How do we learn to become better humans? Tech is the toolkit but *being better people* is the objective. That is our job.'

The task Elizabeth was setting reflected this. She wanted Public Square employees to use their combined brainpower to help aid organisations more accurately monitor the movement of refugees, so that food and medicine and other forms of relief could be distributed more efficiently and fairly.

'These are the sorts of spaces where I want us to be. These are the *people* I want us to be. In times of natural disasters – tsunamis and earthquakes – when dreadful diseases like Ebola are running riot like now, after terrorist attacks – the list is horribly long. In times of great need we should be there – making a difference. *Earning trust and learning stuff.*'

Fred took over to talk through how the day was going to work; he wanted different teams to look at the problem from different angles and come up with solutions.

'Off the top of my head these might include heatmapping, satellite imagery, tracking their phones and any other tech that shows up in the places we usually look . . . you guys know what to do and you'll come up with different ideas. We'll come together every two hours and see what's working best. Have a fun time.'

Some breakout teams headed down to the artificial lake, others stayed in huddles of chairs or sat together on the grass. Everyone had their own laptop, but there were whiteboards and colour markers available too, and some used these to explain stuff to their group. Anyone not directly involved in a project, or simply in need of a break, could go grab something to eat or drink from any number of street food vendors – all the food and beer was free. Alternatively they could spend some time in the old Coney

337

Island-style amusement arcade that Elizabeth and Fred had bought in for the weekend. A tall red and white striped circus tent was filled with pinball machines from the fifties and sixties, arcade games of similar vintage and a line of old peep shows where you dropped a nickel in the slot, wound a handle on the side and saw a series of grainy black photographs showing you what the butler saw, or the fireman or the window cleaner.

After checking in briefly with all of the individual teams and contributing a few of her own ideas to several, Elizabeth went to get herself a slice of pizza. The second-generation Italian guy whose food was proving most popular among the Public Square employees had fitted a wood-fired pizza oven into the back of his sky-blue camper van. The consensus was that the van was cool and the pizza was even better. She was carrying a slice of oily pepperoni thin crust back to her original hackathon group, when she caught sight of Fred; he was talking to a statuesque young woman. The girl looked vaguely Danish or Nordic and Elizabeth had a feeling she recognised her. She walked over.

'Hello, what's this? A two-person breakout group? I'm not sure the rules allow for that.'

Fred introduced his wife to Christy Newmark, who practically curtseyed.

'Mrs Curepipe . . .'

'Please, Elizabeth.'

'Elizabeth . . . you . . . you've been my hero since I was yay high.' She held her hand at waist height to indicate the age. 'My absolute role model.'

Elizabeth smiled.

'I'm honoured. And what brings you over here today Christy? I recognise you don't I? Did you work for us a few years back?'

'You've a great memory.'

Christy explained that she'd worked for Public Square for a

year, straight out of college, but that now she was one of the two people behind Cloud Chancer. 'Perhaps Fred . . . Mr Curepipe mentioned the company to you?'

Elizabeth shook her head.

'He hasn't yet, but I've been out of town, I'm sure he was going to.'

'I hope so, he's being so supportive.'

'Well, it's lovely to meet you . . . again. And exciting that we might be getting involved with your new venture.'

'Yes . . .' Christy smiled. '. . . super-exciting. Your speech this morning, it was so inspiring.'

'I'm glad you enjoyed it.' Elizabeth glanced down at the slice of pizza. 'I better get on and eat this, before it drips all over my dress.' She nodded a polite goodbye to them both and walked away. Her long scissoring stride had taken her halfway across the great lawn before Fred managed to catch up.

'Hey there, Lizzie, wait for me.'

She stopped.

'Hello Fred. She's very pretty. Very talented too I'm sure.'

'Sure, but . . .' He paused. 'Christy . . . her company, you know it's just work?'

'Are you sure Fred? You didn't have your *work face* on when I first saw you.'

Fred shook his head.

'I don't have a *work face* and a *not-work face* Lizzie.'

'You do Fred . . .' Elizabeth smiled. '. . . this face you're wearing right now – talking to me – that's your work face.'

69 Reassignment

CORTES CASA DE HUESPEDES, CHILE, SOUTH AMERICA

They were almost at the guesthouse when Jags spoke again.

'You know what? I think it'd be better if we went and got this thing done quicker – go back now and pick her up. She's more likely to come willingly now, while it's light. I'll tell her that we're taking her to the American diner to talk through the two proposals – *hers* and *ours*. You can gag her once she's sitting in the car, we'll take her out to the derelict mine where I killed her old man and do it there.'

'Sure.'

Jags turned the car around.

They chatted in a relaxed fashion on the drive back to Brochu. Jags found out a little more about Nathan's family, his time in the army, where he'd served and how come it didn't work out. How he deserved more. Jags told Nathan a little about his own childhood in Ohio and his career in the Services. As they climbed the hill that first rose and then dipped down into Brochu, Jags began to drive faster. Then faster still. Fifty kilometres an hour, sixty. Nathan glanced at him.

'What're you doin'. . .' The needle hit seventy kph. '. . .you lost your fuckin' mind?'

As they hit the crest in the road, Jags jerked the steering wheel hard right with his left hand, driving off the tarmac and into the gravel. At the same time, his right hand reached down and pressed the red release unlocking the passenger side seatbelt. Nathan worked out what was happening, but not fast enough to stop it. The Chevy flew across the gravel and smashed into the thick steel support beneath the Brochu sign at high speed. Nathan was reaching for the steering wheel when the car hit; the force of the crash sent him out through the windscreen head first, although the positioning of his arm meant it was his shoulder that broke first. The impact of the crash alone might well have killed him, but if it didn't, then losing the top half of his head – sliced off on the bottom edge of the green metal sign – certainly did.

Jags was shaken by the crash and it took a while for him to regain his senses. Once he did, the sound of a distant siren was the first thing he heard. His chest and abdomen hurt like hell, but there wasn't time to worry about the damage he'd done to himself. He needed to be quick. He climbed from the car, found a nearby rock and smashed out what remained of the windscreen on the driver's side. He distributed the bloodied glass liberally across the bonnet. There was no way this would persuade an experienced accident examiner that it was a lone driver who'd crashed into the sign and killed himself in the process but how many experienced accident examiners were there working in this remote part of Chile? At the very least it would put some doubt in people's minds; at best the police and medics would start cleaning shit up before the accident examiners got anywhere near. More importantly it would buy Soledad some time – the time she'd need to disappear, before the job that this repairman had been sent to do was reassigned.

70 Duck Shit

The guy in front of Carver in the queue for taxis at the airport was holding a live chicken under his arm. William shook his head.

'Welcome to Hong Kong.'

He'd changed some money and bought a couple of new burner phones. Patrick would meet him in the lobby of the Headland Hotel; he hadn't decided yet whether they should stay there or move. He didn't like press hotels as a rule, but he'd agreed to take a look at the place first.

Once in the cab, Carver settled in and stared out of the window. There, in the distance, was the famous Fragrant Harbour, crystalline skyscrapers crammed impossibly close together, the flashing red warning lights on some obscured by cloud. He had mixed feelings about being back.

A combination of rush hour traffic and the various detours necessary to avoid parts of the city occupied by the demonstrators meant the drive took over an hour. Once they were into the city proper, Carver wound down the window and took a breath.

'Duck shit, fried food and petrol – same as ever.'

His driver looked back over his shoulder.

'All okay Mr? You want a different road?'

'No, no. This road's fine.'

They were close to the Harcourt Road, the epicentre of the demos in as much as the demonstrations had a centre. Many traders had closed up as a precaution and the car crawled through the thick traffic past shuttered shops and a long line of police vans. The fact that some shopkeepers had taken fright didn't mean that buying and selling had stopped; the ever-entrepreneurial Hongkongers had adapted and there were street stalls everywhere. William saw vendors selling sweet-smelling spicy crab and sticky rice, general grocery and household products, clothes, fake Chinese Rolex and, of course, umbrellas. Whichever Chinese manufacturer it was that had the lion's share of umbrella sales to Hong Kong was doing well out of this revolution. William looked back through the plastic glass to check how the fare was mounting up. It wasn't too bad, this driver hadn't added the usual stack of extras the way some Hong Kong cabbies did. He found himself starring at the man's arthritic hands, which were resting on the steering wheel like two huge clumps of raw ginger.

The city's Indian summer was hanging on in there, the weather was warm and muggy but his driver left the air con off during the journey. Carver was sweating like a hog by the time the cab dropped him outside the Headland. He paid the fare along with a reasonable tip and stretched his back out before picking up his bag and shouldering his way in through the thick glass door. The bag was heavy and his legs stiff but he refused the top-hatted doorman's offer of help and strode over to where Patrick was reading a newspaper, in a high-backed armchair next to an enormous vase of red roses – a hundred at least and all in full bloom. Patrick jumped to his feet and put his arms around Carver before he could do anything to stop this

343

happening. He stood and tolerated this without reciprocating. After Patrick had finished with the hugging, he put his bag down and looked around.

'What the hell kind of place is this?'

Patrick smiled.

'Pretty swanky, huh?'

'You can say that again. How much is it a night?'

'Er, I'm not exactly sure.'

'Well I think you should find out. It's licence fee-payers' money you're spending, not your own. Are you booked in here for the rest of the week?'

'No, it's just one night's notice I think.'

'Okay, so we'll stay here tonight and then move somewhere else tomorrow.'

'You don't like it then?' Patrick was smiling.

'It's the *press* hotel. And a *posh* hotel. Look around . . .' He waved a hand. '. . . I've never seen so many people pretending to read the *WSJ*. Course I don't like it.'

'Fair enough, I had a feeling you might say that. So I'll go book you in, but just for one night?'

Carver shook his head.

'No need. I'll share your room, we'll ask them to give us a roll-up mattress or something for you to kip on.'

Patrick laughed. He'd expected his old boss's arrival to feel like a breath of fresh air. In fact, this felt more like smelling salts.

'Fine, I'll go ask. How about I see you in the bar? I bet you could use a drink after that trip.'

William studied Patrick.

'No, I don't think so, not now anyway. Let's get upstairs and take a look at the room. I promised McCluskey I'd check something out before I did anything else.'

*

Patrick opened the door to the room with his key card and stepped in. Carver followed, deposited his bag on the bed and headed for the window.

'Nice view. Can I borrow your phone?' Patrick handed it over and watched while William put the mobile inside the minibar.

'What's that all about?'

'I'm here, partly, to help you be a bit more careful and that starts now.'

'But . . .'

William put a finger to his mouth signalling hush then removed his blazer and started unpacking his bag. In among his recording equipment he found the small black plastic device that McCluskey had given him. He fumbled with it for a while, checking the batteries and playing with the buttons before walking around the room waving it in front of various things – the television, Patrick's laptop, the room phone and all the mirrors and pictures and lamp fittings. He climbed up onto the bed, still wearing his shoes, and reached up towards the ceiling light. While he waved the boxy device around, Patrick studied the sweat patches under his arms, which reached almost down to his waist. Carver huffed and puffed before eventually holding out a clammy hand for Patrick to help him down. He jutted his chin in the direction of the door and Patrick followed Carver in silence, out into the corridor and down towards the fire exit. William waited until they were out through the fire door and on the cement stairs before he spoke.

'So McCluskey was dead right, as per usual.'

'About what . . .?' Patrick pointed at the black box. '. . . what is that?'

'It's a radio wave monitor that she gave me and by the looks of it your bedroom's been bugged every which way to Sunday. I got positive readings from your keyboard, the room phone, most of the light fittings and the bathroom mirror.'

'Bollocks.'

'Yeah. So right now you need to think about what kind of conversations you've had in that room these last few days and assume that someone – these repairmen or whoever it is they're working for – heard *all of it*.'

71 Keeping it Simple

CORTES CASA DE HUESPEDES, CHILE, SOUTH AMERICA

Jags got back to the guesthouse quickly enough, with the help of a bribable lorry driver followed by a half-hour hike. He didn't want the guy to know exactly where he was staying and the driver was more than happy to take the money without having to take his rig too far from the freeway. Jags asked to be dropped at a gas station, a place where he'd filled up a few times in the past. It was a throwback to the America of the fifties or sixties and reminded Jags of an Edward Hopper painting he'd seen one time. It had those old-fashioned bubble-headed petrol pumps with rubber elbows and a sleepy-looking guy sat in front of the office who gave no sign of having seen Jags jump down from the passenger seat and slip down the side of the gas station. From there he walked across a field full of scrub and trekked up and down a couple of hills heading west, in the direction of the guest-house.

The hike was an opportunity to think things through and by the time he was back in the room and lying flat on his back on the hard single bed, he had a plan. First – he would wait. Fred would hear about the car crash soon enough, all that Jags had to do was act surprised and stick to his story – he'd been hanging about in his room for hours, he'd tried to call Nathan but heard nothing. The kid had begged Jags to let him go do the job himself, he was cocky, ambitious too and he obviously wanted to impress Fred. Keep it simple, that was the key. Credible. Jags stuck the SIM card back in the Chilean burner phone, put it down on the bedside table, crunched up a pillow until it felt comfortable behind his head and closed his eyes.

By the time Fred rang, waking Jags from a deep sleep, it was the early evening and the room was filled with sunset colours. Fred sounded more exasperated than angry. Jags stuck to the script. He acted surprised, explained how Nathan had insisted on going alone and then just let Fred talk.

'It's annoying as hell . . .' He told Jags the Chevy was a write-off, the police had towed it away, Nathan's body would be repatriated. Jags was to get himself back to Santiago, stay the night there and sort out some paperwork the next day. Once that was done, Fred wanted him to catch the next flight he could back to San Fran. He'd be met. And that was that. The most unusual thing about the call was how calm Fred seemed.

'I could have done without this kind of crap right now but I've got too many other plates spinning to spend any more time on this. Sort out the paperwork then come on back. I want you back here in Cupertino.'

'What about the mine? The visit? What's the plan?'

'The plan is that we leave that new recruit of yours to stew in her own juice for a while. I've ordered a stop on all construction work in Brochu. We'll wait and see who the folks there prefer – *us* and a paid job or *her* and . . . *fuck all*.'

'And Lizzie's fine with that?'

'What?'

'Elizabeth. She's okay with all of this?'

'Of course. Everyone's on the same page.' He paused. 'We've talked long enough, I'll see you tomorrow if the paperwork's straightforward. Day after at the latest.'

Jags took a long, scalding hot shower; there was a greenish bruise coming through diagonally across his chest and another just above his groin. He had a little whiplash but nothing major. He took some more painkillers, packed his stuff up and asked reception to book him a cab back to the capital. He waited on the front porch of the guesthouse, watching the sky turn pink and smoking one Marlboro after another. The more he thought about it, the more uneasy he felt about his and Fred's brief telephone conversation. *Annoying* – that was the word Fred used to describe what had happened. His carefully orchestrated clean-up had turned into a freaking tyre fire and Fred seemed . . . almost indifferent. It didn't stack up. Again and again Jags' mind turned to Elizabeth. How much, if anything, she knew. Whether he might risk calling her. He could tell her what had really gone down: Fred's plan to get rid of Soledad and the steps Jags had to take to stop that happening. She would understand, he was certain of it. But then what? Fred was dangerous at the best of times, if he began to feel cornered there was no predicting how he would react. Better to wait and speak to Lizzie face to face. He let the cigarette drop and ground it out with the heel of his boot. The cab was coming.

72 Old Knights

Carver and Patrick's conflab on the hotel's emergency staircase lasted a while. Patrick ran through the conversations he could remember having in the room and who he'd been speaking to – McCluskey, Rebecca, John Brandon, Naomi and Carver himself, albeit briefly.

'And then Viv of course . . .' He paused. 'Shit, William I didn't tell you yet.'

'Tell me what?'

'She's missing.'

'Viv's missing? BBC Viv?' Patrick nodded. 'Missing since when?'

Patrick told Carver all he knew, which, he realised as he was speaking, wasn't very much. William listened attentively.

'So she went missing from here in the hotel and the last person to see her was this American fellow?'

'Yeah. Dan Staples is his name, she left his room around midnight.'

'You know that how?'

'I've watched the CCTV... seen her leaving his room, going down in the lift and going into her bedroom.'

'Right. And she looks okay? No sign that she was agitated, scared? Nothing like that?'

'The tape's blurry. But no, she seems fine.'

'Dan Staples? That name rings a bell. What do you make of him?'

'I'm not sure. First time I ran into him it seemed like he had no clue ... *all the gear and no idea* like you used to say.' Patrick paused. 'But in fact he's been around a while. Reported from a load of different places in the last couple of years, but never anywhere for long. Viv obviously liked him and he liked her and he seemed sort of all right ...'

'Sort of?'

'There's something about him that doesn't quite fit. Nothing specific – just a gut feeling. He's down in the bar now if you want to go see for yourself?'

William weighed this up.

'Okay, so here's what we do. You go pack your stuff up and take it down to reception. I'll go have a drink with this American bloke. After that, we'll check out of here and go.'

'Where are we going?'

'There's a place I know that rents rooms. Good grub too.'

'Got it. Am I okay to get my phone back out of the minibar?'

'Sure, but don't start calling anyone – remember all those bugs. Better still, leave the thing switched off for the time being.'

'Why'd you put it in the minibar anyway?'

'That's another one of McCluskey's tips. The fridge works as a Faraday cage.'

'Eh?'

'Look it up. On second thoughts, don't. I'll tell you later.'

*

351

Carver wasn't sure what to make of the Purple Bar. It looked like the décor had been done by a westerner with a very fixed idea of what a Chinese-looking bar should look like and too much money to spend. Painted screens and a fake Han era cabinet, tasselled standing lamps and lots of jade – high end chinoiserie everywhere you looked. There were even a couple of the tall brown clay urns that Chinese families used to keep the ashes of loved ones and ancestors, standing against the far wall. It was like decorating the Dog and Duck with a few coffins.

Carver looked around and saw John Brandon, his old colleague and long-time sparring partner, who was sitting on an uncomfortable-looking chaise longue gabbing away to some other hacks. Perhaps one of these unfortunates was Dan Staples? He wandered over. As Carver approached, Brandon glanced up and stopped mid-sentence. The expression on his face was one of genuine surprise.

'William Carver! Blow me, what are you doing here? I thought you'd chucked in the towel?'

'Not quite.'

'Well then I hate to tell you . . . especially because you usually like to be first to a fire don't you? But you're rather late to the show old fruit.'

'That depends what I'm here for.'

'For the same reason we're all here I assume? To watch a lot of young students get seven shades of shit kicked out of them . . .'

'Maybe.' He looked at the rest of the group. 'I'm going to get a drink. What does anyone want?'

Brandon pushed himself to his feet.

'No you're bloody not. This round's on me. A libation for a fellow *old knight*, returning once more to the field of battle.' Brandon was drunk but William appreciated the gesture. 'What can I get you?'

'Just a . . .'

'No, wait . . . I know what I'll get you.' Brandon was off, walking stiff-legged in the direction of the bar. Carver asked the knot of journalists gathered around the gap in the sofa if they knew Dan Staples. They all did, indeed Carver had just missed him, he'd gone to file some copy and run a quick errand. But he'd be back, he was a regular at the Purple Bar – and a popular regular too. Everyone had the same story: Dan worked for one of the big regional papers in the States, based in Colorado, but he was also getting syndicated here and there. Apparently he was making a stack and he was generous with it too, regularly buying rounds for whoever happened to be in the bar. Carver nodded; the prices a place like this charged for a round, it was no wonder the guy was popular.

Brandon arrived back with two huge, bright red cocktails, each in a goldfish bowl-sized glass with a pink paper dragon sticking out of the top.

'Introducing the Headland Hotel's greatest invention – the famous dragon cocktail.'

'Right, thank you.'

'Cheers.'

'And to you.'

The drink tasted like sugared petrol; William sipped at it politely while Brandon gulped his and talked.

'I guess you need time to get settled, but as soon as you have we have to get ourselves down to Lan Kwai Fong. You know it?' Carver knew. 'It's not what it used to be, but it's still where the party is. Last week I met a young lady who claimed that she was the great-granddaughter of the real-life *Suzie Wong!* Imagine that.'

'Right. Feel free not to tell me any more about what kind of night you had. I wanted to ask you about this guy Dan Staples, John.'

'Dan! He's a good man. American, but one of the good ones . . .'

Brandon paused. '. . . I'll tell you all about him, but I desperately need a pee. Don't drink my drink.'

There was no chance of that happening.

Brandon was gone a while – prostate probably – but it didn't matter because the man Carver wanted to talk to him about walked into the bar a few minutes after John left. Dan Staples wore a blue button-down shirt and light brown chinos and a *hail fellow well met* sort of smile, right up until he saw Carver, whereupon he emptied his face of everything. They had never met, William was sure of this, nevertheless Dan Staples recognised him.

Carver watched the American make up his mind whether to approach or not. In the end, curiosity prevailed. He gave a friendly howdee to the group gathered around the chaise before addressing Carver directly.

'Hey there man, I'm Dan . . . Dan Staples.'

'Hello. I'm William Carver. Pleased to meet you, I've heard a lot about you.'

'Is that right? Nothing good I'm sure . . .' he waved a big hand at the group. '. . . not from this bunch of jokers anyway.'

There were smiles and some general chat and Dan was busy taking orders for a fresh round of drinks when William butted in.

'Which paper is it you're working for again Dan? Someone did tell me but I forget.'

Staples looked again at William, still smiling but only with the lower half of his face.

'The *Colorado Guardian*. You heard of it?'

Carver shook his head.

'No, I don't think so. But something about you *does* seem familiar – I think it's your name.'

'Really? Well I guess it's not such an unusual name.'

'I guess not. Have you been in the journalism game for long?'

'Not that long.'

'Where else have you reported from . . . for the *Colorado Guardian*?'

'I've freelanced here and there.'

'Where?'

The American laughed and looked at the assembled hacks.

'What is this? Some kinda inquisition? Do you want me to go print off my resumé Mr Carver and you can just have a read of that?'

'If that's easier for you than remembering where you have or haven't worked before . . . then sure.'

Staples shook his head.

'You know what? I get the feeling you don't like me too much and I have this rule 'bout not drinking with people who don't like me.'

'Makes sense.'

Patrick arrived in time to catch the very end of the exchange. Observing the pair he was unsure which of the two was studying the other more intently. Dan left, taking a few of the other hacks with him. William watched them go before picking up his cocktail and walking to the bar. Patrick followed. Carver flagged down the barman and pointed at his undrunk drink.

'This is a brandy glass isn't it?'

'That's right sir.'

'Then please will you empty whatever that is in there down the sink and put a brandy in it instead?'

'Of course, a single or double?'

'Take a guess.'

Carver turned to Patrick.

'So that was Dan Staples?'

'Yes. What did you think?'

'I think your gut instinct was right. He's lying.'

73 Table Stakes

THE CHERRYWOOD HOTEL, CUPERTINO, CALIFORNIA

Fred had seen more than his fair share of start-ups pitching to investors down the years. Christy Newmark's pitch was among the best. He wondered how many times she'd practised this in front of a mirror before standing up in front of this roomful of suntanned, blazer-wearing venture capitalists. He didn't have to wonder so hard about other aspects of the presentation – or its main influences anyway. Gone was the blue sweatshirt, she was wearing a lemon coloured, knee-length dress and bright red lipstick. The new look suited her. Clever also to have the launch at the Cherrywood, where the men whose money Christy wanted to access would feel most at home. It seemed to Fred that she and her partner had spent the pump-priming money well – not just *front of house* with a swish presentation followed by the tasting menu – all eighteen courses – from Silicon Valley's current favourite chef in the Cherrywood's ballroom, but also on the behind-the-scenes stuff. The important stuff. Her smartest idea, a game-changing idea in fact, had been to buy access to food delivery phone lines across America and several other major territories in Europe, North Africa and the Middle and Far East. Fred could pay her no higher compliment than to say that he wished he'd thought of this himself. With that much data, given a little time there was no limit to what the right voice recognition algorithm might come up with. His first present to Christy had simply been turning up – when people saw Fred Curepipe arrive, pick up a Cloud Chancer prospectus and take a seat near the front, the room began to buzz. His second present came when, just after she'd finished speaking and asked if there were questions she could help with, Fred raised his arm.

'Yes, Mr Curepipe?'

'So what are the table stakes for this next round of funding Miss Newmark?'

'We're asking for two point five million from each primary investor sir.'

Fred nodded.

'Fine, well if any of these other ladies and gentlemen decide they don't want to sit at the table then I'll be happy to make up the difference in return for the appropriate percentage of the whole. Is that acceptable?'

Christy smiled.

'Of course. Thank you sir.'

Fred might as well have taken the VCs' pocket books out and written the cheques himself. Everyone was in.

After she'd finished shaking hands, and while her team were busy taking people's money, Fred asked Christy for a quick word. They walked through the ballroom and out into the kitchen, which was alive with activity.

'I can't stay to eat.'

'I understand.'

'But I wanted to say well done, genuinely well done. I always knew you were a talent, but I wasn't sure about your company. Now I am. Buying yourself access to that amount of voice data, in the places where you've picked – it's smart. More than smart.'

'Thank you Fred.'

'I might have some material that you can road-test that new software on pretty soon, if you're interested.'

'Of course I am. Especially if that'd be helpful for you.'

'It could well be.'

74 The Cookbook

THE HEADLAND HOTEL, HONG KONG

Patrick put his bags in the boot of the taxi and climbed in along-side Carver, who had kept his bag with him, holding it on his lap.

'So where's this place with rooms and great food then, William?'

'Mrs Wang's.'

As soon as he'd established that the driver knew the place, and having given the man some advice on the best way to get there, Carver opened his kitbag and started rootling around. He brought out one of the new phones he'd bought at the airport, unboxed it and dialled McCluskey's mobile number. She answered imme-diately.

'Aye?'

'I'm on a new burner phone, in a cab with you-know-who. Can we talk on this?'

McCluskey sucked at her teeth.

'How urgent is it?'

'Pretty urgent.'

'Fine then, let's go for it. *You-know-who* has bollocksed up the fax machine thing anyway. What can I do for you?'

Carver told McCluskey that he needed her to check something out for him, someone in fact.

'He goes by the name Dan Staples, works mainly for something called the *Colorado Guardian*.'

'Never heard of the paper but his name rings a bell.'

'Yeah, for me too. Have you got everything you need there to run the rule on him for me?'

'Sure. I'll call you back in an hour or so. This phone?'

'I can probably get to a landline if you think that's better.'

'At the hotel?'

'No, you were right about that place – hot and cold running surveillance in every room. We're moving.'

'Good man, call me from the new place then.' She paused. 'Have you had a chance to put an ear over *you-know-who*'s back catalogue of interviews yet?'

'Not yet, that's next on the list. I'll tell you 'bout it when we speak.'

'Magic. Take care.'

The phone went dead. Patrick had overheard most of the conversation.

'I'm sorry about screwing things up with McCluskey and the fax machine.'

'Don't worry about it.'

'I'll set you up with those interviews as soon as we get to Mrs Wang's.'

'Sure.'

'What do you want me to do about my phone, I guess we're assuming that's bugged too?'

'Bugged and trackable and being watched by every other device it gets close to. McCluskey explained it to me. Every piece of tech you can think of is talking to and collecting data from every other device . . . your smartphone, laptop, watch, car, even some of those modern *toasters* are at it apparently.

She told me about an American guy that the cops tracked down with the help of his insulin pump. Anything that's got Wi-Fi or Bluetooth, they can use. It's enough to give you bloody nightmares.'

Patrick's thoughts turned to Eric and what had seemed at the time like a rather paranoid rant about how the authorities were somehow managing to anticipate his and his fellow protestors' every move. He got his phone out and offered it to Carver, who shook his head.

'No. Keep it. Switch it on now, while we're on the move and get any numbers you need . . .' He reached into his bag. '. . . punch them into this . . .' He handed Patrick the second burner phone he'd bought at the airport. '. . . we'll leave your phone stuffed down the back of the seat of the cab. Watching you driving around Hong Kong all day and night might give someone something to think about.'

The rooms that Mrs Wang rented turned out to be just one room that had belonged to her son – now grown up and working in Canada. It seemed obvious to Patrick that the only person she would have agreed to rent it to was Carver. When she saw William standing in the line, queuing up for a corned beef bun, the elegant, white-haired woman handed the waiter pad to an assistant and came hurrying round the counter to greet him.

'Car-ver-ah.'

'Rosamund.'

'I woke up this morning with a powerful feeling you would come. Even though some tall boy . . .' she spotted Patrick sitting at a nearby table, surrounded by luggage. '. . . that boy there . . .' she pointed, '. . . told me you were dead.'

'Dead? No. Not yet.'

Mrs Wang had kept her son's room just as he had left it. There were posters of scantily clad Cantonese pop stars and red Ferraris on the walls, a small white Formica desk with an anglepoise lamp and one double bed. Patrick looked around.

'Are we supposed to share that bed?'

William shook his head.

'Don't be ridiculous. Mrs Wang is fetching us a blow-up mattress, you can sleep on that.'

'Right.' He surveyed the floor space. There wasn't much of it. He'd been transported from the lap of luxury to the sweaty armpit of reality and Carver had only arrived a couple of hours ago.

'No time to waste. Set up your laptop so I can get listening to those interviews of yours. After that, you can go down and fetch those corned beef buns that Rosamund's rustling up for us . . .' Carver sat down at the white desk and got his reporter's notepad out. '. . . and some tea. Milk and three for me.'

Carver listened to Patrick's collection of interviews, now and again skipping forward thirty seconds when he felt he'd got the point, sometimes listening to the same section two or even three times. It took him over an hour and several cups of tea before he was done. He closed down the file, removed the memory stick and handed it back to Patrick who was sitting on the edge of the bed waiting to hear William's judgement.

'You did well getting so many people on the front line of so many different protests to talk to you.'

'Thanks.'

'Now our problem is that you got so many different people, involved in so many different protests to talk to you . . .'

Patrick grinned. '. . . and in so much detail.'

'Yeah, well . . .'

'Listening to it all together, it comes across like . . .' He scratched his head. '. . . have you ever heard of the *Anarchist Cookbook*?'

'Sorry, no.'

'Don't worry, it was well before your time. It was a handbook for assorted troublemakers back in the good old days. It scared the pants off the police and politicians for a while. You could be banged up just for having a copy in the house.'

Patrick looked at the memory stick in his hand.

'You think *this* is like that?'

'Kind of . . . a sort of digital addendum. Whoever it is that's bugging your room and watching McCluskey . . .'

'And Rebecca.'

'And Rebecca, yes. My best guess is it's the contents of *that memory stick* they're interested in.'

75 Cover

McCluskey stared out of the spare room window. Outside the top, left-hand window pane a spider was dancing to and fro, weaving its perfect wheel. Down at the kerb, just outside her front gate, the black Mercedes that Carver had chased away was back. It was a cold day and a mix of fumes and steam billowed from the car's exhaust. She'd been down once already to try to confront the driver – tell him to bugger off – but as soon as she reached her front door, the car would drive away. She'd called the local police station and spoken to the desk sergeant, she gave him the car's registration number and he'd promised to send someone round, but that could take all day and McCluskey guessed the Merc would just scarper as soon as the cops arrived. Or maybe it wouldn't? The car had *D plates* – diplomatic licence plates. Maybe that meant it was allowed to hang around, trying to intimidate old ladies? She wasn't intimidated, she was too busy for that; she checked the time. An hour had passed. She didn't have loads of information on Staples, but she had enough to make it worthwhile updating William. She walked next door to her bedroom and, crouching down alongside her stripped pine wardrobe, pulled out a jiffy bag that was taped underneath. She chose one of the three burner phones she had left and dialled the Hong Kong landline that Carver had sent her.

Mrs Wang bumped the door open with her hip and walked in; she had a plastic tray with two bowls of wonton soup on it in one hand and the phone in the other. She passed the tray to Patrick before handing the phone to William with a smile.

'Thank you Rosamund.'

'Who's Rosamund when she's at home?'

Carver brightened at the sound of McCluskey's thick Glaswegian accent.

'She's our new landlady.'

'Lucky her. So listen up . . .' Carver held the phone halfway between his head and Patrick's. McCluskey's voice was loud enough that both could hear clearly. 'Dan Staples checks out all right when you first take a look. The *Colorado Guardian* exists, he writes for it, he's on LinkedIn, Public Square, Twitter and all that shite. He's even got his own Wikipedia page . . .' Patrick nodded. '. . . but that entry of his was the first thing I found that looks fishy. It's the most carefully curated Wikipedia entry I've ever seen. What working hack has the time to do that?'

'So, what are you saying? It's some kind of cover?'

'Maybe.'

'Right, although I feel like I know the name Dan Staples.'

'Me too. I'll keep digging on that, but there's one other thing.'

'Yeah?'

'This *Colorado Guardian* . . . although it exists, it's as dodgy as hell.'

'In what way?'

'I mapped their office address . . .'

'Right?'

'It's a car park.'

'It's got a car park?'

'No. It *is* a car park, a car park is all there is. Look at the website and it looks like a newspaper but it has no base, no physical presence.'

Carver puffed out his cheeks.

'That's good work Jemima.'

'It's a start anyway, I'll keep looking.'

'Thank you. How are those monster seagulls?'

'Eh?'

'The seagulls. They're everywhere in Brighton, great big bastards, I got dive-bombed by one once.'

'Sounds terrifying.'

Carver paused.

'You're not in Brighton, are you McCluskey?'

'No. No, I'm not. But we'll have no fuss.'

'It's not a matter of fuss Jemima, it's a question of keeping you safe. Viv Fox is missing, we don't know what these people are . . .'

'Your line is breaking up Billy . . . Nope cannae hear you at all now. I'll ring you when I've got more on Staples.'

76 The Fireman

THE NEW FALLINGWATER HOUSE, CUPERTINO, CALIFORNIA

Fred decided to stop off at home before he drove back to the office. Elizabeth was at Public Square and he wanted to do some work without risk of interruption. He sat at his computer and read emails for a while; the message he was hoping to see would be from his Beijing client, but there was nothing from there. He had considered contacting the repairman himself, taking a more direct approach – it was easily done. But it was against protocol, and more importantly his client would think it ill-mannered; the Chinese took things like that so damn seriously. He would wait.

In the meantime, his emails informed him that he had more immediate problems that needed dealing with. He touched a couple of keys to bring up his map sprinkled with silver lights in various cities across almost every continent. Fred pressed his forefinger against the centre of his forehead. He could feel a migraine building. He realised now that he'd been wrong to think of these lights as resembling stars in some sort of grand constellation. They were less orderly than that. Less stable. Looking at the map again now he realised that each light represented a fire and the people sent to fight it – the fires were small at the moment, but they burned increasingly brightly. Unchecked they could develop into a larger, more dangerous conflagration. He couldn't directly affect what was happening in Hong Kong, but he had plenty of resources that could play their part. He nodded. It was time to stamp the fires out.

77 Reading Matter

Carver and Patrick decided to stay in that evening; the long trip from London was catching up with William and he was tired. Plus one of his favourite restaurants in Hong Kong was just downstairs so really what was the point in going anywhere else? They ate in the café.

'We need to find a secure way of getting your material back to McCluskey so she can put an ear over it. Sending it from a white computer somewhere probably makes most sense.'

'I used a place down in Central last time, the King Chung it was called.'

'Right, so we'll use somewhere else this time round. McCluskey told me to work on the basis that nothing's secure. Not burner phones, encrypted messenger services, emails . . . *nada*. She wasn't even sure that fax set-up of yours was safe, but she figured that at least it was *unpredictable*. The people we're dealing with are good at predicting stuff.'

Patrick nodded. He had the new phone that Carver had given him on the table next to his plate of stir-fry and now it buzzed

369

into life. It was a text message. William glanced at the name. 'Who's Eric? Oh, Eric. Is he that rather intense young guy that speaks for *Scholastic?* The last interview on your collection of international troublemakers?'

'That's him, Eric Fung.'

'What's he want?'

'Well, it's possible he wants to thank me for correcting some inaccuracies in the way we were reporting the death of a mate of his. But more likely, he wants something.'

'What?'

'Some of the details from those other interviews you listened to. I told him a little bit about other stuff I'd seen in Turkey and Egypt and elsewhere.'

'I hope you told him to go whistle.'

'Not in so many words. He did me a favour too, he looked at some of the stuff McCluskey sent through. Helped make sense of it.'

Carver shook his head.

'Doesn't matter. He's a contact, that's all. Don't make me give you the extremely boring lecture I give my students on journalistic ethics.'

Patrick smiled.

'I bet you're a good teacher.'

'I'm actually not bad. Not as bad as I thought I'd be anyway.'

'But you're glad to be back?'

Carver made a harrumphing sound.

'I missed certain things.' He slurped some more of his noodle soup. Patrick was about to say something, but Carver got there first. 'How come you're not eating, is that stir-fry no good?'

'It's very good. It's nearly as good as Becs' stir-fry in fact.'

Carver looked up from his food.

'Oh yeah, she said something about that when I went to see her. Your romantic antics at that school auction thing.'

Patrick beamed at being reminded of the story.

'Thanks for going to see her William. How was she when you saw her?'

'She was fine, she was . . . oh, bugger . . .'

'What is it?'

Carver reached for his jacket pocket before realising that he was only in shirtsleeves. His blazer was upstairs.

'Rebecca gave me a letter to give to you, I just remembered. Do you want me to go get it? Or I can give it to you after we've eaten if . . .'

But Patrick was already on his feet.

'I'll go.'

'Okay, it's in my blue blazer pocket.'

Patrick returned ten minutes later, pale as a sheet, the letter still in his hand. Carver pushed his plate to one side.

'Hey, you all right?'

Patrick shook his head and sat down heavily. 'What is it?' William knew what it was. 'Listen Patrick, you've been away too long, she told me that and you know it too. Whatever she's written in there . . .' He pointed at the letter. '. . . that's not going to be the last word on you two. You just need to get yourself back home soon, talk to her and try . . .' He stopped. Patrick was smiling.

'No, William. It's not that . . .'

78 Chemistry

The old pharmacist had a kind look about him, bright brown eyes and those deep laughter lines that make a person look like they're always smiling.

'Forgive me if I'm speaking out of turn, but these tests are pretty reliable these days. If they're giving you a negative result, then negative is probably correct. It isn't usually necessary to keep checking.'

Rebecca blushed.

'It's actually positive results I'm getting.'

'I see. Well obviously the same applies.' He paused. 'You were hoping the tests were wrong perhaps?'

She shook her head vigorously.

'No, not at all, it's just . . . it's a little embarrassing . . . I've got kind of addicted to these things.' This was true. Four times now in the last few days Rebecca had peed on a stick and four times the little blue line had told her she was pregnant. Every time, she felt the same inexplicable rush of excitement and fear and delight. 'I can't get enough of being told I'm pregnant.'

The pharmacist smiled.

'Well then, congratulations. And I'm very grateful that you keep coming back and buying more tests from me – it's good for business. But they're expensive, perhaps you should start saving your money – for baby clothes and pushchairs and so on?'

She beamed. Baby paraphernalia. This was an avenue of adventure that she hadn't even considered until now.

'That's good advice, thank you. I'll just buy one more. Who knew weeing on a stick could be so much fun?'

The pharmacist shrugged.

'Not me, certainly.'

'But then . . . I promise, that will be it.' She looked past the pharmacist at the shelf behind him. 'Have you got anything that you can recommend for morning sickness while I'm here?'

He shook his head.

'There are some drugs that say they help with that, but to be honest I would recommend you try fresh peppermint or ginger tea before anything else. My wife swore by those.'

Rebecca nodded.

'She always said that morning sickness was a good sign by the way, she said it meant you were going to have a big, hairy baby. Although I can't say that I've ever seen any scientific evidence for that.'

Walking back from Highbury Corner to the flat, Rebecca was more aware than ever of the number of buggies and pushchairs and small children on those wooden push-along bikes, out with one parent or both for a Saturday morning walk. She checked her phone, then googled the time difference between London and Hong Kong – just to be sure. William would have landed hours ago, he should have given Patrick the letter by now. As soon as he got it, he would call, she knew that. A big, hairy baby! She'd pee on one more plastic stick, just to make quadruply sure, and if he still hadn't called her by then, *she'd* ring him.

79 The Octopus

Donnie was watching the kid put chocolate sprinkles on his ginger-bread latte when he saw the man with the moustache out of the corner of his eye. The guy was three down in the coffee queue and he was staring. Donnie stared back, expecting the bloke to get embarrassed and look away, but the man held his eye. When his drink was done and he'd paid and was halfway to the door the guy spoke.

'Mr Donald Firpo?'

'Who wants to know?'

'My name's Foster, I'm from the Financial Conduct Authority.'

Donnie looked the guy up and down.

'Really? What can I do for you?'

'I have a couple of questions I hoped you might be able to help me with.'

'Questions relating to financial conduct?'

'Yes.'

'My *financial conduct*?'

374

'That's right. Could we sit down outside for a couple of minutes? I promise it won't take long.'

Donnie looked at the man properly now. A blue tailored suit, white shirt and dark tie.

'You got any identification Mr Foster?'

The man had a laminated card with his picture and the FCA logo on it. He held it up for Donnie to take a look at and then launched right into it.

'This is about some allegations we've had of insider dealing, Mr Firpo.'

'I see.'

'We understand you sold a significant number of shares in Public Square, just before the company announced that they would be paying a very large tax bill.'

'A significant number?'

'I beg your pardon?'

'You said a significant number of shares, yes?'

'Yes.'

'I had about twelve hundred pounds worth of Public Square shares. I sold a third of those – four hundred pounds.'

'Right and can I ask why you decided to sell them when you did?'

Donnie smiled.

'I had this feeling.'

'A feeling?'

'Yup. In my waters. That's how I invest. I get feelings about things.'

'I see. You point out, quite fairly, that your investment was not large. If you were able to help us with some information about how you came to hear about the tax announcement ahead of time then I don't think we'd need to involve you at all, not personally. It might even be to your benefit.'

'My benefit?'

'Yes sir.'

'I see.' Donnie took a sip of his latte. 'You don't happen to have the time on you do you Mr Foster?'

The man from the FCA popped his cuff and glanced at his watch.

'It's a quarter past three. I know you probably need to get back to work, so how about this, I give you my card . . .' He handed a thick cream business card to Donnie. '. . . that's got my phone number and my email on there. Have a think about it, then either give me a call or email me and let me know what you decide.'

Donnie looked at the card, then shook his head slowly.

'I can tell you right now, Mr Foster, save you some time. I know some Financial Conduct Authority people, they're friends of mine. They don't wear suits like yours and they certainly don't wear Philippe Patek wrist watches. You know who wears those?' Foster shrugged. 'It's mainly the people they're trying to catch up with.' Donnie stared at the business card some more. 'I don't want to talk to you and I certainly don't want to find out what shit you're planning to dump onto my phone or laptop if I call or email you.'

'I have no idea what you're talking about Mr Firpo, but I can see that you're not interested in cooperating, in which case I think I'll take my card back.'

He held his hand out. Donnie laughed.

'Nope, I'm keeping this. I got friends in the police as well as in the FCA. I reckon they might be interested in having a look at this.'

Foster shook his head.

'Go ahead then, you have no idea who you're dealing with.'

'Yeah, I do. I have a real good idea.'

Donnie turned and walked back across the piazza towards Broadcasting House. Once he was through security and out of sight he got his phone out and found Carver's number. He thought about calling, then decided on a text instead.

'That octopus of yours, it's twitching its tentacles. Nothing to worry about my end, but you might want to warn any other people who you got tied up in this shit.' He was about to press send then stopped and added a line. *'Take care of yourself. D'*

80 Leave

WANG'S CAFÉ, CENTRAL HONG KONG

Carver asked to borrow the landline again so Patrick could make the call. He took Mrs Wang's phone back up to the bedroom, closed the door behind him, sat on the bed and dialled – the country code, her number without the zero. It seemed like an age passed before she picked up.

'Hello?'

'Rebecca? It's me.'

'Patrick?'

'Yeah, Becs, I'm sorry, I only just . . .' Suddenly he felt his eyes fill with tears. His voice broke. He lifted the phone away from his face and tried to pull himself together. He wiped his eyes dry on the arm of his sweatshirt then tried again. '. . . I'm sorry.'

'Don't be.'

'I only just got the letter. William forgot, I just opened it. I just read it I mean . . . I mean I did both.'

He heard Rebecca laugh. The best sound in the world at that moment. At any moment.

'So you read the letter? And you're happy?'

'Of course. So happy.' He paused. 'You are too aren't you? In the letter you say . . .'

'I'm happy Patrick, I'm . . .' She hesitated. '. . . there aren't words for how I feel right now.'

'Very happy?'

'There you go.'

'It's . . . it's just incredible.'

'It is.' She paused. 'Given how much time we've had together these last few months, I'd say it gives the immaculate conception a run for its money.'

'Well what can I say? I guess I'm just very . . .'

Rebecca tutted.

'Don't go getting *laddish* on me Patrick Reid. Remember, *she* can hear you.'

'*She?*'

'*She* or *he*. Apparently it's about the size of a large kidney bean right now.'

'A large kidney bean? I thought kidney beans only came in one size.'

'Well you're wrong . . . I've been doing a lot of *googling* these last few days. You've got some catching up to do.'

They spoke for a while; Patrick asked about school, asked if she was eating okay, whether she'd been feeling sick?

'A little morning sickness, but nothing serious, the pharmacist says that's good news – it means the baby's big. And hairy. He recommended fresh ginger or peppermint tea, I've bought both.'

'No more weird stuff like with the woman at the gallery?'

'Nothing. Speaking to William helped me feel a bit better about that and there's been nothing else since.'

'He said you were going to go stay with your mum and dad for a few days?'

'I was, I will . . . unless . . .' She paused. '. . . when do you think they might let you leave?'

'I'm going to email Naomi straight after this. And check the flights. Carver's already said that he can get along fine without me.'

'Good. Because I can't. Not me, nor this big hairy baby.' She hesitated. 'So maybe I'll stay here Patrick? If it's only going to be a day or two? I'm happier here.'

Patrick pondered this.

'I suppose so Becs . . . if you're happier in the flat. I'll start looking at flights back straight away.'

Their goodbyes were interrupted by Carver, who arrived in the room with a bottle of whisky in one hand and two glasses in the other.

'To wet the baby's head.' He explained. Rebecca overheard.

'Tell William that's not meant to happen until the baby's actually born.'

Patrick relayed this information.

'Ah, really. Well I've bought the whisky now so . . .'

The first glass Patrick drank barely touched the sides the second drink he drank more slowly, enjoying the heat of it in his mouth, the earthy taste on his tongue. While he drank, Carver talked – old war stories that Patrick had heard before. Before long, William fell asleep, mid-tale and Patrick pulled the duvet across him and turned off the main light. He sat at the desk, got his laptop out, first emailing an urgent leave request through to Naomi and then going online to look at the next available flights back home to London.

Rebecca made herself a cup of fresh ginger tea. She stood by the living room window waiting for it to cool. Down by the fields, sitting on the park bench that she and Patrick always referred to as *Carver's bench*, was a face she recognised. Wearing a quilted navy-blue jacket and grey tracksuit bottoms was the young bloke she'd been chatting to just yesterday. He'd stopped Rebecca while she was walking back home from the tube. At first she assumed he was going to ask her for money and she was already reaching for her purse when he interrupted her. He wasn't begging, he told her. It was nothing like that. He was looking for his dog.

81 Muddy Waters

The harbour handed her back, four days after she'd gone missing. An old fisherman found Viv; his boat had been sitting lower in the water than usual, tugging at its moorings, and he'd found the body underneath the back of the boat, Viv's dark hair tangled in the outboard.

The first that Patrick and Carver heard of it was an email from Naomi – an email in response to his late-night request for urgent leave, but one which left that question unanswered. Patrick understood. Viv's parents were on their way to Hong Kong, they'd arrive the next day, but in the meantime someone had to identify the body. Naomi asked if Patrick would be willing to do that and he said yes.

The morgue, on the lower ground floor of the Causeway Bay hospital, felt like the coldest room that Patrick had ever walked into. Viv was lying on a metal gurney, a thin sheet tracing her body's outline. When the aproned attendant folded the white sheet slowly back from Viv's face and Patrick saw that it was her, a torrent of bile and undigested food jumped from his stomach. The taste of sour whisky and Chinese food burned his throat. He swallowed it back down, confirmed to the man that the dead body in front of him belonged to Vivian Fox and then rushed from the room. Crouched over the toilet bowl in a nearby disabled lavatory, Patrick vomited until there was nothing left to vomit. Viv was dead.

He went back to apologise to the attendant for rushing out and was handed a clear plastic bag with Viv's belongings inside. There wasn't much. The green dress she'd been wearing when they found her, a silver bangle and a couple of silver rings.

Her parents had asked that an embargo be put on the news of their daughter's death until they had a chance to see her, but it did not hold. From the early afternoon, local time, several Hong Kong news websites started reporting that the missing BBC producer had been found, drowned. Within a couple of hours the agencies started saying the same. Soon the news of Viv's death, together with photographs that had been lifted from Viv's various social media accounts, were everywhere. Hard on the heels of this basic information came speculation and then the lies. Patrick sat at the little desk in Mrs Wang's spare room and read the rubbish that was being written. When you typed in Viv's name, top of the list of popular searches was Viv Fox – depression, Viv Fox – suicide, Viv Fox – spy. He kicked the leg of the desk and handed the laptop to Carver, who was sitting on the bed behind him.

'Look at this crap.'

Carver read.

'A spy? Where the hell does all this come from?'

Patrick shook his head. Carver kept reading. 'I mean you only have to read a handful of paragraphs to know that these stories are nonsense, there's no evidence for any of it. Who are they hoping to convince?'

'They don't need to convince anyone. It's not really meant to convince.'

'Then what's the point?'

'It's meant to confuse. To muddy the waters just enough that people aren't sure what to believe. I've seen it before, very recently in fact.'

Carver pointed at the screen.

'Like this?'

'Yes, almost exactly.'

82 A New Song

SANTIAGO, CHILE, SOUTH AMERICA

The band up on the stand was playing covers of American country tunes interspersed with the odd more folky Chilean number. The singer was dressed like a cowboy complete with ten-gallon hat, but the other four band members looked like they'd come straight from work – delivery guys and factory workers Jags guessed. The five could barely fit on the stand and the glitter ball that spun continuously above them looked all wrong, but he had an evening to kill in Santiago and it seemed to him that this basement restaurant bar was as good a place as any to spend it. There were a couple of *no smoking* signs up but no one was paying them any mind and the cigarette smoke helped hold the stink of sweat and stale booze down, like it used to back in America back before the ban. It had taken a whole day and several cash bribes to sort the paperwork necessary for Nathan's body to be flown back home. Jags would fly back to San Francisco himself in the morning.

He had a little round table to himself and a keen young waiter who obviously saw a big tip coming if he kept this American in drinks and food.

'Señor . . . this is our bar tender's famous Pisco sour. The best you will taste. The spirit is from Elqui.'

'Great.'

'Have you been to Peru?'

'Yep.'

'Our Pisco sour is better yes?'

'Sure.'

Elqui was the birthplace of the Chilean version of Pisco. The drink was invented by the Peruvians but perfected by the Chileans in the opinion of every man, woman or child in the country. Jags liked how proud these people were about the food and drink they produced. Their empanadas were the best on the continent, their fish was the freshest, wine the smoothest, fruit the sweetest. The waiter had gone to get some chips and salsa. Jags gulped the drink down; his chest and lower stomach still ached as a result of the crash, but it seemed like the alcohol was helping. He'd have another.

The band were giving Garth Brooks' back catalogue a rest and playing something Jags hadn't heard before. The cowboy guy had taken a back seat and the greybeard of the band, who had been playing bass, had picked up a battered-looking Spanish guitar and was singing unaccompanied.

'*Yo no canto por cantar*
ni por tener buena voz . . .'

His voice was not the best, but still the bar fell quiet and people listened. Jags' thoughts turned to Soledad. She was safe, for now at least. Fred had decided to let her stew for a while. He had ordered a stop to the construction work in Brochu and Soledad had messaged Jags a couple of times to ask why the workmen had suddenly downed tools on the museum and nursery and left. He'd messaged back, saying that there were some issues back in

California and that he was going back there to work things out. This was true. The trick was going to be getting to see Elizabeth before seeing Fred. Jags had promised he'd go straight from the airport to his office tomorrow lunchtime. Several times he'd come close to messaging Elizabeth using the burner phone he'd bought for that purpose but each time he'd changed his mind.

> *. . . canto que ha sido valiente*
> *siempre será canción nueva.'*

Jags ordered the fish tacos. He drank several more Pisco sours and he tipped the waiter well when he left. He walked back to the little motel he'd chosen, filling a bag of ice from the ice machine outside before going to his room. He stopped and listened to the clunking sound of the machine restocking itself. He loved these things; it used to be *his* job to go fill up the ice bucket when he and his mom went on their annual cross-country driving holiday when he was a little boy.

Back in the bedroom he opened a beer, lay back on the bed and looked around. It was a good clean room, with hibiscus-flowered wallpaper, a brown bedspread and rock-hard bed. There were movie star lights around the bathroom mirror. He imagined being here with Elizabeth; he bet she'd never stayed anywhere like this and he had a feeling she'd like it. She would've liked the bar too.

'Fuck it.'

He reached into his pocket and pulled out the phone he'd bought. There was only one name in contacts and now he dialled it. Chances were she'd just ignore the anonymous call, but he listened to the far away dial tone and imagined how good it would be to hear her voice. He could feel his heart pumping in his chest and then he heard the dial tone suddenly end and the lines connect.

'Hello?'

It was Fred.

83 The Rabbit Hole

THE LENNON WALL, CENTRAL GOVERNMENT COMPLEX,
HONG KONG

'The TV doesn't do it justice.' Carver had walked the length of
the Lennon Wall, from the top of the concrete steps, close to the
Central Government Complex to here at the other end where
Patrick was waiting to speak to Eric. Some of the Post-it notes
were looking a little dog-eared, the ink had run on many, making
the messages of hope and defiance hard to read, but Eric and his
fellow protestors had so far succeeded in stopping the Hong Kong
police from pulling the wall down. 'Is that who we're waiting to
see? That short kid in the glasses?'

Patrick nodded.

'He's tougher than he looks.'

'He'd need to be.'

Patrick noticed that almost all of the young protestors gathered
around Eric were wearing masks of one sort or another now – all
except Eric himself. He glanced back at William.

'What do you think of the Lennon Wall then?'

Carver pulled a face.

'Bit of a mixed bag isn't it? There's some plonker from Canada trying to pass himself off as Buddha over there. Have you seen that?'

'I think I might've – *many candles lighted from a single candle?* That one?'

Carver nodded.

'That's it . . .' He raised a finger, pointing back over Patrick's shoulder. '. . . don't look now, here comes your *candle.*'

Eric Fung was walking in their direction. Patrick made the necessary introductions.

'How come *all of* your people are wearing masks now Eric? I thought it was just the Chinese tourists who were worried about that.'

Eric turned and pointed upwards.

'Haven't you seen one of Hong Kong's new *smart lampposts* yet?'

Patrick looked. There was a freshly painted, thick-trunked black lamppost fifteen feet away.

'*Smart?* What makes them smart?'

'Internet connected, very small cameras covering all angles, all manner of different sensors. They will monitor air quality, help regulate traffic . . . all of those beneficial things.'

'Right.'

'And I'm sure you can guess what else they will do.'

'I see.'

'You journalists – you keep describing what's happening here in Hong Kong as a game of *cat and mouse* – between police and protestors . . .' Carver nodded, he'd heard this idiom used often. It had become a cliché. '. . . but it's even more basic than that. It's a game of *hide and seek.* We hide behind masks, we hide ourselves in our phones and our computers.' Eric paused. 'We are hiding *in our own lives.*'

'So why aren't you wearing a mask?'

Eric shook his head.

'They have my face already. It's everyone else's face they want. They know who I am, they know everything about me – they just haven't decided what to do with me yet. The likeliest outcome, when this is all over, is that I will be in prison. In fact, that is probably the best-case scenario. *Generation Jail* . . . just as you said the first time we met. Do you remember?'

Patrick nodded.

'I remember.'

'Never mind.' He attempted a smile. 'I had a feeling that you might come today, I heard about what happened to the BBC lady.'

'Viv.' Patrick paused. 'Yes, she was a friend of mine.'

'I'm sorry.'

'Thank you Eric. She was a good person.'

'I'm sure.'

'And she was . . .'

'She was murdered. Maybe by the same person who murdered Sammy Kwok. I thought that would be why you're here?'

'Well, there are similarities.'

'More than similarities. Exactly the same kind of lies that they told about Sammy are being told about her.'

'Right, yes. So I wanted to ask you whether you'd found out any more about who posted all that stuff about Sammy? I figured it might help me work out what happened to Viv. What's happening now.'

Eric pushed his glasses back up his nose.

'You know what's happening. The people who killed her are spreading lies and sowing confusion just like they did with Sammy. They're telling people your friend Viv was unstable, that she was depressed – suicidal even. They are saying she was a spy. It is exactly the same as Sammy and it will have the same effect. People won't know what or who to believe and so, before long, most of them will stop trying. The only report that got anywhere near the truth of what happened to Sammy was that piece you did. We were grateful, but it was only one report.'

'So where is all this stuff coming from Eric? Have you any idea? Who writes it? Who spreads it?'

'Nameless, faceless people. Me and Sammy's other friends have tried to find out, we managed to trace some of the trolls, but identifying who they are and who they work for is impossible. We've chased a lot of people down many different rabbit holes but sooner or later, the trail goes cold or becomes too tangled. We will keep—'

A dull roaring sound in the skies above the Royal Observatory stopped Eric mid-sentence. They looked up in time to see the green underbelly of a Chinese fighter jet fly low overhead. Eric was about to speak again when the sound of the plane caught up. A thunderous, metallic screaming noise split the sky. Carver saw a man reach down and cover his son's ears with his hands, but not in time to stop the boy bursting into tears, his face a circle of pain.

When finally the dreadful noise receded, Eric spoke again.

'I will let you know if we find out anything else about Sammy's murder, but if I were you, I would focus on what you do know, not what you don't.'

'What do you mean?'

'The reports I read said that the last person to see the BBC lady alive was an American newspaper journalist, is that right?'

'Yes.'

'The same man we warned you about? The one who took the phone?'

'Dan Staples – yes. I know you've never trusted him Eric and I don't either but his story stands up – at least where Viv is concerned. There's CCTV of her leaving his room and going back to hers. There's nothing after that.'

'CCTV?'

'Yes.'

'Closed circuit footage?'

'Yes Eric . . .' Patrick was starting to remember how annoying Eric could be. '. . . thanks for your help but . . .'

'Closed circuits aren't closed to everyone. There are *fakes*, *deep fakes*. You shouldn't believe something just because you think you've seen it. You need to examine it more closely.'

Patrick paused. A thought entered his mind and stuck like a dart.

'Examine it more closely.' He turned and stared at Carver. 'I've just realised something – or I think I have. I need to look at that film of Viv again.'

'Let's go.'

84 Access All Areas

Jags hadn't slept. He'd spent much of the journey back from Santiago to San Fran worrying about the possible consequences of his idiotic drunken decision to call Elizabeth on the burner phone he'd bought. He'd hung up the moment he heard Fred's voice; hung up, removed the SIM and snapped it into small pieces. Nevertheless, Fred could and almost certainly would have tracked the call. Jags couldn't bear the thought that his stupidity had put Lizzie in harm's way. He needed to see her, as soon as possible and definitely before he had to report to Fred.

Inside the huge glassy atrium at Public Square HQ, Jags saw that the digital ticker tape was back. A good sign perhaps? Representing a small victory for Elizabeth and a defeat for her husband.

Announcing himself at reception, he pointed at the green-on-black screen and its endless rolling list of search engine requests.

'I wasn't expecting to see that again.'

The receptionist glanced back over her shoulder and beamed.

'Isn't it cool?'

'It doesn't upset you?'

'What? Noooo, not at all. But this is different from the old one, maybe you're thinking about the old one?'

Jags shrugged.

'Maybe.'

'This one is actually a piece of video art, this Bay Area artist, quite a famous guy. . . he curates it. But it's not boring. It's soooo funny. He takes all the craziest searches, about celebrities and everything, really hilarious stuff and he edits them all together. People love it.'

'I see.'

'Cool. So, if I look at my list here . . .' Her eyes flicked down at her computer screen, embedded in the white Corian work top. '. . . I can see your name but not where I'm s'posed to send you.'

'Yeah, well Fred . . . Mr Curepipe . . . he's expecting me any time now. But I need to get ten minutes with Mrs Curepipe first. D'you know where she is right now? Up in her office maybe?'

'Could be . . . would you mind taking a seat over there while I try and find out?'

Jags nodded.

'Sure. Thank you.'

He went and sat down on the low white leather sofa. The usual selection of glossy magazines – *Wired*, *Vogue* etc – and the international newspapers had been moved to one end of the glass coffee table to make way for a vase of cut white lilies and leather-bound book of remembrance. Jags picked it up. On the inside page was a photograph of a young woman sitting at a restaurant table, smiling. Underneath in black copperplate:

Christy Newmark - 1989 to 2014.
Public Square - 2010 to 2011

He read a few of the messages; there were many, but they all said the same sort of thing. *Tragic, unfair, never forgotten* . . . Jags looked up. The receptionist was calling him back over.

'So . . . I think I've worked out what we're supposed to do with you . . .' She smiled. '. . . if you head on over to the research centre . . .'

Jags shook his head.

'No hold up. I thought you were going to see if Lizzie . . .' He sucked at his teeth. 'I mean Mrs Curepipe, if she's got time to see me first?'

The young woman nodded.

'Sure and I did. It's Mrs Curepipe who's waiting to meet you . . . over at the research block like I say.'

'Oh. Okay. Thanks.'

'A pleasure.' She handed him an *access all areas* pass. 'Do you know where you're going?'

Jags knew. He walked across the campus, past the canteen and the oversized wooden beehive, heading for the research centre, that black metal box of a building, hidden away behind the row of silver birch trees. He was vaguely aware of there being other people around him – walking, cycling, scooting by – but his mind was elsewhere. One moment he was thinking about a hotel bedroom in London, the next a glass-strewn lay-by in Brochu. He shook the second thought from his head and lengthened his stride.

85 The Erasing

The taxi driver that Patrick had hailed a few hundred yards from the Lennon Wall chatted away in Cantolish, occasionally interrupting his monologue about the state of the roads and the state of Hong Kong's political class to point out a local landmark.

'Bruce Lee? You know him?' Carver nodded. 'He lived there.' The cabby glanced back at William and Patrick through the plastic glass to make sure they were looking at the right building. 'Yes, there.'

Carver nudged Patrick with his elbow.

'What was the piece Eric said you put together about Sammy Kwok?'

Patrick shrugged.

'Oh, it was just this little *anatomy of a story* thing that I got Brandon to do. I was trying to put a little weight on the other side of the scale. Balance out some of the rubbish people had said, the stuff we all got wrong. It was too dry really, God knows how many people bothered listening to it.'

'Some I'm sure. And Eric seemed grateful for it.'

'I guess.'

The route the driver was taking back to the Headland Hotel was circuitous. Along the way, he pointed out the street signs that he thought might mean something to the two Englishmen – *Aberdeen, Wellington, Elgin.*

'What are you hoping another look at the CCTV might tell us then Patrick?'

'I can't be certain, but I think maybe I missed something.'

'You're not sure the person on the tape was Viv?'

'No, it was definitely her but . . .' The loud sound of a phone ringing filled the cab and Carver felt the burner phone he'd bought vibrate inside his blazer pocket. Only one person had the number. He took it out and answered.

'Yes?'

'Hello.'

'Are you all right? I thought we were sticking to the landline?'

'I'm fine. I tried calling you on that. This can't wait. It's about your pal Dan Staples.'

'What've you got?'

'Well, for starters I found out why his name rang a bell. Staples was a hack back in the early two thousands, he knocked around a few of the same trouble spots as you, stringing for various American newspapers.'

'I see.' Carver paused. 'You said *was.* Why was?'

'That Dan Staples died three years back – natural causes, nothing fishy. This new version only arrived on the scene at the beginning of last year. They erased the original, took Staples' name and a chunk of his CV and he's been working as a journalist – or pretending to work as a journalist – in some interesting places ever since.'

'Flipping heck.'

'Flipping heck is right. You and Patrick have got yourselves a living, breathing *repairman*. Now all you just have to do is stick him in a jar and bring him back.'

'Seriously. What do you think we should do?'

'Where are you?'

'We're in a cab, on the way back to his hotel.'

'Is that right?' McCluskey hesitated. 'Well then, first of all, I think the both of you need to be bloody careful.'

86 The Main Man

It wasn't Elizabeth waiting for Jags outside the entrance to the research centre, but a lean man in expensive-looking jeans and a sky-blue shirt. Jags recognised him.

'Eldridge?'

'You've got a good eye, Mr Jags. Most folk won't place me unless I've got that chauffeur's get-up on.'

'You're not a chauffeur then?'

'Sometimes I am. Other times, I do *other things*.' He held the door open for Jags. 'Are you okay if we don't take the whole tour this time and just head straight down to Department Eight?'

'Is that where you're from?'

Eldridge gave a thin smile.

'Not exactly, no. But that's where Mrs Curepipe is.'

Jags felt his pulse quicken.

'Okay. How is she?'

'She's good.'

Jags followed Eldridge down the long corridor in the direction of the lift. The place seemed strangely quiet compared to his last visit.

'Where is everyone?'

'Early lunch I guess. Plus a few people off on vacation.'

'Right.' He paused. 'And what about Mr Curepipe, where's he?'

Eldridge didn't hesitate.

'Mr Curepipe's off too. He's taking some compassionate leave.'

'Compassionate leave?'

'Yes. He lost someone close to him I believe.'

Eldridge pressed the button for the lift and the two men waited in silence. Jags was struggling to make sense of what all of this meant. Fred's absence. Elizabeth choosing to meet here, inside Fred's research centre – his *man cave* as she liked to call it . . . The large steel-sided elevator juddered its way down to the basement level and opened out onto a view of the classroom Jags had seen on his previous visit. On the other side of the long glass window was a row of desks – just four of them this time – and behind each was a man, dressed in a white open-necked shirt and black trousers. Another batch of Fred's fuckin' repairmen. But Jags paid them little mind, because sitting at the other end of the room underneath the blank whiteboard, her fingers dancing across the screen of her mobile phone, was Elizabeth. She was wearing her hair in a ponytail, with a black polo neck, faded bootleg jeans and those shoes with the red soles that she liked so much. Her lipstick was the same bright red. She looked up and smiled at Jags – that smile – and he smiled back. Eldridge pushed the door open for him.

'After you.'

Jags walked in but waited on the threshold, unsure what to make of all this.

'Hello.'

'Here he is . . .' She stood, pocketed her phone and strode towards him. '. . . my *main man*.' Elizabeth kissed him on his stubbled cheek and pressed her hand against his chest. Jags smiled and tried not to wince although her hand was pushing hard against the bruise that the car seatbelt had left.

'You look well Lizzie, how're you doing?'

She turned away and walked back to her seat.

'I'm very well.'

'I was worried about you.'

'That's sweet. But you didn't need to be worried about me.'

Jags nodded.

'No . . .' He paused. '. . . I'm beginning to see.'

'Good for you.'

87 Closed Circuits

By the time the car dropped Carver and Patrick outside the entrance to the Headland Hotel, they had a plan. Patrick would take a fresh look at the CCTV footage from the night Viv disappeared while Carver worked out whether Staples was still checked in at the hotel and if so, try to find him. McCluskey had given them clear instructions on this part of the plan:

'I've seen what these fellows are capable of. If you're going to confront him, it needs to be both of yous together and in a very public place.'

Carver would try the bars and restaurants and if he found him, fetch Patrick. The plan was to tell him what they knew, see how he reacted and film the whole thing. McCluskey's digging had uncovered a fair amount, but as yet she'd been unable to find a photograph of the new-look Dan Staples.

'He's camera-shy this lad. Try and get a decent shot of him and we'll see what we can do with that.'

Patrick asked Mr Kip, the top-hatted doorman, to help arrange for him to take another look at the CCTV. Before long he was sitting in a cramped back office staring at a bank of screens. There was only room for two chairs and Patrick sat next to the head of hotel security, a grey-haired man with eyes dulled from too much staring and skin that reminded Patrick of the skin on a cold cup of hot chocolate.

'Can we start with the tape I looked at last time? Viv leaving Dan Staples' room and walking back to hers?'

The security man nodded and shuffled through his stack of minidiscs.

Carver talked the duty manager at reception into confirming that Dan Staples was still checked in at the hotel, although he hadn't seen him that day. William pushed his luck a little further and asked whether Mr Staples was paying for his stay with a credit card? Were they holding the card, or maybe a photocopy of his passport? Unsurprisingly the duty manager told him, extremely politely, to go whistle, but not before William saw his eyes flick in the direction of a box file at the other end of the desk. They had both credit card and passport details and while there was no chance of the manager letting Carver see these, he would undoubtedly hand them over to the police when the time came. That time would come once he and Patrick had gathered more evidence or after they confronted Staples himself.

William scoured the bars and restaurants but there was no sign. He saw Brandon and a gaggle of other journalists drinking in the Purple Bar but left without being seen. He even checked the swimming pool and the hotel gym but Staples was nowhere to be seen. Carver tried one of the house phones and rang the room number Patrick had given him, but it rang out. Staples was either hiding in his room, which seemed unlikely, or he was out and about running one of his errands.

When Carver pushed open the door to the poky security office, ready to update Patrick, he saw his colleague standing with his face almost pressed against one of the small screens, examining it in the greatest detail.

'I'm right, William. At least I think I'm right. Look . . .'

He stood to one side and Carver saw a doll-sized version of Viv leaving a room and walking down a corridor. Then she was in a lift for a few seconds before the picture changed again and Carver watched as she walked down a different corridor, took a key card from inside the front pocket of her rucksack, opened the door and walked in. Carver moved closer and studied the date and time code in the top right corner of the screen.

'I don't know what I'm supposed to be seeing. It looks kosher.'

Patrick nodded.

'It's Viv all right and the time code is right but something else is wrong. That's Viv's regular work outfit, it's not what she was wearing the night she went missing. She was going to wear her green dress – she told me. That's what she wore whenever she saw Dan . . .' He hesitated. '. . . and it's what she was wearing when she died.'

Carver pointed at the screen.

'So what's this?'

'It's what Eric said. It's a fake, film duped from other, older footage, cut together and swapped in . . . somehow. By someone.'

88 Sacrifice

HIJO DE DIOS, CHILE

Soledad had been hiding out at the old mine for two nights now. The only person in the world who knew she was there was her brother, Augusto. She wasn't quite sure why she'd decided to confide in him – their relationship was difficult at the best of times – but it had turned out to be an inspired choice. Augusto had kept his mouth shut and his eyes open. He had cycled up to see her twice already, the first time to update her on the movements of the two strangers from Santiago, recently arrived in Brochu; the second time to bring her some food after she'd told Augusto that she'd been forced to steal some of *El Tio's* supplies and eat those, the previous night.

'You cannot do that sister. It will bring the worst sort of bad luck.'

'Unlike all the good luck I'm enjoying at the moment?'

The strangers had arrived in town the morning after the car crash, but the questions they started asking locals had nothing to do with the accident or the unfortunate American who had been half-decapitated as a result. The questions concerned Soledad.

Where did she live? Where was she now? Which phone number was she using? She left Brochu immediately, taking her father's old sleeping bag, half a loaf of bread and a change of clothes.

The pair sat outside the entrance to Hijo de Dios and ate the cooked sausage and drank the beer he had brought. Soledad smiled at her brother.

'You know what would go well with these?' Augusto shook his head. 'Some of *El Tio's* refried beans.'

'No.'

'Yes.' Soledad jumped to her feet and tiptoed theatrically up to the horrible horned effigy before snatching a tin of rusty beans from out of his lap. The look of shock on her brother's face made her laugh.

'Don't worry Augusto – the worst thing that can happen from eating the devil's beans is indigestion.'

He shook his head and looked around. Just behind the spot where his sister sat, the white rock was stained a reddish brown. There were butchering places like these everywhere once you began to look.

'How long are you going to have to stay up here Soledad?'

'Until those two strangers leave I think.' She paused. 'Or until I can get hold of the American – Jags – and get him to tell me what's going on.'

She had left several messages for Jags using her old Nokia. The shiny new smartphone he had given her, she'd decided to leave back at the house, switched off and with the SIM card removed.

'You think that you can trust him?'

'Yes. I do.'

89 Hubris

'So where's Fred?'

'I thought Eldridge told you? He's on compassionate leave . . . he's doing some bits and pieces back at Fallingwater, but mainly he's resting. Poor Fred.'

'What happened?'

'A woman who used to work here a few years back and who had this interesting-sounding start-up . . . she died.' Elizabeth pulled her red mouth down into a Pierrot-like parody of regret. 'She was very young, it's terribly sad. Especially for Fred, he'd grown pretty close to her I think. He had all kind of plans.'

'I don't know who . . . *her* is.'

Elizabeth shook her head.

'No, I know you don't. The point is Fred is going to take some well-deserved R & R, so I thought we might as well meet over here at his place. Hey Eldridge . . .' She glanced over at the door where *Eldridge-who-was-a-lot-of-things* was standing. '. . . fetch Jags a chair will you?'

A white folding chair was brought and Jags sat on it. Lizzie in front of him, the four white shirt-wearing repairmen along with Eldridge at his back. Five feet between them and him. Jags looked around the room and nodded, taking everything in.

'So this is a funny ol' set-up you've got here Lizzie. It looks like you're getting ready to teach a class.'

She grinned.

'A class? Yes, perhaps I am.'

'Maybe I shoulda brought you an apple or something.'

'Just having you here, that's enough for me Jags.'

'So what's this all about?'

'Well it was going to be a pretty straightforward debrief – like you used to do with Fred. But I think I like your idea better. How about you start the class off with a report? From your trip down to Chile? One of those *what I did at the weekend* kind of things?'

'I get the feeling you know quite a lot already, Lizzie.'

'Maybe. But it's important to know *everything*. Isn't that what Fred's always telling us?'

Jags laughed.

'He didn't learn his own lesson though, did he Lizzie?'

'No.' She shook her head. 'Never underestimate a man's ability to *underestimate a woman*.' She turned to Jags. 'It doesn't matter how much she achieves. How high she climbs . . . still the men around her will assume that she's incapable of finding the next rung on the ladder. Inventing that next rung if it isn't there.' Elizabeth walked the circumference of the room, the clicking sound of her shoes ricocheting off the hard walls. 'Fred was so certain that this place, his *man cave* was the last word in innovation. He was so convinced that *God Mode* was as good as it could possibly get.'

'Hubris.'

Elizabeth shook her head.

'That's you getting all overly poetic again Jags. Truth is – Fred was being a dick.'

She completed her circuit of the room and sat back down.

'So what happens now Lizzie?'

'You go ahead and give us your class report. What happened down in Chile?'

'A lot happened. What specifically do you want to know?'

'Okay. Specifically – at what point did you decide to kill Nathan?'

Jags grinned.

'Well, to be completely honest with you Lizzie . . . pretty soon after I met him. I didn't like him much.'

'Didn't you? That's a shame. I liked him.'

'Is that right?'

'Yup. But more importantly Jags, he was one of us.'

90 The Invisible Man

THE HEADLAND HOTEL, HONG KONG

Carver and Patrick agreed to take turns looking through the other tapes in an attempt to find the original footage of Viv – the segment that had been copied across and recoded to show her leaving Staples' room on the night she went missing. This would constitute one piece of proof. At the same time they'd try to find the clearest possible image of Dan himself. His passport photo would be more useful, but in the meantime it'd be good to give McCluskey something to work with. Patrick wanted to call Rebecca and let her know what was going on, so Carver took the first shift. He sat down next to the hollow-cheeked security man and pointed at the racks of minidiscs.

'I guess we better start the first day Viv arrived . . .'

The old Hongkonger shook his head.

'This was more than three weeks ago.'

'Yep.'

'Every day?'

'All day every day.'

Carver pushed his shoes off and stretched out as far as the wall would allow. The security guard sighed, slid the first minidisc into his machine and pressed play.

Rebecca had been expecting his call.

'I heard the terrible news about Viv, Patrick. I'm so, so sorry. What do you think happened? There's all sorts of odd stuff on the internet.'

Patrick hesitated.

'I know. We're not really sure. Not yet.'

'Well, if there's anything you can do out there to help – then you should do it.'

He wondered whether he should tell her that he'd had to identify Viv's body – he had wanted to tell her this, but now it seemed like the wrong thing to do. He wouldn't tell Rebecca that, nor anything else. 'I read that her mum and dad are on their way?'

'Yeah, they should arrive tomorrow.'

'Well then you should stay and see them. Stay as long as it's helpful. I'm absolutely fine, the ginger tea is working a treat and I'm practising walking with a waddle. That's my main news.'

'I can't wait to see that waddle.'

'I'll have it down by the time you see me.'

Patrick checked the hotel bars once more to make sure that Staples wasn't back, then went and ordered some takeaway food from the restaurant. He arrived back at the security office with a leaning tower of orange polystyrene cartons. Carver looked round, sniffing at the air.

'Smells good, what is it?'

'It's the cheapest food I could find from the hot buffet.'

'Nice work.'

He flipped a carton of meatballs open and ate one with his fingers.

'How are you getting on?'

411

'Not great. Me and Anthony here . . .' He waved a sauce-covered finger at the old security guard sitting next to him. '. . . we've only managed about two and a half days'-worth of tape.'

'That doesn't sound like much.'

'No. I called reception; we can have a room here tonight if we need it. I reckon we're going to.' He ate another meatball. 'The other news, the really bad news is that it looks like Dan Staples is some sort of invisible man. I wanted to try and give McCluskey a look at him, so we skipped ahead and we watched the last few days'-worth of footage from the cameras on his corridor – there's nothing. He's completely disappeared.'

91 Queasy

'I'm sorry about Nathan, Lizzie.'

'Never mind. These things happen. I liked him, but he wasn't my favourite . . .' She smiled at Jags. '. . . you're still my favourite.'

He glanced around the room.

'I can see.'

'*Protect the queen*. That's what you and Fred always used to say, wasn't it? Back in the beginning.'

'It was.'

'And I always felt very protected by you, Jags. Right up until recently.'

'What happened recently?'

She got to her feet again. Her phone back in her hand.

'Fred noticed it first – small changes. I read what he wrote in your file.'

Jags laughed.

'I didn't know there was a file.'

'There's always a file . . .' She glanced at her phone. '. . . *morally queasy*. That's what he wrote. He put a couple of question marks

413

next to it and when I first read it, I thought he was wrong. But you know Fred, he's hardly ever wrong. He saw something in your data – in the *sum*. And I saw it in person, in London.'

'In London? In London you said—' He stopped.

'What?'

'It doesn't matter.'

Elizabeth shook her head.

'No, you're right, it doesn't matter. That's all in the past, what matters is the future. The future of the company.' She put the phone back in her pocket again. 'So, here's what happens next. What we were trying to do in Brochu hasn't worked, it's not your fault – not entirely – but I'd like you to call Soledad Mistral. Tell her you want to meet, say . . . the day after tomorrow.'

Jags nodded slowly.

'I see. So you don't know where she is.'

Elizabeth smiled.

'You need to concentrate now Jags, listen to what I'm saying. You came back here to save me . . . and I appreciate it. But now you need to *save you*. Go ahead and call her and all will be forgiven.'

'Forgiven?'

'That's right. A clean slate, just tell her that you'll meet her at the same restaurant you took her to before. One p.m. the day after tomorrow.'

Jags got his phone out of his pocket. He went to his recent calls, found Soledad's number and dialled it.

92 Deep Fake

THE HEADLAND HOTEL, HONG KONG

Patrick racked his brains for specific days and times when he knew that Dan had been present in a certain part of the hotel. The bars, restaurants and their encounters in the lobby. They checked the CCTV from all of them – there was nothing. All evidence of Dan ever having set foot inside the Headland Hotel was gone.

'Who can do that? I mean who has the capability?'

Carver shook his head.

'I don't know, but I'm pretty sure that whoever it is has also made sure that the credit card and passport details that reception are holding are just as unhelpful.'

'So we've got nothing?'

'Not nothing.' He pointed at the stack of discs. 'Your idea is still a good one; I reckon there's still a chance we find the original CCTV of Viv that they copied and swapped in.'

'And?'

'Well, apart from that we need to hope that Staples himself turns up. I've got a hunch he might. He hasn't checked out and we've still got something he wants. Could be he's biding his time or

415

waiting on a new set of orders.' Carver paused. 'Perhaps we need to chivvy him along.'

'How?'

William got his laptop and old mobile phone out from inside his yellow plastic bag, made a space for them on the desk alongside the cartons of takeaway food and switched them both on. Patrick watched while Carver connected to the internet using the hotel Wi-Fi.

'These devices of ours have been pretty good at attracting their attention when we *don't* want it. Let's see if it works when we *do*. We should eat some of this food before it goes cold.'

Carver persuaded the old security guard, Anthony, to take a break and so he and Patrick sat next to each other, eating takeaway and watching CCTV of Viv, walking up and down various corridors. Now and again Carver's London mobile would vibrate on the desk as a number of unlistened to messages arrived. He deleted several from his students requesting more time to finish their essays before listening to a message from Donnie that was intriguing and troublesome in equal parts, and a couple from Naz reminding William that he needed to send her his Hong Kong contact number. There was a note of excitement in her voice. He flipped his laptop open as well and checked first his emails, then a few stories on the BBC News website before finally taking a look at Dan Staples' Wikipedia page.

Carver shrugged.

'Well, if they don't know who and where we are after that little lot then I don't know what to do. Might as well fire a flare off the roof of the hotel.' He squinted at the screen. 'One thing about being back on the job, I'm getting a much more exciting selection of adverts being pushed my way.'

Patrick looked and saw a glitzy ad across the top of the screen offering VIP weekends at a well-known casino in Macau. On the side was another for a *Gentleman's Club* in Lan Kwai Fong.

'Lucky you. Rebecca thinks these tailor-made ads are terrifying.'

'So do I. Back at home the only ones I get are for Nordic cruises and budget funerals.'

Carver yawned and Patrick looked across at him.

'William, you must be knackered. Why don't you turn in? I'll do another hour or so then I'll do the same, we can pick it up tomorrow.'

'Nah, I'll do a little bit longer.'

'You don't have to.'

'I want to. Viv and I didn't always get along and looking back now, I realise that was my fault. She tolerated me at a time when I was pretty hard to tolerate.'

'Right.'

'She wasn't the only one.'

'Well . . .'

'How about this? You do one more sweep of the bars just in case Staples has come back while we've been cooped up in here, have a pee, get a coffee and then you can take over and I'll go try and sleep.'

'Deal.'

93 Redemption

Soledad's number rang. And rang. Jags listened, praying that his call might remain unanswered, and it seemed that this might be the case. Then there was a sudden click. A woman's voice. Quiet but clear.

'Hola?'

'Soledad? It's Jags.'

'Yes?'

Jags looked at Lizzie and smiled.

'Wherever you are, Soledad . . . leave there now. Ditch this phone and don't go home. Run!'

Elizabeth barely moved. The slightest tilt of the head, but that was enough. Chairs and desks flew in different directions and within moments they were on him. They covered the five feet quicker than he thought they would and Jags only just managed to turn and duck as the first punch flew past his face. He kicked and hit and gouged and fought – if this was going to be his last fight then he wanted it to be a good one. He caught a couple of Lizzie's boys with decent hits – one with a fist to the kidneys and another with a left hook that broke both Jags' knuckle and the man's jaw. A well-placed knee lifted hard into some poor unfortunate's groin left the man screaming in pain and out of the game for the duration and at that point Eldridge reluctantly joined in. Jags gouged a couple more eyes but he was surrounded and tiring and there were too many of them. The four men grappled with him until each had a limb. They were locked hard onto their quarry now and both he and they knew it. He managed a couple more kicks and then suddenly the lights went out and Jags realised that someone at his back had pulled a thick plastic sack over his head. The bag was being twisted tighter and it filled fast with his own panted breath. He tried to slow his breathing but it was difficult. They kicked repeatedly against the backs of his legs until eventually his knees folded and he was forced to the ground. Still he strained against the bag and as he did, the plastic stretched. It was hard to breathe, his head felt heavy but still he pushed – stretching the bag some more – until there above him, standing watching, he saw Elizabeth. Or her outline anyway. A strong hand was trying to force his head down, but he pushed against it, lifting his head some more. She was staring at him and now he heard her voice.

'I'm sorry Jags.'

His head was swimming, he was suffocating – choking on his own fumes.

Oblivion was close now.
Or possibly hell.
It was hell that he deserved.

'Fuck it.'

One of the men who'd come off worst from the fight kicked Jags' corpse a couple of times before being pulled away by Eldridge. He put the bloodied man down in a seat before returning to receive Elizabeth's next instruction.

'Tell them to bring the equipment and do it here. Seal off this floor.'

'Right. And what about the others?'

'Tell Fred's men to continue as instructed. Repair what needs repairing.'

94 Remembrance

McCluskey wore the red poppy for most of October and a good part of November too. She had never missed a Remembrance Sunday service at her local church and she wasn't going to miss this one either. The vicar did a good enough job, although once again the Union Jack outside the church was hanging upside down and she felt she had to mention this as she was leaving the church. She tempered this criticism with praise, in particular for the idea of getting local schoolchildren to read the long list of names of servicemen and women from this parish who had died in action down the years. It was a long list and McCluskey wasn't the only one drying her eyes on a tissue or handkerchief by the end of it. A peal of church bells sounded bright and clear in the cold morning air as she walked back home.

The black Mercedes was parked outside her house, this time with no one in it. She saw a shadow at the upstairs window – inside her *command and control* centre – and stopped. She needed a moment to gather her thoughts. She could call the police again

421

and wait for them to arrive: until they did she could hide around the side of the house.

'Bugger that.' McCluskey opened her handbag and looked inside. 'First things first.' She took the Swiss Army knife that she used as a key ring, pulled out the longest knife and punctured all four tyres on the Merc. That done, she walked around to the rear of the house and silently back in through the kitchen. She took up position in her living room, knowing that the only way the man upstairs was going to leave was via the stairs down into the hall. She armed herself.

The flat-faced man who came down the stairs had a boxful of McCluskey's stuff in his arms and no idea that he was no longer alone in the house.

'Are you the cunt who killed my cat?'

He turned, a shocked look on his face. A golf ball hit him square in the forehead. She threw another, which hit him just above the ear. He shouted – a mix of pain and fury in his voice – and retreated backwards up the stairs. McCluskey yelled after him. 'I've called the police, they're on their way.' This was a lie and now she came to think of it, an oversight. She got her phone out and was through to the operator and about to speak when the man came again, walking slowly down the stairs, a snub-nosed gun in his hand.

'Put the phone down Mrs McCluskey.'

The accent was American or maybe Canadian.

'No.'

'I don't want to hurt you.'

'Then don't, get out of my house.'

'I will. But I need to take that box with me.'

'No chance.'

She had a golf ball in her left hand and she launched it but missed. The man started walking slowly towards her, his hand out in an attempt to calm her. McCluskey reached behind her towards the mantelpiece, in search of more ammunition. Her hand found a snow globe and she turned and chucked it. It bounced off his arm and smashed on the floor. She glanced down and saw what looked like a broken grey tuning fork in a pool of white speckled water. 'That was my *Twin Towers*, you bastard. You'll pay fer that.' She ran at him, hands raised. The flat-faced man turned sideways, stepped backwards and hit her hard on the cheek with the side of his gun as she went by. McCluskey fell.

'Stay down.'

'Fuck you, ya banger.'

She climbed back onto all fours. She had her hands on the edge of the sofa, preparing to stand, ready to fight, when the butt of the gun came down hard on the top of her head. And darkness fell.

95 The Full English

William woke early; the time difference between Hong Kong and home had left his body clock not really knowing whether it was coming or going. He tried his best to wash and dress quietly, so as not to wake Patrick who was sleeping on a fold-down mattress on the floor, but his stumbling about eventually roused his colleague.

'Hey William.'

'All right. How're you feeling?'

Patrick looked at his watch.

'Bit early to say. Okay I think.'

'Good. Did you have any luck with the CCTV last night after I left?'

'Nothing.'

'Okay, I'll check at reception to see if there's been any sign of Staples, get myself some breakfast and then pick up where you left off.'

Patrick rubbed his eyes.

'It's five a.m.'

'Early bird gets the worm. See you later.'

The early bird got a disapproving look from the waiter in charge of breakfast at the Headland Hotel. The man put Carver by a window and offered him a menu, which William waved away.

'Don't need it. I'll have the full English.'

The waiter nodded, removed the second setting from the table and left. Carver flicked through a copy of yesterday's *Wall Street Journal* that he'd picked up at reception. The duty manager had informed him that there was still no sign of, or word from, Dan Staples. Not checked out, but still nowhere to be seen. His full English arrived, looking rather sorry for itself – a single plump sausage, one rasher of bacon, a spoonful of scrambled eggs and a slice of black pudding all gathered closely together – as though for protection – in the centre of a huge white plate. Carver looked up at the waiter.

'Is that it?'

'*The Full English.*'

'Right. In that case I'm going to need more toast. A lot more.'

He demolished the breakfast in no time and then worked his way steadily through the bite-sized quadrangles of toast. He found himself wishing that he'd thought to bring the Dundee thick-cut marmalade with him.

It was almost six by the time he knocked on the door of the security office and the grey-haired security guard opened it.

'It's me again Anthony, I'm sorry to say.'

Carver settled back in, kicking off his shoes while Anthony read the note that Patrick had left, detailing where he'd got to last night. The guard offered him a cup of coffee from his thermos, which William gratefully accepted, and they set the machines running again.

Half an hour passed. Then an hour and Carver started to wonder how much longer Patrick would sleep for. He needed a wee. He glanced across at Anthony.

'Can you pause all this for a minute so I can pop to the toilet? I'll only be . . .' He stopped mid-sentence. 'Fuck me, look! They missed something . . .' Carver pointed at the monitor closest to Anthony's right hand. '. . . they *didn't* manage to erase everything, that's Dan Staples right there, riding that lift. What date is that?'

The old man leant forward, squinting.

'That's not the archive tape. That's now.'

96 Sick Days

Rebecca sat in the nurse's room and tried to breathe slowly. In through the nose, out through the mouth. It wasn't easy, nor particularly pleasant. The cramped room stank of carbolic soap and after school club was still going on out in the hall. She heard kids yelling and the occasional thump of a flat-sounding football hitting a wall. The headmaster poked his head around the door.

'I've booked you a cab, I'm sending you home.'

'No, I'll be fine, really I just . . .'

'It's done. We can do parents' evening without you for once. Bugger off. Come back when you're not such a horrible green colour.'

Rebecca gave him an appreciative smile. The cab took an age to get across London in the evening rush hour and Rebecca slept for much of it. By the time she got out, outside the flat on Highbury Fields, it was pitch black, the orange street lights were on and she felt a little better. Perhaps she might even manage something to eat? There was pesto in the fridge, some pasta in the cupboard. A quick meal in front of the TV, a bath and then bed. She thanked the driver, got her house keys out of her bag and opened the front door. She was halfway up the stairs when she realised that she hadn't heard the front door pull itself shut behind her. She turned round and heard the door to the street, only now, slowly closing. She peered over the bannisters, down into the shadowy hall, but there was no one outside the downstairs flat. She leant out further to get a view of the alcove where people stacked bikes and buggies.

'Hello?'

97 Repairs

The curtains were still drawn and in the half-light, Patrick initially assumed it was Carver standing at the foot of the fold-down mattress, staring down at him. He had a rucksack by his side.

'Hello bud.'

'What the . . .'

Dan dropped into a crouch and in one quick movement leapt forward, grabbing Patrick's wrists and wrenching his arms out to the side before pinning them to the floor with his knees. Patrick tried to kick up at his attacker – his legs flailed around, displacing his sheet and blanket, but nothing more. Dan sat back, his full weight landing heavily on Patrick's stomach and winding him. 'Calm the fuck down buddy, this'll go a whole lot quicker if you just stay calm.'

'F . . . fuck you.'

The words came out sounding reedy and weak and the repairman just grinned.

'Where's the memory stick Patrick? Just give me that and we'll be done.'

'I don't know.'

Dan shrugged. He bunched his right hand, lifted it to shoulder height and punched his victim hard in the face. Patrick heard the bones in his nose break and felt a bolt of excruciating pain, but when he opened his mouth to scream, Dan clamped his thick hand over it, silencing him.

'Let's try again. Where'd you put it?'

Patrick shook his head.

Dan removed his left hand from his victim's mouth and hit him again with the right. Harder this time. Patrick could taste blood in his mouth, sour and metallic. His eyes were streaming with tears, leaving his vision blurry. Dan covered his mouth again and his bloodied nose as well. He couldn't breathe.

'Either you can die here – like your mate – or you can tell me where the memory stick is.'

Patrick was trying to mumble something. Dan took his hand off his mouth.

'I don't have it.'

'Course you do.'

The American turned and reached for his rucksack; he put it down next to Patrick's pinioned arm and unzipped the front pocket. Inside Patrick saw a mobile phone and next to that, something bright – a mirror or . . . Dan pulled out the thick-handled hunting knife and held it close to his face, allowing him a good look. 'I enjoy using this thing, bud. Don't give me the excuse.'

Patrick nodded slowly. He was scared. Terrified. His mouth was moving again and Dan removed his hand so he could speak. At first it was just sounds and bubbles of spit.

'C'mon Patrick. Where is it?'

'It's . . . it's in my kitbag. In the cupboard . . .' He nodded to his right. '. . . behind me.'

Dan glanced at the cupboard.

'I'm going to let you up. You get up slow, get the bag and the memory stick and you throw it over to me. Do it wrong and I'll cut your throat, so try and do it right.'

He leant back and stood, releasing Patrick's aching arms. The American took a couple of steps backwards, his eyes on Patrick all the time and the knife still there in his right hand. They were back where they'd started, Dan Staples staring down at Patrick who was still lying on his back, trying to catch a full breath, his face a bloodied mess. 'Go on, roll over there and get it.'

Patrick pushed himself up onto his side, then his knees and crawled to the cupboard. He slid the door open, pulled his kitbag out and reached around inside – it was in here somewhere, he was sure. Eventually his hand found the plastic memory stick. He turned and held it up for the American to see.

'Good job buddy. Now just toss it this way and we're done.'

Patrick glanced at the memory stick, then tossed it to Dan. It landed at his feet. He was just about to reach down and pick it up when a soft clicking sound stopped him. He stood very still. It was a familiar, but not instantly recognisable sound. Both men had heard it and both figured out what it was at exactly the same moment – they looked over towards the bedroom door, just in time to watch it being pushed open, followed by William Carver, who came charging in holding a fire extinguisher in his hands like a battering ram. He rammed it into Dan, hard enough to knock the knife from the repairman's hand, but not hard enough to floor him. A mad scramble followed, with Carver throwing the fire extinguisher at Dan's head, missing and then crawling around on the floor looking for the knife. He had one hand on the black rubber handle when Dan's right boot connected with his head and sent him flying back against the cupboard. The impact cracked the sliding wooden door cleanly down the middle and Carver fell sideways onto the carpet. Patrick was on his feet now – bloodied but no longer bowed. He moved in Dan's direction, hands held up in front of him in a boxer's pose, but when the American stooped and picked the hunting knife back up off the floor, the sight of it stopped Patrick in his tracks.

'Smart decision.'

Patrick lifted his hands in surrender.

'You've got the memory stick. Please go.'

'I'm going to go bud, real soon. But you see . . .' He picked up his rucksack and slung it over his shoulder. '. . . the memory stick's *a pass*. Your friend here . . .' He pointed down at William. '. . . he's a *merit mark*. I gotta say a proper goodbye.' He turned the knife sideways.

'No! Get the fuck away from him.'

Patrick ran at the American, grabbing for his arms and wrestling him away from William and back towards the wall. There were noises now outside in the corridor – voices and now a loud knocking on the door. Dan punched Patrick a couple of times in the stomach then pushed him, almost lifting him backwards onto the bed. The door to the room opened from the outside and there was grey-haired Anthony and a couple of more formidable-looking members of hotel security. Dan barged past them, reshouldering his backpack and then running, down the hotel corridor and out through the emergency exit towards the stairs. One of the young security guards threw down his hat and set off after him.

98 Lessons

Upstairs in her and Patrick's flat, Rebecca snipped the latch down and pulled the chain across. She walked into the living room, switching on the main light and both the lamps as well. She shuffled out of her coat and chucked that and her brown satchel onto the sofa. Then she stopped and listened. There was nothing to hear – nothing apart from the usual street sounds from outside; the buzz of the fridge in the small kitchen. She walked through to the bedroom and turned all the lights on in there too. She took off her cardigan and opened the clothes cupboard. A shoebox of old letters and photos fell from the top shelf and Rebecca jumped.

'*Pull yourself together woman. Flipping heck.*' She put the box back on the top shelf, hung her cardigan on a hanger and closed the cupboard door.

In the kitchen, she found the pasta and put a pan of water on the hob to boil. She switched the radio on with the volume turned down low. Then stopped and switched it off again.

The sound had come from outside, in the hall – footsteps, on the stairs up to their flat or maybe the half landing below that.

433

But footsteps; she was sure. It could be the downstairs neighbour, Vera, coming to ask for something, that happened now and then. But if she was coming, why hadn't she knocked? Rebecca walked tentatively to the front door, still listening. She checked the latch was down and then the chain as well. She put her ear to the door.

Someone was there. Just outside; waiting. Patrick's cricket bat was propped beside the door. The sum total of their home security system. Rebecca noticed that she was standing with both hands covering her stomach; she removed them and picked up the cricket bat.

It seemed like minutes but most likely it was only seconds that she was standing there. Then, suddenly the light outside in the hall clicked on. Rebecca was sure there was someone right outside her door. There was a shout from downstairs, she recognised Vera's voice.

'Hey you! Matey boy. I can see you up there. What d'you want?'

There was a sound of shuffling.

'Wrong flat.'

The light on the landing clicked off. Then on again.

'Bloody light. Wrong flat my arse. Douglas! Call the police. It's that dickhead I've seen hanging around by the Fields. He's outside Rebecca and Patrick's place.'

Rebecca heard a muttered oath and then the loud sound of feet running down the stairs. She unlocked and unchained the door, opening it in time to see a flash of navy-blue jacket and a crop-haired head two flights down. Vera was standing in her doorway, her five-foot five-inch husband Douglas at her side. She glanced up.

'Oh you're in? I thought you was still out. Are you okay?'

Rebecca nodded. She was as white as a sheet.

'Thank you.'

'Don't be silly. Did you see him? Little toe rag. Don't worry, he won't be back – he wouldn't dare – Dougie here would kick the shit out of him.' She paused. 'Here Beccy, you're looking like you've seen a ghost. How about you pop down here for a mug of sugary tea?'

Rebecca smiled. She went to switch the hob off and fetch her keys.

99 The Lift

Carver regained consciousness pretty quickly. Looking up, he saw legs. Anthony and another hotel security guard were standing in front of the double bed and in between them William saw a pair of bare feet. He tried to stand.

'Patrick, is that you?'

'Hey William, yeah. Are you okay?'

'I'm fine.

'That's good.'

'What happened? He got away? Bollocks. I thought maybe we had him there.' He got to his feet, his head hurt. 'How're you doing?'

Patrick was lying diagonally across the double bed. He lifted his head and attempted a smile.

'Not great I don't think William.' His skin was ashen, his nose broken and bloodied. Carver looked first at the state of Patrick's face and then down at what Anthony and the other security guard were staring at – his stomach.

Patrick had his hands cupped together, holding something.

436

Carver moved closer. The black-handled hunting knife was buried in his gut. Patrick's dark T-shirt and boxer shorts were wet with blood.

'What the hell? We need a doctor, a paramedic.' He glared at Anthony. 'What are you two idiots doing just standing there?'

'The ambulance is on its way, sir, the doctor will come.'

'When?'

'Soon.'

William shook his head.

'Fuck that.' He pushed the two men aside. 'Patrick, we need to get you downstairs, we need to be there as soon as the ambulance arrives. Put your arm around me.'

Patrick looked up at William.

'Are you sure?'

Carver nodded. He glanced again at Patrick's bloodied clothing; he was losing too much blood, too quickly

'I'm sure. We can't wait here.'

'Okay.'

Carver lifted Patrick up from the bed, he didn't know where the strength to do this came from, but it came. He walked him down the short hall towards the bedroom door and pulled it open with his free hand. Anthony and the other security guard followed, but at a respectable distance. Carver and Patrick set off together down the long corridor, moving slowly but steadily in the direction of the lift.

'You're doing great Patrick, this is good. You're going to be fine. The ambulance is nearly here, we're going to meet them downstairs, it'll be quicker. They're going to patch you up.' They were at the lifts. Carver pressed the button and the lift came. The doors opened and they half-walked, half-stumbled in. Patrick's face was contorted with pain.

'Can we sit down again William? I really need to sit, just for a moment?'

'Sure, we can sit. Just for a minute.'

William leant forward and pressed the button for the lobby and then he dragged Patrick backwards until both their backs were against the mirrored wall. Together they shuffled slowly down and sat.

'William?'

Carver was looking at the knife. The blood on Patrick's legs.

'Yeah?'

'I got his phone.'

'What?'

'Dan Staples' phone, I stole it out of his bag. It's under the bed.'

'That's great Patrick. That'll be . . . really helpful. We'll get to that as soon as we've fixed you up.'

'Good. And the memory stick . . . the real memory stick – it's in the curtain. It was the first thing I did. Like you taught me. You remember?' His eyes were wet.

'I remember.'

'William . . . I'm scared.'

'Don't be scared. I've got you . . .' He pulled Patrick's arm closer to his and held it tighter. '. . . we're nearly there, you're going to be okay.'

Patrick was slipping forward. Carver pulled him gently back; the floor of the lift was sticky with blood.

'Tell her I wasn't scared William.'

'You can tell her yourself.'

'Tell her I love her.'

'She knows you love her Patrick. She *really* knows that.'

The lift arrived in the lobby and the doors opened. Carver lifted Patrick up, carried him to a nearby sofa and laid him down. He could hear sirens, the ambulance was coming. It would be here soon.

100 Foundations

The rain fell. It came down so hard that every drop that hit uncovered skin hurt. A needle prick of pain. The tiny hairline cracks in the dam wall were slowly growing wider. Thin trickles of water leaked and dribbled from these cracks, zigzagging down the wall. Trickles turned to rivulets and the cracks grew wider still.

No one was sure why all the waste material inside a tailings dam – the mud, poisonous metals and slurry that had solidified over time and seemed completely secure – could, without warning, suddenly *liquefy*. Maybe the rain was to blame? A little too much rain. Or a minor, almost imperceptible earthquake that had shaken the dam's foundations? Whatever it was, it was happening now. The cracks grew wider, the dam wall could not hold and so it broke, section by section and from behind it came a huge tide of liquid mud.

This dark tide moved slowly at first but picked up speed with every moment that passed. It crashed through the company canteen and plant offices first, crushing the buildings as though they were made of matchsticks and burying almost forty men alive – before the alarm had even sounded. As the tide moved on down the valley, towards Brochu, it lifted cars and cows and goats up, then dragged them under. The alarm was sounding now, but too late for most who heard it. Soledad saw families trying to run, a mother piling her two small children into the back of an old car and frantically attempting to start the motor. Just in the nick of time the engine sparked into life, the car moved and was accelerating but not fast enough – the woman could see the wave of sludge in her rear-view mirror and then it was on top of them. Soledad heard the sound of children screaming. And then silence.

The wave was growing in strength and size and now she saw, in the distance, her own family. They were running. Her mother was being pulled and lifted by the boys while at their back, the wall of waste crushed one breeze block and tin-roofed house after another. Her mother was mouthing something. Soledad strained her eyes to see. Her mother was praying – prayers for her soul, for her brothers' souls. A prayer too for her daughter.

Soledad woke. Her face was wet with sweat. She was trembling. She looked around.

The central Santiago bus station was busy, even at this ungodly hour of the morning. Many of her fellow Chileans were trying to do the same as her – catch some sleep – either stretched out on one of the plastic three-seater benches or curled up in a corner or next to one of the vending machines. She stood and rubbed the heels of her hands against her eyes, trying to wipe the nightmare away. But it wouldn't work. The dreams were getting worse, but at least now she knew what she had to do to stop them. The only way was to stop running. Stop hiding. She glanced at her watch. The bus back in the direction of Brochu was leaving in two hours. Soledad didn't want to sleep any more. She hoisted her rucksack up on to her shoulder and went to find a cup of coffee.

101 The Right Thing

Carver avoided the hotel bars, preferring to stay in the room that the management had provided him. It was on the same floor as the room that he and Patrick had shared and which was now sealed up and decorated with a zigzag of thick yellow police tape. A kindly policeman had asked William to confirm that the room had not been disturbed since the attack had taken place and Carver had simply nodded. He'd gone back to the room only briefly and disturbed almost nothing. He would have preferred to have accompanied Patrick to the hospital, to have ridden with him in the ambulance. But his friend had made it clear he did not want that. It was more important that he retrieve Dan Staples' phone from beneath the bed and the memory stick that Patrick had tucked into the hem of the curtain. So that was what William did.

He'd spent the last twenty-four hours trying to work out what to do next. He'd made one decision, not a decision he was particularly happy with, but which, on balance, felt like the right thing to do. The room phone rang and he answered.

'Hello.'

441

'A Mr Eric Fung is here Mr Carver.' It was the hotel manager speaking. 'He says you're expecting him?'

'That's right.'

It was ten minutes before Eric tapped lightly on the door. When William opened it, he was cleaning his glasses on the bottom of his T-shirt, a drenched-looking anorak slung over his shoulder.

He squinted at William.

'You have quite a lot of security.'

'Yeah. The police wouldn't let me stay where I wanted to stay. They insisted I have a bloody police guard here at the hotel as well.'

'It's probably wise. Also . . . it means there are fewer policemen available to beat up students on the Harcourt Road.'

Carver shrugged.

'From what I hear, you were giving as good as you got.'

'That's incorrect.'

'Whatever. You better come in.'

Best that he do what he'd decided to do quickly – before he changed his mind. He ushered the kid in and offered him the only chair in the room while he took a seat on the bed, alongside his open laptop.

'I want to offer you something . . .' He took a white memory stick from his pocket, and after checking that his machine was not connected to the internet, plugged it into the side of the laptop. '. . . these are the interviews that Patrick collected. The stuff he talked to you about.' Eric nodded. 'If you'd want, I can open the file up on my machine, lend you some headphones and you can sit there and listen to these.'

Eric was, briefly, speechless.

'I would certainly like to do that. I am not sure what to say . . . thank you.'

Carver shook his head.

'Don't thank me. I'm still not sure this is a good idea at all.'

'Then why. . .'

'Patrick talked about your friend Sammy and putting a little weight on the other side of the scale. I think *he*'d want you to have a chance to hear these. That's the only reason I'm doing this.'

'Then I thank Patrick.'

'Fine.' He stood up. 'Here you go . . .' Carver placed the laptop on the desk, handed Eric some headphones, opened the file and pressed play.

It took Eric over two hours to listen to all the interviews. As he listened he made notes in the dog-eared school exercise book he carried around with him. He filled several pages. While he did this, Carver first stood at the window and watched the ferries crossing to and fro from Kowloon, then lay on the bed and dozed. When Eric finished he shook Carver's foot to wake him.

'I've listened to everything.'

'Fine, good.' He paused. 'I'll say goodbye then.'

Eric paused.

'I would like to give you something in return.'

'Yeah? What's that?'

Carver found it hard to imagine that Eric would have anything that he could possibly want. He hoped it wasn't one of those bloody inspirational Post-it notes from the Lennon Wall. He watched as Eric reached into his pocket for his phone.

'We have these . . .'

The photos that the kids involved with *Scholastic* had taken of the man they believed to have stolen their friend's phone were surprisingly good – both head on and in profile. Eric swished through the pictures on his phone, one by one. '. . . we have his face.'

Two weeks later

102 Visiting Hours

McCluskey was sitting up in her hospital bed. It was the best William had seen her, although she still looked a fright. Half her head had been shaved and this made the white, wiry hair on the other side appear all the wilder. Carver remembered what he'd thought the first time they'd been introduced. Jemima's hair resembled a sort of personal antenna – as though she was receiving messages from far-flung places even when the earphones were off.

'Stop staring at me with that pitying look on your face you rude bastard. You're no oil painting yourself, I can tell you that.'

Carver brought a bunch of flowers out from inside his plastic bag and held them up for McCluskey to see. She smiled.

'Freesias. That'll be the bunch of flowers you *nearly* brought me that time will it?'

Carver shrugged.

'I remembered you said you liked freesias or lilies. I was going to buy the lilies but the bloke at the flower shop said those are mainly for dead people.'

'Right . . . don't want to jump the gun . . .' She paused. '. . . are you going to unwrap them and put them in some water or just stand there waving them around?'

Carver removed the paper and rubber bands from the bunch of bright yellow freesias and stuck them in McCluskey's spare drinking glass. He filled it to the brim with water from the sink then looked around.

'Where do you want them?'

'Put them on my wheely table.' McCluskey's table was already overcrowded with get well cards, newspapers, a jug of juice and an untouched fruit basket. 'You can get shot of that presentation basket. I've got fruit coming out my flaming ears.' Carver removed the fruit basket – plastic wrapped and tied with a ribbon. It looked pretty fancy. He put it down next to the door. Jemima pushed herself up in the bed. 'The flowers look smashing William, thank you.'

'You're welcome.'

'Enough of the small talk now though. Tell me where we're at with this story of ours.'

Carver pulled a chair closer to the bed and gave McCluskey chapter and verse. She listened intently, nodding her approval often.

'Well, I reckon you've done *a lot* with much less than that William. What are we waiting for?'

'There are big gaps in what we know.'

'Sure.'

'Losing almost everything you had on the repairmen back inside your house didn't help.'

'You're going to blame *me* for that are you?'

'I don't mean that, I just mean . . .'

'Don't worry about it, I'll be out of here soon and I can start putting things back together.'

'Your consultant said . . .'

'My consultant doesn't know what he's talking about . . . I'm fine. I'm beginning to suspect he might be keeping me in here longer than necessary 'cos he fancies me.'

Carver smiled.

'That's probably it.'

'The point is that you've got enough already to start causing some trouble, maybe smoke them out. I know you've given those pictures of Dan Staples to the police but you should spread them around on social media too . . . make life difficult for him and embarrassing for whichever so-and-sos it was he was working for.' She paused, scratching at the shaved side of her head. 'You can get your woman Naz to help with that, she's smart . . .' Carver nodded. '. . . then soon as I'm out – day after tomorrow or the weekend at the latest – we'll go to work on Staples' phone. I've got a mate at Caversham who can scrape all the data off of that for us. We'll play them at their own bloody game.' She stifled a yawn. 'I'm a touch tired now Billy. You've made me think and talk more than I've been used to.' She glanced up at the clock on the wall. 'Plus visiting hours are almost up . . . you should go.' Carver nodded and stood up from the chair and picked up his bag.

'I'll see you tomorrow.'

'Don't come back unless you've made some progress with this story of ours.' She waved her hand. 'Go on, bugger off.'

He walked down the corridor and caught the lift up to the top floor. The woman on duty at the nurses' station saw him at the door and buzzed him in.

'There's only a few minutes visiting time left Mr Carver.'

'I'll be quick.' He strode to the last cubicle and pulled back the curtain quietly. Patrick was asleep, still hooked up to a drip of some sort, but no longer attached to any other sort of machine. This was a good sign, surely? Carver took the spare fruit basket and put it down on the table next to Patrick's head. He took his reporter's notebook out and scribbled a message:

'I've got a little story. McCluskey and I are cooking up a plan and I know you won't want to miss out. Call me as soon as you can. Say hello to Rebecca . . .' He stopped, then added a PS. *'Rebecca – if you read this first then obviously there's no rush, only when he's ready. Say hello to him from me. William.'*

Halfway across Westminster Bridge, Carver stopped and watched the snow fall. His gloveless hands were red with cold and he bunched them tight and pushed them down into the pockets of his coat. He stared down at the snowflakes falling softly into the dark river. Some of the larger flakes would hold their shape and brightness for a few moments, briefly held up and carried along by the fast-flowing water. But none lasted long. Swallowed by the river and carried away. He picked up his plastic bag and walked on, north towards the Strand. There was a pub he knew. It had an open fire in the winter and a decent selection of whiskies. He'd have one pint of beer and a whisky to keep the cold out. Then he'd get to work.

Epilogue

Dan moved, putting a couple more metres between him and the huge wooden hive. The chauffeur guy had told him to wait here on the lawn, but the noise of the bees – the sound of their humming – was messing with his head. He was already nervous enough. He ran a hand through his blond beard, a temporary measure until the fuss died down. One of several orders Fred had given him.

'*Grow a beard, buy some coloured contacts and keep your head down. This'll blow over and when it does we'll have you in. Fix you up with a new story and send you back out.*'

That was what the message had said.

It hadn't blown over yet – not quite. But they'd called him in anyway. He glanced up the path, towards the glassy egg-shaped HQ. A small knot of people – Public Square execs by the looks of them – were coming his way. At the centre of the group, wearing a knee-length, blue dress and a pair of bright white Converse trainers, was Elizabeth Curepipe. As the group drew level with Dan, she stopped and they all stopped; she issued a brief instruction and the group moved off in different directions, leaving her

451

alone. She strode across the grass to where Dan was standing, staring.

'You like the bees?'

'Er, I guess. They make a good lot of noise.'

'That's true. It's the sign of a healthy hive I'm told.'

Dan shuffled his feet.

'Er . . . I'm Dan Staples. I'm here because your husband asked me in. I don't know if you remember, we met once, just briefly . . .'

'I remember. I like the beard by the way Dan, it suits you . . .' She paused '. . . is Dan okay, for now anyway?'

'Sure. Dan's fine.'

'Excellent. So the only thing you're mistaken about is that it was *me* who called you in, Dan – not Fred.'

'Oh, right. I'm sorry, I . . .'

'Don't apologise. There's no reason you should know. Fred and I are dividing the work up a little differently these days.'

'I see . . . but this is still just a debrief is it?'

'That's right . . .' She pointed at the line of silver birch trees and the black metal box of a building beyond. '. . . we'll head over to the research centre right now if that's okay with you?'

'Sure.'

'Fred's *man cave* I used to call it.'

'Right.'

Elizabeth put her hand gently in the small of Dan's back and led the way.

'There's no need to look so nervous . . .' She turned and smiled at him. It was quite a smile. '. . . we'll make it fun.'

Acknowledgements

The following books were particularly helpful while researching *A Cursed Place*: Shoshana Zuboff's *The Age of Surveillance Capitalism*, Anand Giridharadas' *Winners Take All*, Fred Turner's *From Counterculture to Cyberculture*, Yasha Levine's *Surveillance Valley*, Jamie Bartlett's *The People vs Tech*, Dan Lyons' *Disrupted*, Ander Izagirre's *The Mountain the Eats Men*, June Nash's *I Spent My Life in the Mines*, *Voices of Latin America* edited by Tom Gatehouse, Isabel Allende's *My Invented Country*, Jan Morris' *Hong Kong* and Antony Dapiran's *City of Protest*.

I am grateful once more to Matilda Harrison for the early reading and good advice throughout. Thanks to Jack Hanington and Leila Eddakille for help with the Spanish translations, and to Martha Hanington for reading the book line by line during lockdown. Thank you to John Saddler and to Lisa Highton, Charlotte Hutchinson, Jess Kim, Cari Rosen, Charlotte Robathan, and the entire Two Roads/ John Murray Press team who have been the most patient and perceptive of publishing guides.

Finally, to Vic –

A haiku of deep regard
Seems appropriate
But as you pointed out during the writing of this book I'm not very good at limiting the number of syllables in the final line.

About the Author

Peter Hanington is the author of *A Dying Breed* and *A Single Source*. He has worked as a journalist for over twenty-five years, including fourteen years at the *Today Programme* and more recently *The World Tonight* and *Newshour* on the BBC World Service. He lives in London with his wife and has two grown-up children.